THE BOATHOUSE

Molly Page is only eleven when she tells her father she'll look after him for ever. Since her mother died, it's been just the two of them, caring for each other. Then the Murphys move in next door. Wonderful Nora Murphy is Molly's dream of what a mother should be — and then there are her sons: irrepressible Warren, with his soft heart and grand ambitions; Pete, with his poetic soul and gorgeous voice; and, best of all, Billy, who has the charm and looks of a movie star. Molly grows up with her life entwined with the exciting Murphys — then an invitation to visit her American godmother in The Hamptons changes everything . . .

Books by Caroline Upcher
Published by The House of Ulverscroft:

THE ASKING PRICE

Caroline Upcher has worked in film, publishing and journalism. She wrote two novels under the name Carly McIntyre as well as Naomi Campbell's novel. This is her fifth novel under her own name. She lives in London and Long Island, New York.

CAROLINE UPCHER

THE BOATHOUSE

Complete and Unabridged

CHARNWOOD
Leicester

First published in Great Britain in 2001 by
Orion
London

First Charnwood Edition
published 2002
by arrangement with
The Orion Publishing Group Limited
London

British Library CIP Data

Upcher, Caroline, *1946* –
    The boathouse.—Large print ed.—
Charnwood library series
1. Love stories
2. Large type books
I. Title
823.9′14 [F]

ISBN 0–7089–9405–9

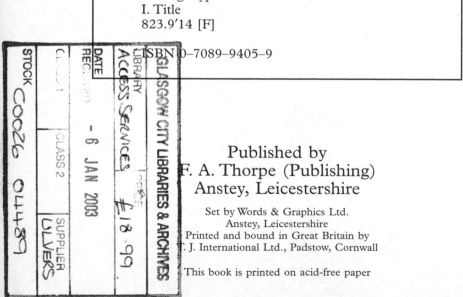

Published by
F. A. Thorpe (Publishing)
Anstey, Leicestershire

Set by Words & Graphics Ltd.
Anstey, Leicestershire
Printed and bound in Great Britain by
T. J. International Ltd., Padstow, Cornwall

This book is printed on acid-free paper

For Emma Sweeney

Part One

VIRGINIA

Long Island, 1979

1

'When I die, I'm going to come back as a seagull and haunt you,' Virginia overheard Sheila O'Mara tell her husband, Virginia's Uncle Hughie, as they sat out on the deck, indulging in their usual early morning bickering.

'Oh, shut up, woman,' Virginia heard Hughie mutter. It was his automatic response to almost everything Sheila said. He'd probably say it if she asked him what he wanted for his dinner.

Virginia was standing high above them on a widow's walk that Hughie O'Mara had constructed, jutting out from a tower. The tower was totally at odds with the rest of the house, if indeed it could be called a house. It was more like a rambling, broken-down wooden shack that Hughie was in the process of fixing up. He had started at the top and was working his way down. A brand new roof was balanced precariously on creaking walls and extending from this roof was the tower, from which you could walk out on to the widow's walk that commanded a magnificent view of the Accabonac Harbor.

The Accabonac Harbor comprised one of the major coastal wetland areas on Long Island, and Virginia found herself looking out over hundreds of acres of shallow water and tidal marsh. Beyond this she could see sand spits and wooded islands with osprey nests rising out of them.

Under the crimson setting sun, it was a breathtaking sight, equal to anything she had seen across the Atlantic on the west coast of Ireland. For a second she was able to shut out the squabbling below her.

Nothing had prepared her for the chaos that awaited her when she arrived at Uncle Hughie's.

He's an eejit, of course. Did we not warn you? The voices of her Auntie Molly and her Auntie Maeve rattled through her head like subway trains and it seemed she was powerless to stop them. Would she ever be rid of all her Irish relatives? Virginia often wondered. They seemed to follow her everywhere. She was the first member of her family to go to university; not only that but she had won a scholarship to Cambridge. Yet even across the water in England, she had to concentrate really hard to banish Molly and Maeve's chatter.

She only saw her aunts three times a year, at Easter, Christmas and in the summer when they came from County Cork to Dublin on a visit. They were several years older than their sister Maureen, Virginia's mother. Poor Hughie was the baby with three older sisters to boss him around. He only came to Dublin for Christmas and Virginia had always looked forward to his visits until they came to an abrupt end when he ran away to America.

Molly and Maeve had never forgiven Hughie for escaping their clutches. He was supposed to look after them in their old age but he had crept away in the night in the summer of 1973, taking nothing with him except Sheila Flynn, a few battered suitcases and two hundred and fifty pounds. This pathetic sum of money — pathetic, at least, for someone starting a new life in a new country — was awarded special mention each time Uncle Hughie's story was repeated, as it inevitably had been several times a year throughout Virginia's childhood. It was important to get the details right. He had taken Molly's bingo stash. This, Virginia understood, was his biggest crime. A close second was the fact that he had absconded with Sheila Flynn.

Sheila was the best fortune-teller in County Cork and her departure left a vacancy that was never satisfactorily filled as far as the aunts were concerned. Sheila it was who predicted the Great Bingo Win of 1962, not to mention the winner of the Irish Sweepstakes three years in a row. Virginia had never been able to work out whether it was the fact that there was no one to tell their fortunes that enraged the aunts, or whether they just couldn't forgive Sheila Flynn for encouraging their brother to flee. Hughie, by all accounts, was hopeless. In the family he was known as Truly Hughie because, as Maureen O'Hare told her daughter, 'He always had a heck of a time getting anyone's attention. He ended every sentence with the words '*Truly* I do' or '*Truly* I can' because he thought no one ever believed what he said.'

But Hughie had surprised everyone. He and Sheila had flown in an airplane — *In an airplane! Did you ever hear of such a thing?* — to John F. Kennedy airport, whence they had traveled via the Long Island Expressway all the way out to

Montauk on the very tip of Long Island. From the station they had gone directly to a bar Hughie had heard about that served draught Guinness. By the time they'd had three drinks, the bartender had found Hughie a job.

Now Hughie had his own little picture framing business and did a bit of furniture repair on the side. He and Sheila had two little boys who already spoke with New York accents that contrasted harshly with Hughie's soft brogue.

Before he left, Virginia had been the only one in whom Hughie had confided about his proposed getaway, but even she had not known about Sheila.

Virginia turned reluctantly from the view of the Accabonac Harbor to the chaos that lay behind her in Hughie's back yard. It looked as if he had brought half of County Cork with him instead of the legendary two hundred and fifty pounds. Virginia noted a rusty mangle, an abandoned hose pipe, a pile of broken ladders propped up against some corrugated iron, and an empty chicken coop, its wire netting torn and rotting. It looked as though anything that no longer worked, instead of being thrown away, had just been chucked into the yard. And that wasn't counting the rowboat with the gaping hole in its side or the van with three flat tires.

But, as Virginia had learned almost immediately, this had nothing to do with Hughie. Sheila's threat to come back as a seagull was in response to Hughie's almost daily announcement that he was going to kill her if she didn't make an effort to clear the place up. As he explained to Virginia, he had long ago given up trying to do the job himself. Any order he restored was destroyed by Sheila in hours.

So he had elected to keep the top of the house as his domain, hence the reason he was working his way down rather than up in the remodeling. Up there, anything he did was relatively safe from Sheila. She wasn't about to make the effort to hoist her 200-pound frame up the stairs unless she absolutely had to. Virginia doubted whether she'd ever set foot in the hexagonal tower room or stepped out of it on to the widow's walk. Virginia saw that Hughie's talent was not necessarily in picture framing or furniture repair. The construction of this tower showed a vision far beyond that kind of work. Hughie had a future as a builder, she thought.

She was sleeping up here instead of in the guest room on the ground floor because on the night she had arrived, Sheila had not got around to making up her bed. And when Hughie had taken Virginia upstairs and shown her the tower, she had been so entranced by the hammock he had hung between two poles up there that she had asked if she could sleep in that. It was a wise choice. Two weeks later the guest room was still in a state of disarray but Virginia didn't care. Every morning she woke to the sight of the dawn coming up over the sand spit in the distance and she savored the few moments of peace before she had to descend to the kitchen for breakfast and the incessant needling that was Hughie and Sheila's marriage.

'One of these days,' Hughie told Virginia, 'I

won't be able to take it any more. I'll go up to the tower, throw myself into the air and hope I fly like a bird away from her.'

Virginia held her tongue. It wasn't her place to ask, *Why on earth did you marry her?*

Instead she asked, 'Why did you leave, Uncle Hughie?'

'Same reason you did,' said Hughie cheerfully, 'Holy Catholic Ireland.'

Virginia could have made him elaborate but she didn't need to. She knew enough about Uncle Hughie to realize his horizon expanded way beyond the confines of the O'Mara family. His ears had long been attuned to the opportunities available to someone like him in America. He had, he told Virginia, spent his whole childhood planning the fresh start he would make as an adult — and here he was.

'So what's your excuse?' he asked her. 'Going to stay over here and make your fortune?'

And throw away Cambridge and the chance of an English degree? What was he thinking of? She didn't really know what she was even doing in Long Island. In fact, only yesterday she had almost started packing her bags to leave. She had come across Sheila painting her toenails. She was making such a mess of it, Virginia had offered to help.

'Ah, there's a sweetheart,' said Sheila. 'I know I'm supposed to put bits of cotton wool in between my toes but I can never be bothered, you know?'

Virginia nodded. 'Is this for something special? Are you and Hughie going out somewhere, will

8

you be wearing sandals?'

'Oh, I wouldn't paint my nails for Hughie. No, I'm going clamming.'

Virginia looked blank.

'Clamming, you know, in the bay,' Sheila explained. 'I dig them out with my toes so I always paint my toenails before I go. Give the little devils a thrill. Pink Geranium here, that's a lucky color. I never get as many when I paint them Dusky Rose.'

'I see,' said Virginia. She had left Cambridge for this. Already she was exasperated by Sheila's constant attempts to read her tea leaves over the breakfast table.

'Leave her alone,' said Hughie, 'she thinks it's a load of rubbish, just like I do.'

'Well, you don't complain about the money I make,' Sheila tossed back at him. 'Now, listen, Ginnie, honey, he'll be tall and he'll be handsome and he's coming your way any day now.'

'Don't call her Ginnie. She's Virginia, always has been. I suppose he'll be American,' said Hughie.

'He will,' confirmed Sheila. 'He'll turn her life upside down.'

'Don't they all?' muttered Hughie.

'I have someone,' Virginia told them.

'You do?' Sheila looked up, surprised. 'I haven't seen him in your tea cup. What's his name?'

'Frank,' said Virginia. 'He's at Cambridge with me. He's going to be a vet.'

'Maybe he is,' Sheila dismissed him, 'but he's

not the one I'm talking about. Now, Hughie, get to work or else you'll never pay the bills.'

Hughie worked painstakingly, taking inordinate care with his caning and repairs. As a result he was very slow. To make matters worse, in the afternoons he switched to working on the house. Virginia could not believe how beautiful the upstairs was compared with the filth and disorder down below. Upstairs were gleaming wooden floorboards, restored antique furniture, quilts, a wall of books. Downstairs were children's toys, piles of old newspapers, a sink full of dirty dishes, a blaring radio.

Sheila certainly paid her way. Hughie worked in the barn across the yard by day, Sheila took it over at night. Every evening, from five o'clock on, there was a knock on the door every hour until ten. Her customers waited in the kitchen while Hughie put the boys to bed.

While she helped out with preparing the supper, Virginia observed Sheila's clientele. They were all women, most of them young. They appeared troubled.

'Well, they would be, wouldn't they?' said Sheila, surprised when Virginia commented on it. 'Why else would they come to see me? They've got problems with the boyfriend or the marriage and they want me to tell them it'll all be over soon. Or they want to know what the man they've just met thinks of them. You're going to meet a woman too, by the way. A girl like yourself. Change your life, she will, turn it upside down, just like the man I mentioned.'

Virginia laughed at this premonition of her

10

turbulent future. Thank God she'd be able to get away from Sheila soon. If she'd known what she was like, she would never have come. But this trip had been planned for years. Ever since Hughie had left Ireland he had promised her a summer holiday in Long Island as soon as she was through with school. Up until a few months ago, she had been looking forward to it. How could she have known that a year at Cambridge would change things?

Uncle Hughie had got her a summer job as a waitress at Gosman's Dock Restaurant in the heart of the fishing port. She was grateful to him, but given the choice she would have preferred to spend the summer in London instead of in a little backwater like Amagansett, Long Island. And if she was going to be a waitress, how much more exciting it would have been to work in a coffee bar on the King's Road in Chelsea or the increasingly fashionable Fulham Road.

It was not an auspicious start at Gosman's. On her first day she tipped a bowl of soup into someone's lap.

She noticed the trio the minute they appeared in the restaurant. A husband, a wife and their daughter. The father waited politely for the hostess to show them to a table. Not *their* table, for, as it turned out, they had not bothered to make a reservation even though it was the height of the summer season. The wife — 'I'm Elaine Alexander', she said, as if she expected it to instantly guarantee her a table — didn't bother to wait. She walked straight to a table by the window overlooking the dock, where diners were afforded the best view of the boats returning from the day's fishing.

Although it had been promised to another party, she would not be moved. A major scene was brewing and the manager had to be called. Finally, after much negotiation, the Alexanders were seated at another table.

It was the daughter who interested Virginia the most. *Thank God I don't look like that, thank God I'm not a great big hulk of a girl with a big nose*, she thought, and immediately felt guilty. But the girl was what Auntie Molly used to call a *galumpher*. She didn't walk, she *galumphed* across the restaurant. It was halfway between a shuffle and a slouch and only heavy people seemed to do it.

Elaine Alexander made as much fuss about what to order as she had about the choice of table. Virginia heard her changing her mind repeatedly. She wanted the seafood platter, then the crab cakes, no, she'd have the steamers, or maybe she'd be better off with just a light salad. The one thing that never crossed her mind was the lobster bisque. Until it arrived.

'I should have ordered that,' she said immediately, when it was placed before her daughter.

The girl clearly knew what was coming and elected to head it off at the pass.

'You can have mine, Mother. I'm happy with your shrimp. Let's trade.'

But she made the offer with a distinct lack of grace and her bad temper showed when she switched the orders with a swift and angry movement. Virginia, who was about to set the seafood platter in front of the girl's father, anticipated what was going to happen and tried to intercept the bisque in mid-air, causing it to upend in Elaine Alexander's lap.

Virginia raced over to pick up a pile of napkins. Speaking softly, she urged Mrs Alexander to accompany her to the ladies' room where they might try to repair the damage to her peach-colored linen shift.

'I don't think so. Victor, we're leaving. Pay the bill. Now.'

Victor was obviously used to doing what he was told.

'What is that?' his wife asked, pointing to the bills lying on the plate. 'Are you leaving a tip after what they've done? They're lucky you're paying the bill after this. Are you crazy? My dress is ruined and you want to leave a tip? After they moved us to Siberia because we're — '

'They moved us because that wasn't our table. We didn't make a reservation, for which I apologize,' he said evenly, hooded eyes staring beyond her, following a boat gliding into the harbor. 'And Mitzi spilled the soup. They had nothing to do with it. Here, honey, thanks for helping out. Or trying to.' He handed Virginia more bills. 'C'mon, Mitzi.'

Mitzi. It was an exotic name for such an awkward creature. As she lumbered to her feet and followed her parents through the restaurant, Virginia felt sorry for her. She'd inherited her father's genes and it was a shame. Her mother was a tiny person, fragile-looking with huge eyes.

With her rouged cheeks, pale skin and lacquered red hair (even at the beach!), she reminded Virginia of an excitable chihuahua: dainty, nervous, prancing her way out of the restaurant, ready to snap at someone's ankles. Her daughter, by contrast, was at least five inches taller with big bones. She had a shock of unruly black hair that flared away from her head in a mass of curls. She seemed to have black eyes to match and a large nose like her father's. She had olive skin, yet she wasn't Latin-looking; Virginia couldn't put her finger on it.

The group at the next table she served were talking about the Alexanders as Virginia approached.

'D'ya suppose she's the girl's mother? Maybe the father married again and this is the kid from his first marriage. You'd never know the mother was Jewish and the father's so good-looking but that girl really got a raw deal. No one could ever make a princess out of her.'

Mitzi could not have heard them but something about the way she walked, head down, shoulders hunched, told Virginia that she must have heard similar comments in the past. Everything about her said she didn't want to be there, she didn't like how she looked, she wished everyone would leave her alone. *And once they'd done all of that could they please give her as much love and affection as they had to offer because, oh boy, did she need it.*

Virginia watched as Mitzi trudged into the car park where her parents waited. As Mitzi got into the car she looked back and Virginia smiled at her and waved. Mitzi paused, looked around her as if she wasn't sure the wave was meant for her. Virginia waved again and this time Mitzi smiled.

For that one moment, Virginia thought Mitzi was the most beautiful person she had ever seen.

2

Uncle Hughie was full of plans.

'California.' He said the name of the state several times a day and each time smiled to himself. 'That's my goal,' he confided in Virginia, 'that's where I aim to be before too long. Land of opportunity. Warm, healthy. That's where we're off to next.'

'Los Angeles?' she asked. 'Hollywood?'

'No, no, no. Further north. San Francisco. I'm thinking about a place called Marin County. Ran into a pal of mine the other day. He left here three years ago and went to live there. Now he's driving a Mercedes 230 SL and living on a mountain top. He says I could make my fortune building A-frame houses all over the canyons out there.'

Virginia had a quick flash of Uncle Hughie leaping about the canyons like a mountain goat. He'd have to speed up a bit, she thought, but refrained from telling him so. No point in spoiling his dream.

'What about Sheila?'

'Oh, Sheila's no problem. She'd make her fortune out there, no pun intended. She'd probably have to learn a bit about astrology and call herself a clairvoyant, a bit of readjustment, you know? But those hippies in California, they'd love Sheila to bits.'

Good luck to them, thought Virginia. She had

this vision of Uncle Hughie always wanting to be off somewhere else. She imagined he would arrive in California, find a job, settle the kids in school and then move on a few years later. If he continued going west, maybe he'd eventually wind up home again in Ireland. She wondered if he'd finish work on this house before he left.

Virginia couldn't understand why he was even thinking of leaving Long Island. If it hadn't been for the undeniable beauty of the place, she would have turned around and gone home. When she'd seen the beauty of the bay across the road from where he lived, she was tempted to stay there herself. She'd arrived with one foot ready to make a dash for the plane back to England. Until she saw the bay.

She woke early one morning and slipped out of the house to explore. For once she turned her back on the view of the Accabonac Harbor and followed a trail through the woods in the opposite direction. A few startled deer leapt away from her, dodging the trees in their haste. She couldn't see the sea but she could smell it. She knew she was close. The trail led to the top of a bluff and suddenly, as she emerged from the woods, she was overlooking the water. The brilliant blue of the sky was reflected in the giant semi-circle of the bay below. A run of breakwaters and jetties had created several smaller bays within the sweeping curve. Each little bay had its own stretch of sand between the lapping waves at the water's edge and the wooden bulkheads protecting the bluff from the onslaught of the sea in storms. The entire bay

— Virginia guessed it to be about three miles long — was deserted. She scrambled down the bluff, fighting her way through gorse and scrub, and jumped down from a bulkhead on to the sand below. It was hard and still damp from the outgoing tide. Looking around her she saw she could have just as easily come down one of the wooden walkways dotted along the bluff, but almost immediately it dawned on her that these led from private houses. Maybe even a walk along the beach would be trespassing.

The bluff petered out in the distance but at the end of it she could see a small shape protruding, a tiny building of some sort standing in the water on spindly legs.

When she reached it, she saw it was a boathouse. Abandoned. No sign of life. At least that was what she thought until she touched the rusty chain slipped through the door and found that it gave in her fingers. She unhooked it, removed the open padlock, pushed the door. Inside were two boats, dorys. Ducking between them, she peeked through a crack in the double doors to see the ramp going down to the water. The dorys took up almost all the space but in the gloom she could make out fishing nets hanging above her, buoys and life jackets on shelves on the walls, and in the far corner a little wood-burning stove. She climbed a small ladder to look in one of the boats and saw a pile of blankets. The stove was faintly warm to her touch. An empty packet of Kents lay at her feet on the floor and beside it a pair of rubber boots. But it was the battered copy of *Rolling Stone* that intrigued her the most.

A deck ran around the outside of the boathouse culminating in a jetty. The rope attached to one of the moorings and tossed along the jetty was wet, as if it had recently been floating in the water. As she looked far out across the bay, Virginia could see a dot on the horizon, a fishing boat.

She climbed the wooden walkway behind the boathouse knowing she had to be trespassing, but when she reached the top she couldn't go any further anyway. The trail was too overgrown with brambles, and hanging vine-like branches had wound their way around tree trunks and spread to form a dense thicket that would have taken her hours to unravel. Clearly no one had been down this path recently.

So whoever had brought the Kents and the *Rolling Stone* had to have come by boat — or walked along the beach like she had.

She daydreamed about the identity of the person who lived in the boathouse as she took orders at Gosman's. It affected her work. She brought customers Little Necks when they ordered Steamers, bisque when they ordered chowder.

'There's someone to see you,' they told her when she arrived for work a couple of days after the Alexanders' disastrous lunch. 'She's been here since noon.'

Virginia had the evening shift and had come on duty at six. Mitzi Alexander was sitting at a table by herself.

'Anything else I can get you?' Virginia asked.

Apparently Mitzi had already downed half a dozen beers.

'You can sit with me. My name's Mitzi.'

'I'm Virginia and I'm afraid I can't. I have to wait tables here.'

'Well, I'll stay till you can.'

By that time she would be under the table, Virginia reckoned.

'You can do whatever you want,' she said gently, 'but I'm going to bring you a cup of coffee along with anything else you order and I'll only talk to you at the end of the evening if you drink it.'

'Deal,' said Mitzi. 'And bring me a bowl of soup. I'll try not to upend it into anyone's lap.'

Her expression was serious and Virginia longed to shake her and tell her how much a smile transformed her face.

It was a slow night and by ten o'clock Virginia was able to sit down beside Mitzi, keeping an eye out for any latecomers or customers signaling they needed more coffee.

'What are you doing over here?' Mitzi asked, still not smiling.

'Working. My uncle lives here. It was arranged years ago, that when I was twenty I would come out here and work through the summer.'

'But why be a waitress?' Mitzi's tone was scathing.

'Beggars can't be choosers. Uncle Hughie got me the job — why should I argue?'

'Because it's demeaning and I'm sure you're not being paid enough. Anyway, you were happy to get away from home, I suppose?'

'Not really. I've already left home. My family are in Dublin. I'm at Cambridge University. Across the water, in England.'

'You are?' Mitzi's face lit up and once again the difference was astonishing.

'Forgive me, but I have to tell you something.' Virginia put a hand on Mitzi's arm as if to restrain her from the violence Virginia's words would provoke. 'I want to take two strips of plaster, band aids as you call them, and tape them to the corners of your mouth, pulling it upward to keep you smiling. Have you any idea how wonderful you are when you smile?'

Mitzi brushed her arm aside.

'I don't give a damn what I look like.'

'Well you should,' said Virginia, hurt by the rebuff. 'That's a pretty selfish attitude. We're the ones who have to look at you after all.'

Mitzi glanced at her quickly and Virginia noted a glimmer of respect in her eye.

'Are you at university?' Virginia asked.

'College. I'm going to Berkeley in the fall. San Francisco. It's a big deal,' she added.

Virginia didn't quite understand what she meant but Mitzi looked pleased so she smiled and said 'Congratulations.'

'Yeah, it'll be great to get away from Mom.'

'You come here every summer for a holiday?'

'We will now.'

'You don't sound too happy about it. What's the problem? It's a beautiful part of the world.'

Mitzi was looking at her as if she was trying to work something out.

'You're Irish, right?'

21

'Right.'

'Catholic?'

Virginia nodded, wondering where this was going.

'I'm Jewish.'

'So? What does that have to do with spending the summer here? There are Jewish people out here, aren't there?'

'Yes,' said Mitzi slowly, 'there are. That's how my mother decided she wanted to get a house here. She came out to stay with friends of ours. Being Jewish doesn't bother *me*. It's my mother who has a problem with it. I wouldn't be concerned if she was prepared to sit back and be Jewish but it's like she's ashamed of it. It's like she wants to be thought of as a WASP. Her parents were Russian Jewish immigrants who made a fortune in the retail clothing business but instead of being proud of this, she seems to want to push them into the background. I can't understand it. I'm proud of what they did. But they never get to meet her friends. It's as if they don't exist.'

'But what do your grandparents have to do with a summer house out here?'

'It's the same thing. Just as she pretends they don't exist, when she gets out here she's going to try and pretend she's not Jewish. Once she's bought a house, she'll probably buy a plot in a Presbyterian cemetery so she can be buried thinking she's taking the secret that she's Jewish with her. Nothing would make her happier than if I were to be invited everywhere, if I played tennis on Lily Pond Lane every day, if I met

22

some nice young Protestant beau and got married at The Maidstone Club.'

'What's The Maidstone Club?' asked Virginia.

'A fancy club with no Jewish members.'

'So why would she want to join it?'

Mitzi shook her head. 'You just don't get it, do you? My mother doesn't want to be Jewish and she imagines if she pretends she isn't, she won't be. What she doesn't seem to understand is that if she just carried on as if she didn't care one way or the other, no one would notice what she was. The fact that she's always trying so hard makes her stand out. It's like when I'm around her, I show her up. Everyone looks at me and when they find out she's my mother, it's a dead giveaway. They know she's Jewish. Frankly, I can't wait to leave and go to San Francisco.'

'She must be pleased about that.'

'Are you kidding? She wants me to get married, stay home, raise a family just like she did. I've told my cousin, whose only ambition is to find a husband, honey, that's your future. Mine's going to be the total opposite.'

'Good for you,' said Virginia.

'So you'll still be here when we're around next weekend?'

Virginia nodded. 'I'm working daytime only next weekend. We could spend time together in the afternoon.'

'I'd like that,' said Mitzi. The smile hovered for a second and then retreated. 'I'll see you then.'

Virginia spent the week wondering if Mitzi would call. After all, what did the two of them

23

have in common? She didn't mention Mitzi to Hughie and Sheila so she had some explaining to do when she arrived home from work the following Friday and Hughie came running out of the barn to tell her: 'There's a young woman turned up to see you. From the city.'

Virginia looked around, saw only a little green coupé parked in front of the house, very much at odds with Hughie's van and Sheila's battered pick-up.

'Where is she?'

'Inside. You'd better rescue her from Sheila.'

Virginia could hear Mitzi's voice as she walked through the front door.

'And *I'm* telling *you* I don't believe any of that stuff. There's no point even trying to tell me. I don't want to know and I'm not going to pay you a penny.'

'I'm not asking for a penny. You're a friend of Virginia's, I'm not going to take money off you,' Sheila wailed. 'I asked you if you wanted a cup of tea and you accepted.'

'I was thirsty, for heaven's sake. I didn't know how long I'd have to wait for Virginia. I didn't know it meant you'd read the tea leaves. Oh, hi, Virginia. Will you please tell your aunt I'm not interested.'

She's not my aunt Virginia wanted to say, and then realized that Sheila was indeed her aunt by marriage. It was just that having never met her before this summer she didn't think of her as family.

'Join us for tea, Virginia. I've been entertaining your friend here. Tell me, Mitzi, are you from

Manhattan or do your people have a place out here?'

'Yes. No. I mean, yes, I am from Manhattan and we don't have a place but my parents have just offered on a house very near here. That's what I came to tell Virginia.'

'Well, isn't that grand. So you'll be our new neighbor. Is it just you or do you have any brothers and sisters?'

'Just me.'

'An only child, just like Virginia here. Did anybody ever tell you, Mitzi, you have beautiful hair.'

'It's a mess.' Mitzi was slouching in her chair, her hands plunged firmly into the pockets of her shorts. But Virginia noticed that she sat up a little straighter at Sheila's compliment, even though she tossed it back in Sheila's face.

But Sheila wasn't deterred.

'Well, of course it is. Who can keep their hair straight with the wind and the sand and the sun? No, it's the thickness that I'm admiring. You'll be thankful for that when you're my age. Won't she, Virginia? And those long legs. Did you ever see such long legs, Virginia?'

Mitzi almost smiled.

Virginia caught on. She began to see Sheila in a new light. She was deliberately coaxing Mitzi out of her shell. The compliments were genuine; Mitzi did have beautiful hair and long legs, but Virginia could see what Sheila was playing at.

'I'd give anything to be a couple of inches taller,' she said, entering into the game. 'Mitzi's like one of those models.'

'She is, isn't she? Did you ever consider that kind of thing? You know, like what's her name . . . Lauren Hutton?'

Mitzi stared at her. 'I could never be a model.'

'Oh, you could, you — '

'No. You don't understand. Models are dumb.'

Sheila didn't miss a beat. 'So I've heard. OK, so I was only saying you *could* be, if you wanted. Nice to have the option. So, will you be inviting Virginia into the city? She ought to see New York while she's here.'

'Sheila!' Virginia was embarrassed.

'No, it's OK. Of course I will. I just wanted to come and tell her about our house.'

'Well, I'm glad you did. I hope you'll drop by again.' And before Mitzi could stop her, Sheila had reached out and given her a hug.

'Thanks for the tea.' Mitzi disengaged herself, her face going a little pink. 'I'll be in touch over the weekend, Virginia.'

Virginia heard the sound of the little coupé's engine accelerating along the quiet roads long after Mitzi had left.

'That's a very troubled young woman,' Sheila commented when Virginia went back inside. 'As I told you, most of the girls who come to see me are troubled but not nearly as much as they think they are. But your friend, she didn't seek me out, she didn't want to hear what I had to say and she's more troubled than any of them.'

'She's Jewish,' said Virginia without thinking.

'Well, that's got nothing to do with it. What a thing to say,' said Sheila. 'No, I saw it all. She's got a tough time ahead of her.'

'Oh, Sheila. Stop. You know we think it's nonsense.' Virginia laughed. She was grateful to Sheila for her kindness to Mitzi, and didn't want to offend her, but neither did she want her to embark upon a dissection of her future.

'You say that but I know deep down you believe it, just a little. Irish girl like you. It's in your blood. And I'll tell you one thing I saw . . . Oh, no, you don't want to know.'

'Now you're teasing me. Go on, you can tell me one thing you saw, just one.' Like it or not Virginia was mildly intrigued. 'Is she going to meet a man too, someone who'll turn her life upside down?'

'Yes,' said Sheila, 'she is.'

'Well, then she won't be troubled any more, will she?'

'Oh, I don't know about that.' Sheila turned to her. 'You see, it's the same man.'

3

Mitzi never reappeared, nor did she issue an invitation to the city and Virginia was disappointed. She had fantasized about the new friendship about to blossom, imagined long telephone discussions over the coming months comparing Cambridge with Berkeley, Jewish mothers and Catholic mothers. *My friend Mitzi.* She imagined being summoned to the phone in Cambridge. 'It's your friend Mitzi,' and the all-important addition, 'calling *long distance. Quick!*' Mitzi's phone tab would grow and grow, and then, next summer, the Alexanders would have their house and maybe Virginia would be invited to stay.

She felt rather guilty about the diminishing role Hughie and Sheila played in her fantasies. She consoled herself with the notion that they would probably be long gone to California by the time she returned.

Mitzi did call her from Manhattan. The conversation was brief. Her parents' offer had been accepted. She wouldn't be coming out any more that summer but here was her number and if Virginia was ever in New York she should feel free to call. Mitzi's telephone voice was strong and confident, revealing nothing of the awkward young woman who was so uncomfortable with her appearance. Only at the end of the call did a hint of vulnerability creep into her voice when she said, 'I like you, Virginia. I don't like many people. I hope I see you again.'

It was sincere, childlike, a little girl in the playground talking. *I don't like many people.* And one of those people is yourself, thought Virginia. Forget about me, try to like yourself.

But she made a note of the number. Her morning visits to the bay had made her realize that she definitely wanted to return to Long Island.

She wondered about Mitzi and men, trying to ignore Sheila's ludicrous prediction. The average male would take one look at Mitzi and run a mile. Not because she was ugly. On the contrary, she was beautiful when she smiled. But her attitude was so offputting, it would take a very determined suitor to break down the barriers.

Virginia's mind wasn't on her work as she served lunch at Gosman's. Mitzi had been right. She wasn't cut out to be a waitress. It only took the slightest distraction and she was muddling up the orders again. Halfway through the day, Rose, another waitress, touched her lightly on the arm.

'Take a break for a second. I'll cover. Something's eating you.'

Mitzi wasn't the only person on Virginia's mind. She kept wondering about the mystery person who enjoyed a cigarette and *Rolling Stone* in the boathouse.

'Where exactly is this place?' asked Rose, and when Virginia told her, Rose put down the tray she was carrying and turned to her.

'Drugs. Be careful. Let me tell you what goes

on around there. See, I cook once a week for a family with a big house at the top of those bluffs. They have ten, twenty people over for dinner three nights a week, but these guests, they never arrive by car. You go by the house at night, you'd think nobody was home. No lights on at the front of the house. All the action's round in back. Anyone who comes to dinner, they come by boat, tie up down on the beach, slip up the walkway. They're bringing drugs in from a boat that's docked at Montauk maybe. Or they're bringing cash.'

Rose was a fanciful girl, given to wild imaginings about Gosman's patrons no matter how mundane their appearance.

'The couple at table five are on the brink of divorce, you can see it. And that man at table eleven is going to ask me to marry him by the end of the season. He's here every day.'

Virginia was about to point out that every now and then the man in question was joined by an exceptionally pretty girl whose hand he held under the table, but she thought better of it. Let Rose dream.

But the notion that there was a major drug-running operation in process on the beach below Uncle Hughie's house remained highly intriguing.

When she approached the boathouse the next morning shortly after dawn there was a little rowboat tied up to the jetty.

Virginia tapped softly on the door but received no answer. The chain was slack and she slipped the padlock free. At first she could see nothing in

30

the dark inside but gradually a shaft of light penetrated through the crack in the far doors and she made her way over to the boat. A hidden form lay huddled under a blanket and she watched its infinitesimal rise and fall in sleep. She leaned against the wall and waited.

The head that emerged about twenty minutes later was that of a man. What struck Virginia was that he did not start or cry out when he saw her. He looked at her for a second or two in silence.

'Well,' he said, stretching in a languid movement, 'you don't look like you're going to give me any trouble. What's your name?'

He hasn't even asked what I'm doing here, why I'm trespassing, thought Virginia. Then it dawned on her. He wasn't supposed to be there either.

'Virginia O'Hare. I'm from Ireland.'

'I'm Shrimp McCarthy.' He stood up in the boat and held out his hand. He had long arms and his reach extended down to her. 'I suppose I'm originally from Ireland too. My grandfather. Something like that.'

The blankets fell away from him. He was tall and wore a sweatshirt with a hood; when the hood fell away, she saw he had fine brown hair, quite long, and a slight growth of beard. The hand she clasped had long, tapering fingers unlike the stubby digits she'd seen on most of the fishermen in the area. Maybe he wasn't a fisherman. His face was slender, his eyes dark brown and sensitive. With his hair framing his face, falling below his chin, he looked almost Christ-like. But we never see pictures of Christ smiling sexily, thought Virginia, and felt Maeve and Molly's admonishing tap on her shoulder. This man's smile was heavenly. Soft and gentle around the eyes, offset by a wide flash of strong white teeth. And as he shrugged off his slicker, Virginia could see broad shoulders and a T shirt stretched across well-developed muscles. How could such a giant be called Shrimp?

'I know what you're going to ask so I'll tell you before you do. I'm the youngest of six boys and when I was a kid I was real little compared to my brothers. They always called me Shrimp. You don't believe me, I'll show you photos.'

He didn't seem about to produce them. *I'll show you photos.* Was he planning to see her again?

'My mother was Italian, from Brooklyn. My father was the Irish one. He used to take the fish in to the old Fulton Fish Market in New York and he met her there, brought her back here and the next thing they knew they had six kids.'

The Italian mother explained it. He was so dark, his brown eyes were like black grapes and his olive skin had acquired a tan that was almost non-Caucasian in its intensity. Virginia had noticed a number of fair, blue-eyed fishermen with rosy cheeks and tufts of straw-colored hair poking out from under their woolly hats. Shrimp McCarthy was no relation to them.

'Want a ginger ale?' he asked her. 'I always have a ginger ale first thing in the morning.'

She shook her head and watched as he opened the doors of the boathouse to let the sun stream in.

'I keep a coolbox out here on the deck. No electricity, you see.'

'Do you live here?' she asked.

'I sleep here,' he replied. 'I fish from here. Yeah, I guess you could say I live here inasmuch as I live anywhere.'

He slept in his clothes — torn T shirt, surprisingly clean, and a pair of faded jeans rolled up to his ankles.

'You like The Beatles?' he asked suddenly.

She nodded.

He pointed to a transistor radio high up on a shelf.

'I like The Beatles. I like 'Strawberry Fields'. Keep going along the bay you'll come to Cranberry Hole Road, go across Napeague Harbor you'll find the cranberry bogs. I sing 'Strawberry Fields' but I change the words, I sing '*Cranberry Fields forever.*'' He grinned at her. 'So what are you doing over from Ireland?'

She explained about Uncle Hughie and Gosman's.

'Anytime you want to bring me a doggy bag, I'd appreciate it.' Another grin accompanied by a wink.

She brought him dessert — apple pie, brownies, and cheese, fruit, chocolates. He provided the fish — blues, stripers, yellow-tail flounder, fluke. She rearranged her schedule at Gosman's so she only worked the lunchtime shift. That way she could be with Shrimp in the evening, sitting out on the deck of the boathouse as the sun went down over the bay: a crimson ball sinking into the water. If Uncle Hughie wondered where she went, he never asked. Once she ran down to the beach in the early morning and witnessed Shrimp about to set off. His sharpy was already in the water and he was standing on the dock, feet planted slightly apart, head bowed, hands clasped in front of him. As she crept up behind him, she realized he was praying.

'Dear Lord, bless this boat and if the water gets rough bless her some more.'

She reached out to touch him and he turned, looking sheepish.

'I always bless the boat, every time I go out. My dad died out there in the Atlantic Canyon.'

'You never take the big boat?' She nodded towards the boathouse.

'My bed?' he laughed. 'That's not mine. If they saw me out in that, then the game would be over.'

That night when they had eaten the bluefish he'd caught, she asked him about his father. She hadn't eaten much. The blues were too oily for her taste. Instead she watched him breaking up crusts of the bread she had brought with his elegant fingers and wondered what the rest of his family looked like.

'What happened to your father? He was on a fishing trip?'

'I guess. Who knows? He was lost at sea is all I know. Of course he was a pirate years before I was born.'

Virginia laughed but saw Shrimp was serious.

'He used to tell me stories about how he was a rumrunner during prohibition. They went in their fishing boats, met the big boats twelve miles out, tossed a roll of bills on the deck and brought back the cargo, the liquor, in the middle of the night. Once he made ten thousand dollars in a single night. He used to tell me, you had to know the exact moment to bring the boat in, how the tide was running. There are sandbars out there that can be treacherous, they shift. You can run aground, be stuck there, a storm can get up. Then there was the local stuff. People around here used to run smaller operations. You could make pretty good whiskey from beach plums if you knew the recipe.'

'Ten thousand dollars,' repeated Virginia. 'That would be in the Twenties?'

'Don't ask,' said Shrimp, 'we never saw a penny. He said the Feds nearly got him once but he slipped through their fingers. That's all we ever learned from him: how to be slippery, how to keep a low profile, do what you want and never get caught. I stay here in the boathouse, keep my head down, no one ever asks any questions. I sell my fish, supply regular customers right around here, cash only.'

No telephone. No car. She'd seen an old bicycle propped up against the wall in the boathouse so presumably that was how he did his shopping. He delivered the fish by boat, tying up at docks along the bay and walking through the dunes.

'But whose is the boathouse? Don't they know you're here?'

'Belongs to a big house up on the bluff. Nobody there. It's on the market. If somebody buys, I guess I'll have to move on.'

He taught her to fish, taking her out into the middle of the bay and showing her how to cast, wait for the bite, reel in. He showed her how to dig for clams in shallow waters with her bare feet and shook with laughter when she told him about Sheila and her Pink Geranium toenails. And then one evening he suddenly stripped off all his clothes and dived off the dock into the clear blue water.

'C'mon. We'll swim along the bay among the fish instead of catching 'em.'

She could see his naked form below her, long thighs working, treading water.

'Don't look,' she pleaded and he obliged her by sinking below the surface and swimming underwater around the dock.

She slipped off her jeans and top and lowered herself over the side of the jetty. As she did so she realized there was no reason why she too should swim naked. He hadn't asked her to. The small pile of his clothes had revealed that he hadn't been wearing any underwear. She, on the other hand, had been wearing a swimsuit under her clothes. She could have left it on.

The sensation of the warm salt water on her skin was blissful. The sea had had all day to heat up and it was like taking a bath. The bay was deserted. Virginia wondered who went up and down the wooden walkways and when. She never saw a soul.

The sun was sinking, sending deep pink slithers across the sky. Shrimp pulled her to him from behind, his slender fingers clasping her and turning her around to face him. His long hair floated on the water as he drew her face to his and kissed her. She slid her arms around his neck and let herself go slack in his embrace. Gradually their legs became entwined and she could feel his penis begin to stir against her. She parted her legs and felt it slip into her. Gently, he released her and took her hand, guiding her as they swam into shore. They lay in the shallows with their arms around each other, and a flock of sandpipers scurried away along the shoreline.

He carried her back to the boathouse. Virginia had never before been picked up bodily by a man. He nudged open the doors and deposited her on to the blankets in the boat. He climbed in with her. It was surprisingly comfortable.

Something scratched her bare leg and she retrieved a piece of paper from under the blanket.

'What's this?' Reaching in, she drew out a dozen pages covered with dense scrawl.

'I write. But I'm a long way from showing anything to anybody. So don't ask.'

His face hardened for a second. Virginia understood. *Don't take this any further.* Then his smile returned.

'You'll stay here tonight?' he said, and it was not really a question. He stroked her body and placed her hands on his own soft brown skin that made a startling contrast with the hard sinew of his muscles. The hair on his chest and arms was as silky as that on his head.

When she screamed as she climaxed, he placed his hand over her mouth and whispered in her ear, 'Tomorrow we'll do this in my sharpy out in the middle of the bay. You'll make the boat rock more than the waves in a Nor'easter. Then I'm going to take you over to Cartwright Shoals and we'll get ourselves stuck on a sandbar like my daddy used to. Only thing different is we'll take our own liquor.'

She met him every day for the last month she was there and knew she was falling in love with him.

On her last evening Uncle Hughie planned a goodbye party and she had to attend. There was another excuse to get drunk: Virginia wasn't the only one leaving Long Island. Hughie had found a job in Los Angeles. The whole family were to move there by the end of the year. Virginia wondered who would buy the house in its semi-remodeled state.

She set the alarm and slipped out of the house at 4.30. The road down to the bay was pitch black but her flashlight caught a fox darting across her path and she heard the raccoons clattering around the neighbors' garbage cans. Down on the beach she could make her way by moonlight to the boathouse. The lighthouse far across the bay on Montauk Point flashed on and off, on and off, its beam sweeping over the water.

She reached the boathouse and slipped round to the front deck. She knocked on the door, four light raps, Beethoven's Fifth, their signal. No answer. She released the heavy chain and slipped inside.

'Shrimp?' she whispered.

Again no answer.

She pushed the boathouse doors wide open so the moonlight allowed her to see that the place was empty.

She walked to the end of the jetty and sat, her legs dangling.

It was so easy to sit there with her back to the land, to look out far across the darkness of the bay with the channel of water illuminated by the moon directly in front of her. She felt drawn to the water, wanted to shed her clothes and swim across the bay, guided by the light of the moon.

Where was Shrimp? Rose's stories of drugs being smuggled in from Montauk danced before her eyes. Could she make out dark shapes on the water? Abruptly, her thoughts shifted to Mitzi. She had called Mitzi on the number she had been given and reached her mother. She doubted Elaine would relay her message but she wasn't worried. She and Mitzi would stay in touch.

She would help Mitzi to see how beautiful she was. She would help her overcome her self-consciousness. She would help the girl escape her mother's hold over her. With a mother like that, it was no wonder Mitzi was teetering so awkwardly on the brink of womanhood. And yet, Virginia recalled, already she had some pretty forceful ideas about women and their role in society, ideas Virginia found intriguing, yet at the same time they frightened her with their intensity. If the world changed in the way Mitzi felt it should, women would never be the same again.

Their worlds would be turned upside down.

How could Sheila have known?

And how was she going to find the words to tell Shrimp what she knew she had to?

'Hey!'

She looked up, startled. Shrimp was rowing towards her in the moonlit path, the oars lapping quietly through the water. Where had he been? She wouldn't ask.

'I thought you'd be here early,' he said as he tied up, 'but I didn't expect you for another hour. Come inside.'

He lit candles, undressed her and lifted her into the dory. The night air was warm and he left the doors open. As they made love they were bathed in moonlight. Afterwards he lay slumped on top of her, his face buried in her neck.

She stroked his back and his long silky hair and, gathering new courage, she whispered in his ear, 'Shrimp, I have something to tell you.'

Part Two

MOLLY

Surrey, England, 1993

4

I married the boy next door.

Bit lazy, you might think, not very adventurous, but it never really entered my head to do otherwise.

His arrival was heralded by the For Sale sign that was put up outside the house next door, but when it was still there a year later, Dad and I began to take it for granted that No. 57 would remain empty forever. It had gone on the market when the old lady who lived there died. We'd never even met her. She obviously didn't have any pets. I say that because Dad is a vet. His surgery is round the corner and down the hill but kids turn up at the kitchen door at all hours with cats and gerbils and even squirrels, so we know most families in the vicinity. Dad never says no but I do get a little angry about the squirrels because he's not allowed to charge for treating wildlife.

Anyway, we never had a visitor from No. 57. To tell you the truth, I never even saw it until it was empty. Chaveny Road is a perfectly ordinary suburban street with two rows of late Victorian family houses. There are low stone walls with an opening in the middle through which you walk up a path to the front door. We all have front doors with stained glass windows and rather gloomy halls with front rooms on either side with bay windows looking out on to the street. The kitchen's at the back and some people have built on, electing to reduce the half acre of garden with the obligatory greenhouse at the end in return for a TV room or an extra bathroom.

But No. 57 is an aberration. The house is a throwback to times gone by, the big house built two centuries ago instead of one, standing alone in its own grounds while all around it land has been sold off and a sprawling mass of Chaveny Roads have replaced the fields that were once there. Whatever the big house used to be called, it's now become No. 57 and you can't see it from the road. All you can see is the entrance to the driveway which by all accounts is pretty long. As a young child I was much too frightened to investigate what lay at the end of it. In my mind the old lady who lived there had achieved witch status, for no particular reason other than no one knew anything about her. The postman never saw her because he just pushed her mail through the letterbox and walked away. The house was huge, he reported, and her name was Miss Everett. Miss Geraldine Everett. And the only mail she received was bills. The milkman delivered three pints a week but he never saw her. Her cleaning lady did her shopping for her, but this was someone from an agency who didn't speak to the likes of us locals. All we saw was her car coming and going.

In fact, the only time we learned quite a lot about Miss Everett was when she left No. 57. We never saw her because she left in an ambulance after the cleaning lady found her collapsed on her bathroom floor and dialed 999.

The next thing we knew there was a For Sale sign at the end of the driveway. I waited a week and then I sneaked up to investigate.

The drive stopped at a high stone wall. At least it must have been high once but now it was just a crumbling mass. Only the two stone portals were still standing and beyond them the grass and brambles were so overgrown it would have been impossible to drive a car through them. The postman, the milkman and the cleaning lady had obviously walked this last bit. The house was a near ruin. Part of the roof was exposed to the rafters. It was clear to me which wing Miss Everett had lived in. It was the only part of the house where the windows had glass. I peeked in through one of the windows and what I saw saddened me. Everything was covered with dust sheets, but I could make out the shape of an old armchair pulled up to the fireplace and I had an instant picture of the old lady sitting there all alone every evening, huddled close to the fire for warmth.

Miss Everett. She had been a spinster. She had never married. She had been left to grow old alone in a house nobody knew about. This sorry image festered in my imagination until it reached tragic proportions and I announced to Dad at breakfast: 'I'm definitely going to get married. I never want to grow old alone.'

'Good plan,' Dad replied. 'The Stewart's tabby at No. 45 is a teenage trollop. This will be her third litter in eighteen months and I don't think she'll survive it. She's very tired. You can tell your friend Lucy that I'm going to make sure

45

she's spayed after this.'

'But I'll still look after you, Dad, even after I'm married.'

'Well, whoever he is he'll be a lucky man,' said Dad. 'You'll make someone a wonderful wife. They don't make 'em like you any more.'

He kissed me on the top of my head and looked rather sad as he walked out the door. At the time I thought it was because he was thinking about Mum, but later I realized it was because he knew they didn't make 'em like me any more.

Mum died when I was very young, too young to really remember anything about her. Dad never remarried and as a result I became the woman of the house. From a very early age I learned to produce simple meals for the two of us and I was a pretty good cook. I could grill, roast, make stews, soups, pasta sauces; I could steam vegetables and I made far and away the best salad dressing on Chaveny Road. Everyone said so. Dad and I went to Sainsbury's every Saturday for the weekly shop and we would run into my school friends' mums and they would always stop and chat in the aisles. Some of them were divorced from their husbands and they were the ones who always spent the longest time chatting to Dad. I knew what was on their minds and they were wasting their time. It would never happen. Dad didn't want to get married again. He didn't need to. He had me. I was the best housekeeper a man could have.

I suppose Dad looked sad that day because he knew one day I'd go off to work and then I'd want a career. After that I'd have no time to bother with cooking, housekeeping, and all the other things that have gone out of style as part of the life of a modern working woman. To be honest, I didn't think Dad was like that, I didn't think he would have expected Mum to stay at home and look after him had she lived. At any rate, we'll never know. Years later, when I was old enough to understand what I was looking at, I discovered her library of feminist literature hidden in the back of a closet . . . Germaine Greer. Betty Friedan. Names I'd vaguely heard of and others I didn't recognize at all. I glanced through the books and they didn't exactly speak to me, as they say. Not my sort of thing.

Looking back, I realize that keeping house for my dad was the best way to distract me from the disadvantages of not having a mother.

But Miss Everett haunted me. As soon as it dawned on me that once Dad died I would be alone like her, I decided there and then to get married. I couldn't wind up like Miss Everett. I just couldn't.

So when a Sold sticker suddenly appeared on the For Sale sign for No. 57 and a month later a huge pantechnicon rumbled tentatively down Chaveny Road and turned into the driveway, I was beside myself with excitement.

Word spread fast. The Murphys were coming. Pat Murphy, apparently, was a fat cat, a big shot in the building trade, who had made enough money to move out of central London and buy a substantial house for his family. No. 57 was going to need a lot of money spent on it but, as the smug what-a-good-deal-I've-made estate agent pointed out, who better to restore the house than Pat Murphy?

Then Moira who cleaned for us — Dad insisted we hire her when he began to spend his leisure hours chipping away at the grime around the bathtub — dropped a bombshell by announcing that she'd been hired to clean at The Big House.

'What Big House and what about us?' Dad asked her, a bit grumpy.

'Next door.'

'Oh, you mean No. 57? Well, why didn't you say so.'

'And I can still go on cleaning for you. It's not as if I have to do anything else here. I'll have time,' said Moira.

'So what are they like?' I couldn't wait for the details.

'Catholics,' said Moira triumphantly. 'Pat and Nora Murphy. Three teenage sons, Billy, Pete and Warren. And I think she's getting on a bit to hold out much hope for a little girl,' added Moira.

'Three brothers,' I said. 'I can marry the boy next door.'

'Good plan,' said Dad, as always. 'Which one?'

That, I remember thinking, was a very good question.

5

I met them one by one about a month after they moved in.

Warren was the first. The doorbell rang one evening at about eight o'clock on a Thursday evening and I opened it to find a skinny boy with black hair and the bluest eyes I'd ever seen. He was clasping something to his chest. On closer inspection it was revealed to be a cardboard box with holes punched in the lid.

'They said a vet lived here.' *They* would, whoever *they* were. 'Can I see him?' He looked at me beseechingly. I assumed he must be about twelve. Younger than me, at any rate.

'Yes, he does. My father. But he's having his dinner right now.'

'Natasha's very sick. Very very sick.'

They always said that, and it was the point at which, if I had any sense at all, I'd say something like, 'Tough. We're closed. See you in the morning.' And give them the address of the surgery. But I wasn't a vet's daughter for nothing, and I couldn't bear to turn away a sick animal.

'Dad!' I yelled. 'Put the lasagne back in the oven. I've got someone to see you.'

'What's your name and address?' I asked him once Dad had taken him into the kitchen, still clutching his box to his chest.

'Warren Murphy. 57 Chaveny Road.' Now

he had my complete, undivided attention. 'Natasha's very sick,' he repeated.

Actually he wasn't. For Natasha, once we'd persuaded Warren to relinquish his box and allow us to open it, turned out to be a male canary. A dead male canary.

Warren burst into tears. And he didn't just cry, he sobbed loudly.

'He can't be dead.'

'I'm afraid he is.'

'Why did you call him Natasha if he was a boy?'

'I didn't know she was a boy. I wanted her to be a girl so I called her Natasha. My mum wanted me to be a girl. I'm the youngest. I've got two older brothers. By the time I came along she was really hoping for a girl.'

'But she didn't call you Natasha,' I pointed out reasonably.

'My father said she never called me anything for the first six months. Not until she'd accepted I was a boy. Then she called me Warren after Warren Beatty.'

'And you've got two brothers?'

'Billy's the oldest. He's in his last term at boarding school. He's eighteen. He'll be going to university soon. He's the bright one. Going to be a politician. Everyone says. Then there's Pete in the middle. He's sixteen. He dreams.'

I didn't quite get this. Did Pete sleep a lot or what?

'So you were a bit of an afterthought?'

'Not really. We're all two years apart.'

'You're fourteen?' I was incredulous. Same age

as me. I'd never seen a fourteen-year-old boy sob before.

'Yeah. I've seen you in school. You're in my year. You know, at St Joseph's?'

Then, of course, I felt really awful because I probably had seen him but I just hadn't noticed him. He was small and skinny and he looked really young for his age. I only registered the tall, good-looking ones. Not that they took the slightest bit of notice of me. I was fourteen but I was plain. I was fat. I had a big nose and a prominent jaw line and although Dad told me these were signs of a strong character I knew for a fact that right now they would do nothing to endear me to the opposite sex.

My hair was dead straight and one of the problems of not having a mother was that there was no one to supervise visits to the hairdresser to get it cut. I'd been letting Moira the cleaner cut it with disastrous results, but she was all I had. And I'd have to have a word with Moira. She had misinformed me. She had told me all the Murphy boys were away at boarding school. I'd had no idea two of them were at my school and one of them was actually in the same year.

'It's OK,' said Warren, 'it doesn't matter if you didn't notice me. No one ever notices me. They don't listen to me either. At least my family never do. Billy's the one they listen to. Because he's so smart.'

'What about Pete?'

'Well, I'm sure they'd listen to him if he ever said anything but he doesn't. I told you. He just dreams and watches.'

51

'What do you mean, dreams? And what does he watch?'

Warren's answer gave me the shock of my life. 'You,' he said, looking me straight in the eye, 'he watches you. In school. He's at St Joseph's too. He told me about you and that your father was a vet. He was the one who said you'd take care of Natasha. But you didn't . . .'

He started crying again and I hugged him. It was instinctive. I was trying to think of suitable words of comfort when a voice said, 'Oh, Warren. What are we going to do with you?'

We were still standing just inside the front door. I'd ushered Warren out of the kitchen so poor Dad could get on with his lasagne in peace, but when Warren had told me we were in the same class, I'd come to a dead stop in the hall.

'Hello, Mamma.' Warren transferred himself from my hug to his mother's. A fourteen year old being hugged by his mother as if he were still a four year old. I almost sniffed with contempt while knowing perfectly well that I often yearned for a mother with open arms. 'Natasha's dead.'

'Well then we'll have to bury him. We'll have a funeral service in the garden at the weekend. Perhaps you'd like to attend?' She turned her attention to me and I had the full impact of her beauty.

It was as if the Madonna above the altar in the chapel at St Joseph's had nipped down and popped over for a visit and on the way she'd had a bit of a makeover. She'd had her long black hair styled to frame her face just so, stopped off at the shops to buy herself a pale blue sweater that set off her very white skin to perfection and a floating sort of chiffony skirt that fell softly over her slim hips and gave you just the merest hint of her long shapely legs beneath it. Dad must have heard her voice because he materialized from the kitchen and she spoke to him above my head.

'Sorry to intrude on your evening,' she said in a soft voice with an Irish lilt to it. 'I'm Nora Murphy. We moved in next door a month or so ago and when my son Peter told me Warren had come down here with his canary, I thought I'd better come and rescue him. Or rather rescue you.'

'Frank Page. And this is my daughter whom you've met. Warren came to the right place. I'm the local vet. Sorry there was nothing I could do. Small consolation but would you like to come in for some lasagne?'

What was the matter with Dad? If he gave Mrs Murphy some lasagne then he'd have to give Warren some too and there wouldn't be enough for me. And I was starving. And why was he suddenly offering lasagne to Mrs Murphy? He hadn't offered poor Warren any when he'd been sobbing over his dead canary.

'We've already eaten,' said Mrs Murphy, much to my relief, 'and Warren still has a fair bit of homework to get through. But we'll have Natasha's funeral on Saturday afternoon. About four? See you then?'

She was looking at me. It didn't look like Dad was included in the invitation and I thought he seemed a bit disappointed. I wished he'd stop staring at her. I didn't know what had got into him. I could see he was making Mrs Murphy really uncomfortable. She was backing away towards the road, pulling Warren and his box along with her.

'Saturday at four,' I cried after them, 'see you then.'

'Fine. Check with your mother first. Sorry not to have met her.'

They were gone before I could say anything else.

'She doesn't know about Mum,' I told Dad when I went back inside.

'Oh, she'll find out soon enough. If that kid's at your school he'll know. Kids find out those sorts of thing immediately. He's probably telling her she put her foot in it right now as they're walking up that long drive.'

My first visit to No. 57.

Everything I tried on looked terrible. What did you wear to a pet funeral? Was it like a human funeral? Did you wear black? The only thing I had that was black was a pair of leggings and they made my thighs look huge. But I couldn't wear my fabulous new bright red shift dress because that would be too irreverent for a funeral. In the end I settled for a beige skirt and my pale pink sleeveless fleecey over a white T shirt. Bit warm for May but I could always take the fleecey off.

As it turned out I was vastly overdressed. Mr and Mrs Murphy were in what I assumed to be their gardening clothes, old jeans and sweat-shirts, and Warren was in shorts because the weather was really quite warm. I stood there in tights and smart shoes — they were new and now they'd given me blisters after I'd walked all the way up the long drive — and felt more stupid than I had in a long while. But Mrs Murphy could not have been nicer.

'How pretty you look. Sorry, we're still in such a mess. We're just going to get changed now, aren't we?' She looked at her husband and Warren and I knew perfectly well they hadn't intended changing at all. They'd be doing it just for me and I felt even worse.

In the event I welcomed the time to myself. It was hard to come to terms with what they'd done to Miss Everett's house. Not that I'd ever been inside before but I still had that picture in my mind of her sitting huddled close to the fire. In the month they'd been there — and they'd probably started long before they moved in — they had completely renovated the house so now it looked very grand indeed. It had been painted, the roof had been fixed, and the windows at the front of the house had shutters. *Shutters!* It gave the house a totally different look, almost Mediterranean. And that was just the exterior.

When I walked through the brand new front door I found myself standing on a black and white tiled floor and seeing myself reflected in at least two mirrors. There were pedestals with flower arrangements on top of them. I felt like I was on a movie set. In fact I felt distinctly uncomfortable. I'd never been in a house like this.

But when Mrs Murphy came downstairs dressed in the same blue sweater and flowing skirt she'd had on when she came to collect Warren, I said how beautiful I thought everything was and she looked rather surprised.

'Oh, do you think so? Nothing to do with me. Pat, my husband, had a decorator come in and overhaul the place. If I had my way, we'd be living in a little cottage overlooking the sea in Limerick. I'm not into all this fancy stuff.'

And nor am I, I hate it, I can think of nothing better than a cottage by the sea, I wanted to tell her, but it was too late.

There were more shocks to come. As she led me out of the front door and round the side of the house, I looked into the room where Miss Everett used to sit beside the fireplace. The walls of the room had now been painted terracotta and the wall beside the fireplace had been knocked through. French doors now led into a newly constructed conservatory. It looked odd to me. It didn't sit well with the rest of the house. It was too new, like those conservatories you see in ads in the Sunday color supplements.

But it was what lay beyond the conservatory that gave me the biggest shock of all. There was a huge gaping hole in the ground, like a bomb crater.

Mrs Murphy saw me looking at it.

'Sorry about that. We're building a swimming pool. It's about the only thing I approve of. My husband is throwing so much money into making our new house look as impressive and flashy as possible and I just couldn't care less. All

56

I need is a big kitchen where I can cook and we can all gather as a family, and beds for us all to sleep in, and I'm a happy bunny. But Pat wants more. Still, the boys are going to love having a pool. Oh, and you must come up and use it whenever you want. It'll be ready for the summer. We're going to have a grand opening, a housewarming party. Tell your parents.'

'My mother's dead.'

It came out all wrong. Here she was being so sweet and warm to me and I had to go and give her a cold shower.

'Oh, my poor baby.' Her arms were around me and she was giving me a hug, right there by the conservatory. 'Why didn't Warren tell me? When did she die?'

'When I was only four.'

'When you were only four,' she repeated. 'I'm so sorry. Warren! Come over here. Where's Pete?'

'In his room. Reading.'

'Did you know Mrs Page was dead?'

Warren nodded, staring at the ground.

'Well, why in heaven's name didn't you tell me?'

'Sorry.'

'Did Mr Page, did your father . . . What I mean is . . . do you have a stepmother?'

'No,' I said, 'just Dad. I look after him fine. He doesn't need anyone else. We have a kitchen like you said and I cook for him and we're a family. It's cool, it really is.'

The expression on her face was so sad that it seemed I ought to be reassuring her about my mother's death rather than the other way around.

'You're very brave,' she said gently. 'Warren, go inside and round up your father and Pete. You'll like Peter,' she told me, 'he's so sweet. Secretly I call him Sweet Pea, short for Sweet Pete. He does nothing but read books all day. Warren's my youngest, my baby, but Sweet Pea is the one I worry about. He's too nice for his own good. You can be, you know? Too nice, I mean. You can let people walk all over you. You have to learn to stand up for yourself and Warren seems to be learning faster than Pete. Warren's a cry baby but he's got a spiky side. He can stand up for himself when he wants to.'

I was fascinated listening to her talk. My father never spoke to me like this. And I was beginning to get excited about meeting Pete. Pete was the one who had noticed me in school. He must like me.

But when I saw him my heart sank. He had the worst skin condition I'd ever seen. His acne erupted all over his face and neck like lava from a volcano. No wonder he hid in his room reading books. I'd do the same if I had a problem like that.

He smiled at me very quickly then looked away and didn't say a word.

They'd already dug a grave for Natasha and we were preparing to form a group around it when Mr Murphy came out.

'Going to wait for me or what? Now, Molly, is it? So where do you live?' he asked. He had a loud voice. In fact, everything about him was loud, from his bright pink shirt with a little man playing polo on the breast pocket to the color of his face which was red and shiny. He had short, cropped blond hair, a chunky face, square jaw, ears sticking out, a wide smile. His smile was probably the only thing I liked about him. It made you smile back without thinking, even though you didn't really want to.

'I live at the end of your drive. No. 59.'

'Do you really? You live in our gatehouse then. What does your father do? Is he our estate manager or something?'

He clearly thought this was a huge joke.

'No, he's a vet.'

'Well, he can't be a very good one if he didn't save our Warren's canary.'

I felt the tears welling up in my throat. How dare this horrible man say my father was not a good vet.

'Pat,' warned Mrs Murphy, 'I think Natasha was dead already. We're here to bury him. Prayers. Let's join hands. Pete's going to read something, aren't you, Pete?'

This was a surprise. I had assumed Warren would be in charge of the proceedings.

It was very strange standing round a little scoop in the earth when beside us there was a huge crater ready to be filled in with the swimming pool. But when Pete began to read I forgot about everything else except the sound of his voice. Unlike Warren, whose voice was at that wobbly breaking stage, Pete's voice was low and deep and utterly mesmerizing. I shut my eyes and listened. When I couldn't see him I was ready to fall in love with him. He was reading Keats. *Thou wast not born for death, immortal Bird! No hungry generations tread thee down.*

The fact that he was reading from 'Ode to a Nightingale' rather than 'Ode to a Canary' was neither here nor there. His voice was dreamy. Rich. Sexy.

But when I opened my eyes he still had his pimples, and try as I might I simply could not reconcile the image of this gangling spotty youth with the voice I'd just heard.

'That it, then?' asked Pat Murphy. 'Shall we fill in the grave?' And without waiting for an answer he began to shovel earth into the tiny hole while Mrs Murphy put her arm round Warren and drew him away. Pete and I followed at a discreet distance. He didn't say anything, just kept sneaking glances at me and I found it very irritating. We were just about to go into the house when Nora Murphy came rushing back out. She was holding the cardboard box that had housed Natasha.

'Pete, for God's sake take this and bung it behind a hedge or something. I found it sitting on the hall table. Warren forgot to bring it out. We had the funeral but we never buried the bird. Take it before he sees it, go on, hurry!'

'Well, there you are,' he said quietly, and his low voice, now laconic in tone, worked its magic once more since I wasn't looking directly at him. 'Welcome to the Murphys.'

6

There was one Murphy I had yet to meet.

Billy the bright one. Billy the one everyone thought would be a politician. Billy the only one to be sent away to boarding school. Billy the eighteen year old.

Warren and I chatted away to each other at school now I had been made aware of his existence, and sometimes we even walked home together. He was quite musical and stayed on after school several days a week for piano lessons, something Mrs Murphy encouraged and Mr Murphy didn't. I barely saw the honey-toned Pete. But I soon learned that Warren's main hobby was gossiping and his family didn't escape his sometimes malicious tongue.

'So our Pete's been dumped by his girlfriend,' he informed me cheerfully one hot afternoon in July as we were turning into Chaveny Road.

'I didn't know he had a girlfriend,' I said.

'Why would you? This is the first time I've mentioned it to you. Anyway. She gave him this ultimatum three months ago to clear up his spots or she'd dump him.'

'But he can't clear them up to order,' I protested, 'that's so cruel.'

'That's so life, you mean,' said Warren, who cried at the drop of a hat. 'I wonder if she'll still come to our party for the opening of the pool. Bad timing to dump him this week if you ask me. Everyone else is coming.'

Mrs Murphy had been as good as her word and Dad and I were invited. I'd hit on Dad for some money to buy myself a brand new one-piece with a halter neck. If I tied the strings really tight it squeezed my non-existent breasts together and gave me a hint of cleavage. When I looked in the mirror I thought I looked amazing — until I noticed there was no space between my bulging thighs all the way down to my knees. This sort of thing had never bothered me before. Just as it had never occurred to me to notice the state of Dad's jeans. He always wore jeans at the weekends, jeans so old and faded they had worn through at the knee. The long drive leading up to No. 57 was now filled bumper to bumper with cars. Fancy cars. I wasn't aware how fancy they were until Dad mentioned we'd passed three BMWs, two Audis, a Mercedes and even a little silver Porsche. Dad drove a Sierra and it was the only brand I recognized. I began to worry about his jeans. Would he be smart enough? I consoled myself with the thought that when I had first gone to the house for Natasha the canary's funeral, I had found myself overdressed for the occasion. Nora and Pat had changed their clothes to make me feel better. Would they do the same for Dad if it were necessary?

But I needn't have worried. Everyone was in shorts or jeans — those who were not already in swimsuits.

They must have been relieved it was such a warm day. What would they have done if it had rained? How did you have a swimming pool opening in the rain? I didn't think anyone in Chaveny Road would be able to answer that one. No one else had a swimming pool.

I didn't think Nora Murphy would remember Dad. She'd only met him once. But she knew him instantly and came straight over.

'Frank Page. Grand to see you. Hope you've got your swimming trunks on under those jeans. The water in the pool's at seventy. Perfect. Run on round to the back,' she told me, 'the boys are all there.'

The sight that met my eyes was what I imagined houses in Hollywood must be like. Where the gaping hole had been, the aquamarine pool now had pride of place in the center of landscaped terraces on descending levels. Rows of giant sun loungers were parked poolside like the cars in the drive. Tables with triangular-shaped sun umbrellas on stands coming out from a hole in the middle were dotted around the place. And away from the water, over on the far end of the lawn, Pat Murphy was in charge of the barbecue. For one awful second I thought he was wearing just a butcher's apron with nothing underneath.

'It's OK, he's got his Speedos on.' Warren appeared beside me.

'His what?'

'Tiny little swimming briefs, dead tight, shows all his equipment. Mum's really embarrassed. He's far too old to be showing if off like that.'

I nodded. I thought I understood. And I hoped Mr Murphy would keep his apron on. I wasn't at all sure I wanted an exhibition of his 'equipment'. I thought of Dad's bathing trunks, as he insisted on calling them. They were like great big bloomers reaching halfway up his chest. But when Pat Murphy turned his back to me and I saw his disgusting flabby buttocks bulging out of his Speedos, I realized Dad probably had the right idea.

Where was Dad? He wasn't here by the pool. Then I saw him walking slowly round the house with Nora Murphy by his side, chattering away as if they had known each other all their lives. I was impressed. Dad was hard work. I knew he was a sweetheart underneath but he never made much of an effort at conversation. I'd more or less had to drag him to this pool opening and I'd been prepared to spend the afternoon keeping an eye on him, making sure he didn't slope off too early. But Nora Murphy had obviously worked wonders. I hadn't seen him so animated in a long time.

'Who are all these people?' I asked Warren, looking round at the guests. I'd never seen any of them before which showed they weren't locals. What struck me was that they all looked tanned and glistening, as if they'd been abroad.

'Flash gits,' said Warren cheerfully. 'Dad's clients mostly. Rich folk. Mamma doesn't like them but she's going to have to get used to them. Dad wants them to become his friends, wants to be one of them instead of working for them. I know this because it's what Mamma shouts at him when she's really angry. She says it'll never happen and he's wasting his time. But he reckons now he has a fancy house like them and a pool and he can invite them to dos like this, he'll be in there in a second.'

Later I would realize that for someone who had only recently turned fifteen, Warren was extraordinarily precocious in his perceptions. Right now all I understood was that Nora Murphy was like me and Dad, and Pat Murphy wasn't.

A trestle table on the lawn served as a bar and a crowd had gathered round it. As I moved closer I caught a glimpse of the barman. He was drop dead gorgeous. Tall, black hair like Warren's but with piercing green eyes and a very wide smile. Every time he handed someone a drink, he said something to them that made them laugh. I gravitated towards him, stood in front of the table gaping at him like an idiot.

'What'll it be, sweetheart?' He smiled straight at me.

'Coke,' I stammered.

'Bit of rum in it? Go on, who's going to know. Only you and me. Be our secret.' He winked at me and I fell in love with him there and then.

'Wherever did your mum find the dreamy barman?' I asked Warren.

'Still asleep in bed about half an hour ago. He didn't get in till four and she was furious. She told him yesterday she wanted him up bright and early to help get everything ready. Oh,' he saw my bewildered look, 'you don't get it, do you? That's Billy. That's my eldest brother. Just left school for good and home for the holidays.'

'Where's Pete?' I asked to cover my surprise.

'Right here.' His unmistakable voice was right

behind me. 'I've been here all along but you never noticed me.'

'He's been following you around like a shadow,' said Warren, while Pete went pink with embarrassment. 'You got some rum in your Coke?'

'How did you know?'

'Billy's party trick. Gets a girl drunk then snogs her.'

'Warren!' said Pete.

But I was thrilled. Was Billy after me?

I went and lay by the pool and after a while I saw Billy leave the bar and start making his way towards me. At least I thought he was coming towards me until he got as far as the springboard where he stopped and put an arm round a blonde girl in a bikini. Then he put his other arm around another girl and a third leaned forward and kissed him on the lips. Soon he was surrounded by women. And that's what they were, I realized. Women, not girls. Maybe a few of them were eighteen like him but most of them seemed far older. They all had sensational figures, long legs, even tans, impeccable manicures and pedicures. And breasts. Perfectly formed and very prominent breasts. Why had I been so stupid as to think he would notice me with a chest so flat you could lay me over the kitchen table and do the ironing on me. Me, a child compared with these glamorous creatures that were definitely a first for Chaveny Road.

'Who are all those girls?' I asked Warren who had come to lie beside me.

'We call them Billy's Beauties. Waste of time

remembering their names since there's a new one every week. They've come from London, mostly.'

'We're in London,' I pointed out.

'No, we're in the suburbs. These chicks have come from central London, sisters of boys he was at boarding school with half the time.'

'Ah,' I said wistfully. I didn't have a prayer but I could still worship him from afar.

Pat Murphy had hefted himself up on to the springboard, causing one of the beauties to topple into the water where she squealed delightfully for Billy to help her out. Billy got his looks from his mother, I thought, observing him beside his overweight, red-faced father whose pot belly hung over his Speedos but not enough to hide his by now unmistakable equipment.

Pat was going to make a speech.

'Ladies and gentlemen, boys and girls, can I have a bit of hush so I can tell you why you're here. First of all, without wishing to sound too much like the Queen Mum,' he paused, maybe he was expecting laughter but if he was he didn't get it, 'I would like to declare this pool well and truly open.' There was a ripple of applause but it was a bit feeble. 'But the real reason I wanted you all here was to ask you to raise your glasses to toast my son William. I say William rather than Billy, because William's a politician's name and that's what he's set his heart on becoming.'

'Dad.' Billy was on his feet, towering above his father on the springboard, trying in vain to get his attention.

'You never know, one day we might all be his

constituents.' Pat Murphy carried on regardless. 'He's going to take a year off and then he'll be going to university and . . . OK, son,' as Billy tapped him on the shoulder again, 'you tell 'em. Captive audience. Here you are, ladies and gents, taste of what's to come. His maiden speech.'

'The thing is, Dad,' said Billy, gripping his father's shoulders, 'you're a bit behind the times. I don't want to go into politics. That was your idea, not mine. I've enrolled at drama school. I start in September. I'm going to be an actor.'

'What does he mean, *going to be*?' muttered Pete behind me. 'The day Billy stops bloody performing will be the day my skin clears up.'

7

A year later I ran into Nora Murphy in the High Street one Saturday. It was a bit awkward. I didn't know whether she'd want to talk to me. Warren and I had been immersed in our GCSEs. I'd done really well and he hadn't and it had caused a bit of a rift between us. I hadn't been invited to No. 57 for ages, not since the year before, really. That summer, after the opening of the pool, I'd practically lived there, going round every day at Warren's invitation for a swim. Of course, the real reason for my visits had been to feast my adolescent eyes on Billy. But he continued to be surrounded by his Beauties. I was fascinated by them and their ability to show off their bodies to their best advantage. Out of the corner of my eye, I would watch the way they reclined on the sun loungers, lying on their side with one arm propping up their head and the other draped casually over their raised haunches. Their legs always reached to the very tip of the loungers and their creamy white breasts spilled out of the bikini tops. If they weren't sunbathing topless, that is. And this was in England so it wasn't always that hot. When the temperature didn't make it high enough, I noticed their nipples stood erect in the cold.

I practised their positions in my bedroom, lying on my side on my bed and looking at myself in the mirror on the door of the wardrobe. But I just looked too sad and uncomfortable for words and after a while I began to stay on the recliners on the patio, watching them from a distance and only venturing into the pool for a swim when they weren't there. I felt too conspicuous otherwise. Not that anyone took any notice of me. I think what hurt me the most was the fact that Billy never even said hello to me. He seemed to operate on a completely different planet to the rest of his family. It was as if Warren and Pete didn't exist and his mother was there merely to provide food and drink for his guests.

Only his father seemed to be able to get his attention. Apparently, after Billy's announcement that he was going to be an actor rather than a politician, Pat Murphy had shown his disappointment by being rather less forthcoming with the funds Billy relied on to finance the seduction of his Beauties. Billy, destined to be a politician in one way if not another, embarked upon a campaign to charm his father back to the bank. He was successful but I couldn't help noticing that Pat Murphy had begun to spend almost as much time making the Beauties at the pool laugh as his son.

'There you are,' cried Nora as we crossed paths, 'I'd been wondering where you'd got to. Why don't we see so much of you these days?'

Actually I had been wondering how I was going to bond once more with Warren now that it was becoming warmer and my thoughts were turning to spending days at the swimming pool, exploitative little minx that I was.

I explained about the GCSEs.

'Oh, that's ridiculous. Warren just doesn't do any work. Not like my Sweet Pea. You come on over on Saturday. We're going to take the cover off the pool. Meanwhile, how about joining me for a coffee right now?'

She was really happy to see me and she looked great. She'd had her hair cut really short, pixie-like, cropped close to her head with a spiky little fringe. It took ten years off her and gave her an Audrey Hepburn look. I commented on it and she smiled.

'Warren did it last night at the kitchen table. He's brilliant. He always cuts my hair. You ought to let him do yours one day.'

'I'm growing it,' I said, a little too defensively.

'Good for you,' she said cheerfully, 'now tell me all about yourself. Have you got a boyfriend? I'm really worried about my Sweet Pea. Must stop calling him that now he's left us to make his way in the world.'

Pete had left school and surprised everyone by getting a place at university. What nobody had known, least of all Nora, was that he had been brilliant at foreign languages. Modern languages as they were known, apparently. I supposed that meant the ones you could actually speak rather than Latin or Greek which were called dead languages. Pete, it turned out, was a whizz at French, German, Spanish and Italian and now he'd gone off to the Continent for a year to perfect them by speaking them. He could read and write in all these languages but he couldn't keep a conversation going for very long. I couldn't help thinking that perhaps this had something to do with the fact that there weren't any French, German, Spanish or Italian people living in Chaveny Road.

His love life, however, appeared to be a disaster.

'I just don't know what to do,' sighed Nora over her cappuccino. 'He's a good-looking boy but he's nice to them and girls don't like that. That's why they keep dumping him.'

I didn't know about the good-looking. I hadn't seen Pete in ages. And where was it written that girls didn't like boys being nice to them?

I called Nora Murphy on this one.

'Ah, I don't mean they don't want the presents and the flowers and the kisses and all that. It's just if a boy's always there when you want him, if he's totally reliable, he becomes boring. You'll see. I'm talking about boys, mind. Not men. I'm not saying it's what girls like but it's what they need somehow to make them really appreciate a boy and Pete doesn't seem to understand this. He needs to learn how to keep them guessing, that he shouldn't call the very next day and say he wants to see them again. He needs to wait a week so they're desperate when he does eventually call and they'll do anything for him.'

'I thought it was girls who had to play hard to get to keep a boy interested.'

'Well, that's exactly my point. They do. It's all part of the fun. But with Pete they don't get much of a chance and somehow it spoils things for them. It's all too easy. They get bored with him. And there's his brother Billy having endless success with girls. It makes it all so much harder for him. And it's happening in Italy, too. He called me last week, poured his heart out over some girl he met in Florence who's now gone off with someone else. Just as well he's moving on to Rome next week. He tells me everything. He always has. He's closer to me than the other two. He's so sensitive, I want to protect him from the world. It was a terrible struggle for me to let him go off on his own on this trip.'

'You love him better than Billy or Warren?'

She looked at me sharply. 'I never said that. Of course I love them all equally. I just worry more about Pete. Warren and Billy can look after themselves.' My ears pricked up. Ever since we'd sat down I'd been wanting to ask her about Billy but didn't want to draw her attention to my interest in him.

'Do they all get on?' I asked her. 'As brothers, I mean?'

'Warren and Pete do. They're more of a kind. They didn't go away to school. Of course it's going to be interesting to see what Pete's like when he gets home. He'll have been abroad, further than Billy. Billy's not like the other two.' You can say that again, I thought. 'Sometimes I look at him and I can't believe he's my own son, despite the fact we look so alike. It's like he's a cut above the rest of us. His dad doesn't see it. It's sort of what he's expected for Billy all along so I suppose it comes as no surprise but it makes me uncomfortable. Sometimes I feel as if I'm not quite good enough for him.'

'And his father is?'

'Oh, you're wise beyond your ears as my granny used to say. No, he treats Pat exactly the same as he treats me. It's just that Pat doesn't notice it like I do. You know something, Billy brings these friends of his over in the summer to use the pool but he never brings them in the winter when we'd all be closeted inside the house together and they'd have to talk to us. By the pool they can just lark around and more or less ignore us. Billy never actually introduces us.'

'But I saw Mr Murphy with them last year.'

'Ah, yes, but that's because Pat goes over and introduces himself.'

'Well, you could do the same,' I pointed out.

'I could. But I'm shy. Like you,' she added, 'I've noticed. We're two of a kind.'

'But you're so pretty, why would you ever need to be shy?' I blurted out.

'Well, you're pretty too. You just don't see it yet. You will. At the moment you probably think your nose is too big and your body's all wrong and you don't notice that you have beautiful long legs and lovely gray eyes. Do you look like your mother?'

I stared at her for a second. It was strange to hear someone ask me if I looked like my mother as if she were still alive. She wasn't in the least embarrassed like most people were. They sort of tiptoed around the subject of my mother as if it were taboo.

'My dad says I do. Once he said every time he looks at me he's reminded of her. But I don't remember her. I just have photos to go on and they're all so old-fashioned it's hard for me to see myself in them.'

'I think it's wonderful the way your dad's brought you up all on his own. Hasn't he ever had girlfriends who've tried to take your mother's place?'

Nobody had ever asked me this before. It was weird how I found it so easy to talk to Nora Murphy. It was like chatting to one of my friends. Yet she was old enough to be my . . .

Would it have been like this if my mother had lived? Would I have been able to chat to her about boys and feelings the way I knew some of my friends did? Dad was Dad. He never talked about this sort of stuff.

'Dad's never had a girlfriend since Mum died,' I said firmly.

'Not as far as you know.'

She had a point. If he had one, would he bring her home?

'But he never goes out,' I told her. 'I cook him his dinner, then we watch TV and we go to bed.'

'That's really sad.'

I didn't see why. I took care of him really well. He seemed happy enough.

'Did you always long for a daughter?' This was a bit daring on my part but I wanted to get off the subject of Dad being sad. 'Warren once told me you wanted him to be a girl.'

'He didn't!' She sounded genuinely shocked. 'How terrible. Yes, of course I would have liked a girl but you can't have everything and I love my three boys.'

'What did you mean when you said you were shy?'

'Just that. I find it hard to think that people will be pleased to see me, that they'll want to spend time with me. I have to wait for them to ask me. Except Pat, that is. He asked me out straight away.'

'Was it love at first sight?'

'Oh, you're a real little romantic, aren't you? That's another thing we have in common. I knew when I became serious about someone that would be it. I'd love them forever. Pat and I have been together for over twenty years. Yes, I think it was love at first sight. I certainly believe in it. Why, have you met someone?'

But of course I couldn't tell her. 'Yes, your son Billy. I fell in love with him the minute I saw him, but I'm shy like you and that's why we haven't got together.' She'd think I was daft. I just nodded and smiled.

'Oh, going to be mysterious, are we? Well, just make sure he treats you right. Don't be too easy, too forthcoming to begin with, but once you've got him just make sure he's a good solid man who can take care of you like my Pat. He always was ambitious, was Pat. It was one of the things I liked about him, his get up and go, but I never dreamed we'd come this far. Tell you the truth, it's caught me a bit by surprise. I'm not sure I feel entirely comfortable in this new house but don't you ever breathe a word of that to anyone. It'll just be our secret. It's the sort of thing another woman would understand. I don't like to be rushed and Pat's success has come a little too quickly but I'm trying my hardest to deal with it because I know it's what he's always wanted.'

What have you always wanted? I found myself wondering as she looked rather wistful for a moment. But I didn't ask her. Instead I blurted out something far worse.

'And are you as in love with Mr Murphy as you were the day you met him?'

For a split second she looked completely shocked and I thought I'd gone too far. Then she recovered herself and said: 'I said you were a romantic. No, or rather, yes, I mean yes, of course I love him but you know, nothing stays the same. Pat and I, we're two very different people to the kids we were when we got married. I love the new Pat as much as I loved the old Pat but he's not the same man and I love him in a different way. Above all, I find I believe in forgiveness in marriage.'

Forgiveness in marriage. What did she mean by that? I must have looked bewildered because she went on, 'I've had to make allowances, allowances I didn't anticipate at the beginning.'

I was mystified. 'What kind of allowances?'

'Oh, you know . . . ' She tossed her hand in a throwaway gesture.

The trouble was I didn't know.

'Is that why you were caught up in a bit of a dream just now? Were you thinking about the way your marriage had changed?' This was taking a bit of a liberty. I barely knew her but I found it so easy to talk to her. 'I hope you don't mind if I, you know, ask you stuff like this?'

She laughed. 'Of course not. No, the reason I

77

was off in the clouds was that with all this talk of boys and love and marriage, I was wondering what your mother would have had to say to you about all that stuff had she lived. Does your dad ever bring up the subject at all?'

'Dad? Love? Boys?' Now it was my turn to look at her in shock. 'I think he'd rather die than talk about romance unless we were joking about it.'

Nora laughed again. 'I thought so. Now listen, and I really mean this, if you ever need someone to discuss these things with, I'm always here. I expect you talk to your girlfriends endlessly, I know I did when I was your age, but if you ever need an older woman's perspective, although I'm not sure how much help I'd be . . . it's just that . . . ' She hesitated. She was embarrassed, going slightly pink. Maybe she was worried that she'd overstepped the mark with me. I was so used to being the one covered in confusion, I found it rather endearing, especially in someone who was supposed to be older and wiser than I.

'It's just what?' I prompted.

'It's just that I always wanted a daughter to chat about this stuff with. And now it's too late.'

'Maybe not,' I said, smiling at her. I deliberately left it open-ended. Maybe she could have had more children (unlikely) — or maybe I could become that daughter.

I couldn't very well come right out and tell her that I was going to be the next best thing, that one day we would be mother and daughter.

In law . . .

8

I couldn't wait to go haring up the driveway of No. 57 for another heart to heart with my new-found friend. Nora Murphy had said I could go and talk things over with her whenever I felt the need. The problem was that apart from needing someone to whom I could unburden myself about my near uncontrollable passion for her eldest son, there was nothing really wrong with my life. If I was going to engineer another chat with Nora I'd have to find an excuse. But before I could manufacture a need out of thin air, help arrived in a totally unexpected form.

Out of the blue I received a letter from Mitzi Alexander.

I'd never met her but over the years I'd heard from her every now and again. She claimed to have been Mum's best friend. Mitzi was American. She lived in New York which was quite an exciting thought in itself. From what I'd gleaned from television and movies, life in Chaveny Road was about as far removed from life in Manhattan as I could possibly imagine, and the idea that my mother's best friend hailed from there intrigued me.

But she wasn't Mum's best friend as far as Dad was concerned. Any requests to him for further information about Mitzi were met with a blank stare. For some reason, he didn't like Mitzi and never wanted to discuss her.

'Don't ask me what your mother got up to with Mitzi. Mitzi thought I was too ordinary for her. Your mother and I weren't on the same wavelength about all that stuff.' But he never explained what he meant by 'that stuff'.

Apparently Mitzi was my godmother, even though she was Jewish, and this seemed to make her think she should keep tabs on me, but not, I noted, to the extent of making a trip to England to meet me or even sending me presents. She did come to London once but all she did was telephone. I wasn't there and Dad didn't tell me she'd called until a couple of days afterwards. Had he put her off or had she just not bothered to try again? Was it too much of a trek for the likes of Mitzi from central London to Chaveny Road?

Her latest letter was a bit heavy. What, she demanded to know, was I planning to do with my life now that I was nearing school-leaving age? What kind of career did I have in mind? The most important thing, she stressed, was that on no account must I fall into the same trap as my mother and allow a man to stop me pursuing my dream.

This posed several questions: Mitzi's own enquiries about my career ideas and plans for the rest of my life were two points I hadn't exactly spent much time addressing. But then I found myself wondering, what had been my mother's dream that had been stopped by Dad? And, somewhat closer to home, what was my own dream?

And where was the man who was going to stop it?

I decided she would think me a bit pathetic if I wrote back, 'Dear Mitzi, no life or career plans, no dream, gorgeous man but bit of a problem there, will get back to you when I've got everything sorted', so for the first time, I didn't answer.

Yet she'd started me thinking and, in retrospect, maybe that's exactly what she had intended.

The problem was that it was becoming clear to me that I was a bit of a misfit when it came to my role in the world of women today. Nowadays, when we'd had a woman prime minister and a woman as head of MI5, and there were countless other females at the top of their professions, it seemed women could do anything. Mitzi banged on in her letter about something called a glass ceiling, and how women were on the verge of crashing through it, which sounded rather dangerous to me.

I didn't want to be prime minister; I didn't want to be head of MI5; I didn't even want to go to an office. And if I were really honest with myself, I didn't actually want a career because I equated having a career with going off to work every morning and sitting in an office some-where when all I wanted to do was stay home.

This whole 'women can make it to the top' thing had got me in a right old muddle. For some time I had been secretly observing my friends' mothers and their careers. It was true, most of them went out to work in offices of some kind and the thing I noticed most about them was how inaccessible they were. If Lucy, Sarah or Josie ever called their mother at the office they rarely reached them direct. First they had to go through a switchboard, then they were put through to an assistant, who invariably told them their mother was in a meeting and couldn't be disturbed so they always wound up telling the assistant what they were calling about and she relayed the message. Even if they had the mother's direct line, she was always in a meeting. And yet they always called their mother, never their father. As I didn't have a mother to call, I had no choice, and unless he was in the middle of performing an operation he always took my call. Although more often I just wandered round the corner to the surgery and spoke to him face to face.

On the odd occasion I accompanied my friends to pick up their mothers from work, we never walked into the office unannounced. We were made to sit in Reception until she was ready for us. Once I had needed to pee and although the receptionist gave me specific directions, I got lost and found myself wandering down endless corridors past rows and rows of offices. Then, in a large corner office, I saw Josie's mother. I was about to go in and say, 'Hi, we're here, did you know?' when I realized she wasn't alone. She was angry, gesticulating, in some kind of argument with the man who sat behind the desk. I caught the words, 'It's a disgrace. Women only earn eighty per cent of the male hourly wage. Haven't you heard of inequality of . . . ' She kept pointing to another man sitting beside her.

Later, on my way back from the ladies', I passed her in the corridor. She was crying and being comforted by another woman. 'It's not fair,' I heard her say several times, and then, 'He's only been here six months. We have the same job title. It's not fair.'

I was confused. Josie had always told me her mother was the boss, that she had ten people working under her. I didn't understand why she had to go and shout at somebody when she wasn't getting as much money as a man. What I did understand was that she was fighting and she was unhappy. Was this what Mitzi and my mother wanted me to do?

Dad explained to me that night that Josie's mother wasn't the overall boss. She just ran a department, she was a department head. Middle management. And that the overall bosses tended to be male as a rule. Did they earn more money? I asked. Probably, was Dad's reply, he'd never really thought about it, and if you wanted to be sure you had control over what you were paid, you'd have to run your own business.

I'd never really thought about it either because I'd never really thought about going to an office, let alone running my own business. What I wanted to do was virtually unheard of these days, and up to now I had been too nervous to tell anyone. Ironically, it was Warren who wormed it out of me.

'Your mum's hair looks really good, Warren,' I told him when we were sitting by the pool one afternoon during the summer holidays. 'Could you do mine one day?'

'Sure,' he said. 'What's more, I'll do it for free.'

I hadn't intended paying; I thought he'd do it for a laugh.

'Did you charge your mum then?'

'No, 'course not. What I mean is I've got a summer job at the hairdresser's on the High Street, start next week.'

'Cutting hair?'

'No, sweeping hair. Off the floor. Making cups of tea. Fetching and carrying for the stylists. But one day I'll have my own salon. I'll be my own boss.'

'Warren, I had no idea you had a plan.'

'I've had it for ages but you're the only person I've told so don't go blabbing.'

'Doesn't your mum know?'

'I'd like to tell her but she might tell my dad.'

'What's wrong with that?'

'I hate my dad.'

It was a shocking thing to say and he said it so matter-of-factly it scared me.

'You can't mean that. Why?'

'Because of what he does to Mum.'

'What do you mean? What does he do to your mum?'

'Never mind,' said Warren darkly, and I suppose if I hadn't been so preoccupied with my future and what I was going to do about it, I'd have quizzed him further. As it was I just asked him: 'Warren, do you think women should have careers?'

'Everyone should have a career if they want one.'

'Well, what do they do if they don't have a career?'

'They just have a job, I guess.'

And yet merely working for a living didn't seem like it was an option for a woman any more. My friends' mothers all had fancy career titles rather than jobs. What does your mum do? She's a senior (never junior) financial consultant, a marketing director, an executive editor, a key accounts manager, a department supervisor. But if I turned round and asked Warren the same question about Nora Murphy, he'd have to say housewife and mother.

She wasn't the only one, but all the other mothers I knew who stayed at home were there because they were on maternity leave or because they'd opted out of their careers to try being at home for a change. And what a big deal they made of it! What a big sacrifice! No one should ever forget that once they had been a vice president or whatever and that the ladder was merely waiting for them to step back on to. What I couldn't understand was this: why did they have to start climbing the ladder before they had their children? What was wrong with getting married, having children, letting them get off to secondary school and then sorting out what you wanted to do in the way of a career? I was forever reading novels in which women searched for the love they couldn't seem to find because they'd spent so much time searching for their careers. Now their biological clocks were ticking away so fast, soon they would stop altogether and it would be too late to start a family.

I'd run a home for Dad for years. Piece of cake. Now I wanted a home with children running around in it while I was young and fit enough to look after them. Was that too much to ask? Then, when I was about thirty, when every other woman was tearing their hair out because no man would commit himself, I would be in a position to pack my kids off to secondary school. That way I wouldn't have to deal with the child minder problem and I'd be all ready to tackle a brand new career.

Because to my mind, being a housewife and mother was a career — just not a very popular one. And no man was going to make me spoil my dream, as Mitzi had warned me they would, by making me stay at home and not have a career because staying at home was my dream in the first place. It wasn't that I didn't want to work . . . I just had my priorities reversed. Right now I wanted to get married and have kids more than anything because I knew that creating a home was what I was good at. OK, so there would be a need to earn money and I would have to address that. But for the time being I had to focus on finding a husband.

Without giving up my independence.

'So now you know,' said Warren, interrupting my thoughts. 'I'm going to be a hairdresser one day and Dad's going to freak out. What are you going to be when you grow up?'

'I am grown up,' I said defensively, 'and I'm going to be a wife and mother.'

'Like Mum,' said Warren cheerfully, 'great!'

And that's when I realized I did have something to discuss with Nora.

I walked briskly up the Murphys' drive. I was a woman on a mission. I had to find out Nora's views on women and careers. I pressed the doorbell once and then again for emphasis. No answer. I waited a second or two and then pressed again. Still no answer. Feeling slightly deflated, I wandered around to the side of the house to see if I could get a response from the kitchen door. An extraordinary sight met my eyes.

Pat Murphy's rather large exterior planted right in the middle of my path.

He was on his knees with his back to me and his butt in the air. I nearly laughed out loud.

'Mr Murphy.'

I gave him such a surprise he nearly fell over. He managed to catch himself and rocked back on his heels, finally coming to a halt and squatting at my feet in a rather ludicrous position. I was staring down at his bald pate until he looked up at me.

'You gave me a fright, you did.' He held out one of his huge hands. They were like giant paws with sausages for fingers. 'Here, give us a hand. I'm all out of breath.'

I wasn't happy about helping him to his feet but I had no choice.

'I was looking for Mrs Murphy.'

'Not here. Gone shopping,' he puffed. 'That's why I've sneaked out to do this.'

We were round one side of the house in an

area of the garden I didn't know. A path of gray slate ran diagonally across the grass to an arbor that I didn't remember ever seeing before. He saw me looking at it.

'I had that specially designed,' he said proudly. 'You can buy them all ready made at the nursery but I wanted something just for her. Look, you can see, it's got her name carved ever so small across the curve of the arch. I was just weeding the grass here so the slate will show. And come and look at what I've done over here.'

Before I could stop him, he'd grabbed my hand again and was leading me along the slate path and under the arbor. What I saw left me stunned for a moment or two. He was in the process of planting a little kitchen garden. He had dug up the soil in a clearing at the edge of the woods and the slate path continued to form a cross dividing four separate areas.

'Herbs,' he said, pointing to the first quarter. 'Thyme, parsley, rosemary, that sort of thing. Cabbages, Brussel sprouts, cauliflowers there. And here we'll have salad stuff, lettuces and that.'

'What about the fourth part?'

'I thought I'd leave that to her, let her plant it herself with whatever she wants.'

'And you did this all yourself?'

'I did,' he said proudly.

'I didn't know you were a gardener.' Of course I didn't. I didn't know anything about him except that he was an ambitious builder and his youngest son hated him, and these weren't exactly prime horticultural clues.

'Well, I'm not.' He looked a bit sheepish for a second. 'Tell you the truth, I took a course. But don't tell the wife. I want it to be a surprise. I could have got the landscapers back, the ones who've done the rest of the place but I wanted to show her . . . '

He faltered and I stopped myself from finishing his sentence for him. He wanted to show her he cared. I thought it was the most romantic thing I'd ever seen.

'You like it then? Think it'll be OK for her?' He was anxious.

'I think she'll absolutely love it,' I reassured him. 'She has no idea?'

'None whatsoever. I sent her off to the West End to the shops to buy herself some nice clothes. Thought that was the safest way of keeping her gone for a few hours. At the last place we lived, we didn't have the space for this sort of thing and it's what she's always wanted. If she's said it once, she's said it a thousand times. 'I'd love to be able to step outside my kitchen door and pick fresh herbs to cook with.' Well, now she's got them. They delivered the arbor first thing. I had to stop them coming up the drive till she'd left. I've been digging all morning. Took time off work for her. When she hears that, then she'll understand. You women, you're always complaining that we don't give you enough time away from our work.' He winked at me. 'You're always saying work comes first and you come second. Well, she can't say that when she sees this, now can she?'

'No, she can't. She'll be really thrilled, Mr

Murphy.' I smiled. 'Tell her I'll be back to see her another time.'

I left him to the last of his weeding and started off back down the driveway.

I was almost home when I met Nora coming the other way. She slowed down when she saw me and leaned across to open the passenger door.

'Looking for me?'

'I came to see you, yes.'

'Well, hop in and we'll have a nice cup of coffee. I need some refreshment. I've been clothes shopping and it always wears me out. Besides, I'd like to show you what I've bought, see if you approve.'

I begged off, said I had to get home and give Dad his lunch, that I'd be back another time. The real reason was that I didn't want to spoil Mr Murphy's surprise. I felt he should be alone with her when he presented something so special.

But once she'd gone I found I couldn't resist seeing her reaction. I wouldn't disturb them. I'd creep back through the woods and watch from there.

I left the drive and slipped through the trees around the back until I found a spot where I could see straight through the clearing, through the arbor to the kitchen door.

Mr Murphy was still on his knees. He obviously hadn't heard the car.

Or maybe he had because he kept glancing up towards the kitchen window, and when Nora's head appeared he called to her, 'Out here, love.'

When she came out I saw her go through the same kind of performance I had just carried out with Mr Murphy. She frowned at the sight of him on his knees, she helped him to his feet, she looked to where he was pointing and her face registered the same look of surprise that mine must have done.

After that it was totally different. I ducked quickly behind a tree as they began to walk straight towards me. They were arm in arm, Mr Murphy talking excitedly and waving his free arm all over the place and Nora giving little 'oohs' and 'aahs' of pleasure. She couldn't stop smiling. When they came through the arbor, she broke free of him and rushed to each of the four areas in turn, and then he came and took her hand and led her back to the arbor. I watched his face as much as hers. With me he had just been a man who was proud of his handiwork, but with Nora the expression on his face was something else. It was one of love. He had made her happy and by doing that he had made himself happy. The bald head, the pot belly, the flabby jowls, all these became insignificant beside the excitement in his face. Suddenly I saw the man Nora Murphy had married. I saw where Billy got his good looks, his charm. Technically, he resembled Nora, same eyes, same color hair, but his sexiness came from his father. Once upon a time Pat Murphy must have been a complete knockout.

When he showed her her name carved on the arbor, she flung her arms around his neck and kissed him. Then, as I watched, mesmerized, he brought his arms around her and began to rub his hands slowly up her back, stroking all the time until they reached her shoulders, her neck, till finally he was cupping her chin. His hands were so large that they covered her ears as well but I could see he was being incredibly gentle.

Until he brought her face forward to meet his and their lips met in a frenzy of passion.

The only time I had seen other couples kissing was at parties, clumsy teenage fumblings in semi-darkness. This was the kind of thing you saw at the movies. They were devouring each other before my eyes. He had begun to unbutton her jacket. She was reaching down to the front of his trousers.

I slipped away. I'd seen enough. This was private. Between two adults. And then I realized something. I had witnessed real passion, and why did it shock me? Because it did, just a little. It wasn't the passion that surprised me, it was the fact that I had witnessed it between two people old enough to be my parents. I had learned something watching them. There was no age limit on passion. Nora Murphy was about to have sex and there was no difference between her behavior and how I'd be if that were me standing there with her eldest son.

'Warren and I have been discussing what we're going to do when we leave school,' I told Dad at supper that night. I kept quiet about what I'd witnessed between Pat and Nora Murphy. Lurking at the back of my mind was the disturbing notion that Dad might have similar passionate urges buried somewhere beneath his placid exterior.

'Is that so? Will I be consulted about this at any stage?'

'Warren's going to be a hairdresser but you're not to tell anyone.'

'I'm the most discreet person in Chaveny Road. A vet is sworn by patient confidentiality. Rabbits are the worst! The things they tell me and do I ever breathe a word to you?'

'Shut up, Dad. This is serious.'

'So Warren's going to be a hairdresser, and judging by your new haircut he'll make a very good one. I assume he's responsible?'

I nodded. 'And I'm going to be a wife and mother.'

'Well, I'm glad we've got that all sorted out. As I recall, we'd already decided you were going to marry the boy next door. Well, now you've met them all which one is it to be?'

Well, I knew the answer to that one.

The trouble was, Billy Murphy was hardly likely to marry someone whose existence he barely acknowledged.

9

Nora Murphy called the next morning and asked why I hadn't been back to see her. 'There I was spending all day wondering what you wanted to see me about,' she said.

I hadn't returned because I hadn't wanted to disturb them having sex. But she didn't know that and besides, how long would they have been at it?

Still, I was anticipating feeling rather embarrassed as I walked back up the drive to No. 57. Would I go pink when I looked at her and imagined what had gone on the night before?

Of course, the first thing she had to do was march me off to her new herb garden and go on about what a sweet thing Pat had done for her, and I had to pretend I knew nothing about it.

'And do you know where he is right now?' she said, and I looked around nervously, expecting Mr Murphy to pop out from behind a hedge and ask her if she fancied a bit of nooky. 'He's gone off to Homebase again to buy me some more plants to put in the empty bit over there. I wanted to go with him but he wants to do it all by himself.'

I couldn't take much more of this and I wanted to get out of there before Mr Murphy came back, so I plunged in with: 'You said I could come and talk things over with you so I wanted to ask you what you thought about women having careers?' It all came out in a rush and she looked a bit taken aback so I added, 'I mean, did you ever think about having a career?'

'Coffee in the kitchen. Come on.' It was a bit abrupt and before I knew it she was striding back along Pat Murphy's slate path and I was following at a brisk clip. But I could hear her loud and clear when she suddenly broke into Carole King's *Tapestry* — as good a song as any while you're walking across the lawn, but it wasn't the lyrics that struck me. It was the fact that Nora Murphy had an astoundingly beautiful voice. Clear as a bell, as they say, carrying right up into the sky. And rich. It was a wonderful sound; all the more so for being so unexpected.

When she reached the kitchen door she stopped, turned and laughed.

'I could have had a career. I could have been a contender or whatever it was Marlon Brando said in *On the Waterfront*. I trained as a singer. Tell you the truth, that's where Pat first saw me, in a club, singing my heart out. He came up to the stage when I'd finished my set and asked if he could buy me a drink. He didn't just buy me one drink. He bought me several and he drank most of them himself. Oh, he was so funny. I couldn't stop laughing and I never looked at anyone else from that day on.'

'But what about your singing?'

'Well, I sang at our wedding. You should have seen me. I sang 'Love and Marriage', you know, go together like a horse and carriage, the old Doris Day hit? Oh, don't tell me you don't know who Doris Day is? I can't bear it. Am I that old?'

'Is she the one in those old movies with Rock Hudson?'

'There you go. Anyway, I had plenty of gigs right after we were married. Pat was just getting started in the building trade and he used to bring his mates along to the clubs. Boy oh boy, did they cheer me on once they'd got a few beers inside them. Nothing like a crowd of brickies for a bit of raucous support.'

'So when did you stop singing?'

'When I had the kids. We couldn't afford childcare and there was Billy waiting for me to breastfeed him morning, noon and night. It just wouldn't have felt right going down a smoky club every night.'

'Did Mr Murphy make you stay home? Did he spoil your dream?'

'What are you talking about? He was the one who wanted me to go on singing. He loved the idea of having a singer for a wife and it killed him that he didn't make enough money to pay someone to take care of Billy so I could go on with my career. I sometimes wonder if that's why he became so ambitious. The problem was by the time we could afford a child minder, I'd got used to being at home with the kids. You see, I had two dreams when I was growing up. To be a singer and a mother. I think I'm really lucky because both my dreams have come true. Just not at the same time. Of course, what would make me really happy would be to see one of my kids become a singer.'

'But none of them inherited your voice?'

'Oh yes, Pete did. He's got a beautiful voice

and sometimes we sing together. But he's just not interested. I dream about going back to singing and Pete understands all about dreaming. He's such a dreamer himself. He's the only one of my family who has his head in the clouds half the time like I do. It's not such a bad way to live.'

I thought she sounded a bit dippy but I didn't say so.

I was about to ask her again about her views on women and careers when we both heard the sound of a car door being slammed.

Pat Murphy's back, I thought, but it was Dad, huffing and puffing his way round the side of the house. He looked rather odd still in his white vet's coat.

'I'm sorry. I'm sorry to interrupt, to come bursting in on you like this but I need you.'

I pointed at my chest and mouthed 'Me?' because he could have meant Nora.

'Yes, you. Come quick. I went home for something and found Buster had got out and ruined Mrs Walker's herbaceous border. Probably a bone down there or something.'

Mrs Walker was the old lady who lived on the other side of us in Chaveny Road. We were sandwiched between the Murphys and Mrs Walker. We avoided Mrs Walker like the plague. She was a crotchety old bag who had hidden herself away ever since her husband had died four years ago. Dad felt sorry for her and tried to be neighborly, found an excuse to check up on her and see if she was all right every so often, but I kept away from her and the feeling was obviously mutual. She glared at me whenever she saw me.

Buster was the McGuires' fox terrier from No. 45. Dad was taking care of him while the owners were on holiday. It was a service everyone seemed to expect him to perform as a matter of course. *We're going away for three weeks, what are we going to do with our pet? Oh, I know, who better to ask than the vet?* As a result, we had a string of canine and feline visitors roaming around the house.

'What did she have to say about it?'

'Mrs Walker's away for the day at her sister's in Kent. That's the whole point. If we hurry, we can get some new plants and pop 'em in before she comes back, appease her a bit. So come on — although I've no idea where we go.'

'Homebase,' said Nora triumphantly, 'where Pat's gone. Go to the end of the High Street, turn right, keep going for half a mile and you can't miss it. Go on, hurry!'

Dad gave her such a look of gratitude, you'd have thought she'd saved his life. For one awful moment I thought he was going to kiss her.

'Have you left them all in the lurch at the surgery?' I asked once we were in the car, to deflect any queries he might have about what was I doing up at the Murphys'.

'Well, I've got to inoculate some kittens before lunch but we should have time.'

He roared into the Homebase car park and leapt out, slamming the door for the second time that morning. Dad was never one for taking his time about things. He was ostensibly a quiet soul but speedy under the surface. When I was very small I dubbed him Silent Superman because he never said much but he flew about the place doing good things for people. Or rather for animals.

When we walked into the giant greenhouse that formed the nursery part of Homebase, I saw Mr Murphy pulling a little cart laden with plants towards another entrance. A pretty girl wearing a Homebase uniform and with long blonde hair tied in a knot on top of her head was following him. She was carrying a bag of top soil. I waved frantically but Mr Murphy didn't see me.

'What are you doing?' asked Dad, sounding surprisingly irritable. 'We don't need him.'

'No, I suppose not.' But I watched Mr Murphy as Dad raced up and down the aisles, plucking terracotta pots seemingly at random.

Pat Murphy arrived at his car and started loading the plants into the trunk. Then he turned and took the top soil from the girl. I could see him quite clearly. His face was glowing with excitement, he was laughing, he was happy. He looked the way he'd looked when he'd shown Nora the herb garden, and as I watched he leaned forward and in one quick movement had whisked the comb out of the girl's hair so that it fell down around her shoulders. She looked totally surprised and he planted a kiss on her lips before she was aware of what was happening.

Then he laughed, got in his car and drove away.

For all his rushing around like a mad thing, Dad took forty minutes to select the right plants to restore Mrs Walker's herbaceous border to its original glory.

'She's probably home by now,' I grumbled as we approached the counter to pay.

The girl with the blonde hair was leaning on the cash register, chatting to a colleague. She had repositioned her hair on top of her head.

'So he says to me, 'where've you been all my life?' and I go, 'Right here at Homebase waiting for you', and he laughs and then he says, 'Want go for a drink Friday? I could pick you up after work.' So I said . . . Oh, sorry, sir.'

Dad was tapping his Visa card on the counter and I never got to hear what she said.

I wondered who she was talking about. Not Mr Murphy, surely.

When we arrived home, Warren was hanging around so we roped him in to help us with Mrs Walker's plants.

'What do you think of your mum's new herb garden?'

'It's OK,' he said, very non-committal.

'Only OK? It was a sweet thing for your father to do.'

He gave me an odd look and I didn't understand his answer at all.

'Dad did it out of guilt,' was all he said. 'Dad gave Mum a guilt garden.'

A guilt garden. What on earth was that? But I soon forgot about it because the two of us had such fun together and talking about heavy stuff like guilt was never part of the agenda.

Warren and I ran wild.

At least that was how Nora Murphy described

it when she rang Dad about us. Warren was in the next room eavesdropping, a particular talent of his, and he heard her say it.

'They're running wild, Frank. They're all over the place.'

She was probably talking about an infestation of fleas or something but we rather liked the idea that she meant us. It made us sound glamorous and exciting, like teenage gangsters running wild in the hood somewhere in America rather than two suburban kids who were strangely content to stick close to home. It's true, we did race all over the place on our bikes and hang about the woefully inadequate record store in the High Street, but we could hardly be described as *wild*.

In any event, Dad and Nora had a conference about it. They went out to dinner to discuss us. They were worried because we seemed to have no inclination whatsoever to want to go to college. Pat Murphy wasn't consulted as far as I could see. He didn't seem to be interested in Warren's future. Nor Pete's for that matter, even though Pete had made it to university. Short-sighted man that he was, Pat Murphy couldn't see past his favorite, Billy. I grabbed every chance I could to get him to wax lyrical about Billy's brilliant progress at drama school because it was the only way I could hear news of him. It wasn't as if Billy was calling me every day to tell me himself. The truth was he never came home any more, not even in the summer, and though I know Nora was bitterly hurt by this, she hid it well. Pat saw him. Pat had plenty of business in central London and father and son lunched together, dined together. But Nora was like us. She was happy to stay where she was. Like Dad. Which was why it was so odd that they had this fixation about us going to college. On and on they went about how important it was, how we'd regret it in the future, blah, blah, blah.

Of course I knew it was all directed at me. Warren was a hopeless case, bless him. No GCSEs to speak of. But his future wasn't a problem. Warren had a gift and a job lined up. Hair and There (cringe!) in the High Street were crazy about him. It had been a question of the understudy's dream come true. During his summer job sweeping up, he'd offered his services when one of the stylists had called in sick on a particularly busy day and never looked back. His summer sweeping job had turned into a cutting and styling trainee job with everyone, clients included, down on their knees pleading to him to join them full time. He'd do three years there and then the world would be his crimping oyster. What did he need to go to college for?

I, on the other hand, was bright, so Dad kept telling me. This was unfair. Warren wasn't stupid. He'd been smart enough to realize what he was good at, to hone his craft by cutting the hair of every female he knew for free until he knew he had put in enough practice to impress professionals. And he'd been proved right. Surely you made the biggest success of yourself if you did something you enjoyed, I reasoned when Dad kept on at me. OK, said Dad, what did I enjoy?

I had enough sense to know that 'staying at

home and looking after you' was not the right answer.

'Animals,' I said, 'looking after animals. I'm my father's daughter.'

Well, he couldn't argue with that, could he?

It was Warren who came up with my plan. Warren was always full of ideas. He was a tonic if you were down. He was such an optimist, he always looked on the bright side. Something always turned up, he reckoned, and if it didn't then he made it. I'd met him for his lunch break and he was regaling me with bitchy stories about his clients.

'Gave me a shock, I can tell you.'

'What did?' I hadn't really been listening.

'The scars. My lady this morning, she's sat there with her hair washed, all ready for me, and I take the towel off and there they are.'

'Accident?' I wasn't really that interested.

'Well, that's what she said, of course, but I thought, accident, my foot, she's had a face lift. Or three. Talk about nipping and tucking, it looked like her face had been to Weightwatchers and had gone down a whole dress size so she'd had to have it taken in. And that girl in the chemist's pregnant. I know it. I nearly stabbed her in the back of the head with my scissors, she leapt out of the chair so quick to run to the bathroom to throw up. Three times. And Mrs Maxwell from that big house on the corner's a chintzy cow. Do you know what? She steals the magazines. She does! Tracy, our useless junior' — he appeared to have forgotten he had been a junior only a few months ago — 'she goes, 'Can

I get you a tea, coffee, magazines, Mrs Maxwell?'
Well, the old bag can't very well take the tea or
coffee home but she puts the magazines under
her coat bold as brass, right in front of me. Does
she think I'm blind or what? She pays forty quid
to have her hair cut but she won't fork out three
quid for *Vogue*? Goes without saying she's the
stingiest tipper we've got. Helloo? Anyone at
home?'

'Sorry.'

'What's up? The usual? You want to stay home
and play house and your dad wants you to get a
degree in tying your shoelaces?'

'He just wants me to do something. I want to
do something. But he knows I don't want to
work in an office. He understands that. And
there's no way I'm going to work in a shop or
something. I'd be bored rigid.'

'Child   minder?   Go   to   college   and   do
childcare? Run a crêche?'

I made a face. It was the college bit I didn't
fancy. I'd had enough school.

'Don't look like that. You're always banging on
about having children.'

I hadn't realized he'd been listening.

'I know. But I can't just have a load of children
just like that. I'd have to go to college and study
childcare to run a crêche. And I'd have to find a
husband or a proper partner to have a big family.
Neither of them grow on trees.'

'I've seen a few who come pretty close,' said
Warren. 'Well, why don't you start with animals?'

They always say the simplest ideas are the
best. It didn't take long to persuade Dad. After

all, we'd been taking in the customers' pets for free while they went on holiday, so what was to stop me extending it into a slightly larger, not to mention fee-paying operation in the back garden? I agreed to a compromise. I would work for six months as a kennel maid at some place Dad knew, and I'd put in a stint working in the reception of his surgery, learning as much as I could about animal care.

Warren built the cages. He was incredible with his hands. I felt a bit bad about doing Dad out of his garden but he'd have the patio. It was all right for me, I could always go up to the Murphys and hang out in their garden if I wanted to be outdoors. Nora seemed happy for me to treat it as my own. I tried to encourage Dad to do the same. I'm sure they wouldn't have minded. But he was uncomfortable with the notion of making free with someone else's property and I suppose it was understandable.

In the end there were twenty cages in all with a fairly big space in the middle to let some of the animals out. I'd take the dogs to the wasteland for daily walks. In fact, I knew perfectly well that unless there was any real friction between my 'guests', I'd wind up taking them into the house as much as possible. Of course I was going to have quiet spells. School holidays would be my busiest times because that's when people with pets went away, but loads of people took off for weekend visits and someone had to take care of their animals. I also offered an at home service, going in and feeding pets and changing their litter trays or whatever.

People usually relied on their neighbors to feed their pets when they went away, and in a suburban community like ours there were plenty of people around. But you could never be quite sure whether the couple next door went in *twice* a day like you asked them to. They didn't even have children of their own, let alone pets. And there'd been those stories about kids replacing dead goldfish with a substitute bought at Woolworths, and thinking you'd never spot the difference. As if . . .

I wouldn't be doing it for free, but where I scored was that everyone knew me. They brought their pets to Dad and I'd always been around. They knew I was familiar with their animals, their animals trusted me and I would take great care of them. They could go off wherever they were going and relax. It was worth paying for. And Dad, the vet, would be right there if they got sick. It was an added bonus and it gave me total credibility.

So I set up shop in the back garden. Actually, it had occurred to me that I could open a pet shop in one of the front rooms of the house but I wasn't quite sure how to go about getting the necessary license. I was still a teenager. Besides, I thought I'd better let Dad get used to doing without his garden before I started carving up his house.

Mitzi probably wouldn't approve of what I was doing. Not exactly a major strike for women's rights. But why should I care what Mitzi thought? Because she had been my mother's friend and part of me had a guilty feeling that I was letting the side down somewhere along the line by not going to college or university and fighting some kind of power battle over a job with a man. The Kennels: my not-so-brilliant career. Well, I would make it work.

Of course, what Warren and I both knew was that it would keep everyone quiet until I found a husband and embarked upon my chosen career. Though Warren didn't know that in my dreams, I *had* found a husband. The only problem there was that Billy was away at drama school and I hadn't heard a word from him. Still, I could always dream. No law against that.

I opened at the beginning of the summer holidays — a smart move suggested by Warren — and found myself inundated with dogs, cats, rabbits, gerbils, tortoises and a white mouse. The mouse was a joke, planted on me by a little boy who lived down the road. I discovered almost immediately that it was made of sugar and I was tempted to eat it to teach the kid a lesson. Instead I went along with the joke and told him on his return from holiday that I was really very, very sorry but his mouse had been very ill and had had to have a big operation. Mercifully, I told him, it had recovered and, hey presto, here he was! I presented the boy with a cage containing a live white mouse and he promptly freaked out.

At first I thought Otto would be another joke but he turned out to be my first big problem. Otto was a Komondor, a Hungarian sheepdog, the oldest of the Hungarian breeds, brought west with the Magyars over a thousand years ago in the great migration from Asia. They were bred for sheep herding, and indeed they looked like sheep with a long woolly white coat, usually matted. Their big advantage was that they could disguise themselves as a sheep hiding in the middle of a flock, and then leap out and surprise a marauding wolf. The fact that there were precious few sightings of either sheep or wolves in Chaveny Road was beside the point.

Otto's master was known as The Refugee because no one quite knew how to pronounce his name. It was something like Mr Pobiskova but everyone just called him Mr P. Mr P was a genuine refugee from the Nazis. He had fled to London in 1939 and wound up in Chaveny Road. He was the only one of his family to escape and we never quite knew the details of their fate. All he had was Otto whom he had suddenly acquired about fifteen years ago and to whom he was obviously utterly devoted. Otto accompanied Mr P each time he went to the shops, and sat patiently waiting outside on the pavement for his master. They each walked so slowly that the whole operation could take them as much as an hour. But Mr P was immensely proud and would never allow anyone to help him. He held himself very straight even though he must have been well into his eighties, and the sight of this almost Chaplinesque little figure shuffling down the road dragging a woolly white monster on a lead behind him was a sight worth seeing.

The problem was Mr P didn't speak much English and he was on his last legs, but that was nothing compared to Otto.

'Someone's going to have to tell Mr P that it's time Otto was put down,' Dad declared at supper one night. 'I just bumped into them in the street and Otto can barely move. I need to get him into my surgery and examine him.'

But before we could think how we were going to engineer this, poor old Mr P had a stroke and keeled over. An ambulance took him straight to hospital and that left Otto on his own.

We had no alternative but to take care of him. To put him on a lead and drag him lumbering down the road to my kennels was out of the question. Without Mr P, Otto just didn't want to know. Besides, I didn't have a kennel large enough. But our access to him did give Dad a chance to examine him and pronounce that it was high time he popped off to the kennel in the sky. The quality of his life was pathetic and he clearly wasn't enjoying a single second of it any more.

But we couldn't do it without Mr P's permission and he was a tenacious old bugger who was still hanging in there. We tried explaining the problem to him, clustered round his hospital bed, but he couldn't understand a word we were saying. Warren tried to execute an unforgettable mime of a Hungarian sheepdog being put to sleep, but all that he succeeded in doing was making us shake with laughter which wasn't very appropriate under the circumstances and left poor Mr P looking even more bewildered.

As usual, Warren came up with the solution.

'Pete's coming home for the weekend.'

I couldn't see what on earth that had to do with the price of beans. To be honest I'd more or less forgotten Pete's existence. He had been away traveling in France or Italy, and except for Nora's occasional yearnings for her 'sweet pea', no one really mentioned him. Or maybe I was too wrapped up in my own yearnings for Billy that I never listened when people mentioned Pete.

'Oh good,' I said.

'Pete's going to be a translator. He came down from uni with a first. He's brilliant. He speaks all these languages. He only has to hear someone speak in a foreign language for five minutes and he can speak it too.' This had to be a bit of an exaggeration, I pointed out. 'Well, maybe just a bit,' agreed Warren, 'but he's our man. He'll be able to get through to Mr P.'

As it turned out, Warren was right. Pete came home and Warren took him in to see Mr P and then called me to report that Mr P had finally conceded it would be a kindness to put Otto out of his misery, but he wanted to see me and Dad first.

'Pete speaks Hungarian?' I was impressed.

'Turns out Mr P is a Czech and yes, Pete does speak a bit of that. Not enough that he could translate a book like he can in French or German or Spanish, but he can get by. But in fact they wound up conversing in Italian as they found that was the language they had most in common.'

'Tell him Dad and I will be there this

110

afternoon and he can translate anything Mr P needs to know.'

I didn't enjoy the walk down to the end of the ward past all the old men lying like skeletons in their beds watching me. They looked so pathetic, it was pitiful to think that once powerful hunks of muscle could be reduced to this. They flashed me toothless grins and to my horror I realized they all looked exactly the same. Which one was Mr P? I couldn't see Warren anywhere and Dad had said he was coming straight from the surgery.

Then I heard it. It was like music. There was a rhythm to the speech. It was melodious and rich and warm. A beautiful deep voice punctuated by soft laughter. It was coming from the end of the ward and I was drawn to it long before I realized I had heard it before.

The man was speaking Italian. I recognized that much. Seeing the back of his head I thought he *was* Italian. He had a shock of glossy dark brown hair and when he turned round to greet me he had beautiful, almost soulful deep brown eyes. But what struck me most was his smooth, tanned skin.

Pete's face had cleared up since I'd last seen him.

He was spotless.

10

It was a totally different Pete.

Once Dad had arrived and reassured Mr P that nothing would happen to Otto until he was out of hospital and could say his goodbyes, Pete and I went off to have a drink.

I kept sneaking glances at him as we walked along the High Street. Now his awful skin had cleared up, it was possible to see him in a different light, not that I'd seen him at all for the last couple of years. He was nothing like his brothers. Billy had toothpaste-commercial good looks, the kind that made you go weak at the knees and pink in the face. Warren was cute but he had the kind of cheeky looks that reminded you of those fresh-faced young jockeys that came over in droves from Ireland, the ones you saw being interviewed on TV after the Grand National: long eyelashes, rosy cheeks, upturned nose, gift of the gab, twinkle in the eye.

But Pete was different. Pete was like a poet. Pete was how I imagined Rupert Brooke must have looked. He appeared sensitive, fragile. A fine-boned face, huge brown eyes, long tapering fingers. His face was very expressive and intelligent. As we were walking along the street, I kept remembering what Nora Murphy had said about him always being dumped by his girlfriends.

'So what a way to meet up again,' he said as

we sat down and ordered our drinks. 'That poor old bloke. I remember him from when we first moved here. He was always shuffling up and down the road dragging that great big dog. I never realized he was a refugee from the war. What's the story on his family?'

I drew a finger across my throat. 'The camps, I assume. No one ever dares ask. Not that we'd have understood. You could have, I suppose. Or maybe not. 'Now Mr P, I'm afraid Otto's going to have to bite the dust and while we're at it, what happened to your family during the war? Mind filling us in?''

I could have died. Pete was staring at me in horror. He obviously found what I'd just said really offensive and on reflection I suppose it was. He was right to call me for being so flippant.

'I'm sorry,' I said, 'that was really gross of me. Poor Mr P. So tell me about your travels.'

'Oh, they were grand. That's how I'd be all my life if I had the choice, you know? A gypsy. A nomad. Roaming from place to place with just a knapsack on my back, meeting new people all the time. I'd travel by train. There is nothing so wonderful as travelling on a train. You can look out the window and lose yourself in what's passing by, and the motion of the train itself is so soothing, I feel like a little baby being taken out in a pram to stop me crying.'

I hadn't bargained for all of this. I thought he'd tell me about the clubs in Naples or something.

'And the other great thing,' he hadn't finished,

'is that with my languages I can pass for a foreigner. Sometimes I'd arrive in a country and give myself a totally different name and pretend to be Swiss or Italian, and do you know what, I think I got away with it.'

'Why would you want to be someone else?'

'Because I'm shy,' he answered immediately, 'and I assumed people would respond better to the fake me rather than the real me.'

'Now why on earth would they do that?' I was genuinely amazed. I'd never had a man admit he was shy before. 'Surely it's much better to be yourself, wherever you are?'

'You know, you're absolutely right. It's just that sometimes I find it hard to know myself, let alone be myself. Don't you ever have that problem?'

Slow down. Now we were really getting in deep. I wasn't used to boys — or in this case, a man — revealing so much about themselves so early on. Pete was clearly someone who waded right in without even thinking to test the water.

'I do,' I answered cautiously, and then, to get off the subject, 'So you're home for a bit?'

'I'm home this weekend for Mum and Dad's silver wedding anniversary. Twenty-five years. Mum's beside herself with excitement. It's so sweet seeing them together. They're really lucky having such a great marriage. So many of my friends have parents who are divorced.'

He suddenly reached out and touched my shoulder.

'Oh, I'm sorry. How stupid of me. Your situation is much worse than divorce. Your father's a widower, isn't he? You grew up without a mother.'

I nodded. 'It's OK, really. I never knew her. I'm fine talking about it.'

'Do you ever wish — ' He stopped.

'What?'

'Maybe I shouldn't ask this, but do you ever wish your father had married again? Given you a stepmother?'

'There's two ways of looking at that,' I said honestly. 'In a way I'd like him to be happy with someone, but then again maybe I wouldn't like her. As it is, we're fine as we are. Actually,' I looked at my watch, 'I ought to be getting back. Dad'll be home from the surgery soon. I need to feed the animals in the kennels and then cook him his evening meal.'

'Of course. I'm so sorry. I didn't realize I was keeping you.' He was on his feet, putting on his jacket, fumbling in his pocket for some change to leave on the table.

'Not at all. It was really great to see you again.'

'Was it? Do you mean that?'

As I came to know Pete better, I realized that he took everything literally. If someone was introduced to him and said something like, 'Oh, how nice to meet you, I've heard so much about you,' Pete would immediately ask, 'What have you heard about me?' He didn't seem to understand that there were things people said that didn't really mean anything. They were just ice-breakers. He might be an expert at conversing in French, Italian or Spanish but small talk was a foreign language to him.

115

I saw quite a bit of him one way or another but he didn't actually ask me out on a date for over six months. And even then I didn't immediately recognize it as a date. He just wandered into the kennel area one afternoon and announced: 'A friend of mine who happens to be one of my favorite poets is giving a reading on Thursday night. It starts at 7.30. I'll pick you up at seven, OK?'

Then he wandered off before I could even give him an answer. And I would have done because seven o'clock was a highly inconvenient time for me to be out. I fed the animals at seven and then I fed Dad.

'Oh, go on,' said Dad, 'I can take care of business here once in a while. Go out and enjoy yourself.'

I was a bit hurt to be honest. Dad didn't seem to need me.

But I was even more depressed by the event itself. It was at the back of a large bookstore in central London. Ordinarily I would have been thrilled at the thought of being taken into the West End for a night out but sitting on a hard chair at the back of a bookshop was not my idea of a fun evening. The trouble was I could sense that the whole thing was a bit of a failure. There were at least twenty-five chairs arranged in a semi-circle around a lectern but only seven were occupied, dotted self-consciously along the rows like people who go to the movies on their own on a wet afternoon. Pete and I were the only couple. Pete had mentioned that we might go for a meal with the poet afterwards. Looking at him

I felt even more despondent. These people were not my type. Literary, earnest, intellectual. None of them looked like they'd had a good laugh in years.

I didn't understand the poem. It didn't rhyme. And in any case we could barely hear it because the bookshop was still open and late-night shoppers were milling around in the back-ground. I wanted to leave and join them. Anything but this miserable creature droning on in front of me.

When he finally finished Pete leapt up and ran over to shake his hand and congratulate him. There was a table with piles of the slim volume and of course Pete bought one. The other bastards in the audience looked like they were getting ready to leave without buying anything. One of them actually had the nerve to stuff a newspaper in his pocket. He'd been sitting there reading it instead of listening to the poem. The girl from the publishers looked a bit glum. I wasn't surprised. Only one copy sold.

Pete introduced me to the poet who had a clammy handshake. He thanked me over and over for coming and I knew I was supposed to buy a book, but then Pete did the guy out of another sale by suddenly turning to me and saying, 'I've bought Matthew's book for you. Would you like him to sign it?'

Matthew was overcome with gratitude and in return he insisted Pete read one of his own poems.

My ears pricked up. Nora had mentioned it but I had forgotten Pete wrote poetry, although

117

it didn't surprise me.

'Not a chance,' said Pete, 'no one wants to hear my crap. I'm not a published poet. But I tell you what, I'll read one of yours if you like.'

My heart sank. More droning on.

I couldn't have been more wrong. When Pete began to read I realized he knew exactly what he was doing. The voice was mesmerizing as always and suddenly I understood what Matthew was writing about. When he'd read his poem in his own reedy voice it had come across as a pointless whine, but Pete turned his work into magic. Sad, moving evocations of the agonies of lonely urban living. A bit bleak, perhaps, but punctuated by savage language every now and then that struck home. Pete read four poems in all and suddenly I noticed that chairs were filling up. Unlike Matthew's, Pete's voice carried and the book-shop customers were drifting in to listen. Matthew wound up selling twenty books.

Later, we went round the corner to a French bistro and I couldn't help but be impressed by the way Pete knew his way around the menu and the wine list, chatting to the waiters in French. The meal was all about Matthew. A first-class wimp as far as I was concerned. When the bill came I watched, astounded, as Matthew let Pete pay without so much as a token attempt to wrest it away from him. From where I was sitting, Matthew owed Pete, not the other way around.

It was a pattern. Pete did things for other people and didn't seem to realize life was about give *and* take.

Warren confirmed this. 'He's always been like

that. Dad and Billy never lifted a finger till Pete went to university. Pete was always the one who remembered Mother's Day and all our birthdays. Needless to say he was the one who organized everything for Mum and Dad's wedding anniversary recently. Even Dad forgot but it was OK because Pete had booked a place for Dad to take Mum to dinner and organized flowers and everything. Billy didn't even send a card let alone show up.'

'Don't you ever get jealous?'

'What about? The fact that Mum and Pete have so much in common? Why should I? Suits me fine. Dad's thick as thieves with Billy. Mum's got lots to talk about with Pete. Leaves me free to get on with my own life without any parental interference.'

What *was* that life, I wondered, not for the first time? What did he have in his life that he didn't want his family interfering in?

Warren was still chuckling away about Pete. 'We trained him to get up and make us all breakfast every morning. He did all the chores around the house. He let us walk all over him, especially Billy. Mum always stuck up for him, said we ought to treat him with more respect. But if someone's there right in front of you, offering to sort your Latin homework out for you or pick up your dry cleaning because he just happens to be going right past it, what are you going to say?'

'Well, what did you do for him in return?'

Warren looked sheepish. 'Not a lot. He never seemed to need anyone else's help, or if he did he never let on. The only time he wouldn't do something was if his horoscope indicated he shouldn't or if the date added up to the wrong number or something.'

'What are you talking about?'

'He gets it from Mum. Haven't you noticed? They're both into astrology and numerology and they're both so superstitious, they make up their own. They've both got birthdays in July so they're both Cancer. Emotional. Home lovers. Moody. Ruled by the moon so they go nuts every time it's full. That's just an excuse, as far as I can see. July is the seventh month of the year so seven is their lucky number. Everything they do has to add up to seven. If they're climbing a flight of stairs and they notice there are eight, they'll jump the last one so they've only climbed seven. Or if there are eighteen, they'll jump two so it makes sixteen because that's a six and a one and it adds up to seven. They'll only fly on dates that add up to seven.'

'Sounds like a load of rubbish to me.'

'Not to them. Superstitions rule their lives. Pete has to sleep facing a certain way otherwise he won't wake up again. If Mum sees a hearse she has to cross her fingers until she sees a four-legged animal or she'll be the next one in the hearse. We went to Newmarket races one day when we were kids and she saw a hearse driving out of London. Well, she didn't see a four-legged animal till the start of the first race. Drove the whole way there with her fingers crossed and nearly killed us kids four times. I had a terrible fight with them once when I wanted to look at an especially large full moon and they said it was unlucky. I thought they were freaking out because they always went nuts about the full moon, but it turned out it's unlucky to look at it for the first time through glass. The trouble was it was before I got my contact lenses so I was wearing specs at the time and if I didn't look through them I wouldn't be able to see it at all. I can't remember how we sorted that one out.'

I was amazed. Pete seemed so together. I would never have thought of him as being someone who would take something like astrology seriously. I felt a little spooked.

'I don't get it. *Astrology!* Pete's a grown man.'

'In some ways. There are times when I wonder if he's ever done it.'

'Warren!'

Warren and I discussed sex endlessly. That was one of the great things about Warren. It was like having a good gossip with a girlfriend. But it occurred to me we only ever talked about boys. Warren was very good at getting me to talk about my haphazard relationships but he kept his own pretty much to himself.

He never revealed who he was seeing and I began to wonder. But if I asked him straight out who they were, he'd say something evasive like, 'No one you know.' And this was entirely possible. His work had drawn him into a whole new crowd of people he seemed to keep pretty much to himself.

'OK, so I compartmentalize my life. Many people do, you know?' he protested when I challenged him about it. 'I know an awful lot of people and I just sort of know some of my friends wouldn't mix with others so why bother to introduce them?'

He *was* a hairdresser, but then so what? Did that automatically make him gay? Not at all. But there was something about him. He wasn't exactly queeny in appearance but he was feminine. He liked chatting about girly things. He loved flowers and clothes and cooking and he was always giving me recipes to try out on Dad. I studied him surreptitiously for a moment. It was hard for me to think of him *like that*. He was my buddy, part of the furniture, as familiar to me as my old school uniform. But I had to admit he was attractive because he was always so alive. He had so much energy and it was infectious. I always felt good when I was around Warren and he had a smile that could really light up his face. He had, I realized, the most charm of all the brothers. Not the kind of charm you turned on when you wanted something, the kind that Billy had in spades, although, God knows, it was potent enough. No, Warren's charm was totally natural.

'Well, you can say *Warren!* like you're shocked that I would think such a thing, but Pete never talks about his girlfriends. I don't know what he gets up to away from home but now he's back we never hear a thing. Mind you, after having Billy giving us a running commentary, it's a bit of a relief. What with Billy and Dad, there's enough testosterone flying around for one family, thank you very much.'

I liked the fact that Pete didn't brag about his

conquests — if he had any. Except of course I knew he told Nora and she wouldn't have told Warren about the times Pete had been dumped by his girlfriends. She wouldn't betray Pete's confidences to his brothers. But why had she told me, I wondered?

As for me, I loved the way Pete listened.

The reason he was home, apart from timing his arrival for Pat and Nora's anniversary, was to work on his first job. It was the translation of the memoirs of a Swiss woman climber who had been caught in an avalanche on Mont Blanc or some other lofty peak. It was one of those amazing survival stories because she had been trapped for days before anyone found her. But the main point of the story was that she was pregnant at the time. Not very far gone, otherwise she wouldn't have embarked on the climb. But would the baby survive?

The baby, a girl, had indeed survived and was now grown up and living about eight miles away so Pete was home to spend time interviewing her for the book. He'd already done the translation for her mother whose English was too fractured to cope with writing her own book, and now the publishers had had the idea of interspersing comments from the daughter who had also been caught in the avalanche, protected inside her mother's womb.

During this time Pete took me out for meals a couple of times a week and suddenly I realized I was coming to look forward to seeing him and telling him about my day.

'The Johnsons have gone away for three weeks

and left their cat with me and it's covered in fleas. They could have told me. It's a particularly nervous cat. I can't hold him down by myself with one hand. The only place a cat can't get to with its tongue is the scruff of its neck and that's where I have to spray it with flea stuff but I always have to get Dad to help me. And Mrs Roberts' labrador has got diarrhoea and I can't figure out why and nor can Dad but it's getting to be a nightmare cleaning out his kennel, I can tell you.'

'But you love it, don't you?' said Pete, who'd listened to all of this, enthralled, as if I were telling him State secrets.

I nodded. 'But what about you? How's the book going? And what's the daughter like?'

'Well, it's a bit tricky because she's not in the least bit interested in her mother's climb and why should she be? She wasn't even born. She's got her own life in England. She married an Englishman and came to live here and between you and me I think she did so to get away from living under her mother's shadow. She didn't like being 'the daughter of the woman who . . . etc. etc.' She wanted to be someone in her own right. She's a highly independent young woman, commutes every day to a job in the City. She's bilingual, unlike her mother. It's all she wants to talk about. How quickly she can get to the top. It never dawns on her that she's doing exactly the same as her mother only with her it's managerial ladders instead of mountains. She divorced her husband soon after arriving in this country, married her laptop instead as far as I can make out.'

'No kids?'

'No kids. She breeds floppy discs.'

'I want kids more than anything in the world,' I told him.

'So do I,' he murmured.

'You do?' I'd never heard a man say this before.

'Oh, yes, I want a large family. I always have. I want to work from home, translating great big tomes in my study and hear my wife clattering about in the kitchen and see my kids frolicking on the lawn. No one ever thinks men want that sort of thing but they do. At least I do.'

'Well, women aren't supposed to want it either any more. Not now our mothers have fought so hard to pave the way for our brilliant careers, climbed mountains and all that.'

'It's always hard not following the herd. I know everyone thought that just because I got into university I'd be a high flyer somewhere and now they're all disappointed because all I want to do is sit in a room by myself and translate books into English. It's not as if I'm even a simultaneous interpreter for the United Nations or anything.'

'Or a tour guide in some far flung corner of the world,' I teased him.

'Well, to people in central London, Chaveny Road *is* a far flung corner of the world, but the truth of the matter is I like it fine and I wouldn't mind staying here for the rest of my life.'

It was spooky the way he echoed my own

thoughts. I had found a soul mate. I'd always thought Warren was my buddy but I enjoyed talking to Pete. I had the feeling that whatever I told him, he'd listen and understand whereas Warren — well, Warren was good for a laugh.

Mr P died. We'd had Otto put down a few weeks before and buried him near Natasha the canary in the Murphys' garden because Mr P lived in a flat and didn't have any land. Dad and I took photographs of the grave covered in flowers and brought them into hospital to show him. Apparently he died holding one of them in his hands. He'd left money for a funeral so we organized it. Warren, Dad and I contacted a rabbi to come and take the service, and since poor Mr P had no family to speak for him, we asked Pete to.

But on the day, ten minutes after the service had started at the local synagogue, Pete still hadn't turned up. Had he forgotten? Surely not. That wasn't like Pete.

'Where is he?' I hissed at Warren.

'He left early this morning to go over to that woman's daughter for a final interview. He'll be here. Don't fret.'

Of course he arrived minutes later. But in a way I wished he hadn't. He had the daughter in tow.

'Had to bring her along as we're on our way to lunch,' he explained in an aside as they slipped into the pew in front of us.

The woman was a stunner. It had never occurred to me that she might be. She was tall with long dark hair and creamy white skin. Her

126

long legs were encased in sheer stockings and her high-heeled shoes were just this side of 'fuck-me' pumps. She had on huge dark glasses which made her look very glamorous. The simple sleeveless gray dress was tailored and fitted her slender figure perfectly. She exuded class and made me feel very Miss Chaveny Road, as Billy Murphy had mockingly dubbed the local talent.

But when Pete leaned forward to catch something she whispered in his ear, his arm slid along the back of the pew behind her and he let it rest there when she leaned back.

Maybe it was an accident, maybe he felt more comfortable sitting like that, but whatever it was it gave me the shock of my life.

I found myself faced with an emotion I hadn't hitherto encountered in connection with Pete.

Jealousy!

11

My friend Maria had a theory.

She reckoned that blokes were exactly the same as us when it came to feelings. She maintained that they think the same way we do, that they agonize over what to do just like we do: shall I make a move or not? Does she fancy me or doesn't she? Shall I call her or wait for her to call me? How long should I wait? What does she really think?

Maria then went and blew it by saying things like, 'Of course, they haven't a clue what the word commitment means. That would be too much to ask.'

What if she was right about the feelings thing? Because while it became quite clear that I needn't have worried, that Pete and the woman weren't involved in any way, he still showed no signs of making a move on me.

And as for Warren's theory that he was probably still a virgin — at 22? Please! Even this was proved to be sheer fantasy when Maria said she knew a girl who had slept with him and pronounced him to be one of the best lovers she'd ever had.

'How many has she had?' I asked miserably.

'That's not the point and you know it,' said Maria, bossy as ever. 'But it means that he's worth going after if only for the sex.'

The trouble was that the Pete I knew wasn't

the type to do something 'just for the sex'.

'So what happened? Is she still seeing him?'

'No way. She dumped him pretty fast actually. Said he was too intense, took everything much too seriously for her liking.'

That was when he'd probably gone running to Nora and cried on her shoulder. Metaphorically, of course — although I wasn't even sure about that. Funnily enough, even though I'd thought of Warren as the only cry baby when I'd first met him, I knew I would have no difficulty picturing Pete crying. He was so sensitive. It took one to know one.

Of course now when we went out for a bite or a drink all I could think about when I looked across the table at him was that he was reckoned to be a good lover. I found myself, on a Thursday evening, sitting in a pub that served rather good food, asking Pete to pass me the salt, the pepper, the ketchup, the fizzy water, just so I could get a buzz from the brush of his fingers on mine as he handed them over. Because that was as much contact as I was going to get. He never touched me and I was beginning to wonder why on earth he persisted in taking me out. Was I just someone to keep him amused while he worked on this book? When it was finished at the end of the summer would I never hear from him again? It was impossible to tell what he felt about me and I was beginning to despair.

'I've had a letter from my godmother in America,' I told him in an effort to start up some kind of conversation that would take my mind off matters physical.

'I didn't know you had a godmother in America,' he said.

Why on earth should he know a thing like that? He always acted as if we were really close, as if we shared everything. Except . . .

'Oh yes. She's a feminist.'

Mitzi Alexander was back on my case. Not answering her letters hadn't worked. She had simply continued to write demanding to know why she hadn't heard from me. What was I doing with myself? Had I gone to university? What had I majored in? In what area was I going to seek work? What did I have in mind as a career path?

'Are you?' asked Pete, surprising me as always.

'No,' I said firmly.

'Oh, come on.'

What did he mean, *Oh, come on*?

'I'm not. Honest.'

'You don't believe women should be paid the same as men? Be treated equally?'

'Do you?' I challenged.

'Well, I don't suppose I'd like it if I found a woman was being paid more than me so I can understand how women get angry when they do the same job as a man and are paid less. Of course, since I want to stay at home and work for myself it's all a bit academic as far as I'm concerned. The problem with the younger generation of women today is that they don't appreciate what their mothers and grandmothers and great-grandmothers have done for them.'

'Oh God, don't you start, Pete.'

'I'm serious. Suppose you wanted to move away from your dad and buy your own home.

Don't look like that, I know you'd never leave him, but just imagine if you wanted to. You'd go down the estate agents and look at what they'd got and you'd find something you loved and then you'd apply for a mortgage. Now imagine what it must have been like when you couldn't do something like that just because you were a woman. All those thirty-something women we keep reading about who own their own homes, cars, businesses even, but they're wailing and moaning all over the place because they can't get a man. Well, you know what? I think if they bothered to examine themselves for half a second they'd realize they don't even want a man. They're far too selfish and spoiled and independent and having a man around the place full-time would seriously cramp their style. But I don't think it ever dawns on them that they owe their freedom to the women's movement. They wouldn't be seen dead being associated with the women's movement. So what's your godmother like?'

I gulped. Pete always jumped right in and went straight to the point of something. I might have guessed he'd have a view on feminism.

'Don't know. Never met her.'

'*Never met her?*'

'She was my mother's best friend. I may have seen her when I was tiny but since I don't even remember my mother . . . '

'What's her name?'

'Mitzi Alexander.'

'Wow! Can you imagine the kind of woman that name conjures up?'

'But she's a committed feminist.' As soon as the words left my mouth I knew what his reaction would be.

'So she has to have a butch haircut and wear dungarees?'

I didn't say anything. To be honest I no longer knew what to think.

'So what does Mitzi have to say?'

'She's invited me to spend the summer in America. She wants to get to know me.'

'Great! So when are you off?'

Did he look a little crestfallen for a split second — I was going away for the summer — or did I imagine it?

'Hang on. I don't want to have feminism rammed down my throat for the entire summer. Besides, I don't think she'd approve of me if she knew I was still living at home with Dad instead of being out there carving a name for myself in the big wide world. She keeps asking about my career plans.'

'Well, what have you told her?'

'Nothing. I haven't been in touch for ages. Anyway, I don't have any career plans. She'd be horrified.'

'What on earth are you talking about? You run your own little operation with the animals. It's small-scale but it's innovative and it's successful. She'd be proud of you. Write back and tell her about it.'

'So you think I should go? For the whole summer?'

'I think you should do whatever you want to do. But at the very least make contact with her.

And get rid of all these knee-jerk reactions to feminism. You're an independent woman. You do what you want, don't you? I read somewhere that Germaine Greer said all intelligent women are feminists. So there you are — whether you like it or not.'

He thought I was intelligent. I suppose that was something. But as to what else he thought about me, I was still pretty much in the dark.

Nora Murphy telephoned me that evening in a state of high excitement.

'I'm taking you out to lunch tomorrow. Luigi's in the High Street. One o'clock. Don't be late.'

'What's the occasion?'

'You'll find out.' She was being uncharacteristically mysterious.

She was already waiting for me when I arrived. A bottle of champagne stood open on the table.

'I'm not taking a sip until you tell me what all this is about,' I said.

'I'm taking up singing again. It's a secret but I thought I could tell you.'

I grabbed my glass and took a large swig of champagne.

'That's wonderful. How did it come about and why does it have to be a secret?'

'Oh, only from Pat. And only because I want to surprise him,' she laughed. 'If I hadn't told you about my singing, this idea would never have popped into my head and now I can't get it out.'

'What idea?'

'That I could go back to singing. Oh, not right away. I mean eventually. When Warren's finally flown the coop.'

I wondered if she realized that Warren was perfectly capable of flying the coop right now, that he only stayed at home for the benefits of Nora's home cooking and the luxury of having his laundry taken care of.

'And then I thought to myself, why wait?'

I could see she was really excited. That was the thing I liked about Nora Murphy. She looked like a beautiful, peaceful Madonna but her serenity masked a childlike excitement, as if she'd never really grown up, a sort of innocence.

'I've started having lessons again. I mean, I can't just walk back into some club and expect them to hire me after fifteen years away from the scene. But I'm definitely going to sing again and I have this vision of singing at the wedding of one of my boys. We'll have the reception here in the garden and we'll have a platform in the marquee — or on the lawn if it's a nice day — with microphones for the speeches, and then I'll get up and amaze everyone, especially Pat, by singing.'

Now, I thought, is not the right moment to point out that the wedding is usually in the hands of the bride's parents.

Then I had an idea. When I got married there would be no room to have the reception at our house in Chaveny Road. Even before I'd appropriated the back yard for the animals there hadn't been room for anything like a marquee. So maybe I could have my reception at No. 57, at the Murphys'.

I said as much to Nora.

'Hey, that's a great idea. But there's one

condition.' She winked at me.

'What's that?'

'You'll have to marry one of my boys.' And she laughed. Huge joke. To her.

'So what brought all this about? What started you thinking about singing again?'

'Billy.'

'Billy?'

'He's rehearsing for this play in the West End. His first big part. That's the good news. But the bad news is it's a musical and he has to sing. Well, he's obviously inherited his desire to be a performer from me but, as I said, if anyone's got my voice, it's Pete not Billy. So Billy's having lessons, I met his teacher not long after you and I talked and the rest is history. Or it will be. I sneak off twice a week to London. I haven't had so much fun in years.'

I was happy for her. She was positively glowing, prettier than ever.

'She's a lovely woman and do you know what, I've invited her for the weekend. It's my birthday in a couple of weeks so I've invited her down for that. I thought we could all have a singsong with her.'

'You must be thrilled. Billy hasn't been here for ages.'

'Oh, we're all thrilled. Well, not Pete perhaps.'

'Oh, why not Pete?'

'Well, there's a bit of a problem there but don't tell anyone I told you. The only time Pete ever becomes remotely disagreeable is when he's around Billy. I don't know if it's jealousy or what. They're so different. Billy's so carefree and

Pete's always got the troubles of the world stacked on his shoulders. He tries to get Billy to be serious and Billy just tells him to lighten up and Pete goes off in a sulk.'

'At twenty-two?'

'You'd be surprised. Men are quite capable of sulking at seventy-two I should imagine. But maybe Pete will be more relaxed now he's got you.'

'Now he's got me?'

'I've been dying to have a gab about you and Pete. Are you as keen on him as he is on you?'

'I don't know,' I said truthfully, 'how keen is he on me?'

I held my breath. Had Pete been talking to Nora about me? Apparently, yes.

'He's really interested in you. He likes all the things about you that I do. Your simplicity, the fact that you want to stay around here and live a normal life. That you have real solid values, you're not looking to rush off to London in search of some powerful office job. He respects you. He says he finds you refreshing. He really appreciates how you listen to him.'

'But he's the one who listens to me,' I protested.

'Well, there you are then, you listen to each other. You obviously have a lot to talk about and he likes that. Pete's always been a talker. He doesn't like bimbos and I think he's finally learned to stay away from them. He's realized he likes women who have a brain.'

But is he attracted to me, I wanted to ask her, does he fancy me?

'Have you . . . ? I mean, has anything . . . '
Nora was actually giggling. 'No, it's not the sort
of thing a mother should ask but I'm dying to
know.'

She wants to know if we've slept together, I
thought. Chance would be a fine thing.

'I'm not altogether sure he wants to.' Best to
tell the truth.

'You mean he hasn't made a move on you?' I
shook my head. 'Well, what about you? Don't
you fancy him?'

'Nora, please. He's your son.' I smiled just in
case she thought I was really angry.

'So? If you do, why don't you make the move?
It's probably what he's waiting for. He's quite
shy, you know, and men can be as insecure as we
are about what the other person is feeling.'

This was echoing what Maria had told me as
well as Pete's own confession that he was shy.

'So you think I should give him some sort of
clue that I like him? Going out for a meal or a
drink with him twice a week isn't going to do it?'

'Does he at least kiss you goodnight?'

I shook my head.

So did Nora. 'I despair,' she said. 'My Sweet
Pea. Will he ever learn? Would you like me to
have a word?'

'No!' I said firmly. The idea that a man would
kiss me because his mother had told him to was
too sad to contemplate.

But in a way she had already opened the door.
Telling me that he respected me, that he liked
my brain, that he understood why I had chosen
to stay in Chaveny Road, that he found me

refreshing, all these things gave me confidence. It was only a small leap to thinking he must find me attractive, and I doubt I even had time to consciously register it before I saw Pete again.

We went to the movies and we discussed the film over a Chinese takeaway at No. 57. Nora and Pat were in the next room watching television.

I had a couple of dogs to walk before I went to bed so at about eleven I got up to leave.

'Want to help me take the Johnsons' Border terriers around the block?' I asked Pete.

He was awkward with dogs. He kept getting pulled into the road when they wanted to pee and his legs became entangled in the lead. It was almost comical and I think when I kissed him it was more out of friendly affection than anything else.

I'll never know whether Nora did say anything or whether he was just knocked out by such close proximity to me but he responded immediately. He pulled me to him and probed gently with his lips.

I don't know how I managed to hold on to my lead while he was kissing me. And kissing me in broad moonlight to boot. Anyone coming down the road could have seen us. But what surprised me most was that he knew what he was doing. I had never been kissed like that before. He began slow, so slow I thought his heart wasn't in it but then, gradually, he began to exert a little more pressure with his mouth before I felt the tip of his tongue begin to trace my lips. By this time I was melting, oblivious to Chaveny Road, and it was only when I felt the dogs winding themselves impatiently around my ankles that I came to.

Just as well. Pete had let go of his lead and we spent ten minutes searching for the wandering Border terrier. Then we put them back in the kennels and kissed good night.

That night and every night after that.

I wrote back to Mitzi Alexander, told her all about my kennel 'business', made out I was quite the young entrepreneur. But I turned down her offer of a trip to America.

There was no way I was going to leave Pete for a whole summer.

12

'Singing teacher, my ass, he just wants to get into her knickers,' was Warren's comment after Julie had been for the weekend. I didn't meet her. I was a bit hurt not to be invited to Nora's birthday celebrations but, as Pete explained, Pat Murphy had taken everyone out to dinner and there was no real reason for him to include me.

I wondered when Pete would make it official that I was his girlfriend. He'd discussed me with Nora. I'd told Warren about us, of course. I told Warren everything. He made no comment about the relationship, which slightly threw me, but when I asked him why Pete seemed so keen to keep quiet about us, he came up with a reasonably satisfactory answer.

'What you have to understand about Pete is that he's not Billy. He's had a real problem with girls. He's been dumped all over the place plus he's superstitious. So he probably reckons that if he makes it official, it'll be a bad omen. You'll dump him or something. And then Billy will taunt him and he couldn't take that.'

Warren didn't have a clue about Nora's singing lessons. He described the moment when Billy 'introduced' Julie to Nora.

'Mum liked her, I could tell. Surprised me. She's quite a looker but she's not Mum's type. Quite tarty. Red hair. Big boobs. Very theatrical. But Mum was all over her. It was Julie, come

140

and do this, and Julie, come and do that, morning, noon and night. And as for Billy, he was following her around like a lovesick puppy. I've never seen him like this. He was positively drooling. It's probably because he hasn't made it with her. Yet. She's keeping him dangling. The funniest thing was when she made him try out a few of the songs she's taught him. She really is trying to teach him but he's having to talk his way through them like Rex Harrison did on Mum's old record of *My Fair Lady*. Anyway, he's asked her back for Pete's birthday party on July fourteenth so you'll get to see her then.'

What was I going to give Pete for his birthday?

The keys to a hotel room?

It had certainly crossed my mind. If Nora hadn't been planning a birthday party for him I'd have suggested I take him away for a dirty weekend.

Because he sure as hell wasn't going to do anything about it on his own.

I felt as if we were back to square one. I'd finally got him to kiss me but now I was going to have to figure out how to persuade him to make love to me. I knew from his kisses that he wanted to. But we both lived at home so that meant renting a room somewhere and Pete clearly had a problem with that. I yearned to be able to ask Warren's advice. It was the sort of thing Warren would know. The perfect place to have an affair. As far as I could make out it was the sort of thing he discussed endlessly with his clients while he was cutting their hair. They trusted him with the most unbelievable confidences, most of which he passed on to me on condition that I kept my mouth shut. I was impressed by Warren's progress. He seemed to have bypassed the normal three years as a trainee and become a stylist pretty quickly. He was already muttering about 'when I have my own salon'.

'I'd never have thought you'd be so ambitious,' I told him. 'When we were kids you seemed the least likely of all of you to succeed.'

'Well, having Billy around didn't really give the rest of us a chance to shine. All the focus was on him. Now, in a way, the joke's on him.' Warren looked mischievous.

'What do you mean? I thought he'd worked solidly since he left drama school.'

'Sure, but he goes to this fancy drama school for three years and what does he wind up being? A presenter on QVD, the shopping channel. He doesn't have to act, he just has to look good.'

'Oh, OK, but what about his first job, that dippy kids TV series where he played a vet and he had to get on a horse?' I hadn't seen it but he had rung Dad for advice on how to play his part.

'He was so scared of the horse they had to film him separately. That wasn't Billy you saw getting on the horse, that was the back of some other guy. Billy was miles away cowering behind a bush.'

'What about when he was on *Family Affairs* on Channel Five?'

'What about it? Everyone knows the acting's terrible and you're only on it for your looks.'

'But he's got a good part in this musical, hasn't he? Your mum's really pleased.'

142

'Yes, but have you heard how he got that part? He was out of work so long he took a job as a dresser for one of the leads in that musical. He never made it out of the dressing room but he told everyone he was actually in it, never thinking anyone would want to go and see it. Of course there's this girl who has such a crush on him, she blows all her money on tickets going to see him in it every night and after about a week, when she's completely run out of money, she has to ask him where he is because she can't see him on stage. That's when we all find out the truth. She hung around backstage and asked someone else in the cast.'

'You mean he's still a dresser?' I was wondering why he needed to take singing lessons. 'Your mum's going to be really disappointed. Someone ought to tell her.'

'No, no. He finally made it into the cast. But of course he can't sing a note. That's why Julie's been brought in. But even she was walking around the house this morning singing 'There may be trouble ahead . . . ' '

I had to laugh. If only Pete had Warren's sense of fun.

I'd decided to take Pete out to dinner in the West End the night before his birthday party.

I'd picked Japanese because I remembered when we'd had a Japanese meal once before, Pete had got quite drunk on sake. If I plied him with enough, maybe I could steer him towards a night at Maria's. Maria was away for the weekend and had given me the keys to her little flat in Parson's Green.

To be honest, dinner wasn't much fun. At least not for me and I don't think Pete enjoyed it much either. He was in an odd mood. I could see what Nora meant about him and Billy. The entire evening was not about us. It wasn't about Pete and his birthday. It was about Billy.

'It's always the same. You'd think he'd grow up a bit but no, he always has to play the clown to get a laugh. The minute he walks through the door the attention's on him. Always has been, always will be.'

He ranted on until he revealed what the real problem was.

'Only Mum saw through him. At least I think she did. She's so loyal that she never showed it but she always made me feel as if I were just as important as Billy. Now she's all over him and that stupid redhead.'

Of course! He didn't know about the singing lessons so he couldn't understand Nora's sudden interest in the woman Billy had brought home.

'What does Warren think?' I asked him, trying to deflect his interest elsewhere.

'Who knows what Warren thinks?' Implying 'who cares?'.

Poor Warren, I thought, always pushed to the side just because he's the youngest.

'Of course I wouldn't mind,' Pete went on, 'if Billy had any brains at all. I just can't stand the way he knows he can always fall back on his charm and his looks.'

What you really mean, I thought, is that you can't stand the way it always works. You can't come to terms with the fact that you're so

144

awkward and gauche with women. At least, based on my experience you are.

Even as the thought crossed my mind, I realized I was being critical of Pete for the first time. Pete was real and straightforward and honest. But, and I made a mental promise to wash my brain out with soap and water for thinking such a thing, he was hard work. I liked him. I respected him. I fancied him. But my patience was beginning to wear a bit thin.

I had got Pete pissed but not in the way that I had planned. The sake had made him belligerent and sulky. In an effort to cheer him up, as we left the restaurant I put my arm through his and reached up to kiss him on the ear.

'I have a surprise for you,' I whispered.

He smiled at last. 'I didn't want to say anything but I was wondering where my present was.'

I hailed a cab, bundled him into it and gave the driver the address of Maria's flat in Parson's Green. In the cab I snuggled close to him but he kept asking where we were going, oughtn't we to be getting back home, we'd miss the last tube if we didn't hurry.

Admittedly, Maria's flat was not exactly the perfect setting for a night of passion. It was a shoebox and she was untidy by nature. When I'd visited her in the past I'd never really noticed her tights flung all over the room and the piles of magazines and books stacked on the floor ready to trip you up. Worst of all was the kitchen with the washing up still in the sink. She'd done as I asked and left a bottle of champagne in the fridge but I had to wash up a couple of glasses before we could drink any.

Then he said something which made me want to curl up and die.

'Why are we here?' he asked, as if he had absolutely no idea.

'I thought we could be together. For your birthday.'

'You want us to spend the night here?' He looked incredulous.

I nodded miserably.

'You're trying to seduce me?'

'Well why not?' I shouted, suddenly angry. 'It's what happens, in case you didn't know. People who are seeing each other usually like to spend the night together.'

'But not here. Not in a sad little bedsit surrounded by someone else's dirty underwear.'

Typical Pete. He couldn't compromise. He couldn't draw a veil over the drawbacks of a night in Maria's flat. He had to go and spell it out. He had to go and make me feel even worse. Even his beautiful voice had suddenly developed a bit of a whine.

'Well, I wanted to do something. It wasn't as if you were going to find us somewhere to go.'

'I would have done if you'd given me time. You're not like other girls. I can talk to you,' he said in the kind of voice that implied I was being totally unfair. 'Sex isn't everything.'

'Well, obviously not to you,' I shouted and ran into Maria's bedroom and slammed the door.

Childish. Stupid. The kind of behavior I knew Pete would absolutely loathe.

To give him his due he did try and reach out to me. After about twenty minutes he knocked on the door and asked me to let him in so we could talk.

Talk! I didn't want to talk. All we ever did was talk. I wanted to take it a stage further and he just wasn't getting the message. Or maybe he was but he didn't seem to be able to handle it.

Eventually he let himself out of the flat and left me to cry myself to sleep on Maria's cheap candlewick bedspread.

Of course he was the first person I saw at his birthday party the next day. I had been deliberating as to whether or not I should show up but I had come to the conclusion that it would look very odd if I didn't. I was furious with him, I was hurt, I was angry, but a small part of me couldn't forget that he'd said, 'You're not like other girls. I can talk to you.' A small part of me also knew he was right about Maria's flat, that it was totally inappropriate for our first time — and for any other time for that matter — that I'd got it wrong. But then I'd console myself with the fact that he'd been too much of a wimp to sort out where we would go himself and saying 'sex isn't everything' was just pathetic.

It didn't help that Pete, bare chested in his swimming trunks, looked surprisingly strong and muscly. He'd filled out since we were teenagers hanging round the pool. He wasn't exactly a hunk but he was definitely a man rather than a boy.

'Hello, Gorgeous!'

I had been about to go over to Pete to try and

smooth things out before the barbecue got underway, but Billy Murphy stopped me in my tracks.

Immersed as I had been in trying to get a relationship off the ground with Pete, I had actually forgotten the impact Billy's looks made on me. Pete's endless moaning about his brother had had the desired effect of making me think of him as some irritating dumbo, the person I'd had a crush on for twenty seconds when I'd been a kid, before I'd needed a brain to engage me in conversation.

But I was still a woman.

Billy's looks had improved if that was possible. When he smiled at me I could feel his warmth radiating towards me like some heat-seeking missile and every pore of my skin was basking in that warmth and being drawn towards him. I was melting. I was smiling back. I was searching for something witty to say. I was aching to flirt.

'Boy, have you grown up,' he said, appraising me from top to toe. 'I tell you, Julie, she was just a kid when I last saw her. Now look at her.'

Julie did look at me. I hadn't even noticed her standing beside Billy. This was Nora's singing teacher. Billy's too, of course, but more important, this woman was Nora's ticket to success. Warren had been right. She was tarty. She was voluptuous. To translate: she had gigantic breasts.

'This is Julie, my singing teacher,' Billy introduced her. After all, how would he know that I knew all about her. 'She's giving me lessons for my new part. I'm never going to get the hang of it, I'm not a natural singer.' He smiled in such an engaging way that I doubted anyone would want to be a natural singer if they could look like Billy Murphy. 'I'm going to have to speak my lyrics.'

'And that's pretty hard,' Julie chipped in, 'you have to be quite a good actor to make that work.' There was a pause before she said quickly, 'And of course Billy is a wonderful actor.' But she hadn't said it fast enough, hadn't sounded too confident about Billy's acting ability. 'So introduce us properly, Billy. I don't know who this is.'

And that's when I realized Billy couldn't even remember my name, so I introduced myself quickly and went in search of Nora.

Pete's birthday was on 14 July. Bastille Day in France where, as he'd told us, having had first-hand experience on his travels, they celebrated with massive firework displays so that's what Pat Murphy had planned. Huge poles had been erected on the far side of the swimming pool, the idea being that we would all stand on one side and imagine the pool was a lake. We would watch the fireworks explode into the sky pretending we were in the middle of the beautiful French countryside instead of a suburban English back-water like Chaveny Road.

'Has Pete been enjoying his birthday?' I asked Nora innocently.

She looked at me, suspicious. 'He's in one of his moods. He didn't come home last night. We all came down to breakfast to celebrate his

149

birthday and he wasn't even in the house. I don't want to pry but what on earth did you two get up to? When he did come in, I'm afraid Billy started teasing him, calling him a dirty stop-out, all good fun, but Pete just stomped upstairs and slammed his bedroom door like a teenager having a tantrum. I notice you two haven't spoken to each other this afternoon. What's going on?'

I shrugged, didn't answer.

'OK, be like that. But you'd better cheer up later on. It was going to be a surprise but I can't keep it to myself. If I tell you something, promise me you won't breathe a word.'

'I promise.'

'Right before the fireworks I'm going to go round there on the far side of the pool and sing. Julie's been coaching me. She's got Pat to set up a microphone and she's told him she's going to sing but in fact it'll be me. I'm going to do Julie London's 'Cry Me a River' and Shirley Bassey's 'Hey Big Spender', really raunchy. It's one of Pat's favorites. He's going to absolutely love it.'

'That's wonderful,' I said with as much enthusiasm as I could muster. This was all for Pat's benefit but it was Pete's birthday, I thought sadly. What was anyone doing for him?

The barbecue was sensational. The best I'd ever eaten there. Billy was in charge of the food. He was a great showman, flipping the sausages and steaks in the air and on to people's plates. There was a separate grill for fish and he danced between the two, catering to whatever the guests requested. He was hogging the limelight and the

150

birthday boy was nowhere.

'Who are all these people?' I asked Warren. 'I don't know any of them.'

'Haven't a clue,' said Warren cheerfully. 'They're all Dad's clients as usual and Billy's actor friends.'

'But it's Pete's birthday. Where are his friends?'

I had expected to see the poet whose reading we'd been to, even the daughter of the mountain climber whose memoirs he'd translated. But none of these people at the barbecue had anything to do with Pete.

'You know something?' said Warren, winking at me, 'You're right. It's Pete's birthday but where is it written in Pat Murphy's book that anyone should take any notice of Pete? Or me for that matter?'

While everyone was eating, Nora took my hand and asked me to slip away with her into the house to get changed. I thought she meant a swimsuit because the plan was that everyone could take a moonlight dip in the floodlit pool before the fireworks began. They were going to be given special silver foil capes to wrap around them over their wet suits while they watched the display. But from her bedroom closet Nora took out a tight-fitting gown. It was silver and it shimmered, and when she put it on she looked like a mermaid.

'This is my costume,' she said proudly. 'I've had it made specially. As well as a microphone, Billy's rigged up a spotlight so this dress is really going to stand out. I'll feel like Marilyn Monroe singing 'Happy Birthday' to Jack Kennedy in Madison Square Garden.'

She was so excited it was a joy to watch her. I began to feel excited too at the thought of Pat Murphy's face when she walked out across the lawn and up to the microphone.

The crowd on the lawn gasped and parted like the Red Sea when she came out. She really was a beautiful woman. I didn't notice Pat Murphy's reaction because I was too busy looking at Dad who stood there with his mouth open. I'd never seen an expression like that on Dad's face, at least not when he was confronted with a human. He generally reserved such emotion for animals. Then he did a very sweet thing. He raised his hands and began to clap and everyone else followed suit. So Nora was applauded as she made her way across the garden and around the pool.

When she began to sing I couldn't understand why she had needed lessons. It was as if she had been singing for a living for the last twenty years. She had them all spellbound as she sang 'Cry Me a River' and when she sang the words, 'I cried a river over you', I could see she was searching for Pat in the crowd.

I couldn't see him anywhere, and with the opening bars of 'Big Spender', belting out the words 'The minute you walk in the door', she was caught up in the momentum of the song, giving it all she had, Pat Murphy forgotten for the time being.

But Warren was searching for him everywhere. 'This is dynamite. Can you believe it's Mum up there? Where the hell is Dad? We need him to start the fireworks as soon as she's finished and he's got to hear her sing.'

'I saw him going into the house. Must have been going to get something for the fireworks.' Billy was looking irritated. 'He could have stayed to watch Mum sing after all I've done for her.'

'What do you mean, all you've done for her?' demanded Pete, who had been staring at his mother, literally worshipping her as she'd been singing. If anyone had given him a surprise birthday present, it was Nora.

'I arranged for her to have singing lessons. It's a surprise for Dad, but where the hell is he?'

I saw Pete's face disintegrate. For one awful moment I thought he was going to cry. Billy had dealt him the biggest blow of all. Nora had done something without telling Pete, her confidant, and worst of all she had involved Billy.

We went into the kitchen, shouting. Warren, Billy and me. Pete following at a distance, reluctant to leave the sound of his mother's voice.

'Dad, where are you? It's time for the fireworks.'

'Mr Murphy! Mr Murphy!'

'He's probably gone to the bathroom, the en suite off their bedroom. He'll never hear us if he's in there,' said Billy. 'Come on.'

Warren got there first but there was no sign of Pat Murphy. We were all bumping into each other on the landing, trying to get back downstairs when the Murphy family cat eased its way out of a door at the far end of the corridor.

153

I'd never been in there.

Warren held a finger to his lips and I didn't understand why until we reached the door and I remembered it was the guest room. Was there someone sleeping in there?

Warren pushed open the door and we had a front row view of the Murphys' guest-room. Warren turned round and tried to head Billy off at the pass but he was too late.

As Billy rushed into the room yelling, 'Come on, Dad . . . ' he was confronted with the sight of Mr Murphy standing just inside the door, locked in an embrace. Pat Murphy's tongue was halfway down Julie's throat and it took him a second to realize what was happening as we all trooped into the room and lined up to look at him.

As he disengaged himself and Julie began to fumble with her dress which was hanging open at the front, Billy stepped forward and shouted in his father's face, 'Having a good time, are you, Dad? Enjoying the party?' before pushing past us and out the door.

13

I steered clear of No. 57 for quite a while after that.

After we witnessed Pat Murphy and Julie together, I ran out of the house and found Dad happily devouring a large chunk of Pete's chocolate birthday cake. To his great surprise, I didn't leave his side for the next half hour and when he finally asked me what the matter was I pleaded an upset stomach and we went home.

I spent a great deal of time wondering what happened in the Murphy household that night after everyone had left. When I called Nora to thank her for the party, I thought I detected distance in her voice but maybe I was imagining it. I know I should have asked to speak to Pete but I couldn't bring myself to. We hadn't said a word to each other at his party.

Needless to say it was Warren who eventually put me in the picture.

I went in to Hair and There to buy some nail polish — it was the only place that stocked my favorite brand, at least that was my excuse — and he came straight over and suggested we go for a coffee when he was on his next break.

'Billy's completely crushed,' he said before I had taken my first sip. 'I told you he wanted to get into Julie's knickers. Well, I was right. He told me everything. First time he's ever taken me into his confidence. I was dead chuffed.'

I gave him a withering look. This was not the time to get into a celebration of brotherly love. Billy and Warren? It wouldn't last longer than a morning. Besides, I was dying to find out what had happened since the party. But Warren would not be rushed.

'Billy thinks about sex almost every minute of the day. That's what he told me. He has to have it every day, or as often as he can. And Julie was holding out on him. First time it's ever happened to him. Normally, he told me, he strikes out immediately. But not with Julie. Well, now we know why. Apparently the first time he took her home Dad was on to her like a shot. She likes older men. Poor old Billy had never encountered one of them before, the type who goes for the sugar daddy. Julie gave Dad her phone number and he was up to London like lightning. They'd been having it away long before Pete's birthday party. Billy's devastated. I'm telling you. He's completely gutted. His ego's down by his ankles. Makes a change from his Y fronts.'

'Warren!'

'OK. OK. You were there. You saw what happened. There's no point trying to pretend it didn't but this time it's mega serious. This time Mum knows about it.'

'What do you mean, this time? There've been others?'

'Is the Pope Catholic?' He saw my face. 'OK, strike that. Sorry. How would you know about the others?'

He looked sad. A first for Warren.

'Do you want to talk about it, as they say?' I

asked him. 'I mean, I don't want to pry . . . if it's personal.'

'Yes you do,' he grinned. The old Warren was back. 'Yes, as a matter of fact I would like to talk about it. I never really have — to anyone. There's a kind of complicity of silence between us. Billy, Pete and I never talk about it amongst ourselves but we know all about it. Dad plays away. It's one of the reasons we moved here. He had a scene with the woman next door and it was all getting pretty heavy. I thought he'd pull his socks up once we started a new life here. But no. Here he is, at it again.'

Suddenly I remembered the blonde at Homebase with her hair tied in a knot on top of her head.

'And you've always known about it?'

'Well, I have and I imagine if I do, since I'm the youngest, Billy and Pete have known about it for longer than me. And to tell you the truth we all think Mum knows too but the golden rule is that we do our utmost to keep it from her. We protect her. We pretend it isn't happening, that everything's fine, we're one big happy family. And to a certain extent we are. Mum and Dad get along fine, you'd never suspect anything when you see them together. I suspect many families are like us. Poke about a bit and you'll fine the odd infidelity, jealousies, bitterness, ups and downs. But we brothers sort of made a pact a few years ago that we'd keep Mum in the dark. It's the closest we've come to being brotherly in any way, if you know what I mean. And now Billy's gone and blown it. His nose was so put out of joint about Julie, he had to go and spill the beans to Mum.'

'How did she take it?'

'She went totally berserk. It was a shock. We expected her to creep away and weep in a corner, but oh no. She started wailing and yelling and she told Dad to go upstairs and sent us all out of the house. Of course we waited about five minutes then we went back in. You could hear them yelling and screaming at each other. I'm surprised you didn't hear them down at your house, and then when Dad came downstairs he had one of those little boxy suitcases. He tried to say something to us but we all looked away, we were so embarrassed, and then he went out of the front door and we haven't seen him since.'

'Where is he?'

'Who knows? Who cares?' I remembered when he'd said the shocking words '*I hate my dad*' and I hadn't understood. Now I did. 'You should have seen Pete. He turned on Billy and it was pretty unpleasant. Pete only loses his temper once every five years but when he does you don't want to be around. He was furious with Billy for telling Mum, for making her open her eyes and see what she's married to. She's thrown Dad out and it's a terrible thing but I can't help thinking Julie's brief appearance in our lives might have done us some good, cleared the air a bit.'

I waited several days hoping that Nora would call me. I had to tell myself there was no reason why she should. It wasn't as if we were the same age and I was her closest friend, but somehow I'd felt we had become quite close through our chats. But I didn't hear a word and I began to fret. I didn't want to call the house in case I got Pete. I felt awkward about Pete. I hadn't heard a word from him since his party. It was interesting that for the first time I was keeping something from Warren. I hadn't told him about the fiasco at Maria's flat. I found I didn't really want Warren's take on the situation. It was all too embarrassing. And I guessed that Pete was really depressed about his birthday. My instinct told me that I should leave him to get in touch with me in his own time.

But my curiosity got the better of me about Nora and I went to see her.

I could tell at once that she was completely devastated. She didn't look me in the eye. She didn't smile. Her face was drawn and sallow. There were dark shadows under her eyes.

'You know what's happened,' she said immediately, leading me into the kitchen and putting the kettle on like an automaton, barely aware of what she was doing. It was a statement, not a question. 'The boys will have told you. Everyone knows. Everyone.'

I didn't know what to say. I had come beetling up the drive hungry for information but now that it looked like I was about to be given it, I was at a loss to know what to do. This was a different Nora and I didn't know how to handle her.

'Does your father know, has he said anything?' she asked suddenly.

I shook my head. I hadn't a clue what Dad knew but this seemed like the right answer.

'Pat and I had an agreement.' She sat down at the kitchen table and I busied myself rescuing the kettle she'd left boiling on the hob. 'I'd look the other way. I knew. Of course I knew, but I always said to him, do what you want but if I find out, that's it, finito. I wish I could be one of those women who refuses to put up with it, but the truth is I genuinely believe Pat still loves me. Maybe because it's what I want to believe, who knows? The way I look at it is whatever happens when he's away from me, well, that's not part of him and me. Some men need more than one woman. I know about leopards changing spots and all that. Never happens, my granny always said. Well, Pat's my leopard. I can't change him. But I told him, I said, 'Pat, what we have between us is special. You screw that up, that's it, you're history. And the only way you're going to screw us up' ' — That gave me a jolt, Nora never used words like screw — ''is if you fall in love with someone else and tell me so. Or if you fall in love and you don't tell me and I find out from someone else and that would be worse.''

I realized she was talking to Pat, not me, and it was odd having her be so aggressive to me.

''Maybe it's just an illusion, this thing I think you and I have between us, Pat, but all I'm asking is just don't shatter it. These past few years being married to you, it's been like living through an earthquake. Every time you have a woman — and even though I don't have proof, I always know, I always sense it — it feels like my nerves are one big picture window about to shatter. Will she be the one? Somehow my picture window is still intact but don't push it. One notch higher on the Richter scale and you're out. Just don't do it, Pat.'' Now she looked straight at me. 'But he had to go and do it, didn't he?'

I remembered what she'd said about forgiveness in marriage and I wondered if she still believed in it.

'Mr Murphy's gone?'

'You bet he's gone.'

'But you have your sons. How are they taking it?'

'Billy's ignoring me. Gone back to London. Pat took his girl. In a way Billy and I ought to be consoling each other but of course Billy doesn't see it that way. Warren's too young to understand. Pete's the only one I've got to talk to. He's being wonderful.'

'Warren's not too young to understand,' I burst out, then stopped. I couldn't betray what Warren had told me. 'Well,' I finished lamely, 'I just came up to say I was sorry and that I was here if you — you know — wanted a daughter to talk things over with.'

The Nora I knew returned for an instant. She got up and hugged me, her cheek wet against mine.

'Thank you. You're so sweet. I'm sorry to have burdened you with all this. I'll be fine in a few days and then we'll get together.'

I sat with her for a while and then left, pleading Dad's supper as an excuse. I met Warren coming up the drive.

'I just saw your mother. She's in pretty bad shape.'

'Tell me about it. The house is like a morgue. She's off weeping in her bedroom half the time with Pete being very proprietorial and taking trays of food up to her.'

'He wasn't around.' It was the first time I had thought of him.

'He went up to London to see his publisher. Some big new translation job.'

'So what about Billy? He's back in London with a new singing teacher?'

'But he's coming home at weekends with his tail between his legs. The thing is, Billy never actually made it with Julie, they weren't a couple, so he can't play the wronged son with Dad. He could have a go at Dad for being unfaithful to Mum but since Billy's known about Dad's philandering for years and, if anything, for all I know he's egged it on, he can't very well start preaching against it. No, our Billy's hoisted by his own petard or however the saying goes.'

So it was that having heard all this from Warren about Billy, I was completely taken by surprise one Saturday morning when I was cleaning out the kennels and Dad called to me from the back door, 'Someone to see you,' and there was Billy looking unbelievably handsome.

'Hi, Gorgeous. I was told you treated poor sick animals who were looking for a cure.'

'A cure for what? Where's the animal and in what way is it sick?'

He looked straight at me. 'I'm the animal and I'm lovesick.'

'Good-looking boy like you? Never.'

I laughed, aware that I was flirting and thinking, what the hell? It felt good and it meant nothing. That was the thing about Billy. Flirting was probably the only language he understood.

'So what happened to you?' he asked.

'What do you mean? Nothing happened to me.'

'Yes it did. When I last saw you, you were this kid who ran around with Warren and you had your hair all scraped back behind your head and you used to skulk around our pool and never talk to anyone.'

Probably because you and your stuck-up friends never spoke to me, I thought, but didn't say anything. I hadn't even been aware that he had noticed me 'skulking' as he put it.

'And now look at you.'

I knew I should have left it at that but the temptation to know exactly what he saw when he looked at me now was too great.

'Have I changed that much?'

'Are you kidding? You're a beauty now. You've got those long legs and a knockout body and those beautiful gray eyes that always make you seem so wistful and dreamy, as if you're miles away thinking about an age gone by.'

This was more like it. Then I realized that as he'd been talking to me for less than five minutes, either he was a clairvoyant or this was an incredible line. Besides, how could I possibly look dreamy while I was cleaning out the kennels?

'Shall I give you a hand with that?' He was

163

moving towards the kennel I had just been raking out.

'Hold on, aren't you afraid of horses?'

'This is a kennel, not a stable. There's a dog in there, right? And what makes you think I'm scared of horses?'

'Warren told me,' I said sheepishly, 'when you were in that series playing a vet, the one you called Dad about. You didn't like mounting a horse. And the dog in that particular kennel is trouble. The owners have been away for three weeks and I still haven't entirely won her over to my side. Wouldn't go near her if I were you.'

'OK, so I am a little scared by horses,' he said, disarming me with his candor, 'but that beast in the TV series was a real nightmare. It didn't want anybody on its back. There was only one day when they used a double, after that they got a new horse because even the stunt guy complained. You don't want to believe everything Warren tells you. He rewrites history like there's no tomorrow. Last of the great embellishers, our Warren.'

He had opened the kennel door before I could stop him. The McIntyres' cocker spaniel immediately went crazy and began racing round and round the small kennel space, yapping excitedly before backing itself into a corner and growling. To my surprise, Billy collapsed on the straw on the kennel floor and began speaking quietly to the spaniel. He inched closer, still on his knees until he could reach out his hand and almost touch the dog who hadn't stopped growling. I was convinced that any minute it would dart forward and bite one of Billy's fingers off. But even as I was wondering what I would do if this happened, the growling began to subside and within minutes Billy was stroking the animal under its chin and reaching forward to gather him up into his arms.

'There. You see?' he said triumphantly. 'Ferocious little dogs, temperamental actresses, what's the difference? They need to be treated to a little of the Murphy charm. Works wonders. This little creature was just scared, that's all, weren't you, sweetie? You're OK now, Uncle Billy's going to take you for walkies.'

'She's had her walk already this morning,' I said hurriedly. I didn't want Billy absconding with my charges. I still couldn't quite come to terms with the fact that my teenage idol was dropping by our back garden as if it were the most natural thing in the world.

'Did you come over for anything special?' I asked him. 'Did you want to ask Dad about something?'

'No. I came to see you. In fact, I've dropped by a couple of times when I've been home for the weekend but there was no sign of you. When I saw you at Pete's party, I was knocked out by how you'd changed. Then you ran away right after we found Dad with Julie. I looked for you but you'd gone.'

I was surprised he brought it up like this. I had been wondering whether I should mention it.

'How's your mother?' I didn't tell him I'd been to see her.

'Spends all her time with her darling Pete.

You'd think she'd spare a thought for me. I'm the one who really lost out. I lost my singing teacher.'

'Since when was a singing teacher more important than a husband?'

He looked at me, amused. 'Oh, I see. You're a live one. Got a mouth on you, have you? Well, let me tell you something. Mum has not lost Dad. She may think she has. She's always been so wrapped up in her romantic dreams and now they've been shattered. For the time being, anyway. What she doesn't realise is that to Dad Julie is just another bit of skirt. He'll have lost interest in her a week next Tuesday. He's not going to leave Mum. He adores Mum.'

'But what about her? She may not want him back.'

Clearly this thought had never crossed Billy's mind. He looked a bit startled and then said: 'So anyway, I'm at a loose end tonight, thought you might fancy going to a movie or something?'

I don't know why I said no but something told me not to make it too easy for him. I could never forgive Pat Murphy for what he had done to Nora. And Billy Murphy supported his father. So if he thought I was going to roll over and fit in with his idea of how women behaved with Murphys, he had another think coming. I might be a romantic dreamer like Nora but I was wise to his beguiling ways. I wasn't a moonstruck teenager any more. He couldn't just beckon me with his finger and expect me to come running.

I took the spaniel from his arms and wished he would stop grinning at me like he knew exactly what was going through my mind.

'Got to wash your hair or something, have you? Does look a bit greasy. You should try that new citrus shampoo that smells like grapefruit. Warren gave me some to try. It's amazing.'

He was about to leave. I put the spaniel back in its kennel and walked him to the door. Just as he was about to walk through it he darted back and kissed me on the cheek, lingering just long enough for me to breathe in the smell of his hair falling over my face.

Grapefruit.

Of course, when he called about a week later and said did I want to meet him for a drink after rehearsal in a Covent Garden bar, I was there like a shot. Whichever way I looked at it, being asked out by Billy Murphy was an opportunity I wasn't about to pass up twice.

I liked Covent Garden. I liked the mixture of old and new, the restaurants, the outdoor cafés, the almost Parisian atmosphere. At least it appeared Parisian to someone who had never been to Paris. Floral Street was a perfect example. Such a pretty name and so narrow you felt you were right there in the last century. But it was filled with the coolest fashion shops.

He had told me to meet him in a bar beyond the piazza and when I reached it, I found him surrounded by a crowd of seemingly beautiful people. He saw me over the tops of their heads and summoned me from afar. They parted to allow me to walk right up to him and once again I smelled grapefruit as he kissed me on the cheek. He would have kissed me on the lips but I turned my head very slightly and he must have seen this coming — or maybe he saw the alarm in my eyes — because he switched at the last minute.

His friends — they turned out to be the chorus in the show — all called him Will.

'How long have you known Will?'

'Oh, you're Will's neighbor.'

'So do you think Will's going to make it as a singer?' Followed by raucous laughter.

'Will?' I said, looking at him. 'What's this Will?'

'Will Murphy sounds better than Billy Murphy. More professional. More grown up. More like a serious actor. My agent suggested I lose Billy.'

'You mean like Will Shakespeare?' I said. 'Good Will Hunting?'

'Very funny. So,' he bent down to whisper to me, 'I thought we'd have a quick drink with this lot and then move on to have some supper. That OK with you?'

I nodded.

'So when do you open?' I asked a member of the cast who seemed less threatening than the others. Billy's Beauties had been replaced by Billy's Cute Young Actresses, an altogether more sophisticated breed. Brunettes rather than blondes. Hip clothes, very street. Noses, lips and earlobes pierced. I felt as if I stood out a mile as the kennel maid from Chaveny Road.

'Couple of weeks,' she said. Then she turned away. I didn't know how to talk to these people. It wasn't my world, not that I really had a world beyond Chaveny Road. That, I was beginning to realize, was the problem. Billy — I mean Will — was no longer one of the Murphy brothers. I'd never known him well in the first place, not like I knew Warren or Pete, and here in central London he was even more of a stranger. He had a life I knew nothing about, a life that was totally beyond my experience, surrounded by these strange-looking people. Someone had ordered me a drink and I didn't know what it was. It was dark pink in a frosted glass. It looked very enticing but supposing it knocked me out cold?

'What's the matter?' Billy saw me looking at it.

'What is this?' I whispered, not wanting to appear too provincial in front of his friends.

'That's a sea breeze. Vodka, cranberry juice and, wait for it, grapefruit juice. You're drinking my shampoo.'

Of course once he'd said that, when I took a sip, it tasted like shampoo to me and I must have made a face because he said, 'Come on, let's get out of here.'

Once outside the bar he took my hand in his as if we'd been going out for ages. We went to a place called Joe Allen's which was clearly something of an actors' hangout. They greeted him warmly on the door and several people called out to him. I felt curiously proud to be with him.

We sat at a corner table with a red and white checked cloth and he ordered me a burger and fries without even asking whether it was what I wanted.

And then he began to talk.

It's just as well I'm a good listener. I had to be. He talked about himself non-stop, but he was so open and candid that once again I found myself disarmed. I had not expected him to be self-deprecating, to paint himself in less than an ever glowing light. But I was wrong.

'I'm so glad you came,' he began. 'I couldn't believe it when you said no last Saturday. I've always thought you were the sweetest girl, I've always wanted to get to know you better, but I figured you were more Warren and Pete's friend.'

I looked at him. How much did he know about me and Pete? I'd tried to reach Pete once but I hadn't heard a word back.

'I know I was a creep when we first moved in. I had all those girls hanging round the pool and I know how it must have looked to you. But I noticed you even then. What you have to understand is that when a guy's that age and he finds he's attractive to those kind of women, it's like a drug. I couldn't have walked away from them even if I'd wanted to. And then when I found out about Julie and my dad and I was devastated, I thought of you. I knew you'd be kind and you'd listen. Then, when you said no, I went into a panic.'

It sounded like a load of bullshit. It probably was a load of bullshit. I doubted whether Billy had given me a single thought before Pete's birthday party. But he looked so appealing that I wanted to believe every word he said to me.

So I smiled at him in what I hoped was a sympathetic and encouraging way.

'The thing is I'm a hopeless picker of women,'

he told me. 'I always fall for bitches who treat me badly. I get hurt.'

Like hell, I thought.

'I really thought Julie liked me. I mean, I asked her to come to my mother's birthday dinner so that has to show her I'm serious about her, doesn't it? And what does she do? She goes off with my father. What kind of birthday present is that for my mother? You wouldn't do a thing like that, would you?'

I shook my head.

'The problem is my singing's really suffering. The new teacher's no good for me. But she knows everyone. She gave my name to this casting director and I'm going for a reading tomorrow for a part in a movie. And she knows this photographer and she got him to take these amazing pictures of me, and she knows this publicist who's going to place some stories about me in the press.'

'So why aren't you out with her tonight?' I couldn't resist asking him.

'Because she's a real dog and you've turned into a beauty,' he said immediately. More bullshit but it made me feel good.

'Don't you have any dreams?' But before I could begin to think of an answer, he went on, 'I want to be famous. I admit it. I crave fame. I crave recognition. I want to be a star. That's the whole story, really.' He grinned.

'Don't you want to be a good actor?'

'Of course. It's a means to fame. I suppose you think I'm an idiot, cashing in on my looks.'

He was vain. I could have told him that for

nothing. But his looks were extraordinary, so what was the point of denying them?

'I think you *are* very good-looking and it would be insane not to take advantage of that.'

'Thanks,' he smiled and put his hand over mine. 'I was right. You're a sweetheart. I'm not a bright guy like Pete, I'm not funny like Warren. All I have is my looks. I've always been insecure inside but I've never told anybody about it. I'm not really even sure why I'm telling you.'

'I'm sure that's not true. Beauty isn't only skin deep.'

'You're very sweet. Now, tell me about you. Are you happy doing what you do?'

'You mean am I happy living a humdrum existence in dreary old Chaveny Road? It's my life. I know no other.'

'Just you and the animals. Do you sometimes pretend you're on a safari with them? Bit of an adventure?'

'Billy, they're dogs and cats.'

'Yes, but you could build them up in your mind to being big dogs and big cats.'

He was like a kid. Maybe he got his childlike sense of fun from Nora. I'd never really thought about it before but he was right about himself, he probably didn't have a huge brain. But he was rather sweet and while he might claim to be insecure, there was one area where he was totally confident. He knew how to handle women. Even the McIntyres' spaniel bitch had responded to his charm.

'OK, eat up. Now we're going to go and have some fun.' Outside in the street, he took some balloons out of his pocket. 'Here, give it some puff.' He handed me a balloon and began blowing one up himself. It was something I'd never been able to do so I let him blow them all up and tied the string he produced around the rim to keep the air in. He attached the strings to some ribbons.

'Follow me,' he yelled, suddenly taking off and tearing down the street.

We crossed the Strand, dodging the traffic with death-defying agility, ran down to the Embankment and raced along the river like a couple of kids.

He was right. It was pure unadulterated fun.

'What we do now,' he took a Magic Marker from his pocket, 'is we write your name on this one and my name on this one and we let them float away across the river like this . . . ' He let go of both of them and they rose up into the night air and floated gently off towards the South Bank.

'What do we do with the rest of them?'

'We tie them round lamp posts. It's a race. Last one to tie all their balloons gets the booby prize.'

He was way ahead of me, leaping up on the Embankment wall and down again in a manic burst of energy that was exciting to watch.

Needless to say he won. I was still clutching four balloons when he came towards me empty handed.

'OK, so I get the booby prize,' I conceded. 'What is it?'

'This,' he said and kissed me.

There's an old song called something like 'It's In His Kiss' that said you could learn whether or not a boy loved you from his kiss. I had never really understood how you could tell so much from just a kiss. Kissing was kissing.

Wrong.

With Billy, kissing was an art form. He kissed me very slowly, as if he was savoring a delicious piece of fruit. He licked tentatively, he liked what he tasted, he peeled my lips, he sucked out the juice and came back for more.

And I just stood there in his arms and melted.

I had known when I first set eyes on him that I would fall in love with him and I'd been right.

14

I could not get Warren's words out of my mind.

Billy thinks about sex all the time. He has to have sex every day or as often as he can.

That night he had hailed a cab right there on the Embankment and taken me back to his flat. So refreshing after Pete and his endless procrastination. Billy's flat was so impersonal, we might just as well have gone to a hotel room. There was no furniture, just bare floorboards, a wooden chair and a TV set. In the bedroom there was only an enormous bed and a lamp standing on another wooden chair. In the kitchen, the pile of empty takeaway pizza cartons stacked against the wall had grown to an alarming height. The fridge revealed a carton of three-week-old milk and a bottle of champagne.

'I'm saving that for a celebration.' For one moment I thought maybe I was going to be something he wanted to celebrate until he said, 'You know, when I get my first movie part.'

We made love four times and I thought they ought to write a song called 'It's In His Foreplay' because once again he amazed me. Out of bed it was all about him, but between the sheets it seemed the only thing that mattered to him was pleasing me. I missed the last train and had to stay the night. Just before he fell asleep, Billy told me I was very sexy.

'Four times,' he whispered, clasping my head

on his chest, 'that's amazing.'

I wasn't quite sure if he was crediting me with this amazing feat, or himself. I wanted to tell him I loved him but I managed to resist. He had to say it first.

In the morning when I got home Dad was in the yard feeding the animals. He gave me an odd look. Of course I'd stayed out the whole night many times but I'd never missed the morning feed before. But then I'd never had to get back from central London. I wondered if he'd guessed who I'd been with. He didn't say anything but then he never would.

A week went by and I didn't hear from Billy. Warren had said he had sex every day, so who had he been sleeping with since seeing me? But then Billy himself had told me Warren was the last of the great embellishers and I thought he might be right.

Because that's what I wanted to believe.

I was as bad as Nora, preferring the illusion to the reality.

Nora seemed a little better, to the extent that she had begun to worry about how other people were feeling and here we had a problem.

She had decided that what she needed to take her mind off her troubles was a holiday.

'I've always wanted to go to Italy. I'd like to go to the opera in Milan. I'd like to go to Tuscany and wander round the churches looking at all those frescoes I've heard about. I want to wander through olive groves.'

She was looking all dreamy and I had no problem picturing her standing in a church, holding a candle and wearing one of those lace shawls around her head, gazing up at a stained glass window. Nora didn't need to go to Italy. She was the Madonna of Chaveny Road. I nodded my approval.

But I hadn't heard the whole story.

'And I was thinking,' she continued, 'what if you and Pete came with me? I keep on thinking how Pete's birthday was ruined by what happened and I owe it to him. I'll use Pat's credit cards to pay for it and we can stay in the best hotels and won't we have such fun?'

She was looking at me with such expectation that I knew it was going to be hell to say no. She was so out of the loop, she hadn't a clue about me and Billy. She still thought Pete and I were an item. And why shouldn't she? It wasn't as if we had broken up. We just hadn't seen each other for ages, and presumably Pete, guessing I had been seeing Billy, was avoiding me like the plague.

'What does Pete say?'

'Well, you know, he was a little strange about it. He said I should take you on your own. Just girls together. I don't get it. He's always wanted to go to Tuscany with me. We've talked about it.'

'Then I think you should go with him and I would be butting in if I came. To be perfectly honest,' I lied, 'I am not terribly keen on threesomes and I have no particular desire to go to Tuscany, not like you and Pete obviously do. So why don't you two go?' It all came out in a rush and she probably wasn't fooled for a second but she just shrugged and said, 'Well, if that's what you want. I'll ask Pete again. I don't know what's got into the two of you. I never see you together any more.'

So she went off to Italy for a week with Pete and I went back to worrying about Billy and sex and when I'd hear something from him.

Warren was the link as usual. He stopped by the house on the way home from work one night with a box of citrus shampoo for me.

'Billy told me you liked this stuff. Don't ask me how he knew but it is good, I can tell you that. So where have you been all week? Want to come up for a swim? I had a dip this morning and the water's great. Dad always moaned about the cost of heating the pool but ever since he left home, we've all been able to do exactly what we want.'

'How is your mum?' I asked as we walked up the drive. 'Where is your father?'

'Well, he's in London, we think. Billy's in touch with him. And Mum's away. Get this, Pete's taken her to Italy for a week. Tuscany. He's going to show her frescoes in churches and olive groves. Sounds like a barrel of laughs. Should cheer her up no end.'

Warren might treat the whole thing as a joke but I could see Nora in Italy — not that I'd ever been there myself. Maybe she would be swept off her feet by some handsome Italian romeo. But with Pete cramping her style, maybe she wouldn't.

'Now come with me and be impressed,' said Warren. 'I want to show you something.'

He led me out to the pool and collapsed on

one of the sun loungers, donning a pair of outrageous sunglasses.

He reached into a little cabinet I hadn't seen before and produced a phone.

'See, we have a pool phone. I can lie here pretending I'm a movie producer in Hollywood making deals.'

'That's supposed to impress me?'

'No, this is.'

He had placed a case on the lounger in front of him and from it he took out a laptop.

'See, I can unplug the phone out here and plug in the modem and be online by the pool.'

'Whose laptop is that?'

'Pete's. Look, here's what I wanted to show you. I've been working on the computer at the salon to design our own website. That grapefruit shampoo is our own and I think we ought to be selling that and other products online. I wanted to check out what else is on the market. Hey, hang on, I've got mail. Or rather Pete has. Oh, it's from Billy. He's at his agent's, using their computer. I suppose he thinks Pete's taken his laptop with him to Italy and he can contact him and Mum there.'

'Maybe he doesn't even know they are in Italy.'

'That's right. On e-mail you could be anywhere. Let's chat to him.'

I watched while Warren pecked away at the keyboard with two fingers, electronically connected to the person I was desperate to talk to.

'Oh, I told him I was here with you and he wants to talk to you.'

Warren got up and motioned for me to use the laptop. I was clueless with e-mail.

'What do I do?'

'Read the message he's sent you. Hit Reply. Type your message to him and hit Send.'

I looked at the screen, peering at it in the sunlight. Mercifully this would obscure it from Warren's view.

Meet me at the Embankment tomorrow night. Eight o'clock. Our spot.

Our spot! How would I ever find it?

I replied that I'd rather come to his flat. He could make of that what he wanted.

OK. See you then.

'Let's swim,' I said to Warren, 'you can do this later.'

He abandoned the laptop much to my relief, I didn't want him seeing my message from Billy. No doubt he'd find it later and I'd have to come clean. I never kept anything from Warren. But for the moment I wanted to take my liaison with Billy one step at a time, with no outside interference.

Billy had his cell phone clamped to his ear when he let me into his flat the following night. I had imagined him opening the door to me and taking me in his arms but he just motioned me inside and walked away, still talking.

And within seconds I knew he was talking to a woman. His voice was hushed but I could still make out the words.

'You're so sweet, no, really you are. I knew you were smart the minute we met. I'm so lucky to have met you. What? No, I'm serious. I had the

180

picture of your face in my mind right in front of me the whole time I was reading. I know you're good for me. I do. So when can we meet? How about dinner tomorrow night? No, I don't want you breaking dates on account of me. I don't want to interrupt your life. We only just met. I have no right to do that. Let's just meet for a drink and see what happens . . . OK, I'll call you, OK, first thing in the morning. What's that? What . . . '

He was literally purring down the line to her. I turned around and walked right out the door. On the train home I began to cry. Silent heaving. I didn't make a sound because I didn't want the other passengers looking at me, but the tears streaming down my face gave the game away. More than anything, I was angry with myself for being so stupid. How could I have imagined that I could mean anything to Billy Murphy? I would force myself to forget about him and pretend the night of the Embankment had never happened.

He turned up at the house the very next day and if Dad had had his suspicions about him before, they were confirmed now. Billy banged on the front door while Dad and I were preparing supper together in the kitchen. It was a ritual of ours if I didn't have any plans — Dad never went out — and we tried out new recipes together, simple pasta dishes, soups, made-up stuff. It gave us a chance to chat about our various animal charges and compare notes. I'd ask Dad's advice if one of my pets was ailing and occasionally there were more serious problems,

181

like when people dumped their pets on me and never returned. It happened. They said they were going away on vacation but in fact they were moving and didn't want to take their pet with them. It was left to me to find a new home for them whether I wanted to or not.

I had just removed a chilled tomato and basil soup I'd made from the refrigerator when Billy showed up. He came charging into the kitchen, pumped Dad's hand up and down a few times, saying, Hi, how are you?, but not looking at him, and then he started following me round the kitchen, barking questions at me.

'What happened? Go on, tell me? What happened? I open the door to you and then I look round and you're not there. I was rushing up and down the street making a complete fool of myself, waited for you to call, I waited for your explanation. Nothing.'

'I was supposed to call you?' I shouted at him, suddenly furious.

'Well, you were the one who ran out on me. Why did you leave?'

'You honestly don't know?'

'Why else am I here?'

'Will you stay for supper? We're having cold tomato soup with — ' Dad was looking anxiously from me to Billy.

'No, he is not staying for supper.' I was very firm on that one.

'Thanks. I'd love to,' said Billy, 'I'll run up to the house and pick up a bottle of wine. That should give you time to cool down and think of an explanation. Back in a second.'

182

He ran out the door and I turned on poor Dad.

'He is not staying for supper.'

'Yes, he is,' said Dad, 'otherwise we won't have any peace. I can tell. I'm going to eat my soup and my bread and then I'm going to take myself off to see that new Julia Roberts movie. I like Julia Roberts and she'll be in a better mood than you are.'

'You never told me you liked Julia Roberts. And since when have you been sneaking off to movies on your own?'

'Since they invented Julia Roberts. Mmmm, soup's good.'

'Don't bolt your food, Dad. Bad for your indigestion. You'll burp all the way through the movie and disturb the audience. Hey, leave some for Billy.'

'So you're going to let him stay?'

Of course I was going to let him stay. One look at his gorgeous face when he walked back into the house and my heart was aflutter, pathetic creature that I was.

'Just going out to see the new Julia Roberts movie,' Dad told Billy.

'Good for you,' said Billy. 'When we want to get Mum in a good mood we tell her she looks like Julia Roberts.'

'Well, she does,' said Dad to my amazement. 'See you later.'

'Let's open this wine.' Billy was brandishing a bottle of Pinot Grigio.

'I'll do it. Sit down there and eat this soup. Did anyone see you up at the house?'

'Warren was out by the pool fiddling with the laptop. Who cares if anyone saw me? Now, if I eat it all up like a good boy, will you tell me what's bugging you?'

'You invite me to see you. I walk into your apartment and you're flirting with a girlfriend right in front of me.'

'And you're upset because we slept together and you think that means you own me?'

'Well, no, I . . . ' I didn't want to appear possessive but yes, that was exactly it. And maybe I didn't have the right to expect that. Maybe that wasn't how it worked in his world. Well, if that was the case I wanted out.

'Don't say no because you're absolutely right. You're new and you're special. That was a casting director I was talking to. It was work.'

'But you were flirting with her.'

'Of course I was flirting with her. I have to keep her sweet. She's just sent me up for a very important role. She's a little in love with me. They all are.'

Except for Julie, I thought.

'I have to be like that for my career. My agent says — '

'Is your agent a woman?'

'No, he's a Shetland pony.'

'But he's male?'

'Yes, but I flirt with him too. I'll flirt with anyone if it'll get me the part. It has nothing to do with the women in my real life. I've moved on from those bimbos I used to bring home when I was a kid. I want a grown up, someone who respects my career and can help me. Julie could have helped me. And now you walk out on me. That's a first. I have never had that happen. But the truth is I like it. I want a challenge. I like an independent woman.'

'You like feminists?'

'Feminists? God, no. I wouldn't go that far. All that men and women are equal stuff? Takes the fun out of romance. I like a woman to respect a man. That's only natural, isn't it? But I like a woman who has her own life, earns her own money. Like you do.'

'But I like a man who respects women,' I countered.

'Of course you do. But you want to get married and keep house for your husband like you keep house for your father, don't you?'

'Then what would happen to my father?' I said, dodging the question deliberately.

'You'd liberate him to find himself a new wife.'

'You think I'm what's stopping him from doing that? I asked, horrified. 'He's not seeing women because he thinks it'd upset me?'

'I never said that. What I'm saying is he probably hasn't even thought about it because you're always here and it's easier for him to ignore the issue altogether. How long ago did your mother die?'

'Over twenty years ago.'

'And he's never dated?'

'No one he's ever told me about.'

'Well, maybe you need to spend some time away from him. Give him a chance to breathe, spread his wings a little. We had a good time the other night. Come and stay with me two or three nights a week, let him get used to you not always being here at night, see what happens.'

'I suppose he could do the morning feed and I could walk the dogs once I got back.' I was unaware that I was already falling in with Billy's plans. 'So what about this audition you went for? Did you get the part?'

He shook his head. 'But there'll be others and in any case, we open with the show next week. I have to concentrate on that. What are you going to wear for the opening?'

I went back to London with him that night, leaving a note for Dad on the kitchen table. I felt awful thinking that maybe I had been stopping Dad from finding someone of his own all these years. I would make a point of talking to him about it.

I couldn't help myself. I set about bringing more warmth to Billy's flat almost immediately. I bought cheap junk shop furniture and repainted it and generally prettied the place up. Rugs on the floor, cushions everywhere, flowers in vases, plants, books, curtains. Every time I was there I brought something new.

'See,' he told me triumphantly, 'this is just what you adore doing. Making a home. You're a natural nest builder.'

'I have a job,' I told him indignantly, 'I have my own business.'

'Your own *business*? You call that a business? Well, whatever you want, but this makes you happy. You're not exactly looking to run the world. I hate businesswomen.'

'Casting directors are businesswomen in a

way,' I pointed out. 'You like them well enough. And women producers.'

'I like them if I can flirt with them, charm them into giving me what I want. I don't like the other kind, the butch kind, the ones who think they're equal to the men.'

'What makes you think they aren't?'

He never answered me. He refused to get drawn further into the argument. I could not make him understand that just because I was happy to live at home and keep house for my father, it didn't mean that I wasn't an independent woman, equal to any man. It didn't mean that when I married and had kids that I would be content to stay home and care for them forever. And even if I did, it would be my choice, not because some man wanted me to. I would always want to control my own income. I just wasn't in any hurry to rush out and plunge into a career until I knew exactly what it was that I wanted to put my energy into. I could see Billy hated the idea of feminism because he was scared of it. He associated it with a type of woman over whom he had no control and he didn't like that.

In the meantime I was falling more and more in love with him and I marveled at the way that however much I might disapprove of his views about women, it didn't stop me enjoying the way he treated me. I was a woman. He was a beautiful young man who showered me with attention and I basked in it. It was my teenage dream come true and I couldn't resist it. Being in love, I decided, now I was the great expert, was a bizarre experience. Suddenly you were the most forgiving, understanding person in the whole world. You had an explanation for everything your partner did wrong. If Billy liked his women to be girly and to defer to him, then that was his father's influence and he'd grow out of it. He was lucky he had someone like me to help him understand how independent women had become since Pat Murphy was a boy.

But then the moment arrived when he really did need me and it felt great.

He had always claimed that he had come looking for me as a shoulder to lean on when Julie had walked off with his father, but we had both known that that was just a line. He'd needed his ego to be bolstered on a temporary basis and I'd been in the right place at the right time. That it had grown into something more meaningful was just one of those things.

At the end of the day we could put that down to sex and we knew it.

The real test came when the show opened, his reviews stank and he was fired within a month.

He blamed the producer. *The fucking cunt of a bitch of a producer* was what he actually called her several times a day. I did too. It was utterly ridiculous, as he pointed out to me repeatedly and I agreed with him, that he should be fired because so many members of the audience had written in to complain about his singing. They knew he couldn't sing when they hired him. They hired him because he was a hell of a good-looking guy and that hadn't changed, had it? It was their fault he couldn't sing, they'd found him such a crap singing teacher. No mention was made of Julie. It was all the new singing teacher's fault — and the woman producer's.

I assumed he would get a job waiting tables or something like other out-of-work actors. Not a bit of it. Billy stayed in bed till noon then went to the gym. The rest of the day he spent moping around his flat until I arrived to make him supper or, when I had the cash, to take him out.

But I was secretly pleased that Billy had been fired because it brought us closer together. I began to wonder what he would have done if I had not been around to boost his flagging spirits. I felt needed and important when I arrived at his doorstep every evening with a bag of groceries and a determination to cheer him up.

'It was meant to be,' I told him over and over again, 'you're not supposed to be in silly musicals, you should be — '

'It wasn't a silly musical. The reviews said it'd run forever. According to them I was the only thing about it that stank.'

'They said you couldn't sing, there's a difference. What does your agent say?'

'How do I know what he says when he doesn't return my calls?'

'I'm making chicken parmigiana. Won't that make you happy?'

'Happier,' he said grudgingly, but he ate two platefuls and we climbed into bed to watch TV.

Of course there was a downside to my playing house with Billy. I was neglecting Dad.

'Are you crazy?' Billy was contemptuous when

I brought this up. 'You're a grown woman. He can take care of himself. High time he did.'

It never occurred to me to suggest that Billy could also take care of himself. And, Dad being Dad, he never said anything about my sudden absence. I was rushing home every morning, feeding the animals, returning people's calls, taking more bookings, walking the dogs, whizzing through the paperwork, and then rushing back to be with Billy.

And it wasn't as if I was getting much sleep. Billy talked into the night and although I wasn't required to do much more than listen, I had to stay awake to give him the occasional reassurance that he was absolutely right, they were complete bastards, they didn't appreciate him, he was incredibly talented.

But eventually something had to give. I didn't return two of my favorite customers' phone calls for over a week — it just slipped my mind each day — and they took their pets to kennels five miles away. I knew I had to spend a few days at home.

Billy looked thoroughly dejected. He had a way of sitting with his huge shoulders hunched over and his head hanging down, occasionally glancing up at you. It really got to me. There was something so pathetic about seeing a big man looking miserable and vulnerable.

'I'll be back soon and I'll call you every night,' I promised.

I did and he was never there.

By the fourth day I began to wonder if something dreadful had happened to him.

'Look,' said Dad, 'I'll keep an eye on things. Get on back to him if you're worried. All your summer bookings are in. Everyone who's going away has already planned their summer holidays, they've been in touch. Spend an evening doing the billing and I'll send out the invoices. I'll be here for the animals at night and providing you're here during the day, everything'll be fine.'

'Do you like Billy, Dad?'

'I don't really know him.'

'That's not an answer.'

'He seems to make you happy. That's important to me. I can't pretend I've ever had much time for his father, but his mother's a saint and maybe something of her has rubbed off on Billy.'

I had the sense Dad was searching around for something nice to say about him. Then he surprised me with one of his out-of-the-blue questions. About once every two or three months Dad shot a query at me that invariably put me on the spot and in one fell swoop negated the weeks he'd seemingly been turning a blind eye to what I was doing.

'Tell me, why do you like him? What does he bring to your party, smart, independent girl like you?'

It was ironic that while Billy made no secret of the fact that he thought I was a wimp for still living at home, Dad always thought of me as being highly independent.

'He's given me confidence. He's so good-looking and sophisticated and yet he wants to spend time with me. And he needs me. He makes me feel there is so much I can do for him and it makes me feel terrific about myself.'

'Just make sure he gives you something back,' Dad muttered.

I went to London the next evening. As I walked from Covent Garden Underground station to his flat, I realized I should have let him know I was coming. He might not even be there and I didn't have a key.

He was there — and so was his father.

Pat Murphy was drunk and Billy was not far behind him. In the ultimate ironic twist, Julie had dumped Pat Murphy and he had come to drown his sorrows with his son, as Billy explained quickly when he opened the door.

'Hello, sweetheart. What are you doing here? Little shopping in town?' Pat was red in the face as usual. I thought of poor Nora and resisted the urge to deliver a major put down. He was Billy's father after all. I looked from him to Billy, waiting for Billy to explain. He said nothing. Didn't even offer me a drink.

'Where've you been all week? I've been calling you every evening.'

'Ooh, you've got a little jailer here, lad,' said Pat. 'He's not your pet monkey, sweetheart.'

'Mr Murphy, please don't call me sweetheart.'

'Sorry, honey, I've forgotten your name. Billy's been out working. Casting directors. We've been taking them all out for a drink. Well, just the pretty ones. They're all in love with our Billy. Hey, Billy, we're out of ale. Want me to go down the off licence and pick up some more?'

'No, I'll go,' said Billy, staggering to his feet.

'Last time you found your way to the pub and I never saw you again. Stay here and keep Dad company.' I was pulling on my coat. I didn't want to be left with Mr Murphy.

But I stayed out of politeness.

'How is she?' asked Pat Murphy the minute Billy was out the door. 'I call every night. She won't talk to me.'

'Nora?'

He seemed to have sobered up in a second. 'Yeah. I miss her. I love her. Will you tell her? You see her, don't you? She told me about your little talks. She likes you.'

I was a bit taken aback, although whether it was because he had elected to use me as a go-between or because Nora had told him about our 'little talks', I couldn't say.

'I will tell her,' I said slowly. I was beginning to feel a little sorry for him but then he went and blew it.

'It wasn't my fault, honest. Julie came on to me. Threw herself at me. Told me she liked older men. I never encouraged her. I swear I didn't.'

But you didn't exactly fight her off. Who did he think he was kidding?

When Billy returned he looked at me in surprise as if to say, 'You still here?'

'Billy?'

'Look, I wasn't expecting you. There's something I've got to take care of. I'll give you a call, OK? You didn't make a special trip to see me, did you?'

'Course she did,' said Pat cheerfully, 'they all do, Billy, lad. You know that as well as I do.'

'No, I was on my way somewhere,' I lied, and Billy knew I was lying. 'Call me soon.'

I felt wretched on the way home. Dad didn't say a word when I walked in the door. For once I wished he wouldn't be so bloody understanding, that he'd interfere, ask me what was going on, tell me how to handle Billy. Would I ever hear from him again?

Stupid question. I heard from him the very next day.

'I wanted you to be the first to know,' he said as I clutched the phone. 'I couldn't talk about it last night. It would have jinxed it.'

'What? What? Tell me.'

'I might have been fired from that dumb musical but some good came out of it. Before I left the show a director saw it and reckoned I was just what he needed for his new picture. He told his casting director to check me out and it turns out she's one of the ones who's crazy about me. She fixed me a meeting with this guy and next thing I know they're talking to my agent. I get to go to New York for a month's filming. Not the starring role but a great cameo. Mega exposure. And good money.'

I was devastated. Struck dumb. Shell shocked. I wouldn't see Billy for a month.

'Are you there? What's the matter? Aren't you over the moon for me?'

'Of course,' I stuttered, 'it's the best thing that could have happened for you. When do you leave?'

'Tomorrow.'

Total shock horror!

'I'm coming home to say goodbye to Mum tonight so I'll call in on you. Will you be home?'

He breezed in and Dad tactfully made himself scarce, but what could we do in half an hour? He said all the right things — 'I'll be home before you know it; I'll call; I don't know what I would have done without you these past few weeks' — but he couldn't help but whoop for joy at the same time.

His goodbye kiss was heavenly, but somehow that only made things worse. I had a taste of what I would be missing — literally.

'Call my agent. He'll tell you where to reach me.'

Yeah, great, the one who never returned calls.

I cried myself to sleep like a four year old. It was so tantalizing having him just up the road. And then I awoke in the middle of the night with a brilliant idea.

It took me two days to pin Warren down.

'OK. Nothing easier. The good news is Pete's gone off again and left his laptop behind so we can do it at the house. Who do you want to e-mail?'

'My godmother in New York.'

It was simple. I would change my mind and take Mitzi up on her invitation to join her at her summer house in The Hamptons. It was only two hours from New York, she had told me.

Only two hours from Billy.

Part Three

MITZI

Long Island, 2000

15

My first introduction to Mitzi's attitude was her total refusal to come and meet me at JFK airport.

'But I've never been to America before,' I wailed down the phone during one of the numerous telephone conversations I had with her before I left.

She had responded instantly to my e-mailed reminder that she had invited me, full of stumbling, tentative hints that if the offer were still open, then if it wasn't too much trouble and if she still had room for me, and if she didn't I'd quite understand, but then again if she did it would be quite wonderful . . .

She responded by phone and this was a surprise. To date she had always written letters, but perhaps the urgency of the situation required her to pick up the telephone. Mitzi, I would learn, talked constantly on the phone; her cell phone was like some growth attached to her ear. My expression of interest in visiting her seemed to have liberated her to use her favorite form of communication. Fine, except she called in the middle of the night. Dad picked up the phone thinking it must be an emergency and was greeted by a screeching American accent.

'Of course you can come. I said so, didn't I? I'm going to send you a ticket. I have these air miles I need to use up before they expire. That's why I asked you. Truth is I booked the ticket already. I had to. I told my friend Sylvia in London she could come visit. Now I'll call and tell her she can't. So, are you packed? You leave in two days. You'll have a night in the city then we go to The Hamptons for August. So — '

'Stop!' I heard Dad yell. 'I think you have the wrong number. It's some crazy woman calling from America,' he hissed at me. I had come into his room to see what the commotion was about. I knew at once who it was. The trouble was I hadn't told Dad I'd contacted Mitzi Alexander.

When I took the phone from him I heard Mitzi's voice for the first time. It was quite a shock. Raspy, much older than I had expected. She growled rather than talked and she sounded like she was in a thoroughly disagreeable mood even though she was the one who had woken us up. Once I'd had her on the phone two or three times, I decided she always sounded like she was complaining about something. Her words were drawn out — 'so what do you *waa-aunt* to see in New *Yooorrrik?*' and her voice went up at the end of each sentence so everything she said was like a question, as if demands were constantly being made of her and she had to challenge them.

Dad was tricky about my going.

I suppose some instinct had told me that he might be because I had not mentioned to him that I'd e-mailed her. It was awful. He never interfered in my life but he always knew about it. And if I chose to talk about it, he'd always listen. But even if I knew he wasn't as ecstatic about something or someone as I was, he always accepted what was going on. Like I knew he wasn't crazy about Billy but he'd been nice to him. But as soon as he found out about Mitzi he clammed up. He didn't say 'you can't go' and it wasn't as if I had to ask him to lend me money for the ticket because she'd organized that. At first I wondered if he was resentful of the way she'd taken matters concerning me into her own hands. Maybe he felt he should have offered to send me. But we both knew how I reacted when he offered to do anything for me. I was always Miss Independent, I can do it myself, thank you very much.

But I needed him on this one. I wanted his approval, his blessing. And I wanted to share my nervousness with him. I'd never been to Edinburgh or Paris, let alone New York. I had been on a school trip to Normandie so I did have a passport. But whenever I brought up the trip, he just said something non-committal like, 'Are you all packed? Take cool clothes, I hear it gets pretty hot out there this time of year,' and walked out of the room. Finally I cornered him.

'You don't want me to go to New York.'

'I never said that.' He sounded peevish. Rare for Dad. 'It's a wonderful opportunity for you. Why would I not want you to go?'

'Then it must be Mitzi. You don't like Mitzi.'

'I don't know her.'

'Dad, she was Mum's best friend.'

'So she says.'

'You mean she wasn't? So why is she my godmother?'

'We only have her word for that.'

'So in your eyes she isn't?'

'Auntie Susan is your godmother.' Auntie Susan was Dad's older sister who lived in Newcastle. She came for Christmas every four or five years and it was a nightmare. She was ten years older than Dad and she attempted to boss him around just as she bossed around her poor henpecked husband, Uncle Norman.

'Dad, the truth is I don't really have any godparents because I didn't have a christening.'

'I had you baptized,' said Dad, 'you know perfectly well I had you baptized.'

This was true. He had me baptized when I was in my teens so I could be confirmed. Auntie Susan had made a special trip.

'But I've never understood why you and Mum didn't do it when I was a baby like everyone else.'

No answer. But I wasn't going to give up.

'I just don't get it. If Mitzi was Mum's best friend, why don't you know her?'

I expected another immediate rebuttal of the suggestion that Mitzi was Mum's best friend but his answer surprised me.

'Your mother didn't marry the boy next door as you're planning to do.' I glared at him. Chance would be a fine thing. I pictured a dreamy scene where Billy proposed to me at the top of the Empire State Building and it made me go weak at the knees for a moment. 'She had a life before we married, as you would expect,' Dad went on. 'Mitzi Alexander was part of that life. Your mother met her when she was on a working holiday in America one summer. Your mother was from Dublin, as you know, and she had relatives who had emigrated to Long Island. Mitzi's family had a summer house out there. I can't remember how the story goes, your mother was waiting tables at the restaurant as a summer job or babysitting. Whatever, she was serving Mitzi or Mitzi's parents and they became friends. They kept in touch by phone and letter. But Mitzi put all kinds of ideas into your mother's head, how she had to fight for her rights as a woman. She turned your mother's head completely. Came to Cambridge and London, did the same thing all over again, had her going on marches and sloshing around in the mud at Greenham Common. And your mother went back there once or twice. I think she might even have gone to see Mitzi in California. Her relatives moved there too as I recall.'

'So did you keep in touch with these relatives? Why have you never mentioned them? Maybe I can meet some of my mother's family — my family?'

'I wouldn't know.' Again the evasive attitude. So unlike Dad. 'They've never been in touch with me.'

For some reason my mother's family had always been a closed book. Her parents were dead and she didn't have any siblings. She came from a Catholic family so I had assumed there had to have been brothers and sisters. I had wondered about them, pestered Dad to get in touch, but when he showed no interest in doing so, I'd always dropped it. Characters in novels go rushing off to look for long-lost relatives they've never met but people in real life tend to just get on with things.

'Well, Mitzi will know where they are,' I said confidently. 'Tell me, Dad, did I ever meet Mitzi?'

'You were going to. Your mother went to stay with her one last summer.' Dad's voice had suddenly gone quiet.

'After I was born?'

'Yes.'

'Why didn't she take me?'

'She was going to but you developed earache right before she was due to leave. The doctor advised against it, her taking you on a plane. She went on her own. As it turned out it was for the best.'

'What do you mean?'

'She never came back.'

'She drowned in *America*?'

I had always known my mother had drowned but I had never known exactly where. I had assumed it was somewhere in England. Death by drowning was so awful to contemplate that I had never wanted to see the spot, the dark waters that had claimed her, in case it matched the horrendous whirlpool that surfaced in my nightmares from time to time.

'You might have drowned with her but I had you safe and sound.'

'She was with Mitzi when it happened?'

'Who knows who she was with?' He said this wearily, as if he'd gone over it a thousand times in his mind.

I recalled what little I had been told. It was a boating accident of some kind. Surely he had to have known the details, but I understood his reluctance to go over it all again.

'So that's why you hate Mitzi.'

'How can I hate her? I don't know her.'

'But you hold her responsible for my mother's death? If my mother hadn't gone to visit her, she'd still be alive.'

He never answered me on that one. But something in his mood seemed to have lifted, as if he'd got something off his chest and could relax a little. I let it go at that. We had a lot of other stuff to organize. After all, it was Dad who was going to run the kennels for me while I was away. As he pointed out, half his patients were going to be in them for the month of August anyway while their owners were on holiday. And Warren, bless him, had offered to pitch in and help with the evening feed after his last shampoo and cut.

So I was all set.

And terrified.

'Meet you at the airport? Where am I going to find the time to do that?' growled Mitzi. 'You're clearly not your mother's daughter if you can't get yourself into the city from the airport by yourself.'

Dad, of course, drove me all the way to Heathrow and Warren announced he was coming too for moral support. Then, when we stopped to say goodbye to Nora, she joined the party as well.

'I can't say goodbye to you on the doorstep. Is

there room for me in the car?' She grabbed her coat and came out in her slippers. 'I won't get out of the car. Can't have you missing the plane and we can have a nice chat on the drive out.'

But of course we couldn't — at least not the kind she had in mind — because Dad and Warren had their ears flapping. I hadn't seen Nora since she had returned from her trip to Italy with Pete, although needless to say, Warren had filled me in on all the gossip.

'Pete said she was out of control.'

'What on earth do you mean?' I had visions of Nora on rollerblades hurtling along marble floors in Venetian palazzos.

'She flirted with the waiters, apparently. Made eyes at them while they were serving her spaghetti carbonara or whatever it's called. Batting her eyelashes and smiling too much. Pete was shocked. Typical Pete.'

But I understood. Nora's husband had been caught with a younger woman and she'd lost her confidence. She needed a little reassurance and if even a waiter found her attractive, it was something.

'Other than that it was a success? Good churches, frescoes, that sort of thing?'

'Oh, yeah, fine, no problem,' said Warren vaguely. Frescoes weren't exactly his thing.

I made Nora get out of the car in her slippers — they were pretty fancy leopard skin ones, not the pink fluffy bunny variety — and accompany me on an urgent last-minute dash to the ladies'.

'They have them on the plane, you know,' Warren called after us.

After I'd had a glowing report of all the works of art and churches she'd seen, I butted in with: 'Nora, there's something I have to tell you. I saw Mr Murphy.'

'You did? Where?'

'In London. I went to see Billy,' I saw her eyes widen but I didn't want to get into that now so I rushed on, 'and Mr Murphy happened to be visiting him. Anyway, while Billy was out getting more beer, Mr Murphy said he was really missing you and he told me Julie came on to him, not the other way round. He said it wasn't his fault.'

For a moment I thought I saw her face soften a little, then she turned away. When she spoke again I hardly recognized her voice, it was so much tougher.

'Of course it was his fault. Everyone thinks I know nothing of what he gets up to, everyone tries to protect me and I've had enough. I'm not a fragile little flower. I'm a grown woman, middle-aged maybe, but I'm still attractive and I'm not going to waste any more time on Pat. He's had his chance, God knows I've made allowances for him but enough's enough. If he's pining for me, fine. Let him pine.'

'What was that you told me about forgiveness in marriage?'

'Well, all I can say is that I've been forgiving for twenty-five years and it's become a little boring.' She sounded hard, flat, and it scared me.

'We'd better be getting back to the others. I need to check in if I'm going to make this flight.'

She looked at me for a minute as if she might

relent a little but when we stepped outside the ladies', Dad appeared on the scene.

'So this is what you do when you go off to take a leak.'

Nora's face brightened. She smiled at him. I thought about what Warren had said about those waiters in Italy. Maybe it applied to any man who came Nora Murphy's way these days if she was this close to flirting with Dad.

'Look up our Billy while you're over there,' Warren called as I went through the gate.

Can he be that stupid that he hasn't worked out that's why I'm going, I wondered, as I settled down in my seat to try and figure out how to work the in-flight entertainment remote control.

I had never flown before, but scared as I was I wasn't about to tell anyone I was so inexperienced. But the noise on take-off caused my heart to stop. And when we landed at JFK, we hit the runway with such a bump I thought we'd crashed. But the passengers cheered and clapped and the woman sitting next to me told me they did that when the pilot made a good landing. If that was a good landing, I didn't want to imagine what a bad one was like.

No one had warned me about Immigration. The line was endless, snaking back and forth behind barriers throughout a vast hall. I had read about Ellis Island and I felt a momentary pang of fear. This was a foreign country with its own rules. Maybe I wouldn't be welcome. I tried to imagine what immigrants a hundred years ago must have felt like. Whole families whose futures depended on being accepted by this strange country. And what had happened if they were not accepted? Ellis *Island*! The island aspect of it made it sound like Alcatraz — if they didn't get in did they have to leave by swimming? Manhattan was an island . . .

'Wait behind the line!' The official was a woman and she was pretty tough. Somehow I had reached the front of the line without noticing and had moved forward to the booth to show my passport.

When I was finally allowed into it and they asked for my forms and I hadn't filled them in because I didn't know I had to, I had to go all the way back to the end of the line. Three more flights had landed since I first entered the hall and the line had tripled in length. The heat was sweltering despite the air conditioning and this time I'd finished with my romantic Ellis Island reverie, so the waiting seemed endless.

When I finally made it back to a passport booth, I shook while the official looked my name up on a computer.

'You here for business or pleasure?'

'Pleasure.'

'Vacation?'

'Yes.' A whisper.

'What's that? Speak up please.'

The passenger in the booth beside me was being led away. He was protesting but it seemed his papers weren't in order.

By the time I was released into customs I was exhausted. My bag was the last to come through on the carousel and I barely had the strength to lift it. When I finally staggered into the Arrivals hall I wanted nothing more than to be released into the care of someone who had come to meet me. I watched people being hugged and kissed and others being swept away by the drivers of limousine companies. I clutched someone's arm and gasped 'Taxi?' as if I needed oxygen.

Another line, and once I was in the back of a yellow cab it took me another five minutes to make the driver understand where I wanted to go.

'Eight-hundred West End Avenue.'

'Where's that? Ninety-seventh, ninety-eighth Street?'

'New York,' I said desperately, 'Eight-hundred West End Avenue, New York, New York 10025,' I read out Mitzi's address.

'You're giving me zip codes. What am I? The mailman?'

The cab did not have air conditioning and we hit rush hour traffic.

'You want to take the Fifty-ninth Street bridge or the Triborough?' asked the driver.

I wanted to take an overdose, I was so hot and miserable.

But then I saw one of the most stunning sights in the world — the Manhattan skyline — and my heart soared. It was nothing short of majestic, and the sun going down behind it bathed it in a deep crimson glow.

'Where are we?' I asked the driver.

'Queens,' he said as if I was mad.

People lived here. We had passed streets of rather sad-looking houses. How awful it must be to live here and look across the river at another world. Manhattan looked like a city of towering silver palaces and it seemed the cab was crossing a drawbridge reserved for the privileged.

But we soon left the river behind, only to be glimpsed occasionally between skyscrapers at the far end of long cross streets. Mitzi's building was rather imposing. West End Avenue seemed to be a residential street, no shops, not much color. I dragged my bags into a marble hallway and the doorman looked at me suspiciously.

'Mitzi Alexander,' I told him.

'Fifteenth floor but I think she's finished by now. She finishes at six.'

Finished what?

Her door was open. He must have called and told her I was on the way up.

As I walked in I heard the sound of weeping.

I called out, 'Mitzi?'

No answer.

I walked towards the weeping. The door was ajar. I could see into the room.

A woman was lying on a chaise longue, curled in a foetal position, rocking herself backwards and forwards, her grief harrowing to watch.

I rushed over and put my arms around her.

'Mitzi, what's wrong? Tell me what's wrong? What can I do to help?'

The woman stopped crying abruptly, probably more in shock than anything else. Who was this woman with an English accent who had appeared out of nowhere? She pulled away from me.

'Mitzi?' I asked again.

'I'm Mitzi,' said a voice behind me, and I

turned to see a striking-looking woman with a mane of wiry black hair fifty per cent streaked with gray. 'Dr Mitzi Alexander. That's my patient you're attempting to console but her time's up. You look a lot like your mother, you know.'

And with that, out of sheer exhaustion or being likened to the mother I would never know, I flopped on to the chaise longue with the patient who had begun to whimper again and joined her in a long overdue bout of sobbing.

'Welcome to America,' said Mitzi, 'welcome to New York.'

16

Mitzi was a talker.

A shrinking chatterbox. Or a gabby shrink, whichever way you wanted to look at it. The combination didn't fit, somehow. Weren't shrinks supposed to listen?

Actually, it suited me fine that I didn't have to say much as the car inched its way along what I understood to be The Long Island Expressway. I was exhausted and confused by jet lag and I was happy just to listen intermittently to Mitzi's constant chatter. It was as if she'd been unleashed from some kind of imprisonment and allowed to talk for the first time in months and I suppose in a way that was true. All week long she listened to her patients and now it was her turn to let rip with what was on her mind.

But I was the one who was imprisoned now and Mitzi was my jailer. I felt trapped and, every now and again, terrified. But worst of all was the knowledge that with each mile we were moving farther and farther away from New York — and Billy. I hadn't really taken into account the fact that Mitzi was going to whisk me away from the city so soon after my arrival. I had thought she would plan some tourist stuff for me which would give me a few days in New York and allow me to contact Billy. I wanted to surprise him. But Mitzi, as I would learn, was far too selfish to spare a thought for what might be interesting to me unless, of course, it involved something that was also interesting for her. She didn't have to work for the whole of August so she couldn't wait to get out of the city, and that meant she wasn't about to hang around and show me the sights.

I suppose I must have known that Mitzi was a shrink. I mean, she had to have mentioned it in one of her letters. It never dawned on me that she would practice from her home. The sound of her doorbell had shattered my sleep at seven a.m. and I'd had to tiptoe down the corridor in my robe to get myself some breakfast in her tiny kitchen while she saw her first patient. She managed to see another two before we finally left Manhattan, and once again I heard sobbing echoing through the apartment.

I felt trapped because of what she had sprung on me the night before.

'So,' she said, turning to me after she'd got rid of the depressed patient, 'here you are. My daughter.'

'Goddaughter,' I corrected automatically.

'Whatever, when I adopt you you'll be my daughter.'

I stared at her, too stunned to speak, and aware that at the same time I was impressed by her striking appearance. Mitzi was very tall, probably about five-ten, five-eleven with long, well-formed limbs. She had a strong face, full of character, long nose, wide mouth, bushy black eyebrows above piercing dark eyes. There was a flush of rosy colour on her cheeks although her skin was basically dark olive. But her hair was literally her crowning glory. It was a huge mane of thick curls flowing out around her head and past her shoulders, an odd style for a woman who had to be in her forties, but it suited her. With her height she could carry it off. At one stage she must have been raven haired but now it was streaked with gray and white strands that made it even more dramatic. There was no make-up on her face and her height and her flashing eyes gave her an allure that was unmistakable despite the unflattering trousers and scuffed Keds she was wearing.

'Could I have something to drink please?' I stammered. 'A glass of water would be fine.'

'Help yourself. The kitchen's through there. There's seltzer in the fridge.'

Wasn't she even going to feed me? Not that I was hungry. I'd eaten on the plane and it was two in the morning on my English time. And what on earth was seltzer?

She followed me into the kitchen.

'I told your mother I'd step in when the time was right, that I'd adopt you. I guess we don't really have to go that far. You're a grown up, you can decide for yourself, but from now on I get to have a say in what you do with your life whether you want it or not.'

'I am over eighteen,' I pointed out and laughed. She was joking, right? Apparently not.

'You think I'm kidding? I'm not. I don't expect you to heed what I say all the time but I'm going to give you advice all the same. I've always wanted a daughter. Not kids, just a daughter, and everyone kept saying I should adopt but I guess I've left it too late. And I knew I always had you even though I'd never met you. You were Virginia's daughter, how bad could you be? If you had even half of her genes you were going to be the ninth wonder of the world and here you are, exactly that.' She smiled and her whole face lit up. She was extraordinary looking.

For a second the question formed in my mind. 'Who's Virgi — ?' Dad and anyone else who talked about her always said 'Your mother'. It felt good to hear her name spoken as if she were around somewhere. It made me feel a part of her. And I was reminded of why I had made such a seemingly lunatic, impulsive decision to come and stay with Mitzi. It wasn't just about Billy. It had been informed by the knowledge buried deep inside me that, after Dad, this awesome creature standing in front of me was my closest link to my mother.

And now that I thought about it, there had always been something rather proprietorial about Mitzi's letters to me, as if she had some kind of claim over me, which she obviously thought she did. Would we get into a long Q & A about my mother? Had I unconsciously been assuming that Mitzi would supply me with all the answers?

I had fallen asleep right in front of her on her patients' couch while she talked and talked. At some point I was aware of her hoisting me to my feet and half carrying me down the hall to the spare room in her apartment. I think I heard her talking to me in my sleep, in my dreams. And now here she was again, talking away as I sat beside her in the car, the maternal theme still on her mind.

'Aren't you furious with Virginia for deserting you? For dying so young and leaving you to fend for yourself?'

Shrink claptrap, I decided. Not worth dignifying with an answer. And it was the right decision because Mitzi carried on regardless, going off at a tangent, as she was wont to do, to talk about her own mother.

'Of course, you'll want to follow in Virginia's footsteps and that's where I come in, but you know, there's no way I would ever have done as your mother did. When I was growing up, my mother was a typical America suburban house-wife. She gloried in the post-war boom, she lived for her appliances — her washer/dryer, her dish-washer, her housework, running her home and looking after me and having a meal on the table for my dad every evening. That was her whole life. She never had a job. She never even thought about it. She had it all so dumb! Her only joy in life was her Martini. My dad was having an affair with his secretary ever since we could remember. I knew about it, but my mom acted like it wasn't happening. By that time my father had taken over my mother's family business because she didn't have any brothers and we had moved to the city, to this big apartment on the upper west side. Then she turned the running of the household over to the staff. I went off to college — Berkeley, you know, I was smart — and I left them to it. Barely saw my mother after that. She became really ambitious, not in any kind of career, but socially.'

Mitzi wound the car window down and rested her elbow on the ledge. She had my attention now because I had detected a bitterness in her tone. I still couldn't quite come to terms with the fact that I was in America for the first time. It was as if Mitzi had suddenly materialized in Chaveny Road and was whisking me away to Cornwall. My cultural uprooting was not important to her. Apart from her brief 'Welcome to America', she'd made no effort to acclimatize me. She expected me to slot right into her life as if I'd been part of it forever, which, in her eyes, I probably had.

'All my mother cared about was that my father was successful and they were invited everywhere — everywhere except Jewish homes. Mrs Victor Alexander *At Home*. That was her world. My father's success was her passport to New York society.' Mitzi's tone was now openly contemptuous.

'But she married him. She must have loved him.'

'Love!' Mitzi spat out the word. 'You think marriage is about love?'

'Of course,' I said, astonished.

'So are you *in love*?' She drawled the words and winked at me.

At last I could talk about Billy. I had been thinking about him constantly and it was an unbelievable release. And for the first time I silenced her. I told her about the Murphy family, about the swimming pool opening where I had seen him for the first time, how he had gone

218

away to drama school and become a famous actor. I added the *famous* on instinct, although it wasn't strictly true. Billy, I knew, hoped this film in New York would make him famous, would bring him the stardom he craved. I described his looks in glowing detail, and with barely concealed pride I told her how he'd sought me out and begun a relationship with me.

'A *relationship*? Are you crazy?' She more or less laughed in my face. 'That's a crush. You've got a stupid crush on him. That's not love.'

How would you know, I wondered?

'You're not married, Mitzi?' It was ludicrous that I knew so little about her but Dad had always refused to supply me with any details.

'Nope.'

'Never have been?'

'Nope.'

And no kids, as she'd already told me. Just 'me'.

'I really want to get married,' I told her.

'Oh, no, here we go.'

'What do you mean?'

'Just like your mother. All she ever wanted to do was find a nice guy and raise a family.'

'What's wrong with that?'

'Everything if you were as talented as your mother was. She was so clever. You know she read English at Cambridge? She had a place at Trinity College, Dublin but she wanted to get out of Ireland, away from her family. She did the right thing. The last thing she needed was to be trapped in Holy Catholic Ireland.'

I nodded. Secretly I was horrified to think that

Mitzi had influenced my mother in her thinking against her family. But I smiled and said, 'Sure. Cambridge. That's where she met Dad.'

Mitzi made a face. 'So how is Frank?'

'Fine. He sends his best,' I added for the sake of politeness.

'No he didn't. You don't have to pretend. I don't even know him. But I blame him for what happened to Virginia.'

For a moment I thought she meant she blamed Dad for my mother's death which was impossible since he had been in another country. And also ironic since I'd sensed that Dad blamed Mitzi.

'What do you mean?'

'If Virginia hadn't met Frank at Cambridge and he hadn't asked her to marry him, she'd probably have a brilliant career by now.'

It was as if my mother's death didn't matter. The fact that she hadn't achieved a brilliant career was the tragedy.

'You see,' Mitzi went on, 'we had a choice between the mother/housewife role and the career woman. Back then the career woman role still had a bit of stigma attached to it. If you were a married woman, it wasn't a given that you would also want to work, to make something of your self, that you might want more out of life than cleaning the house and cooking for your man. When I met Virginia she had a summer job, working as a waitress in a restaurant on the East End of Long Island out at Montauk Harbor. I'll take you there. You can sit and watch the fishing boats come in while you eat dinner. I noted her accent and the way she seemed so much smarter than the other young girls working in the restaurant. I befriended her right there in the restaurant. And later I invited her to the house, my family's house . . . '

'Where we're going?'

'No, I take the boathouse down by the water. I rent out the family house but we'll go there. They're having a big party while you're here. It'll be a big Hamptons summer benefit, if that sort of thing would amuse you? It's the only way to get into the Hamptons scene, the charity route.' Again the contemptuous tone. 'And to think when my parents first bought the house my mother was obsessed with playing down the fact they were Jewish. My mother's biggest sadness was that she wasn't allowed into the Maidstone Club. So anyway, I befriended your mother in order to raise her consciousness.'

'Raise her consciousness,' I repeated. I didn't understand where this was going.

'Virginia had no idea about sex discrimination. Equal opportunity. She was a waitress but she never noticed the waiters were paid more. I had to spell it out to her what was going on. Do you realize what it was like once upon a time? A woman would walk into a bar in America and be told, 'We don't serve women.' Can you imagine? Women served. Nobody served them. But by the time I got through with her, your mother understood what it was all about. By the time she went back to England she had wised up. She was going to fight for her rights. If she got a job she was going to demand to be paid the same as a man. Didn't happen, of course. Once she married your father, she was in his clutches and that was that. But I didn't let go of her. I kept in touch with her long after you were born. I became your godmother.'

I wondered if my mother had had any say in the matter.

'So you think getting married to this Billy or some gorgeous piece of meat just like him and having his children is going to make you really happy?'

I decided to keep quiet. It wasn't so much that I was taking the line of least resistance as that I sensed there was little chance of stopping her in her tracks once she got started on something. This woman had been my mother's friend. Maybe she wouldn't be if my mother were still alive but she had been then, and I felt that by listening to her I might learn something about my past.

'You can't live your life for a man,' continued Mitzi. 'I can't believe I have actually invited someone who would be so girly and romance obsessed. Men are the enemy of all we want to achieve in our lives. You've bought into the mystique about marriage and motherhood and dating sold by all those women's magazines, haven't you? When you get a crush on a guy you get all dippy and goo-goo-eyed and you can't think about anything else so all the important stuff in your life gets put to one side. Tell me I'm not wrong.'

The truth was she wasn't. I knew I had been guilty of neglect in my work when I had been rushing off to see Billy in Covent Garden. I had forgotten to take care of the billing and I hadn't returned people's calls so they had taken their business elsewhere.

'What will happen is what happened to your mother. You'll have one kid, you'll have another, you'll get caught up in domesticity, you won't work, your husband will have affairs because you don't give him enough attention, you'll hate him. Why do it to yourself?'

'Did my mother hate my father?' I asked, incredulous. 'I know that's not true. And why wouldn't I go on working? I love my work and I do it at home so that takes care of childcare. I'd be there for them. And besides, my husband would help out. Men see themselves very differently now. They take it for granted that they will look after the children sometimes, they enjoy it. I think a man would ask himself the same question a woman would these days. He'd think: I want to have a family but how am I going to have time for my career, my wife and my family? I'm going to have to make some adjustments. If a man doesn't think like that, then he shouldn't get married. And nor should a woman.'

I realized I'd never really thought about what I'd just said before. It just sort of came out. But it sounded right.

'Will this wonder husband clean the toilet, too?' Mitzi sounded skeptical. 'So tell me something, who's your role model in life? Has to be a woman. Bet you can't come up with a man.'

'As a matter of fact I can,' I said immediately. 'My Dad.'

223

'How's that?' asked Mitzi, clearly thrown.

'Because he quietly goes about his business, because he's successful at what he does, because he's respected by the community and because he raised me as a single parent without fuss and gave me confidence in myself.'

She didn't have a leg to stand on. I felt rather sorry for her.

'So who's your role model?' I asked by way of compensation. 'If it's a woman it has to be someone who's around now,' just in case she picked one of those old feminists I'd never heard of.

'Hillary Clinton,' she answered automatically.

'Aha!' I could see that one off easily. 'Hillary's not a real feminist. She's a fake. She got where she is today on the back of a man.'

'Yeah, so what if she did? Although she was always a lawyer, she always had a career of her own from the get go.'

'You've never had a female president of America, have you?' I goaded. 'Not like our Mrs Thatcher, and then there was Indira Gandhi and Golda Meir and even Mary Robinson in Ireland. American women are a bit behind on that one.'

'We're waiting for Hillary,' said Mitzi predictably. 'First the Senate then back to the White House as the first woman president in 2004. Now, more of this later. We're here.'

I hadn't even noticed that we'd left the highway, although I had become aware of some pretty wooden houses with sloping roofs, shingling, wraparound porches, shuttered windows glimpsed here and there through the trees.

Suddenly I could see the sea ahead of us on the horizon at the end of a long road. Mitzi swung the car into the forecourt of a very grand house fronted by beautifully manicured lawns and sprinklers spraying in every direction. It could only be described as a mansion, the kind of house I had imagined Jay Gatsby might have lived in when I had read Scott Fitzgerald's novel. My heart sank. Growing up in Chaveny Road had not prepared me for this.

But then I remembered. Mitzi had said something about a boathouse.

'This is my old family house, the one I rent out and virtually live off,' Mitzi explained airily, driving past it without a glance and veering off down a sandy dirt track leading off to the side through the woods. We emerged on to what seemed to be a bluff overlooking the most beautiful bay I had ever seen. Mitzi drove furiously until I thought we'd shoot over the cliff into the sea. She braked abruptly and leapt out, leaving the door hanging open.

'Come on, come on, help me unload.' She was round the back of the car, hurling stuff on to the ground. 'Follow me.'

I grabbed my bag and my knapsack. She had disappeared over the edge of the cliff and as I looked down I could see her hurtling down a steep wooden walkway that seemed to go on forever. As I followed her, taking one step at a time, treading cautiously for fear I would fall, suddenly I saw the water far below me. Then, as I was about halfway down, there, right beside the bottom step, I could see a little wooden shack on stilts, the waves lapping gently beneath it.

I stopped in my tracks and gazed down at it. This was the most romantic house I had ever seen. A little rowboat was tied up to one of the stilts. Beyond was a jetty with another boat with an outboard motor moored alongside it. Also built on stilts was a deck running along the front of the house with a motley collection of old and extremely comfortable lounging chairs. A hammock had been strung up between two trees in the shade behind the back door, surrounded by rhododendron bushes.

Viewed from above it was magical but when I climbed down and reached the house itself, it was even better. All I could think of was that it would be the perfect spot for a romantic interlude. Then I caught myself. I was acting out everything Mitzi had said about me. Maybe she was right, maybe I was just a silly little romantic dreamer.

But she surprised me.

'Beautiful spot, don't you think? It's the old boathouse. I converted it into a place where I could spend the summer once I started renting out the big house, got permission to add on the two bedrooms. Maybe you might want to invite this guy Billy out for a weekend if he has some spare time from his filming? Take him as your date to this damn benefit they're having up at the house. Lord knows, it's movie stars they're after, and maybe if I can rustle one up I can charge them more rent.'

Me and Billy in this little paradise. It would be a dream come true.

But how on earth would Mitzi fit in?

When I awoke from a deep sleep the following morning, Mitzi was not around. A note from her pinned to the fridge by a magnet with a sign on it saying, 'Surfs up!' told me to help myself to whatever I wanted for breakfast. She'd gone out, she wouldn't be back till lunchtime. I had the morning to myself.

I was sleeping in a little square box with nothing in it but shelves crammed with books and a sleep-sofa, as Mitzi had called it. It was surprisingly comfortable but my efforts to convert it back into a sofa during the day had proved futile. The hinges were old and rusty. I suspected it hadn't been used as a bed for some time and now it had been forced to unfold, it was damned if it was going revert back to its less conspicuous status. There was no wardrobe, just a coat rack with pegs on which to hang my clothes. In order to get out of the room, I had to clamber over the sleep-sofa to the door.

But in fact I didn't mind a bit. The main living area was sparse, with a kitchen counter running along one wall and beside it a beat-up dining table where we'd eaten scrambled eggs before I'd once again fallen asleep in front of her. Other than that there were just a few chairs, a TV set, a radio, the odd lamp, more bookshelves and one entire wall of plate glass looking out to sea.

Mitzi's room was as small as mine, on the other side of the living room. She slept on a futon and the only improvement on my quarters was that she had more coat racks and more pegs on which to hang her clothes.

The most basic thing about the place was the bathroom. In fact there wasn't one as such. There was an outside toilet reached by a quick trip through the kitchen door, but by way of compensation it had ultra modern fittings including bright yellow tiles on the floor. There was a basin and a mirror but nowhere to wash. Round the other side of the house, hidden from view behind another rhododendron bush, was an outside shower. You stood on a little deck under a nozzle sticking out from the wall. The water, Mitzi promised, was hot. I was looking forward to showering by moonlight.

Mitzi had left a sliding door open on to the deck and I took the carton of grapefruit juice I had found in the fridge outside. There was a rocking chair on the deck and I sat and rocked while the gulls swooped and landed on the deck railing and studied me for a moment before taking off again. I staggered to my feet and walked to the end of the deck and peered round the house. The car was still standing at the top of the bluff high above me. Mitzi couldn't have gone far.

Her laptop lay on the dining table.

I could use it to contact Warren, find out where Billy was. I couldn't believe that Mitzi had said I could invite him here. And I ought to call Dad and tell him I'd arrived safely. Mitzi had said I could use the phone to do so. She'd probably be more comfortable if I did it when she wasn't there.

And, I realized, I felt more comfortable when I got Dad's answering machine and was able to leave a quick message saying all was well. Somehow I didn't want to talk to Dad just yet about being here with Mitzi.

She returned in a rage.

'I do not understand why I go on doing this. What is wrong with me? They're even worse than they were last year.'

I didn't have a clue what she was talking about so I said nothing. It wasn't as if she'd even said 'Good Morning' to me or asked if I had slept well. Not that I could keep quiet forever. Far from it. As I had worked out while she had left me alone that morning, I was entirely dependent on her. I needed to ask her a million things, not least how her laptop worked and could I use it?

'My renters. I had to go up to the house and play landlady, check they had everything they needed. Not that I care, you understand, but they're paying me forty thousand dollars. Their demands are endless. When is the pool man coming? When is the landscaper coming? Why isn't there a dry cleaners in Amagansett? Do I look like I'm God? And the fuss they're making about this fund raiser!'

'What's it in aid of?'

'Who knows? Who cares? They have my blessing to invite two hundred people at five hundred dollars a pop to my house. They're going to ruin the lawn with a marquee and then complain the landscaper's not doing his job. I imagine they're even going to pretend it's their house, that they own the damn place. I come across people all the time who've been there and been told that. If I say it's my house, they say,

'We didn't see you', so I say, 'No, I live in the boathouse', and they look at me as if I'm mad. But these people I rent to, I know them, they've been coming to the house for five years and they still haven't climbed far enough up the Hamptons social ladder to be accepted, so what makes them think they will be now? Just because they're giving a benefit. My parents had that house for fifteen years and nobody invited them anywhere. My mother had this dream that I'd meet a cute blond, blue-eyed WASP in East Hampton and she'd be able to plan a white wedding in June for me on the beach. Didn't quite work out that way as you can see. If she'd wanted Doris Day she should have given birth to her in the first place.'

I laughed. Mitzi looked great to me, although she could have done with some softening. She had braided her hair into a long silver plait down her back and was dressed in a man's shirt with the sleeves rolled up and a pair of baggy cutoffs held up by a piece of string threaded round her waist. Her nails, toes and fingers were unpolished and she had rather unsightly bunions. I'd never encountered anyone like her before. She strove to look masculine but she could not hide the fact that she was 100 per cent woman.

'That woman up at the house is just like my mother. I can't believe such women still exist. There's a ditsy young daughter hanging around looking bored and I swear if the benefit is even half the success it's meant to be, there'll be a wedding planned next. I might as well sell them the house.'

'Why don't you?'

'Because then I'd have to go across their land to get here and they'd be renting me this house instead of the other way around. This house is part of the land. I'd have to include it in the sale and I could never bear to part with it. Now, come on, I'm going to take you fishing.'

She was out the door and running to the jetty like a teenager.

'Bring a sweatshirt in case it gets cold out on the bay.'

She must have put the rods in the boat early that morning along with a coolbox filled with sandwiches and cans of Coke because she was all ready to leave.

'Can you swim?' she asked casually as she gunned the motor and steered the boat out towards the middle of the bay. I thought of all the time I'd spent doing laps in the Murphys' pool. Could I swim? What a question! The water was so calm I imagined that if I stood up in the boat and stepped on to it I could walk clear across the bay to the thin strip of sand I could see in the distance.

'What's that island?' I asked dreamily. This place was sheer heaven.

Mitzi had dropped anchor and was standing up in the boat. She was casting her line, flicking her arm back and then far out into the water and reeling in over and over again. She had the grace of an expert and when she caught something and delivered it flapping at my feet I looked away, hating to see its popping eyes staring at me. She gripped my arm, hoisting me to my feet and opened a locker that I hadn't known I'd been sitting on. She threw in the fish and went back to her line.

'That's not really an island. That's a sandbar. Pretty treacherous. Known as Cartwright Shoals. That's where they think your mother drowned. Why do you think I brought you out here?'

Suddenly my skin felt like ice even though the sun was beating down upon it.

'What happened?' I whispered. Did I really want to know?

'I have no idea,' said Mitzi. 'I wasn't here. She called up out of the blue and asked me if she could use the boathouse and she wanted to go when I would be away at a convention. But I said, 'Sure, go ahead.' It was awful to get back and learn what had happened, to go into the house and see all her stuff lying around.'

Suddenly I couldn't take it any more. The shock was too much. I was this close to the place where my mother had disappeared beneath the surface. Had it been a calm or a rough sea? Had she struggled? Had she been eaten by fishes?

I knew I shouldn't be tormenting myself like this but I couldn't help it. I snapped.

And the next thing I knew I was in Mitzi's arms, my shoulders heaving. She was cradling me and rubbing my back and the boat was rocking from side to side.

It was only later that night, lying awake listening to the waves breaking on to the sand, that it dawned on me that this strange, gruff woman also had a very tender side to her.

For the first time I could see why my mother had been close to her.

17

'Who's Nora?' Mitzi asked, looking up suddenly one morning as we were having breakfast on the deck.

In the week I'd been there, we had quickly fallen into a routine, our mornings following a pattern I suspected Mitzi had mapped out years ago. We woke around seven, took turns to stand naked under the outside shower and let a blast of cold water wake us up and then we pattered about the kitchen fixing our own breakfasts which we took outside to eat on the deck. The sun was always up and showering the bright blue water on the bay with little glinting diamonds of light. I sat, mesmerized, watching them and sipping endless cups of tea while Mitzi, athletic and lithe, went for a run along the water's edge before returning to drink juice and coffee. Then we ate something together — eggs, bacon, pancakes and maple syrup, corn muffins, exotic American goodies I'd never even contemplated having for breakfast.

Around ten o'clock Mitzi brought her laptop out to the deck, plugged it in and checked her e-mail. As we were both on AOL I was allowed to check mine quickly before she got started — and delete it before she saw it. I say I was on AOL but of course it was Pete's laptop, appropriated by Warren, that I was sending e-mails to. But this morning Mitzi had logged on before me and had opened up my daily e-mail from Warren without thinking.

'Nora?' I said. 'Nora Murphy?'

'Whoever. You've got an e-mail here from someone called Warren — sorry, I'm reading it — and it says, 'Have you spoken to your father? Has he said anything? I can't get my head round it. I actually heard someone refer to them as Frank and Nora the other day. Apparently it's been going on for some time.' What is he talking about? What's been going on for some time?'

I didn't have a clue but I wasn't about to let her see that. 'Nora's Warren's mother. And Billy's. Can I see it?'

'Go ahead.' She pushed the laptop towards me and I tried not to grab it from her. I had been getting e-mails from Warren, the online junkie, twice if not three times a day. 'Billy's brother,' I explained when Mitzi started rolling her eyes. He'd done me a real favour by telling me how to contact Billy in New York.

Billy had been taken completely by surprise when I'd tracked him down at his hotel. I'd left messages for two days before he'd finally called me back, making the excuse that he was filming all day and at night he was exhausted and fell asleep immediately he got in.

But he was thrilled to hear from me.

I twittered away to him. 'I'm having such a great time. It's the most beautiful place, you just can't imagine how beautiful it is. You'd love it here. You have to come out.'

'Been to any clubs, any good bars?' He yawned. Poor lamb, he must be so tired.

'No way, I'm so zonked from all the sea air, I'm tucked up in bed by ten-thirty.'

'How sweet.' He was supposed to say he wished he could be there with me. But he didn't.

'So how's the filming going?'

'Great. They love me. Who did you say you were staying with? It's so wild you're in The Hamptons.'

I could tell he was impressed. 'My godmother. I told you. Mitzi Alexander. She was my mother's best friend and I'm sort of getting in touch with my mother through her. Getting in touch with myself really.' I could tell I was sounding a bit New Age but I wanted him to understand how important it was for me to be there.

'It's just you and her? You're not in a group or something? Isn't it kind of boring?'

'Of course not. We're bonding. Until you get here, of course. There's going to be a big benefit up at the big house her family owns and — '

'Gotta run, hon.' He sounded American already. 'Got an early start tomorrow morning. We'll talk. OK?'

He called back the next day and was so sweet.

'I'm sorry I couldn't talk longer yesterday. It's so great knowing you're here and so tantalizing having you so close but not being able to see you.' This was better.

'I could come into New York,' I offered immediately, aware of Mitzi listening in and glaring at me disapprovingly.

'Well, you could,' he sounded doubtful, 'but I'd hate to drag you away from such a beautiful place into the hot, sweaty city. I'd be busy most of the time and we wouldn't get to see much of each other, but hey, did you tell me you were staying with Mitzi Alexander?'

How clever of him to remember her name.

'My godmother.'

'And she's rented her house out to the Rothsteins?'

'Is that their name?' How did he know all this stuff?

'They have a daughter? Jessica Rothstein? And they're having a big Hamptons benefit next weekend. Going to be the place to be seen . . . '

'Well we wouldn't have to stay long but I feel I owe it to Mitzi to put in an appearance,' I whispered, glancing sideways at Mitzi. She didn't seem to be listening.

'No, it's cool. I have that weekend off. It's the perfect time for me to come and see you. I can't wait.'

Now, as I read Warren's e-mail, I wondered if Billy knew about my dad and his mother.

It had started, according to Warren, when they went out to dinner to discuss what to do about the pair of us running wild and doing nothing about going to college. Years ago. Of course, nothing had happened and, by the sounds of things, it still hadn't. But they'd been seen together having dinner several times. And Nora was round at our place helping Dad with the animals in my absence. Warren had promised to help out but he reported that Nora had offered to take over. It all made sense when I remembered the way she'd behaved towards Dad

236

at the airport. She probably realised he'd always been keen on her and now she was turning to him, on the rebound so to speak.

Dad and Nora Murphy.

I wasn't quite sure how I felt about this. I ought to have been over the moon that Dad had found someone, if indeed he had, but there was that funny little niggle that tweaked away at the back of my mind. He didn't need anyone else. He had me. I'd never been away before. Was this what he had been waiting for? I adored Nora. But why hadn't he said anything? Nora had talked to Warren, admitted they were 'sort of seeing each other', whatever that meant, that they'd got on so well when they had that first dinner that they'd begun meeting on a fairly regular basis. Talking, making each other laugh, sharing stuff about us kids, everything she ought to have been doing with Pat Murphy, except of course Pat Murphy was Mr Invisible. But Dad hadn't said a word to me. Should I call him and ask him about it? Did Nora see him as just a substitute for her absent husband? How did he see her? Why hadn't he ever said anything? Was he angry about me going to see Mitzi? Should I wait till I got back to talk to him about it? All these questions. And why did it all have to blow up when I was so far away and could do nothing about it?

But there was one person I knew for sure I was not going to discuss it with. Mitzi and I had been having some pretty good heart to hearts but a relationship between Dad and a woman other than my mother was an out-of-bounds subject as far as Mitzi was concerned. She'd see it as a betrayal of my mother even if my mother wasn't around to be betrayed. Besides, it was none of Mitzi's business.

'So what about your dad and Nora Murphy?' Needless to say she was curious.

'Oh, she's just helping him out at the kennels in my absence. Now I'm going fishing.'

This was what I did every morning after breakfast on the deck. I went and sat on the end of the jetty and dangled a rod over the water and pretended to fish. Mitzi had told me that's what my mother used to do and somehow sitting in the exact same spot, doing what she had done before me, brought her closer to me. I looked out over the bay to Cartwright Shoals and I imagined her body lying somewhere on the ocean bed.

'They never found her,' Mitzi told me bluntly. At first I found her direct approach when talking about my mother rather disconcerting. I had expected her to be more gentle, more tentative, to test the waters with me to see how much I could take without getting upset. But after a while I began to appreciate the way she was so matter-of-fact. After all, I had never known my mother. It was as if Mitzi were talking about a stranger who might interest me. Getting straight to the point could be viewed as being economical given the short amount of time we had together.

'That's maybe why your dad never remarried,' she speculated. 'He kept hoping they would find her body. We all did but I guess I was too much of a realist to go on believing she'd turn up. Someone saw her set off in the rowboat. She used to go out on her own even when I was there because she said there was nothing like being out on the water where no one could bother you, no one could get to you. She had that right. You find peace out there all on your own. Trouble is Virginia found a little too much peace, the kind you rest in. She'd got herself these waders, thought they would make her a serious fisherwoman. You had to see her. She looked so dumb in them, dainty little thing that she was. The guy on the beach saw her stand up in them on the prow and she overbalanced, fell straight into the bay. Seems she was treading water, her head bobbing away. But it's hard to discard waders. She was dragged under, towed away by the current. It's pretty treacherous out there. Looks calm and serene from here but that's an illusion.'

Mitzi told me all this the first morning, coming to sit beside me on the jetty.

'We used to have such fun together on this beach, your mother and I. We used to sit right here on this jetty and smoke dope till we were so stoned, we fell in the water. That woke us up.'

I wanted to do everything with Mitzi that my mother had done but she didn't have any dope.

'Tell you what, though. We can go ride the elevator.'

I didn't understand what she meant until she took me along the beach, clambering over breakwaters, our bare feet crunching on shells, giant horseshoe crabs scurrying away from us, to what looked like a covered walkway.

'See? It's an elevator all the way from the top of the bluff down to the beach. My mother had it built when she suffered a stroke and couldn't manage the stairs any more. It used to bring her down to the beach in her wheelchair. Your mother and I used to ride up and down in this elevator naked. We'd go down in our swimsuits, have a swim in the bay and then rip off our wet suits and ride up and down, singing at the tops of our voices, till we were dry. Wanna give it a try?'

It was the best fun. But when the elevator reached the top of the bluff, we could hear the sound of construction coming from the house. Chainsaws, nails being hammered, workmen shouting. Harsh, raucous sounds, shattering the calm. I was momentarily shaken. Mitzi ventured forth to get food now and then but most of the time we were ensconced in this cocoon at the bottom of the bluff. Every day I looked out over the bay, never up and back. Apart from Billy's sleepy calls from his New York hotel bedroom and Warren's e-mails, I had forgotten there was another world up and beyond the bluff.

'For the benefit,' Mitzi said. 'You should see the vans parked outside the house. They're importing new shrubs, they're building a new porch, the marquee's going up, it's never ending.'

'What do you wear to a benefit?' I asked her. 'I'm not sure I have anything with me that's suitable.' What I really wanted to know was what would Mitzi wear. She looked stunning now. Her olive skin had tanned quickly and her white streaked hair looked very striking against her nut brown face. But she never wore make-up and she dressed in faded jeans and mens' workshirts. This total lack of interest in appearance was part of what gave feminism a bad name for my generation. We wanted to be independent women, we could take care of ourselves, but no way did we want to be seen as hairy, unattractive women. We didn't see men as the enemy.

'Well, I guess we'll need to wear something clean,' Mitzi grinned. This was probably going to be her only concession.

Would she ever wear a dress, I wondered? I had challenged her about her appearance during one of our many arguments about feminism.

'It's all changed now, Mitzi. Don't you see? You can wear whatever you like. Nowadays we are women through and through. We embrace our femininity. That whole thing that if you look all pretty and wear make-up and stuff means you can't be equal to a man is so out of date. Don't you see that by dressing like a man, what you're doing is trying to be a man. If you can't beat 'em, join 'em — that's what you're doing. Do you see men dressing like women? I think we should be proud to be women. I think it's about being a woman and choosing to look like one and still holding your own in what used to be a man's world.'

But Mitzi wouldn't budge. 'By dressing provocatively, you just can't be taken seriously,' she maintained. 'We still need more women to have power. The more women we have in power, the more they are going to fight for a better deal for women everywhere.'

I couldn't argue with that but I still couldn't see what that had to do with making yourself look unattractive. Why would a woman gain power by making herself ugly? And shutting men out of her life?

'Mitzi, you don't have to choose between having a man and being a feminist.' But even as I said this I realized that in a way whenever I was around Billy my behavior was different. I became more girly. But I enjoyed it.

One thing I was certain about was that I refused to be identified as a victim. Somehow I had always thought of Mitzi's type of feminist fighting for victims, acting on behalf of women who couldn't stand up for themselves.

At night, lying in my little room, listening to the waves lapping beneath me, I tried to work out what was wrong with all the feminist arguments Mitzi was handing out to me every day. Finally, I decided to try and make her understand how things had changed. We were out fishing and as the boat chugged out to the middle of the bay, she had been having another go at me about my non-existent career.

'I don't want a career right now,' I protested. 'It's not as if I don't work. I have my own little business and it's what I choose to do. I'm not political or radical, Mitzi. I'm not out to change the world because I know I wouldn't be much good at it. I'm just an ordinary girl, I live in suburbia and I'm happy there. We exist. You probably haven't come across many of us but we're the women for whom you fought the war.'

She was standing up in the boat, casting away, but I could tell she was listening.

'From what I can make out,' I went on, 'back then you seemed to think it was a choice between a career or motherhood. But now everything's changed. Thanks to you and everything you did in the women's movement you've been telling me about, my generation now has a choice and men respect that. They know they have to because of what you did. We can choose whether we want to work, be a president, be a mother, wear a slip dress or dungarees, have kids or not have kids and it's that *freedom of choice* that's important, not what it is we actually choose. Don't you understand? You're so judgmental but you shouldn't judge me, Mitzi. It probably looks to you as if we take our freedom for granted. But you have to appreciate how things have moved on. It's not so different from the way you take for granted all those appliances that changed your mother's life back in the Fifties. We appreciate what you all did for us but we shouldn't be penalized for it by being made to act exactly as you did. What's the point of you having won that freedom for us in the first place if we can't enjoy the fruits? Just because you sacrificed yourselves, we shouldn't be made to feel guilty for being able to choose. I don't have to rush into a career. I can take my time to explore my choices and you should be happy for me, not resentful.'

For I could see that's what she was. Resentful, bitter and somehow unfulfilled. And I was astonished at the way I was standing up to her. If only she could understand how just being with her this short time had brought out a side of me I never knew I had.

'OK,' she muttered, 'I take your point, but all I ask is that you take yourself seriously. That's what drove me mad about your mother. She was so bright but she just didn't take her potential seriously.'

Probably because she was happy being ordinary, like me, I thought to myself. Surely if I was destined to be a high-flying crusader I would have felt the call by now? I was content to live the kind of life I did and marry the boy next door. Why not? Someone had to. Had Mitzi forced my mother to be someone she wasn't? Well, she wasn't going to get the chance to do that with me.

'Fine,' I countered, 'but just so long as you have some fun once in a while, Mitzi. You sneer at me being ditsy over Billy but romance is *fun*! I enjoy it. So do millions of women all over the world. You should try it some time.'

Might loosen you up a bit.

Mitzi and sex. I wondered about that too and then, one night, I had my answer. And I wasn't entirely sure I was happy with it.

She went out sometimes, late at night after I had gone to bed. I couldn't stay awake after ten-thirty. She told me she had trouble sleeping, that she had got into the habit of going to Salivars Bar in Montauk to have a nightcap. She enjoyed chatting to the locals.

'Maybe I'll get you up early one morning, I

mean really early, like around four a.m. and we'll go have breakfast with the fishermen before they set off. It's the place to go. It's a bar till four a.m. then it turns into a restaurant and serves breakfast so you get the partygoers going out overlapping with the fishermen coming in.'

'That'd be great,' I said, thinking I'd have something to tell Billy. But it never happened.

In the middle of the second week I was there, I woke up suddenly in the middle of the night and wondered if maybe Mitzi had roused me to go to Salivars after all. I called out but she didn't reply. I lay still for a moment or two wondering what had dragged me out of my deep sleep and then I heard them. Voices. Coming from the deck.

I slipped out of bed and moved to the window to look outside. And stepped back quickly. I didn't want to be caught watching.

Mitzi and a man were walking down the steps from the deck on to the jetty. *Mitzi and a man!* I couldn't resist it. I had to see what was going on. I squinted through the crack in the blind.

She was kissing him. She was wearing just a shirt, hanging open. I think they would have been oblivious to me even if I had opened the window and yelled at them. They kissed for what seemed like several minutes before pulling apart and I saw him get into a boat tied up to the jetty. I had a shock when I had a proper view of the man. He was pretty rough-looking. A fisherman maybe.

Then it dawned on me. He was leaving. They

had come *from* the house. He had been here with her.

The next couple of nights I couldn't sleep. I kept lying awake waiting to hear if he came back. I heard her returning each night from the bar, the car door slamming in the night air at the top of the bluff, her footsteps coming down the walkway, the front door opening and her bedroom door closing and then silence.

But on the third night I heard her move to the front of the house and open the slider that led out to the deck. I was at the window immediately. She was going down the steps and along the jetty holding a flashlight above her head. I watched her signaling to someone in the darkness of the bay.

There was virtually no moon and it was a while before I made out a boat approaching, a murky shape emerging out of the night. She guided him in with the torch and I ducked back as they came up to the house.

I heard them having sex, I heard her cry out, and I felt awkward and excluded even though she had no idea I was listening.

Maybe I should have been pleased for her, glad that she had someone even if she did choose to keep him a secret, smuggling him in in the middle of the night.

I didn't begrudge her sex. Far from it. What I had a problem with was that that night, and each night I heard her with someone, when I tiptoed to the window to watch him depart, I saw a different man.

18

My one consolation after discovering that Mitzi was a closet nymphomaniac — maybe I was exaggerating but how else could I explain what I had seen? — was that soon I too would have someone to curl up in bed with.

Billy was due out at the weekend. I couldn't wait.

Now I knew about Mitzi's secret life — even though I couldn't confront her with what I had observed — I felt no compunction about showing my mounting excitement. The more I fussed about getting just the right amount of sun to acquire a nice tan and what color I should paint my toenails, the more Mitzi growled at me in exasperation until one morning she opened a closet and threw a whole pile of old magazines on the deck.

'Bury your cute little nose in these for a couple of hours and give me some peace, OK?'

'OK,' I said and watched her bury her own nose in a newspaper. I had noted that she barely glanced at the *New York Times* which she had delivered and always seemed far more interested in a more downmarket paper called the *New York Daily Post* which seemed to appear in the house with strange regularity.

'Hey, I think this is your guy,' she said suddenly and not without a certain amount of triumph. 'Listen to this.'

She read out loud to me: '*Which infamous box office star has been seen out on the town with Will Murphy, an unknown Brit actor in town for his first screen role and young enough to be her son? Pity it's just a five-minute walk-on role, Will. Maybe you'll last longer with her off-screen?* I thought he was supposed to have quite a big part in this picture.'

And I thought he was working so hard he was exhausted every evening with no time to spend with me, but kept it to myself.

'I'd better call and find out what time he'll be arriving so we can go meet him off the train,' I said.

'Movie stars don't take the train,' said Mitzi mischievously. 'He'll come by private plane or at the very least he'll take the Hampton Jitney, that's an air conditioned bus that fancy folks take.'

He was taking neither. He was coming out by car with a load of other people. And he wasn't staying with us.

'There's a whole bunch of us coming out. These friends of mine, they've taken a group share in a house on the ocean. That's the place to be, babe. You're not on the ocean, are you? And you're north of the highway and that isn't cool at all. But don't worry, you can come visit, it'll be a gas.'

But I thought the whole point was that you were coming out to be with me, I whined inwardly. *What happened to that plan? And since when did you call me Babe?!*

'Oh, great,' I said, trying to sound cheerful, 'so

248

who are you coming out with?'

'Oh, a bunch of people. About ten of us actually. Guys I've been working with on the film, friends of theirs, couple of dot com millionaires in the making and some girls who want to come along.'

'Well, that sounds wonderful. I can't wait to meet your friends.' I was aware I sounded rather formal.

'And the girls know Jessica Rothstein so it's great. We all get to go to the same benefit.'

'Mitzi saw a piece about you in the *New York Post*.'

'Oh *that*! That was hilarious, wasn't it? This actress who's in the movie had me, like, walk her to a premiere one night and they turned it into a rumor that we were an item. Can you believe it?'

I laughed.

'But they said she was a star.'

'So that's great, good for my career to be seen with a star.'

'So I'll see you tomorrow night? What time will you arrive?'

'Pretty late. We'll drive out after dinner to avoid the Friday weekend traffic. I hear it can get pretty hairy going out to The Hamptons. I'll come get you Saturday morning, take you to the beach.'

'OK.' I tried not to sound too disappointed. 'I'll wait for your call Saturday morning.'

'Not long now,' he whispered down the line. 'Maybe we'll get in a little skinny dipping in the ocean. That'll be something to tell them about in Chaveny Road.'

I hung up, smiling to myself, and Mitzi glared at me. That was one problem I was going to have to deal with. Mitzi meeting Billy. If he was going to come and pick me up it was inevitable they would run into each other. Well, I would deal with that when the time came.

Meanwhile I had 48 hours to while away. I began leafing through the magazines. *Redbook. Good Housekeeping. Ladies Home Journal.* I wondered why Mitzi had copies of these kinds of magazines. They didn't exactly seem her style.

I found the article about an hour later, by which time I had become totally absorbed in learning how to have *No Fuss Patio Gettogethers, A Relationship That Really Works From Day One, A Stress-Free Camping Vacation With All The Kids.*

Orgasm: How To Tell Him What You Really Want by . . . I had to read it twice before it sank in. Dr Mitzi Alexander.

Mitzi, the great feminist, wrote sex tips for girls in women's magazines. *Oh please!* Mitzi was becoming more transparent every day. Then I looked at the date on the magazine and saw it was several years old. Maybe it was early on in her career and she had needed the money.

I suppose it shouldn't have come as a surprise to me when I walked out on the deck to have breakfast on Saturday morning and almost didn't recognize her.

Instead of her usual cutoff jeans and work shirt, she was wearing a pair of elegant khaki shorts that displayed her terrific legs — *shaven,* I couldn't help noticing — to perfection. And the

250

halter top allowed me to make another discovery. Mitzi had great tits, or rather she was exhibiting a pretty impressive cleavage. Her hair was even more unruly than usual but she'd tossed it back in such a way that it looked incredibly sexy, tumbling down over her shoulders.

'You look fabulous,' I told her, but instead of the 'thank you' most people said when paid a compliment, Mitzi immediately went on the defensive.

'It's the benefit tonight. It's at my family house. So I have to show them a thing or two. You know?'

Of course she did. But the benefit wasn't until the evening. So why the shorts and the sexy halter top this morning? Mitzi was full of surprises.

I kept hoping she'd suddenly remember some shopping she had to do, and not be there when Billy arrived. He'd called. He sounded really up and breezy and he was on his way over to pick me up. But Mitzi was glued to the deck. Furthermore, she was on the side of the deck that had a clear view of the walkway.

'Hi babe, you down there somewhere?' I had heard a car drive up and there was Billy's voice up above us.

'Hi yourself. We're here. Just keep on coming down those steps,' Mitzi called out before I could answer, sounding just as light and breezy as he did.

'What a seriously cool house.' Billy came pounding into view, taking the last few steps of the walkway in a single jump on to the deck.

'Thank you,' said Mitzi. 'Too early for a beer?'

'Never,' Billy laughed. 'I'm Will Murphy.'

'Mitzi Alexander. Pleased to meet you. Heard a lot about you.'

'Good? Bad? Indifferent?'

'Bad enough to make you sound really good.' I'd never heard Mitzi come out with lines like this before.

He looked utterly gorgeous. And so American. As I was beginning to understand, Billy was something of a chameleon, switching his clothes and manner to fit wherever he found himself. He stood there, chunkier than I'd remembered him, tanned (where'd he acquired that?), a reversed baseball cap on his head and sunglasses with blue mirror lenses covering his green eyes. He was wearing a very tight white T shirt with short cap sleeves that emphasized his broad chest and bulging muscles (as with the tan, I wondered where had they sprung from?) and long loose Bermuda shorts resting on his hips and falling almost to his knees. On his feet were what Mitzi had informed me were called docksiders. He looked deliciously fit.

I was unbelievably thrilled to see him again. But I was also a little frightened. I couldn't quite put my finger on it but I felt a little out of my depth with him. This wasn't the Chaveny Road Billy, not even the Covent Garden Billy, this was a different, altogether more grownup Billy.

And so far he didn't even seem to have noticed me.

'Hi,' I said, my voice shaking a little. Why was I so nervous? This was my guy. Come to see me.

'Oh, there you are. What are you doing hiding over there? Come and give me a kiss, for God's sake.'

He stood there while I got up and went over to him. I put my arms around his neck and raised my face to his.

He gave me a quick peck on the mouth. I stayed put expecting his arms to go around me for a hug, and when they didn't I peeked up at him and saw he was looking over my shoulder, watching Mitzi inside the house.

'It's OK,' I whispered, 'she seems to like you.'

'What's that?' He had released me and joined her inside. All I could do was follow. 'So what are you going to do with yourself today, Mitzi?' he asked her. His tone amazed me. It wasn't the respectful tone I would have expected someone of his age to use with my godmother. It was the same bantering, confident tone he used when he was chatting to those casting directors and women producers. I was proud of him. He could handle Mitzi, no problem. I don't know why I had even worried for a second.

'Expect I'll go fishing,' she said casually. 'Wanna come along?'

I held my breath.

'Maybe some other time. Got a crowd of people waiting for me to get back and entertain them on the beach. You'll be at the benefit tonight, right?'

Mitzi nodded. 'For my sins.'

'Oh, don't be like that. It'll be fun. But I can understand how it must feel to see your old house turned over to a crowd of upstarts. I'd hate it if they did that to our family house back home.'

What was he talking about? You could hardly compare No. 57 Chaveny Road with Mitzi's Long Island mansion.

'It's no longer really the same place,' said Mitzi. 'I hardly recognize it now. You know the Rothsteins?'

'I'm out here with some people who know Jessica.'

'Oh, it's like that,' said Mitzi. 'You're not really one of *them*?'

'Yes, it's like that,' and Billy laughed. They seemed to be speaking a different language, one I didn't understand.

'Well, see you tonight,' said Mitzi.

'You bet,' replied Billy. He actually could be an American, I thought, listening to him.

'What was that all about?' I asked him on the way up the walkway. '*You're not really one of them?*'

'Haven't a clue,' said Billy, 'but it seemed to hit her spot.'

'It's a great little house though, isn't it?' Somehow I wanted his stamp of approval.

'You think? Beats me why she doesn't live in the big house. Why does she want to hide away in a crap little shack no one even knows about?'

'Oh, you know,' I said casually. It wasn't as if I'd had a proper look at the big house. Maybe he was right. But I was just a little bit sad that he hadn't fallen in love with what I had thought was the most romantic place I'd seen in years. He'd sounded so convincing when he'd told Mitzi what a cool house it was, but that just showed how charming and sensitive he could be.

He took me to the ocean and right away I grasped that it was a whole different scene. A great expanse of golden sand and white crested breakers rolling massively into shore. A lifeguard sat on a high white chair. The car park was packed with buzzy little Jeeps and convertibles. Flash young men and blondes in bikinis. Surfboards, wet suits, jet skis roaring across the water sounding like a flock of chainsaws riding the waves.

Billy's friends were just like him — or maybe he had become just like them. Come to think of it, he spent an awful lot of time in the gym in London. What was to stop him doing the same thing in New York? Except he was supposed to have been working so hard — or that was what he had told me. These were fit guys he was with, guys with tans and biceps, and Billy looked every bit as good as they did, if not better. The girls all had that model look and despite my days spent preparing myself, I felt plain and mousey beside them, the only one wearing a one-piece swimsuit in amongst a bevy of bikinis. It was back to Billy's Beauties all over again. He introduced me hurriedly and I smiled but they didn't really pay me much attention, except for one girl who said: 'Oh, you're staying with Jessica's landlady? The crazy woman the Rothsteins rent that house from, the one they pretend is theirs?'

So Mitzi had been right about that.

I smiled, expecting Billy to step right in and say how wonderful Mitzi was. He had got on so well with her.

'Crazy,' he said. 'You should see her! Dressed in this old halter neck with her sagging tits almost down to her knees. And veins all over her legs.'

I was shocked. Had I heard right?

'You're staying with a legend,' one of the men informed me.

'One of those eccentric spinsters who've gone back to nature in a big way, wink wink,' said Billy. 'They've been telling me all these stories about her and the fishermen. Turns out she really gets around, drinks herself stupid at Liar's Bar or Salivars and then propositions the nearest available guy.'

'Another middle-aged mess,' said one of the girls. 'I'm never going to let that happen to me. Sounds like she's desperate.'

'I only have to look at you to tell you it could never possibly happen to you,' said Billy with his usual charm.

'Well, I really love being there,' I spoke up firmly. And I realized I was speaking the truth. The ocean was impressive and dramatic but I sensed before long I would be yearning for the calm and beauty of the bay side. Besides, I felt protective of Mitzi. They had her all wrong. They didn't know her like I did. 'I'm having a great time. I really am.'

'You British,' said one guy, putting his arm around me and laughing at Billy. 'Whatever turns you on.'

'OK,' said one of the girls, a tall strawberry blonde and the one most likely to be the leader of the pack, 'why don't you all take off and do your guy thing and leave us girls to have a catch-up gossipfest.'

I had a moment of panic. Did that include me? Was Billy going to leave me with strangers? And what on earth was a gossipfest?

He didn't even wave goodbye, just grabbed a surfboard and took off with the other men.

I laid out my beach towel rather nervously and stretched out. I closed my eyes.

It didn't take me long to realize that these girls had come out to The Hamptons with one thing on their minds: to look for a husband. And not just any husband. He had to be rich. He had to come with the right credentials. He had to own the right things. These girls didn't talk about men as if they were human beings. They made them sound more like credit cards.

'So Wayne got a Sea Ray. A 410 Express Cruiser. Takes nine passengers. Stateroom has a queen-sized bed with mirrors all around and a bath with a stand-up shower.'

'Johnny's buying this place on the ocean out by Watermill. Twenty acres. There's a domed dining rotunda. What's a rotunda for Christ's sake? He says he wants to start giving dinner parties every Saturday night. For real conversation, he says.'

I opened my mouth to explain what a rotunda was but before I could get a word out, another girl cut in.

'Like you can cook, Melissa?'

'Or talk!'

'Get out of here. I know how to call a caterer.'

'Jamie bought a new Ferrari.'

'Mickey bought me stock options in . . . in . . . actually, you know what? I don't know what in, but who cares?'

'Rudy bought me a pair of diamond studded handcuffs. They are so cute, they're like a child's. He wants me to wear them as a bracelet and eat pasta with my hands tied together when we go out to dinner. And he's having his cell phone number engraved on them.'

'You talking about Rudy White? I dated him last year and he bought me an anklet. Same deal. Watch out. He's a sicko. Made me want to barf, some of the things he suggested.'

'Well, they'll all be there tonight. Jessica says her mom has forced every available male in The Hamptons to buy a ticket to this thing, she's so desperate to find Jessica a husband.'

'Meanwhile little Jessica's still servicing her cute little Cuban doorman in the elevator?'

'You got it.'

'So what about Will Murphy?'

'Cute-looking.'

'Does he have a bean? What'd he do back in England? I talked to my friend at Miramax who says he's nowhere in this picture he's doing right now. It's just a walk-on part. My friend said he was shopping around for an agent here in the city, not having much luck.'

'So he's toast. Pity. I repeat, he's cute.'

'Mrs Rothstein's not going to like this. We've brought him out here for her little Jessica. Jessica saw him at some club the other night, fell so hard for him we had to yell *Timber*! She's sold her mother the line he's the new hot Brit actor with a multi-million dollar Hollywood contract. Perfect husband material.'

'Oh no he's not. I hear he's kinky. Violent. Gets off on beating girls up. Better not let Mrs Rothstein hear that.'

I couldn't believe this. They were talking about Billy as if I wasn't even there.

'He's not kinky at all.' I opened my eyes.

Five pairs of gleaming white veneered teeth blazed down on me.

'He isn't?'

I sat up. 'Of course not. He's the most gentle, the most tender lover I've ever had.' Not strictly true but I loved him so that made him gentle and tender to me.

'You've slept with Will Murphy?'

I looked at them. What did they mean, had I slept with him?

'You know him really well in London?'

'I live next door to his family,' I explained. I was about to add, 'I'm his girlfriend', but surely that was obvious.

'Oh, so you're the little girl next door. I think he did mention that.'

Something wasn't right. Hadn't Billy told them all about me?

'So how much of your body is your dress going to cover tonight?'

'All of it but it's transparent. Totally.'

I lay back down on my towel and listened to the endless, mindless twittering about clothes and hair and depilatory and beauty parlors. And for the first time since I had arrived in America I had the feeling: *I do not want to be here.*

I get like this sometimes. It's weird. It's an instinct. I just know I don't fit in and nothing I say or do is going to make it any better. It's just an awful realization that there are many people who have nothing in common with you and somehow you have become separated from the people who know and understand you. You're not in any kind of real danger but you feel isolated, trapped, and a tiny panic sensation is beginning to niggle at the back of your mind.

I had that now. I needed to get back to Billy. More important, I needed to get back to Mitzi and the calmness of the bay.

I was in luck. One of the girls had a hair appointment in East Hampton. *A hair appointment! At the beach!* In fact, they all had hair appointments but the rest of them were booked for later in the day.

'Are you leaving now? Going back into East Hampton?' I asked.

'You're having your hair done too? Wanna ride?'

'I need to get back to where I'm staying. I'm feeling a little . . . you know. I need to lie down for a while.'

The way they looked at me, I wondered if these Beach Barbies ever had their period. They shrugged. Whatever.

'Will you ask Billy to give me a call. About tonight?'

But if I had thought getting back to Mitzi's

would make me feel better, I was wrong.

As the day progressed, my sense of doom grew. A feeling of dread was developing and I couldn't make out why.

I suppose I got a real sense of the drama that would play itself out over the course of the evening when Mitzi began to drink.

When I arrived I could see her boat approaching the jetty as I was coming down the walkway. She'd been fishing out in the bay. I noticed she'd changed back to her jeans and work shirt.

She'd caught a couple of bluefish. Normally, I was sickened by the sight of her slicing deep behind their heads before she filleted them for our supper. But now, more than anything, I wanted to light the grill beside the deck, marinate them in fresh tomatoes, parsley, oil and garlic, as we had been doing every night, throw them on the grill and wash them down with a few glasses of Chardonnay.

But tonight would be different. Tonight we would have to 'frock up' as Dad called it when I put on a dress and applied make-up. I wondered about Dad and what was happening with Nora Murphy. Would it make a difference to the two of us? Dad was the only person I had ever talked to about my 'little panics' as I called them. He had understood immediately. He was uncomfortable around certain people too. At first, he said, he had thought it had something to do with insecurity, but later he had figured out it was more to do with boredom.

'We're not phoneys, you and I,' he had

explained, 'and we don't want to be anywhere near people who are.'

So maybe this was why Mitzi was hitting the bottle at four o'clock in the afternoon. She was anticipating spending an evening with a bunch of phoneys.

I kept waiting for Billy to call and make a plan. When would he be picking me up? The more I thought about the benefit, the more relieved I was I would have Billy as my escort.

At 6.30 there was still no word from him and Mitzi retired to the outside shower to wash her hair. I noticed she took the half-empty bottle of wine with her and I imagined her standing there, stark naked behind the rhododendron bushes, swigging away while the water pounded down on her. It wasn't such a bad idea. When she reemerged, I followed her example.

While I showered, Mitzi dressed. Correction: Mitzi dressed to *kill!* When I joined her on the deck, feeling rather pleased at the way I looked in my pale pink linen shift, my little pearl earrings and my new mules with their kitten heels — or at least as much as I had been able to see of my appearance in the tarnished-looking glass which had bits of mirror chipped away — I had the shock of my life.

Mitzi was wearing a skin-tight black dress, sleeveless, with a scooped neck and a skirt that reached to her ankles but had a slit up one side to her hip bone. My first thought and, I imagined, everyone else's who looked at her, was 'she can't be wearing any underwear'. Her deep tan had accentuated the mass of freckles across her ample chest. Her hair was tied in a long black and white bushy pony tail down her back and long turquoise drop earrings dangled from her ears. She looked stunning. Exotic. Gypsy-like.

'OK,' she said, 'now or never.' She stood up — and nearly fell over.

'But Billy hasn't called,' I protested. 'We can't leave yet.'

'Billy hasn't called, Billy hasn't called,' she parroted in a mocking voice. 'Sweetie, you exist as a person in your own right. You do not have to wait for Billy to lead.'

'You look great,' I told her.

She shrugged as if this was something she already knew. She didn't tell me what I desperately needed to hear: that I looked OK. I felt my confidence ebbing away like the tide beyond the jetty. The sun was sinking gracefully towards the water. It would be a beautiful sunset. How I wished we could stay here and watch it with the calm water lapping beneath us.

Getting Mitzi up the walkway was no joke. She was drunk and her dress was too tight. I had to hoist it up for her and push her butt from behind. She cursed me with every step. And she insisted on driving, so the fact that we made it to the big house at all was something of a miracle. As it was, we had to leave the car almost at the top of the walkway since the lane was jammed with cars and chauffeurs milling around, smoking and tossing their butts into the woods.

Jessica Rothstein was not a pretty sight but at least she was better than her mother.

There was a reception committee waiting to receive us just inside the door. Whether they were all Rothsteins I couldn't say, but Mrs Rothstein was standing there like a politician, introducing herself and pressing the flesh. She had dyed red hair. I suspect she had been aiming for strawberry blonde and missed. She was wearing something white and diaphanous and floaty which was clearly meant for someone twenty, if not thirty years her junior. Like Jessica. Except Jessica was so large that it would have made her look like the marquee I could see on the lawn in the distance.

If you averted your eyes from the guests, the grounds looked rather beautiful. There were lanterns everywhere and little round tables with lace tablecloths draped over them and an arrangement of blush roses in the middle. Eight spindly little white chairs had been placed at each of them. There was an open marquee with a podium inside it and in the middle a bank of microphones had been set up. Speeches were clearly in order.

Waiters in white jackets pranced about everywhere bearing trays of drinks aloft. A band was playing in another marquee with a small dancing area. I took a glass of champagne and wandered over to look at the buffet. An officious-looking woman saw me and informed me: 'I'm serving supper at eight o'clock. I have pâté de foie gras mousse followed by a mixed green and nasturtium salad followed by poached salmon with new potatoes and wild asparagus and claret jelly and biscotti for dessert.'

'What else?' said a voice behind me. Mitzi had lurched up to the buffet.

'Coffee,' said the woman.

'Five-hundred bucks a ticket and you're not giving them a choice?' Mitzi shouted. Several people turned to look in our direction.

'Cappuccino or espresso and I have decaff, of course.'

'Jesus!' said Mitzi.

I led her away. I realized she had got the dress part right. The women were all in clingy long dresses with plunging necklines, most of them revealing crêpey cleavage. Everyone was tripping about the lawn, the women air kissing, the men slapping each other on the back. I felt sorry for Mitzi. The results of the construction sounds we'd been hearing all week were very much in evidence. A brand new porch had been added to the back of the house. It didn't belong and clashed violently with the old clapboard style behind it.

'Bet you they didn't get a building permit for that. Hey, Loretta,' she called loudly to Mrs Rothstein, 'you got a permit for that thing?'

Mrs Rothstein ignored her, mainly because her attention had been distracted by the arrival of Billy and the Beach Barbie Beauties. I gasped at their appearance. They were wearing skimpy little petti-coats, and if they had been to the hairdresser it could only have been to have their hair lightened since their blonde wisps blew freely about their faces.

I tried to signal to Billy but he was taking an inordinately long time greeting Mrs Rothstein.

And Jessica.

Jessica's big and fat, I found myself thinking meanly, what is he doing fawning all over her?

He's being polite, I decided. He's so sweet. It's her party and he's making her feel good. It occurred to me that his father would have been proud of him. The whole scene played out before me was exactly what Pat Murphy had been aiming for with his swimming pool parties back at Chaveny Road. If Billy had fulfilled Pat's dream and become a politician, then Pat would have no doubt foisted endless fundraisers on the neighborhood.

'What's this benefit in aid of?' I heard a man behind me ask his date.

'I never really looked but it's gotta be something to do with the theatre. Loretta Rothstein's an angel. No, no, no, don't look like that, she's not *angelic*, it's what they call people who put up money for plays. I bet you there's a million actors here tonight all trying to get on the right side of her.'

'Poor little Jessica. No actor's ever going to look at her.'

But if they opened their eyes they would see they were wrong. Billy was all over Jessica, leading her over to a table for supper, sitting down beside her. My heart went out to him. He was being kind to her. He was making her feel wonderful, you could see it in the way her face lit up. Probably nobody had paid so much attention to her in ages.

I went over and sat down beside him, slipping my hand into his.

'Oh, there you are, hon,' he said, turning briefly to look at me and breathing a fleeting kiss on my cheek. 'That's Mrs Rothstein's seat, I think. You're probably over there at another table.' He gestured towards the far end of the lawn, 'Go take a look.'

I obeyed meekly. I understood. I was only the house guest of the hostess's landlady.

Speaking of Mitzi, where was she?

The men at my table had one topic of conversation: Nasdaq, Nasdaq, Nasdaq. I didn't have a clue what it meant and I was too scared to ask since all the girls — and they were definitely girls not women — were nodding in agreement each time a man opened his mouth. But when one of them got up to go to the bathroom, Mitzi suddenly slid into the vacant chair beside me.

'Gonna storm,' she growled.

It was true the Weather Channel had predicted a storm and the heat was indeed oppressive by now, but as the sky had still been a clear blue at the beginning of the evening, I imagined Loretta Rothstein had decided to risk it. What else could she do with the marquees up and running and 250 guests at $500 a ticket arriving on her doorstep?

I saw Loretta Rothstein glance nervously at the sky several times and then suddenly she was on her feet beside a man who was tapping at a microphone to check the sound.

'Ladies and gentlemen,' he smirked at everyone in a typical MC way, 'please fill your glasses and raise them to this wonderful lady on my right, Loretta Rothstein! We want to thank

Loretta,' he drew her to him, squeezing her arm, caressing her shoulder while she tried not to look embarrassed, 'we'd like to thank her for the loan of her beautiful house for this benefit.'

'IT'S NOT HER HOUSE!'

Mitzi was on her feet and lurching towards the podium. The MC ignored her.

'We'd like to thank Loretta not only for opening her house but also for letting us roam freely about her stunning property. We'd like to thank Loretta for — '

'It's not her house and it's not her fucking property. It's mine.'

'Loretta, maybe you'd like to say a few words.' As soon as the going got rough, the MC chickened out. He handed Loretta the microphone.

Loretta took the only way out.

'I'd like to introduce you to the person you really ought to be thanking,' she said graciously, signaling Mitzi to the podium. 'Dr Mitzi Alexander is kind enough to rent me her house every summer. The Alexanders have been part of the summer season on the eastern end of Long Island for as long as we can all remember.'

'That's a crock of shit and you know it. Nobody spoke to my parents for the first ten years they were out here.' Mitzi was literally reeling drunk. She grabbed the microphone and waved it from side to side, her rangy body swaying along with it. 'But you know what, my mother would have been happy to see this nightmare taking place. It's the kind of pretentious bullshit they craved. But they never got to participate in it. Now I have a question for you, Loretta.'

'What's that, Mitzi?' Loretta beamed at the crowd. She was trying to make them appear like a comedy double act, as though this dialogue was scripted, something she and Mitzi had prepared together.

'This porch addition, you never got a builder's permit, did you?'

'I never what?'

'You heard. I checked at the Town Hall and I know you didn't. Now everybody knows you didn't so you're going to have to tear it down, aren't you?' Mitzi was enjoying herself. Who cared if Loretta had spent $100,000 on her new porch? When Mitzi was finished it would be rubble and Loretta knew it. 'The trouble is, Loretta, you just don't know how to do things properly out here. You can't just step right in and do whatever you want. That's what my parents believed and how wrong were they? Wise up, Loretta. You're a big joke. You have to spend a great big fortune before anyone begins to take you even remotely seriously. Look at everyone laughing at you! They'll eat your food and drink your wine and trample all over my lawns but they won't love you. Nobody loves you . . . '

'Who is that crazy woman?' I heard a voice behind me. 'She's projecting, that's what she's doing, I'll bet you.'

A shrink phrase. Very fitting. Mitzi herself had told me what it meant only the other day when we were out fishing. If Mitzi was projecting then what she was saying about Loretta was what she really felt about herself. She was projecting her pain on to someone else.

It was a first for me. I had never seen an older woman out of control before. I had never seen someone I looked up to make a fool of themselves. I had never seen someone I thought was stronger than I was disintegrate before my eyes. It could have been a salutary experience but instead it was a total shock.

I knew I should go to her but I couldn't. I sat in my chair and looked down at my feet. I let Mitzi go on ranting and screaming. I heard her voice dissolve into drunken sobbing. I didn't move. I was embarrassed and I was ashamed of myself.

'The weird thing is that she's a good-looking broad,' said the man behind me. 'Bit over the hill but sexy as hell. Wonder who she is?'

I should have stood up and told him proudly that this was my godmother and that everything she said was true. I should have made my way to the podium and taken my place by her side. But I didn't. I was aware that someone was walking up there. Someone was taking her by the arm and leading her away. Whoever it was was comforting her, soothing her as if she were a horse that had bolted and been recaptured.

It was Billy.

As they went past I heard him saying to her over and over again, 'It's OK. Take it easy. It's OK. Take it easy. I'll take you home.'

I stood up to follow them but they had been swallowed up by the crowd and I lost sight of them.

Once again Billy had surprised me with his expert handling of a tricky woman. I remembered the McIntyres' cocker spaniel and smiled to myself. He had the gift, no doubt about it.

The truly sad part of the evening was that Mitzi did not get to see the total — and entirely natural — destruction of all Loretta's efforts. When the storm hit, she and Billy were long gone. It was a Nor'easter, they told me. Hardly ever saw one in summer but when you did, the only thing worse was a full-blown hurricane. The winds were terrifying, 40–50 mph gusts at least. The marquee came down, collapsing almost gracefully as if it knew its time was up. Then came the rain. As the women were drenched, their naked bodies were exposed as their flimsy dresses, soaked and ruined, clung to their skin. $200 coiffures were reduced to drowned rats' tails. Men sloshed through the mud and slipped, falling on their butts.

Frantic, they sought shelter, stampeding like a herd of cattle towards the porch. There were too many of them. They squeezed into the octagonal shape and crashed out again through its windows. There was the sound of glass breaking and makeshift plywood (for that's all it seemed to be) splintering as the porch surrendered to the weight of Loretta's hysterical guests.

Mitzi would have loved it but she never saw it.

I watched for a while from a secluded corner of the house and then when the rain and the wind had subsided a little I made my way cautiously back along the trail to the top of the walkway. The party was over in more ways than

271

one. Loretta would never rent the house again.

As I made my way along the path, brushing aside the overhanging branches weighted down by rainwater, I thought about poor, disillusioned Mitzi. I wondered if she really despised Loretta and her guests as much as she made out or if she secretly yearned to be one of them? I hoped it was the former, that she had the courage of her convictions. I would support her. I would make up for being such a coward earlier in the evening. I would tell her how much I admired her, how much I loved her little house and how I felt she belonged there. I would ask her to tell me more about my mother and I would ask her to let me come back and stay with her again and again.

And best of all was the fact that Billy had come to her rescue. Now she would be bound to accept him as part of my life.

By the time I arrived at her house I had totally put the world to rights and was humming happily to myself.

I gripped the handrail and descended the walkway, one step at a time. I went barefoot with my kitten heels in my hand.

The house was in darkness. Had she not yet made it home or was she already asleep?

The back door was locked. I did not have a key. I had never needed one as I had always been with Mitzi.

With luck, we had left the sliders leading to the front deck open. I padded round the house and climbed the steps to the deck. The door was ajar. Even better.

I had my back to the bay. I was about to enter the house when I heard a moan and knew immediately that it was a sound I would be able to recreate in my memory for the rest of my life.

I should have kept going. I should have gone into the house and put myself to bed. I should have pulled the pillows over my head and blocked out the sound.

But tonight was clearly not the night when I was going to do anything I ought to. I turned around slowly and gazed out to the jetty, my eyes drawn as if by a magnet to the couple writhing on the thick wooden planks. The normally calm waters of the bay had been whipped up by the storm and were slapping against the dock below them.

They were not naked. Clearly they had been in too much of a hurry to remove all of their clothing but Mitzi's dress was ripped and Billy had one arm free of his shirt.

I watched them but I did not see them.

All I saw was my mother's face somewhere out there beyond them, lying on the bed of the bay.

Part Four

LOVE THY NEIGHBOR

Surrey, England, and Montana, 2000

19

Dad and I were a sorry pair.

Everyone was expecting me to be climbing the walls with excitement on my return, bursting to talk about my trip. Diaries had been cleared in anticipation of long evenings spent listening to me boring them to tears. After all, not only was it the first time I had been to America, it was the first time I had been abroad on my own.

Instead I called no one and whenever I ventured out I looked the picture of abject misery. Over Billy, of course.

Dad wasn't much better. He put on a brave smile when he met me at the airport but I knew that something was up when he didn't immediately quiz me about how I'd got on in America. He seemed lost in his own world, as miserable as I was. If he noticed something was wrong with me, he didn't mention it, but then that was just like him. He never interfered with my life. So we skulked around the house for two days, avoiding each other as much as possible, before I discovered the reason for his gloomy face.

I deliberately avoided any contact with the Murphys because they would only remind me of Billy.

Until I bumped into Warren in the High Street.

'You're back!' he yelled and passed his

fingertips from his lips to mine in a welcoming kiss. They smelled of a mixture of pungent hair lotion and salt and vinegar crisps. I nearly threw up on the spot. 'Let's go and get a coffee and you can tell me all about it.' He was bouncing up and down on the balls of his feet, executing a little dance in his excitement. It was rather heartwarming to have someone so pleased to see me.

'Don't you have clients waiting to be transformed into visions of loveliness back at the salon?' I asked, trying to escape what I knew would be the Spanish Inquisition.

'Oh, who cares about them? They can wait, silly old moos. I want to hear all about it,' he insisted.

He dragged me into the Ye Old Coffee Shoppe, a place we normally avoided like the plague, but he obviously couldn't wait to hear my gossip.

'Why are you home so early?' was his first question. I had forgotten I wasn't due back yet. 'A whole week,' he confirmed. 'Were you worried about your dad?'

I nodded, glad of an excuse even though I had no idea how Warren knew what was wrong with Dad. But I jumped at my only chance to escape being quizzed about Long Island. Warren might say he wanted to hear all the gossip but he had always been much better at imparting it than sitting still and listening.

'How has he been?' I asked.

'Well, of course I haven't been with him. I've only seen Mum's side of it and needless to say she's fine.'

'She is?'

'Yes, of course she is. She's got what she wanted.'

'What's that?'

'She's got Dad back, stupid. Right where she wants him. Full of remorse and eating out of her hand, promising he's a reformed character. He just appeared one day, let himself into the house when she was out and was waiting for her when she came home. I don't think they realized I was upstairs. They screamed at each other and what was so surprising was the way Mum went for him. I've never heard her like that. Tell you the truth, I was a bit scared. They went at it hammer and tongs and then all of a sudden they went a bit quiet. I listened from the top of the stairs but I couldn't hear much, just their voices, still talking but muffled. When they came upstairs, I scooted back into my room and they didn't reappear for a couple of hours. *It was the middle of the afternoon!*'

Warren looked so disgusted, I had to laugh.

'But I'm worried about where that leaves your poor dad. They were really getting close and I think he was pretty smitten. How is he?'

'Looks so glum all the time,' I said, glad to have the attention taken off me. 'What can we do?'

'Not a lot. It's none of our business. And in any case I suppose I should be happy my parents have got back together. In a way I am. It's Pete who's having the real problem.'

'Pete's home?' I hadn't fogotten Pete. I just hadn't thought about him in ages. Suddenly the thought of seeing him again was very appealing. I needed to talk to someone solid like him. I would enjoy telling him all about my Long Island summer.

But our situation was unresolved and I was a little nervous about picking up the phone and saying something like, 'Hi, want to pick up where we left off?'

'He doesn't know what to do with himself. All he wants is for Mum to be happy but he can't bring himself to trust Dad to keep his word. Pete's such a disgustingly reasonable guy, he's trying his best to give Dad the benefit of the doubt for Mum's sake, but what he can't handle is the change in Mum. She gave him quite an earful about being overprotective of her and how he's got to give her a chance to sort things out with Dad, stop butting in. This is all new, Mum standing up for herself. Good for her, I say, but it leaves Pete without a role to play in her life. She's toughened up and faced the music but the problem is, Pete hasn't. It's just not his style to act tough. So he's wandering around pretending everything's fine and looking suicidal at the same time.'

'Rather like my father,' I said. 'He hasn't said a word about Nora. But then he never has to me. I'm not supposed to know they've even had anything going together.'

'Are we going to play cupid?' asked Warren mischievously.

'Oh, Warren, grow up,' I said impatiently.

He looked rather hurt and I felt bad. The truth was that somehow he had grown up in the short time I'd been away. He was sporting a little shadow of a goatee beard and moustache and it suited him, brought out the intensity of his eyes. He had these piercing blue eyes which looked great against his jet black hair. He had good clothes too, but then he was a hairdresser and hairdressers kept up with the times, didn't they? All those magazines lying around the salon, they couldn't help but dip into them and learn about the latest trends.

I didn't take Warren seriously, I thought sadly as he sat across the table from me, throwing out ideas about how we could get Nora and my father back together again. Warren saw things in black and white. He didn't see the gray that made up most of our lives. His father had cheated on his mother therefore his mother should send his father packing again. His father had done wrong and should be punished. That was the black and white version. Well, yes, fine as far as it went. But if you looked into the murkier side of the picture, you'd see that Nora was probably still in love with Pat and wanted him back under any circumstances. Warren had probably never been in love so he didn't understand that love makes you act irrationally. Pete was older and wiser and he understood that his mother's feelings for his father were complicated.

Just as my feelings for Billy were complicated.

'So did you get in touch with Billy after I told you how to find him? How's he doing over there? We've only had a post card. Even Dad hasn't had a phone call. Nothing. Big fat zero.'

I thanked God for Warren's kangaroo mind. He tired of topics easily and invariably moved on to another long before he'd exhausted the last.

'I believe he's doing pretty well,' I said. After all it was probably true about his sex life if not his career. 'He's very busy, that I do know. And no, I didn't see much of him.'

That was the truth I had faced up to on the way home, sitting in the plane for six hours. I had made Mitzi drive me to the airport the morning after the benefit. After what I had seen, there was no point hanging around.

Mitzi knew I'd seen her with Billy on the jetty and she and I could barely bring ourselves to exchange eye contact. We sat in stony silence side by side in the car, driving along the Long Island Expressway. She attempted to talk to me. To draw me out. To begin with I froze her out but then I relented in my eagerness to tell her about the collapse of the porch and the absolute wreck the evening had turned out to be. But she made a fatal mistake. She took this as an invitation to try to explain her behavior.

'About last night — '

'Everyone gets drunk once in a while,' I said quickly.

'I don't meant the drinking. I mean about me and Billy. I went after him deliberately, to see if he'd bite. And he did. Like a fish.' She was breathless, talking very fast, very nervously. Guilty as hell. 'I was middle-aged bait. I wanted to see if he would respond. If he'd go after anything. If he was that type of guy. He's a complete shit. You must know that. I wanted to

282

show you what he was like. I'm glad you saw us. Now you can't deny it.'

'Mitzi, that's a load of garbage.' I was outraged. How dare she pretend she had my best interests in mind when she seduced Billy? 'I hope you won't deny it when I tell you that your problem is that you have absolutely no self-respect. You throw yourself at any man. Standing up there last night accusing Loretta Rothstein of wanting to be loved, it was quite clear that it was you who was desperate to be loved. You sleep with a different fisherman every night. You behave like trash. And yet you're so hypocritical. You preach about how women should be their own person, independent of men, and yet your own life seems to revolve around finding solace in as many fucks as you can find. Surely if you want men to respect you as a woman, you have to (a) respect men a little more and (b), most important, show them you respect yourself. It's no secret, you know. Everyone knows about you and those fishermen.'

I was shrieking at her and by now I was also crying.

'And you think you're going to be so different?' she hurled back at me. 'Virginia was exactly the same. Always so high and mighty. She disapproved of the way I behaved with men and then look what happened to her. Turned out Virginia liked fishermen just as much as I did.'

'What do you mean?'

'Forget it. So I fucked Billy. So what? You're well rid of him. I did you a favor. One of these days you'll look back and thank me. You're a kid.

You're an innocent. Just like Virginia would have been if she hadn't met me.'

At the airport I thanked her much too quickly for having me to stay and I ran. I wanted no more association with her than courtesy demanded. I hated her. I hated her for not living up to my expectation of her, for disillusioning me about so many things I didn't know how I would ever begin to deal with them. In the beginning this holiday had meant so much to me. I had had so much to look forward to. Seeing Billy again. Discovering my mother through Mitzi. And to begin with it had all seemed like heaven. But even the calm of the early morning mist over the bay was shattered for me when I awoke that last day. Now it seemed like a sinister film covering the murky waters where my mother had drowned. I couldn't wait to get away. One by one Mitzi had crashed into my dreams and knocked them down like ninepins. Billy couldn't possibly still be my idol, not after she'd finished with him. And worst of all, at the last minute, she had tried to suggest that my mother was not the angel I had built her up to be. What was that all about?

That was why I had run — literally — away from Mitzi. She was poisonous. I felt that if I stayed in her presence another minute I was in danger of becoming infected by her.

Dad had been wary about talking about her. Now I knew why. I couldn't wait to tell him he was right, to thrash it all out with him and make myself feel better.

But Dad was in such a strange mood when I

284

got home, we hardly talked at all.

And now, having seen Warren, I was reminded of the other failure I had to confront: my relationship with Billy.

Relationship was the wrong word. I knew that now. I could face up to the truth. I had never had a relationship with Billy. It had all been in my mind. I kept on thinking of all the signs I had had that Billy didn't care a damn about me, signs that I had totally ignored because if I did so I could continue with the fantasy that we were a couple. If anybody ever asked me that question, 'If you were an animal, what kind of animal would you be?', I'd have to say ostrich. Billy could have told me where to reach him in New York instead of leaving me to track him down. He could have phoned the minute he got there. And once I'd made contact with him and told him where I was, he could have called me every night at Mitzi's. He could have arranged for me to be with him when he came out to the island. I was no one to him. I had been a stupid idiot. A complete innocent. Mitzi was right on that one. Maybe what Mitzi had been trying to make me understand was that if you didn't watch yourself, you could get snared into marriage and a life of subservience by these types of men. Then you were trapped for life. They had a hold over your feelings and you reacted to them even if you knew it was wrong. But I knew that if Billy had tried to contact me before Mitzi drove me to the airport, I would have let myself be talked into

285

seeing him. If he called me now, I'd probably still go to the phone, wouldn't I? In spite of the fact that I knew it would all end in tears. Even though I knew Billy didn't give a damn about me.

And I despised Mitzi for placing so little value on herself that she let herself be picked up by man after man and then thrown away again, for not being true to herself and what I thought had been her beliefs. Or did I despise her because she had made me realize that my own dreams might not necessarily come true? That this was something we all have to face up to at some point.

Except that I didn't really despise her at all. Not deep down. In her own gruff down-to-earth way she had been incredibly kind to me. She wanted the best for me, I could tell. It was just that what she thought was the best for me, and what I thought, might not necessarily be the same thing. But those hours shared fishing with her in the boat, and those long discussions on the deck when we had grilled what we had caught and eaten it washed down with bottle after bottle of delicious wine — looking back I realized Mitzi had downed the bottles and I had had a few glasses, and still I hadn't noticed her drinking problem — there was no getting away from it, those moments had been wonderful. Mitzi had forced me to talk to her, she had treated me like an adult in a way that other older people like Dad and Nora Murphy never had. I would miss talking to Mitzi, I realized. I would miss Mitzi. Yet I was furious with her. I was in a terrible muddle.

Pete Murphy was the last person I expected to pour my troubles out to.

It was an uncanny rerun of the time when Billy had turned up unexpectedly at the kennels after Julie had run off with his father.

Except this time when Dad said, 'Someone to see you', and my heart lurched for a fraction of a second thinking that Billy had come rushing across the Atlantic after me, a voice behind him said, 'Only if she wants to.'

And my heart paused in mid-leap because it'd been a while since I'd heard his gorgeous voice.

Despite the fact he was supposed to be an actor and had had voice training, Billy's voice had always slightly irritated me. It was always too smooth, too 'on', as if he were acting all the time.

'Hello, Pete,' I said and added quickly, 'Good to see you.'

And it was good to see him. Pete wasn't traditionally chocolate box handsome like Billy but he was definitely attractive. Billy was muscular and chunky but Pete was fine-boned. He had a thin, sensitive face. In fact everything about him was thin and sensitive. His fingers, for instance, were like a musician's, long and tapering. And his eyes were soulful and expressive, not twinkling and flirtatious like Billy's. The adjective that always came to mind when I thought of Pete, once he had said goodbye to his acne problem, was one that was usually applied to women rather than men: beautiful.

And then he did what I had been secretly hoping someone would do ever since I'd arrived home. He opened his arms and said, 'Come and let me give you a hug.'

Of course when his arms went around me and he gave me a great big bear hug, I crumbled. All the misery and confusion I'd been allowing to well up inside me, while maintaining a stoic 'I've had a wonderful holiday' front on the surface, came pouring out in a watery mess of tears all over Pete's chest.

'Go on, let it all out. Take your time. Don't worry. I'm here. Don't worry.' He was stroking my hair all the time and he never let go of his firm reassuring grip of my shoulders, holding me to him. I kept waiting for him to say, 'There, there', as if he were soothing a crying baby. Which he was, in a way.

'So,' he said when my sobbing finally subsided and he was able to hold me at arm's length and look me in the face, 'let me take you to lunch and you can tell me what all this is about.'

Firm, decisive, confident. And gentle. That was exactly what I needed.

'Just let me go and do some repair work on my face.'

'I'll go on down to The Lotus Flower and get us a quiet table. You can meet me there in ten minutes. Is Chinese OK?'

'Fine. Totally fine.' I didn't tell him I didn't give a fig where we ate since I was too wound up to swallow anything.

Wrong.

The minute he ordered Peking Duck my mouth started watering. I loved crispy duck and I never even bothered with the little pancakes and chopped up greenery they bring you. I just bung the duck on my plate, smother it in plum sauce or whatever it is and dive straight in. I was munching away, feeling better by the minute when Pete said, 'So is this all to do with Billy? Has he gone and made you miserable in his own inimitable way?' and I choked.

'Why should it have anything to do with Billy?' I looked at him across the table.

'Oh, come on. I know you were seeing Billy. I found a message from him amongst the e-mails on my laptop. 'Meet me on the Embankment. Our spot.' At first I thought it was to Warren. I knew Warren had been using my laptop. But *Our spot?* That was a bit intimate so I quizzed Warren who recalled you'd been with him that day at the pool. Then you go rushing off to America ostensibly on some wild goose chase to see a godmother whose invitation you've already refused once. What made you change your mind? I got it in one. You fell for Billy's magnetic charms and went chasing after him. And by the looks of things you've had the same treatment he's doled out to virtually every woman who's surrendered to him.'

For a split second it crossed my mind to say something like, 'Well, if you'd been more of a man that night, if you'd been more decisive, if you'd only gone to bed with me, none of this would have happened', but was that really the case? I had a sneaking feeling that whenever Billy chose to turn his attention on me I would have responded as I did. With luck, my brief association with him would turn out to be like a measles injection. I had been inoculated against something by being given a small dose of it and now I would be immune.

But I could not discuss Billy with Pete. I just couldn't.

Instead I told him all about Mitzi and when I'd finished I sat back and waited for him to sympathize with me about what a rough time I'd had.

I was in for a shock.

'Poor Mitzi. You have to see her side of it.'

'Oh, thanks a lot. That's really helpful, Pete. *You have to see her side of it*. What side is that, exactly?'

'People are usually poisonous because they're unhappy. You're being very judgmental about her. So she drinks a lot. So she screws fishermen. So she says one thing and does another. We're all guilty of that at one time or another. She sounds really bitter and that's sad. Quite clearly she had very high ideals at one point in her life and she's stuck to them, but somehow life hasn't quite worked out as she planned. If she has any major fault, it sounds as if she's a little inflexible. Feminism has changed, she should have changed with it. She's obviously one of those women who is perfectly capable of having a career and, in this case, ironically, it happens to be a shrink, and everyone thinks they're totally in control but if you poke around a bit in their private lives you find the most awful mess. And you can't handle wanting to look up to her and feeling sorry for her at the same time. You can't handle the fact that she needs you just as much as you need her.

Back in the Seventies, she probably relied on all the 'Sisters' in the women's movement to talk to but now they've moved on and married and have families and she's been left behind.'

'What?' I was astonished. It had not dawned on me that Mitzi needed me but Pete was probably absolutely right. I'd accused her of having no self-respect. The fact that I had bothered to stand up to her showed that I cared about her. She had probably got as much out of our conversations as I had. She was probably missing me just as much as I was missing her. Because she had found someone who had challenged her to take a good look at herself, and just as I would never have expected my own godmother to wake me up to the fact that a woman of strength and character can be flawed and vulnerable, she had undoubtedly never dreamed that a woman over twenty years her junior could teach her a thing or two. Was she, even now, sitting on her deck reflecting on everything I'd said to her? Who else cared enough about Mitzi to tell her the truth about herself, to tell her in so many words that she was as much of an ostrich as I was? I knew nothing about her life in the city, the time when she wasn't cocooned in her own little paradise on Long Island. She listened all day to other people's anguish. But who listened to her? As Pete was listening to me now.

But Pete was probing as much as listening and he had a knack of sneaking in a question when I was least expecting it. Shock tactics employed to catch me on the hop and it worked.

'So what did Mitzi think of Billy?'

It was a natural enough question. He knew I'd seen Billy. And I still hadn't mentioned him. I looked away and didn't say anything. Stupid thing to do. I could have just said, 'Fine. They didn't see much of each other.' I could even have pretended they never met. But I dug my own grave. I had something to hide and he was on to it.

'Oh, no, don't tell me. He didn't go after Mitzi too, did he? Because with Billy no one's sacrosanct, you do realize that, don't you?'

Well, I do now, now it's too late, I thought.

'So that's it.' He didn't even need to be told. 'I don't know if you realized it but you mentioned several times how attractive Mitzi was. She would have been a real challenge to Billy, an older woman, not one of his usual bimbos. He would most likely have been pretty threatened by her and his only way of dealing with that would be to seduce her. I'm right, aren't I?'

I nodded. I still couldn't look at him.

'Well, don't blame Mitzi,' he went on, 'Billy's a complete bastard. Look at him, he can have any woman he wants and he has to go and shit on his own doorstep.'

'Now who's sounding bitter?' I couldn't resist it.

'I'm not perfect, you know.' Pete looked very hurt. 'I never said I was. I'm as flawed as the next guy. I hate my father and I hate my brother. I'm doing OK but to all intents and purpose I'm still living at home with my parents because every time I finish a translating job abroad or wherever it is, all I ever do is come rushing home to see if Mum's OK. Although I tell you, now Dad's back I may well make more of an effort to move out once and for all. Billy may be a creep but in the eyes of the world he's out there being an actor, going places. And where am I? Nowhere.'

'Pete, you're not exactly over the hill.'

'Doesn't matter. There's a tremendous pressure on youth to succeed these days. I don't have Billy's ambition. I don't have Billy's way with women. I don't have my own home.'

'Nor does Billy,' I pointed out.

'Maybe not, but he's not still based at Chaveny Road, is he? I mean, look at that guy over there,' he gestured to an old Chinese waiter hobbling over to one of the tables, bearing a tray that looked much too heavy for him. 'He shouldn't still have to be doing that sort of thing at his age. He's obviously a guy who never got anywhere. I have my dreams like everyone else but I have my fears too and one of them is that if I don't push myself, I'll end up like that waiter. Yet I don't want to behave like Billy and sometimes that looks to be the only way to get on in life. Trample over other people and the road to success will miraculously open before you.'

'But, Pete, I like you precisely because you are like you are. And because you know who you are. Do you suppose Billy has ever had the intelligence to stop and think what a shit he is and how it might rebound on him later on in life? Of course he hasn't. Just as Mitzi hasn't really figured out where her life stopped moving forward as it should. You're ahead of the game, Pete, because you've confronted your fears and you'll do something about it.'

Pete was looking at me thoughtfully. 'Sounds like you've been doing a little figuring out about yourself too. Come to any grand conclusions? Anything about yourself that you're going to do something about?'

'Well, I'm never going to let myself become like Mitzi. I'm going to try and stick to my beliefs but if I feel they need a bit of an overhaul because the world has changed then that's what they'll get. You may want to get away. I don't. I know I want to stay in Chaveny Road, at least while Dad's still here. But I do know one thing.'

'What's that?'

'It'll be a long time before I trust a man again.'

'Then it looks as if Billy's done his damage. And Mitzi too in a way,' said Pete, 'sleeping around with a different man every night, surely that means she doesn't trust any member of the opposite sex.'

'OK, I meant men like Billy.'

'Meet a lot of men like that, do you? Spot 'em immediately you clap eyes on them? That's the real danger. Men like Billy, as you call them, never seem what they really are when you first meet them. That's their secret. Idiots like me on the other hand take care to tread gently until we know the girl really trusts us because the girls we go for are the ones who are genuine and sensitive and intelligent, the ones who like a guy for who he is not what he is. We tend to hang back a bit at the beginning just in case they might run off

294

with our sexy, charming older brother if he decides to make a move. Stupid, I know, but it does happen. Then we're hurt. And quite frankly we've had enough of it. Men can get hurt just as easily as women, you know. They may be so chockablock with silly masculine pride that they'll go to extremes not to show it but believe me they hurt.'

He was speaking in the third person and it sounded daft because he was obviously talking about himself. I wondered if Pete had any idea how attractive he was. It was something I'd thought about before. Billy wore his good looks with an easy grace but he was very much aware of them. Pete's face was so expressive, it was a joy to watch.

When he was pensive, he was little short of beautiful. Nora Murphy's sad, fine features reproduced in a masculine version, long black lashes shading penetrating eyes. And then when he smiled, his face lit up and so did everything else. It was extraordinary, his mouth turned up and looked suddenly mischievous, his eyebrows rose, his cheeks lifted and while his eyes creased with laughter his lashes seemed to part to show a twinkle. Pete was a warm man and a serious one. I had, I realized, enjoyed sitting talking to him in much the same way as I had enjoyed talking to Mitzi. His interest in me seemed genuine.

And what he was saying — in a roundabout way — was that I had hurt him.

'Are you around for a bit now? Are you working on anything at the moment?' I tried to change the subject.

'I'm here for a month and then I'm going to America.'

I was silent for a moment. I had a pang of something and it took me a minute to recognize what it was. It was disappointment that he was going away just as I had found him again. But what did I care? Hadn't I just announced I wasn't going to trust a man again? Pete had just finished explaining to me why he wasn't like the kind of man I shouldn't trust. But he hadn't exactly come right out and said I could trust him, had he? Better tread carefully. Especially if he would be disappearing soon.

'Whereabouts?' I asked casually.

'Montana.'

'They don't speak English there?'

'Sure they do but I'm going to meet a woman who is Austrian. She's married to an American, a psychiatrist who runs an extraordinary school out there in the mountains for kids with psychological problems. She has written a book on the effect divorce and shared custody has on the child. It's an amazing book in that it addresses a very common problem in a way that is both academic and accessible. It should be a bestseller and it's the first time I've worked for a New York publisher. My agent sent them the manuscript of my mountain climber's book and they hired me straight away.'

'But why Montana? Why is the school there of all places?'

'It's out in the wilds. As far away from the temptations of the city as possible. If the kids do succeed in running away they'll have to make it down a seven-mile trail and then hitch a ride to the nearest town forty miles away.'

'Well, then, there's your chance. Instead of running home when you've finished the job you can become a cowboy in the wilds of Montana. Crush your fears for ever. Obviously if we see you again in Chaveny Road, it's a cinch you'll wind up a little old Chinese waiter.' I said these words lightly but inside I was shrieking, 'You have to come back as quickly as possible.'

'We'll see,' was all he said. 'Come on, I'll walk you back to the kennels. I've got to go back and e-mail them about flights anyway. I haven't a clue where I fly to. Do you want to borrow my laptop?'

'What for?'

'Well, don't you want to write to Mitzi? Or have you already done so? Don't you want to keep in touch?'

He was right, of course. E-mail was the perfect way to keep in touch with her. And it was something I realized I very much wanted to do.

'Come up to the house,' he said. 'Mum would like to see you and we can send her a quickie right now.'

But I never got around to it.

At the far end of the drive a man was standing looking up at the house. He had his back to us and before we could comment on him, we were joined by a rather agitated Warren, emerging from behind the box hedge at the side of the drive.

'He's been lurking around here for about an hour. I came home for lunch and I saw him from the kitchen window. He was wandering round the garden, staring up at the house.'

'Well, didn't you go and ask him who he is?' said Pete in exasperation.

'No,' said Warren, 'he might be a murderer on the prowl. I was about to call for back-up then I saw you two coming up the drive so I snuck out of the house and ran down behind the hedge to tell you.'

'He doesn't look like a murderer to me,' I said. Trust Warren to overdramatize everything.

'Like you'd know one when you saw one,' said Warren.

Pete glanced at me and grinned. If I couldn't tell a scheming womanizer like Billy when I met one, what chance did I have with a murderer?

'Oh, for God's sake, I'm going to go and introduce myself,' said Pete. 'If he murders me I want to be buried alongside your wretched canary, Warren.'

The man turned round as Pete approached. He was on the thin side with obviously dyed blonde hair. He was very tanned and wearing a cream-colored suit. He had discarded his jacket and he wasn't wearing a shirt. Just a fancy brocade waistcoat covering his skinny bronzed torso. His bony shoulders protruded awkwardly from the sleeveless waistcoat. He wasn't wearing socks either, I noticed, looking down at his feet, just a pair of loafers. As we moved closer I could see he wasn't as young as he was trying to look, probably in his early forties. But he was attractive, although one glance told me he'd probably be more interested in Warren or Pete than in me.

'Can we help you?' enquired Pete pleasantly. 'I understand you've been here a while.'

'Do you live here?' asked the man.

'Yes,' said Pete.

'Have you lived here long?'

'No. Just a few years.'

'Oh.' The man looked crestfallen.

'Sorry to disappoint you,' said Pete.

'Oh, not at all.' The man smiled. 'I'm looking for someone who's lived in the area for at least twenty years. I used to come here rather a lot. I'm on a nostalgic visit you see. Or rather I was on my way somewhere and suddenly realized where I was so I made a bit of a detour to come and look at the house.'

'Who are you?' asked Warren.

'My name's Ferdy Everett. My Aunt Geraldine lived here and I used to come and stay with her. I never made it to her funeral. I was living in Switzerland at the time. But I've always intended to come back here. I adored Aunt Gerry. Good Lord,' he looked straight at me, 'Virginia? It can't be.'

'Virginia was my mother's name,' I told him. 'Did you know her?'

'Not really. And of course you couldn't be her. You'd have to be older than me. But of course I knew all about her because Aunt Gerry never stopped talking about her. Where is she living now? She's not still in that house at the end of the drive, is she? Do tell me she is. I'd love to see her again. She was so beautiful.'

Warren and Pete looked at each other.

'She's dead,' I said simply. I never had a

problem telling people my mother was dead. It was worse for them in a way because they always thought they'd put their foot in it.

'She died when I was about four,' I explained, 'in America.'

'Oh my God, you mean she never came back?'

'Never came back?' I echoed.

'From America. She went to find him and she never came back?'

'Went to find who?'

'Your father, of course. That's why she went, to look for him. Aunt Gerry told her not to go but she didn't take any notice.'

Then he saw my face.

'Whoops! You don't know what I'm talking about, do you? Aunt Gerry always said she was going to take it all to her grave with her but I never believed her for a second. Seems like I was wrong. I can see I'm going to have to tell you the whole story.'

20

Ferdy was a chatterbox.

I was desperate for him to tell me the 'whole story', as he had promised, but for some reason he clearly wasn't going to be rushed into it.

We went into the house and he began exclaiming about how much it had changed. It was rather spooky the way he knew his way around, even though we'd never seen him before.

'Oh my goodness, look what you've done here. Aunt Gerry used to have this as her little study in the days when she still wrote her short stories but you've gone and made it into a breakfast room,' he commented. And, 'Was there always a wall here? Didn't it used to be one big room?' And of course he was right. I sensed then that we all relaxed a little. Up to that moment Ferdy had been a stranger, someone we were prepared to trust but still a stranger. The fact that he so obviously knew his way around the house somehow made him legitimate. 'I won't say a word about the swimming pool,' he said and then proceeded to tell us how his aunt would have turned in her grave.

'Where is her grave?' asked Pete, direct as usual. 'Seeing as how you've mentioned it twice. You mentioned the secret she took to her grave and now she's turning in it.'

Ferdy had the grace to go a little red. 'I'm not

entirely sure, to tell you the truth. As I said, I never made it to her funeral. In fact, I feel pretty awful about the fact that I didn't come and see her as often as I ought to have done in the last years of her life. I hope she wasn't too lonely.'

I had this sudden picture in my mind of what I'd seen through the window as a child, the armchair pulled close to the fire in the midst of furniture covered in dust sheets. It dawned on me that Ferdy probably had no idea that we had never even met Geraldine Everett, that we'd let her sit up here on her own and never bothered to get to know her. I couldn't very well say, 'I thought your aunt was a witch so I never went near her.'

'You said you had a story to tell me,' I prompted.

'Oh, I do,' said Ferdy, 'but as you'll see it's not something I can just trot out in one line. I'm trying to think how best to explain it to you. The last time I saw you, you were a toddler, and your mother was about your age which was why I mistook you for her. She lived down at the end of the drive and she used to come up and have these long talks with my aunt. Aunt Gerry adored her, the child she never had and all that. I know I became quite jealous at one point. Aunt Gerry was my mother's sister and when my mother died I sort of attached myself to my aunt. I didn't get on with my father at all so I came out here at weekends when I was first living in London. Then when I got my shop — I'm a decorator, you know? — I was so busy I could only come occasionally. When I started going abroad to look after my clients who had houses on the Continent, I more or less stopped coming altogether. And then she died.'

He looked so forlorn that for a moment I thought he might actually shed a tear. I was becoming rather impatient with all this chat about himself. I wasn't sure how long I could endure listening to his life history. I wanted to know about my mother.

Then he smiled again and I acknowledged what a charmer he was. He was one of those people whose face lit up when they smiled. I think what happens is their mouths actually do turn up at the corners and it gives the impression of their whole face lighting up. At least it did in Ferdy Everett's case.

'Why don't I make some sandwiches?' asked Pete. 'Tomato, ham, cheese with a bit of lettuce in amongst it? How's that sound?'

Warren announced he had to be back at the salon, his lunch hour was nearly over. I could see he was furious that he had to leave.

'Nice meeting you,' he said to Ferdy, 'are you around here for long?'

'I was just passing through, as they say,' said Ferdy. 'I have to be in Bath tonight. But I imagine I'll come back.'

While Pete made sandwiches, Ferdy stood at the window and watched Warren as he went down the drive and disappeared out of sight.

'Very cute,' he said, 'just my type. Too bad he's not gay.'

I glanced at Pete. We'd never come right out and talked about it but I think we'd always

303

assumed Warren *was* gay. I'd been uncomfortable with the assumption, the way we'd based it on his being a hairdresser, but he'd never given us any evidence that he wasn't. He kept his private life extremely private.

'He isn't?' I said. It was risky talking to a near stranger like this and I felt disloyal to Warren but it was too good an opportunity to pass up. 'How do you know?'

'Because I am gay and I looked at him several times and he never reacted. Takes one to know one, you know?'

'Maybe he just didn't . . . ' I stopped, aware that I was about insult him.

'Didn't fancy me? No, he didn't, because he likes women. In fact . . . '

'Yes?'

'Oh, never mind. Here we are talking about these intimate matters and we've only just met, but I've always been like that. I chat away to strangers and tell them my innermost secrets within twenty minutes of meeting them, less sometimes. Aunt Gerry was always ticking me off about it. 'Ferdinand,' — she always called me by my full name — 'Ferdinand, you must learn a little discretion.' She hated indiscreet people. She was always going on about so-and-so being so nice and self-contained. That's what she liked about your mother. 'Virginia's so wonderfully self-contained.' I can just hear her saying it. But she still managed to get Virginia's secrets out of her, didn't she? Oh yes! Mine too. That was the thing about Aunt Gerry, she could get you talking. She was a great listener. She was crafty.

You couldn't accuse her of being a gossip because she didn't dish it out but she liked hearing it all. That was when I heard the truth about your mother, at the end of a long revelatory evening, the day I came out of the closet. It was only natural that Aunt Gerry should be the first person I should tell. We'd had quite a lot to drink and she started talking about your mother. Only this time she told me things I didn't know.'

I was going crazy. How much longer was he going to meander on about himself? Pete winked at me as if to say, 'He'll take his time but he'll get there in the end, be patient.' It seemed so natural to have Pete at my side. Not once did it occur to me to send him away, that he shouldn't hear what I sensed would be life-changing information for me.

'This may come as a shock,' he warned, 'but I think you have a right to know. And I think Aunt Gerry wanted you to know but somehow she just couldn't bring herself to tell you. She didn't know you, did she? She kept her distance after your mother died. I think that was deliberate. I think she knew if she got to know you, she'd have to tell you. As for me, I can't go on any longer carrying it around with me. I want to get it off my chest. I couldn't tell you when I last saw you as a toddler, you were too young, but I knew if I ever met you as an adult, I'd have to unburden myself if you hadn't already found out.'

Get on with it, I pleaded silently. I was a little irritated by the way he seemed to feel he had a burden to unload. His actions were not entirely altruistic.

'Your mother had a friend called Mitzi,' he began.

My head shot up.

'You know her?' Ferdy asked, surprised. I nodded. 'Well then, you'll know who I'm talking about. Your godmother. Oh, I never met her but I heard about her. As far as I could see your mother was caught between Aunt Gerry and this Mitzi. They both adored your mother and they both had totally opposing views as to what she should do with her life. I doubt Mitzi would ever have come to this house. She wouldn't have wanted to run into Aunt Gerry.'

That explains it, I thought. That's why she never came to see us.

'What was it Mitzi and your aunt disagreed about?' I asked Ferdy.

'Feminism. Aunt Gerry was one of the original feminists. She and your mother used to discuss it for hours. Your mother had this young baby — you — and she was happily married but she felt guilty about it and Aunt Gerry used to tell her she shouldn't.'

'She *shouldn't*? That's not what Mitzi felt.'

'Precisely. Aunt Gerry was always trying to make your mother understand that she herself had been programmed to be radical but she wasn't at all sure it was necessary for Virginia's generation. Aunt Gerry didn't believe in all the bra burning and man hating that was going on. She felt they were making a mockery out of feminism, that they'd lost the plot. She believed in women having a choice and if Virginia wanted to get married and raise a family then she shouldn't be ashamed to do so. My aunt thought she had a fine mind and it was sad that she dropped out of Cambridge early to have you, but then she knew what had really happened, that it wasn't planned.'

So my mother had cut short her university education to have me. That must have been a blow for her.

'I didn't know,' I said. 'Maybe that's why Mitzi blames my father so much. She really seems to hate him.'

'She doesn't even know who he is,' said Ferdy.

'Of course she does. You should hear her going on about Frank Page.'

'Oh, Frank Page.'

It was the way he said it. Suddenly I dreaded what was coming.

'My father,' I said.

'The man your mother married,' he said. 'Here's what happened. Your mother, as you probably know, was a nice Catholic girl from Dublin who amazed her family by getting into Cambridge. She met Frank Page there and they started seeing each other pretty early on. Then Virginia goes to Long Island to stay with some Irish relatives during one of the long summer vacs, gets a job waitressing or something. When she comes back she's a changed woman. She's met Mitzi Alexander, she's spouting feminism all over the place. But what no one knows is that she's also pregnant. With you.'

'But Mitzi said she was in America for quite a

while, over a month. I never knew Dad went out there too.'

'He didn't. It was a fisherman. Your mother told Aunt Gerry all about it years later. She slept with a fisherman. She came home to Frank Page's arms but she was carrying another man's child.'

'Mitzi never told me,' I wailed.

'Mitzi never knew. Nobody ever knew except Aunt Gerry. Virginia never told Mitzi, she never told Frank Page, and since nobody knew, nobody could tell you. You grew up thinking Frank Page was your real father. Frank Page thought you were his real daughter. Virginia told him you were the result of their reunion celebration when she came back from America. He proposed immediately. They had always intended to get married. They just brought it forward by a year or two because she was pregnant. Mitzi came rushing over from America and tried to put a stop to all of it, tried to make your mother have an abortion, tried to make her get rid of you. But your mother went ahead with both the wedding and the baby and when Frank Page finally graduated, they moved here and he set up his practice. That's when your mother met Aunt Gerry. Aunt Gerry told me she could sense at once that your mother needed a friend, needed support, needed to be told she was doing the right thing. She encouraged Virginia to come and talk to her, to bring the baby — you — up to the house every day. She kept your mother's agile mind alive by engaging her in discussion. She made your mother understand that what was done was done and she had a fine baby daughter as a result, something she, Aunt Gerry, had never achieved. There was plenty of time for your mother to go to work at a later stage providing she didn't start vegetating in Chaveny Road, and Aunt Gerry saw to it that she didn't. She hated the way Mitzi kept coming over and trying to make your mother dump the baby and go off on marches and protests, trying to make Virginia feel guilty for being a wife and mother.'

Pete had moved to put his arm around me. He was holding me, trying to stem the awful shuddering that was wracking my body. Ferdy was right. It was a terrible shock. My father was not my father. But worse than that was the knowledge that my mother had had to carry around this terrible secret. Should she have told her husband? Had she done the right thing?

'It took its toll, needless to say. One night she came out with the truth, broke down and told Aunt Gerry everything.'

'But my real father? A fisherman? Out there on Long Island? I could have looked for him while I was out there.'

'You wouldn't have found him.'

'Why not?'

'I'm going to be cruel to be kind. What are the chances of finding the man your mother had a quick fling with twenty odd years ago? Virginia never even told Aunt Gerry his name.'

'But if she knew she was pregnant why didn't she tell Mitzi? Why didn't she look for him there and then?'

'Isn't it obvious? If she'd told Mitzi, Mitzi

would have marched her off to an abortionist the same day. Your mother wanted this baby. She wanted you. She didn't tell Frank Page in case he made her do the same thing because it wasn't his. Don't forget she came from a good Catholic family. She probably didn't know if the fisherman would marry her. She knew she had a chance with Frank Page. She wanted to be married. She didn't want to cause a family scandal back in Dublin. Although from what I've heard about Frank Page, I doubt he'd have been so cruel as to make her have an abortion if she didn't want one.'

I couldn't handle the way he never said 'your father', always Frank Page. Dad was Dad. I'd never known any other. In order to hear about my mother, I'd had to learn about my father too.

But Ferdy wasn't finished.

'She went back to Long Island one last time to look for your father. That's how long I was out of touch with Aunt Gerry in that I didn't even know Virginia never came back. She was always talking about finding him, according to Aunt Gerry. She felt he had a right to know he had a daughter. Aunt Gerry tried to talk her out of it. She didn't think any good would come of it even if Virginia did find him. And she didn't like the idea of your mother falling back into Mitzi's clutches.'

'Instead it was far, far worse. Did she ever find my — the fisherman?'

'We'll never know. She took all her secrets with her to the bottom of the sea leaving Aunt Gerry to fret away about whether to tell you or not.

Instead she told me and as I said, I always thought she did that knowing I would pass it on to you one day.'

When the time came for Ferdy to leave we expressed fervent hopes that we would stay in touch, that he would visit frequently and how wonderful it was that he had found us. But I think we both knew that we would probably never see each other again. You could tell Ferdy was like that. Full of promises — and he probably meant what he said at the time — but promises that he never followed through on. You could just see that he flitted in and out of people's lives, blinding them with his charm and moving on. There was nothing malicious or exploitative about him. I suppose if anything he was just feckless. And he was embarrassed about the shock he had given me, the secret he had withheld for so long. As soon as he had delivered his revelations, he wanted to be gone. He couldn't handle my obvious pain.

I let him go. I had Pete. And Pete could not be more different.

Pete was like a rock. I think it was the fact that he shared my secret that drew me closer to him than ever before in the days immediately after Ferdy's brief, disruptive pit stop.

Just as I knew that Ferdy, whatever he might have promised, would never return, I also knew that I was never going to tell anyone what I had learned from him.

I wouldn't say a word to Warren, to Mitzi, and least of all to Dad. Ferdy had come and gone so fast that a week later I had moments when I actually wondered if he had come at all.

But Pete had been there. Pete had witnessed everything and he knew what I was going through. Needless to say I fell apart after Ferdy left and Pete was there for me.

It happened when I saw Dad for the first time.

He had been away for a couple of nights at some kind of vet convention. Pete and I were sitting on the sofa in our sitting room when he walked through the front door.

I burst into tears. All I could think of was that he wasn't my real father. But then again he was and I loved him and I didn't want anyone else as a dad. Just him. In fact, there was no one else. Dad *was* my real father and always had been. And yet he wasn't.

I had done some serious thinking about the whole situation and come to the decision that I would not tell him what I had learned from Ferdy. Dad knowing wasn't the same as me knowing. Dad was the only father I'd known and I accepted him as such. But if I told him, he would have to come to terms with the fact that my mother had lied to him. The sins of omission. He'd had enough to cope with that she'd died. I didn't want him to have to deal with anything else.

As to the question of who my real father had been, I couldn't face thinking about that now. I had no doubt it was a bone I'd worry to death at some stage but now was not the time.

Because I knew who I would have to talk to about it: Mitzi.

I was more confused than I had ever been in

my entire life and Pete was the only one who knew why. He supported me in my decision to keep everything to myself. Or rather to ourselves.

'I understand,' he said, 'you have me to share the burden with and what good would it do to upset Frank. Because he would be upset. No doubt about it. If he was uncomfortable about you going off and spending time with Mitzi, just think what he'd be like if he learned about what your mother got up to over there. You probably wish you'd never found out yourself.'

'No,' I said firmly, 'I'm glad I know.' And I meant it.

As well as leaning on Pete, I took refuge in my animals. They seemed to sense something was wrong. For a start they were unusually well behaved. I walked the dogs in the woods every day but at eleven o'clock every morning I also let all the animals out into what I called the playground. This was the yard at the back of the house. I watched the new arrivals closely and if a particular cat or dog showed signs of vicious behavior towards my other 'guests', I popped them back in their cage until they calmed down. Then I let them out again. Each day I allowed them to mingle a little more until they were fully integrated. Naturally, some animals preferred to sit on the sidelines watching, maybe growling a little, feeble protests that the other animals ignored, but very soon after I started my kennels, I proved that the idea that cats and dogs cannot coexist peaceably together is a complete fallacy.

Indeed, after the pets had returned home, I often received phone calls from the owners asking me what wonders had I performed?

Now, in the playground, the animals gravitated towards me as if they wanted to help. Dogs placed their heads on my lap and looked mournfully up at me. They licked my hands. Of course they were probably begging for an early helping of Pedigree Chum but it was comforting. The cats rubbed themselves around my legs and purred, another way of saying, 'Where's my dinner?' but it made me feel wanted.

Dad noticed I was not myself, of course, but his only comment was, 'Something's upset you', and when I didn't reveal what it was, he didn't take it any further. That was his way.

Warren was surprisingly sweet. I'd expected him to pry but he didn't. I suspected Pete had had a word, told him not to quiz me about what Ferdy had said and to go easy because Warren was very gentle. I felt bad about the fact that we had automatically assumed he was gay. Not that there would have been anything wrong if he was, but somehow, having thought he was gay, I had not bothered to concern myself with his relationships in the way a true friend would. I had assumed the reason he kept them private was because he was gay and didn't want to discuss it. But by thinking I was respecting his privacy, had I unwittingly shown a lack of interest? Did he think I was cold, unfeeling? In the old days, pre-Billy, I had been close to Warren. We'd chatted about everything, but since my return from America I had neglected him. The old intimacy was no longer there. Now I talked to Pete. Did Warren resent that, I wondered? If he did, he didn't show it.

The big surprise was that there was one person Warren did appear to have grown close to and that was Dad. While I'd been in America, Warren had been helping Dad out, exercising my animals, taking over the evening feed when Dad was held up at his surgery. He'd got into the habit of popping round at the end of the day on his way home from work to see if Dad needed anything and he still dropped in most evenings. In the old days, had Warren turned up at the front door he and I would have gone straight out for a drink. Now he came in and sat down and Dad produced a couple of cans of lager. I sat in on a couple of sessions but I have to confess I soon left because it was so unbelievably boring. The hairdresser and the vet. You'd think they would have nothing to talk about but they did. The thing about Warren was that unlike Billy or Pete, he had never strayed very far from Chaveny Road and nor, for that matter, had Dad. They were local boys, members of the community who had a lot to talk about. And talk they did. Endless hours of gossip about their respective clients who, more often than not, were members of the same family. I was grateful to Warren for giving Dad something to look forward to. Of course, I couldn't help wondering whether Dad entertained Warren in the hope of receiving news of Nora, but then that was a decidedly cynical side of me emerging, a side I wasn't at all happy about. I had wised up in America, learned a lot about myself. I knew that I no longer trusted people as implicitly as I had in the past and it saddened me. I found I looked more for people's ulterior motives rather than accepting that they were just being nice. But for whatever reason, Dad liked Warren, about that there was no doubt in my mind.

Pete announced he was going flat hunting and why didn't I come with him? Thinking it would take my mind off everything, I agreed.

It was soul destroying. Until the money from his Montana book came in, Pete was broke. He had a permanent cash-flow problem as far as I could make out. He could only afford a studio flat, i.e. one room, kitchen and bathroom. We traipsed round the area looking at pokey little rooms above shops that smelled of leftover curry and dodgy drains. I was appalled.

'You can't live somewhere like this,' I told him in disgust.

'Why not?' he said cheerfully.

'Do you seriously think you could adjust to being cooped up in a little hole after living in a spacious house with a large garden and a pool? Why don't you look further into central London?'

'Are you mad? That would be three times the price. Here I can get away from Dad but I can be close enough to pop back home for a swim if I want. And see Mum.'

I wondered how Nora would feel about that.

And then I almost shook my head in amazement. How times had changed! A few months ago I would have been thinking how thrilled Nora would be to have him close to her. She had all but admitted he was her favorite, the one who shared her love of singing, the sensitive one she felt protective of.

But a new Nora had emerged while I had been away in America. I had gone to see her, of course, and told her an edited version of my stay with Mitzi and my experience with Billy. I had been rather apprehensive as I walked up the drive. How much should I tell her about Billy? Would she detect my concern about Mitzi?

As it turned out, I needn't have worried. Nora, who had been such a great listener in the past, now appeared to want to dominate the conversation. Although she didn't do much talking for the first half hour.

When I arrived at the house she was singing. I could hear her as I let myself in through the kitchen door. She was in the living room standing beside a brand new grand piano.

One of the ugliest men I had ever seen was seated at the piano, head bent over the keys. I listened for a while. It wasn't very entertaining. He was having her sing scales, up and down, over and over again. And breathing exercises. They didn't see me and I was just about to slip away and come back another time when the man said 'OK, enough of that. Let's have some fun. You've earned it, Nora.'

And with that they took off, launching into what had obviously been developed as a repertoire of old Beatles songs: 'Hey Jude', 'Blackbird', 'The Fool on the Hill', 'Penny Lane' and ending with 'I Am the Walrus'. The pianist joined in on the last one, rather appropriately. With his fuzzy hair sprouting from the side of his head and his droopy moustache, he looked rather like a walrus.

They were laughing themselves silly when Nora suddenly noticed me.

'Hello, stranger! How long have you been there? Come and meet Marcus.'

We shook hands and I saw that he had an enchanting smile that made all the folds in his chubby face wobble. It was all I could do not to laugh.

'Pat found him for me,' Nora told me proudly after he had left. 'He's my new singing teacher. A little different from Julie, you have to admit. But wasn't it sweet of Pat to hire someone for me?'

'So Mr Murphy came home?' I said, looking directly at her.

'My Murphy came home,' she repeated, 'to Mrs Murphy, who was very happy to see him at the end of the day.'

'Forgiveness in marriage,' I said.

Her face hardened just a fraction.

'Not completely. I let him come back on the understanding that he was on probation. I know I've said that before but this time he's back after I've actually thrown him out. He knows I won't hesitate to do it again. Now we play by my rules. I've always wanted a piano in the house. Pat wouldn't hear of it before. Now he's changed his tune, forgive the pun. Now he's here every night for supper, no more hopping about staying near the site. No more motel rooms where he can get up to God knows what. And in return, I give him more attention than I give to my boys. He strayed, he cheated on me, but fair's fair — I was so wrapped up in my sons, especially Pete — that I wasn't being much of a wife to my husband, if you know what I mean. Well, let me tell you, that's all changed.'

And she actually winked at me.

But the message was clear. She wouldn't be needing Pete as much as she had and I wondered if that message had filtered through to him.

In the end he didn't have to live above a fish and chip shop. We found the perfect place for him, so perfect in fact that I was rather envious of it myself. But I would never leave Dad. I had resolved to take care of him for the rest of his life.

'You're mad,' said Pete. The first time he had said anything other than comforting words concerning my father.

'What do you mean?'

'Well, when you get married, have kids, what are you going to do then?'

'The house has four bedrooms.'

'Even so. Maybe your Dad won't want you all crowding him out. Maybe he'll want a bit of peace and quiet. Maybe he'll have found himself a new wife and want his privacy. Most children want to leave home.'

'Warren's still living at home.'

'Warren's just bone idle. It suits him to walk five minutes down the High Street to work and back again and have Mum take care of his washing. He won't move until he has to. You're a different kettle of fish. The only reason you're not thinking of moving is because of what you know about your father. What you are not taking into account is that he doesn't know it too. So he's not bothered.'

Ever practical Pete. Of course he was right, damn him, but I still couldn't think about moving. Not just yet.

Not even if I found somewhere as perfect as Pete's place. I decided he was blessed. The chances of finding a place like that in the area around Chaveny Road were extremely remote. His landlord was a widower whose children lived a long way away. He was an independent old bugger who resented them fussing over him but he was quite old and infirm. To relieve their anxieties, they had got together and converted the garage at the end of the garden into a self-contained living area. Of course this meant the old boy didn't have a garage any more, but since they'd long since sold his car behind his back to stop him going out and driving into a lamp post, this was just as well. They'd gutted the garage and turned it into one big living area with a shower and toilet in one corner and a kitchen behind a half-wall in another. They'd turned the roll-up garage door into French windows leading out to the garden. All Pete had to do was find furniture, promise to alert the children living up in the North if there was no sign of life from the main house for more than a day, and the place was his for a very reasonable rent.

I recalled Billy's bare fridge in Covent Garden and resolved to go round as soon as I had a few hours free to work some kind of magic over Pete's new home and make it cosy and welcoming for him. Sounding rather bemused, Pete said he'd leave the key under a flower pot for me.

I was in for a shock.

Pete had already furnished the place. But it wasn't just any old furniture. I recognized a few pieces from No. 57 but he'd picked up a beautiful antique trestle table from somewhere, placed some candlesticks and a tall vase of flowers in the center and it had become the focal point of the room. It took your eye away from his bed in the corner and the clutter of his desk. He'd already had bookshelves delivered from Ikea and assembled them so his books lined the walls. On one wall he'd hung a tapestry, something I knew he'd picked up in Italy when he'd gone there with Nora. She had shown it to me with great pride but I hadn't got the point of it at the time. Now I was presented with the full beauty of the faded woven landscape depicting a bygone Tuscan scene. A pair of comfortable-looking armchairs were placed facing each other in front of it with a little table between them. There wasn't room for a sofa but it didn't matter. The walls had been painted a muted terracotta and the place was so warm and welcoming, it was almost impossible to believe it had once been a garage. It had the feeling of being a rather grand room within a much larger house.

But the biggest surprise of all was when I opened the fridge. I had brought goodies from the only delicatessen in the High Street but there was no room for them. Every shelf was crammed with pasta, Parmesan cheese, sauces, cold salamis and ham, salad, fresh raspberries, cream. The scent from a basil plant wafted towards me and I saw a bowl of tomatoes and another of fruit and jars of olive oil and vinegar, earthenware pots of rice and pulses.

The phone rang. I moved to answer it and then remembered it was Pete's phone. The machine picked up and I heard his voice play into the room.

'Are you there? If you are, pick up.'

I was embarrassed. I had gone round there assuming that he would need me to give his new home the 'feminine touch' and I'd discovered that he was more capable than I of making a nest for himself. I remembered how he'd talked about his dream of having a large house with a wife and children frolicking on the lawn while he worked in his study, translating. This was his study, outside was the lawn. All he needed now were the wife and the kids.

'I'm here, Pete. You've done wonders. It's so great, I wouldn't mind living here myself.'

There was a short silence. Had I said the wrong thing?

'In that case you'll accept my invitation to cook you dinner? You'll be my first guest. I had intended to ask Mum but she's elected to savor the delights of Dad's new electric grill so good luck to her. I'll be home in twenty minutes. Go ahead and open a bottle of wine. You'll find some Chilean Chardonnay knocking around somewhere. It's surprisingly good. Help yourself. Tagliatelle alla vongole sound OK?'

It sounded more than OK. I was starving, and because of that I found Pete's subsequent behavior in the kitchen a bit irritating. I felt mean even thinking such a thing when he was being so sweet and cooking me dinner, but he was such a perfectionist, the meal seemed to take an eternity in the preparation. I am more of a slapdash cook. A pinch of this and a dash of that together with constant tasting to see if I like it, never mind how it's meant to be. I never follow recipes but I have an instinctive feel for ingredients, what goes with what — or at least I think I do. At any rate I always produce something edible as far as Dad's concerned.

But with Pete it was all about preparation and presentation. He moved about the kitchen as if he really knew what he was doing with a dishcloth tossed casually over his shoulder. He chopped and diced away for hours, holding his instruments with both hands, his long fingers hovering above the chopping board while he moved his body from one angle to another, attacking from the right, then from the left, till everything on the board was reduced to little piles of different colored dust.

The smell of herbs and garlic began to waft around the room and my mouth watered. He gave me a glass of wine but didn't encourage conversation. This was very Pete. He was the intellectual version of Gerald Ford who apparently couldn't fart and chew gum at the same time. As far as I could make out, he couldn't do anything and make conversation at the same time. On the other hand, as I experienced later when flopping warm and sleepy in one of the armchairs after making a complete pig of myself, going so far as to rather inelegantly mop my plate clean with a piece of bread, this was a plus when it came to people. He gave them his full attention.

'That doesn't happen very often,' I said, aware that I might burp at any second. 'Nobody ever cooks for me.'

Even as I said it, I recalled Mitzi producing those perfect Long Island fish suppers and felt guilty. She hadn't made such a song and dance about it as Pete had. Men in the kitchen, I decided, were a mixed blessing. I noticed Pete had left a mountain of dirty dishes and pans. Surely he wasn't expecting me to clear it all up? That was the problem with the garage. There was no room for either a washing machine or a dishwasher.

'You need spoiling,' said Pete. 'I have this irresistible urge to take care of you. You've had some bad breaks recently. But I have to be honest with you, apart from being near Mum, one of the reasons for getting a place round here and not moving into central London was to be near you. I wanted somewhere you could visit without the rest of the family watching our every move.'

One minute I was feeling floppy and satiated, the next I was fully alert.

'What moves did you have in mind exactly?' It was a bit coy, not really the kind of talk Pete went in for but it didn't stop him coming over and standing behind my chair and running his long fingers through the hair on my crown in a soft scalp massage.

I went floppy again.

'Did you learn this from Warren? I feel like I'm at the backwash.'

'No, he learned it from me,' said Pete, and he leaned over to kiss me upside down. He undid my blouse at the same time and moved the massage down to my breasts. My arms were reaching up of their own accord and pulling him down with such urgency that he toppled over and lay sprawled all over me.

We moved to his bed pretty swiftly after that and it didn't take long for me to learn the difference between Pete and Billy between the sheets. I hated myself for even comparing them but I couldn't help it. Billy had been an extremely attentive lover but the truth was, I could have been anyone. He had, I realized with the clarity of hindsight, just been going through the motions with my body, fine tuning it like an expert mechanic so that I was in such constant physical ecstasy that I didn't notice that he never said my name.

Whereas Pete made love to me. He didn't necessarily say my name every ten seconds but he murmured things that indicated that he knew who he was with and that he was happy about it. It seemed there was one area where he could talk and act at the same time and it was certainly the one that mattered.

'You understand why I didn't want our first time to be in that horrible little place you took me to for my birthday?' he asked me, stroking the inside of my thigh. I've agonized ever since over whether I did the right thing saying no. I wondered if I'd ever get another chance. Then Billy stepped in and took you away from me. I thought I'd had it then. But I've always believed in perseverance.'

With this he inserted his fingers into my wetness again and closed his mouth over mine.

We talked for hours and by the time dawn broke, I knew whatever feelings I had had for Billy had been nothing more than infatuation.

With Pete I knew it was love.

And it had absolutely nothing to do with the fact that he never asked me to do the washing up.

21

Pete and I were an item and everyone seemed so happy about it. The thing about Chaveny Road was that not many of its inhabitants ever strayed very far from home. They accepted that it was sometimes necessary for people to make the forty-five minute trip into central London in order to find work, but beyond that they became suspicious. Pete had lost ground by traveling to foreign parts but he had made up for it now by taking up with a local girl. Was it my imagination or did everyone smile at us when we went into shops in the High Street together?

Whatever, we had entered into an idyllic time as a couple. I think all couples have it at the beginning. The trouble is you're so busy enjoying it, you rarely remember to stand back and appreciate it. I felt unbelievably secure with Pete. He always called when he said he would, he consulted me about what we would be doing together; if I was prepared to sit through *Gladiator* with him then he was happy to go to *Magnolia* with me. The fact that we each enjoyed both movies and that neither of us had any desire to see *Mission Impossible II* seemed like the icing on the cake. I accepted that he was a better cook than I and could teach me a thing or two. But then he conceded that he was a bit pedantic in the kitchen and allowed me to be his sous-chef in order to loosen things up a little.

And in bed, nothing needed loosening up. We just went from strength to strength.

So I was happy in my personal life, as they say, but what was I to do about the kennels? It was the one area of my life Pete had absolutely no interest in whatsoever and it bugged me slightly. I wasn't particularly interested in how he translated his books but I always wanted to know about the people he was dealing with. The woman in Montana whose book he would be translating sounded absolutely fascinating. The school her husband ran dealt with kids as young as twelve who had been involved in drugs and alcohol abuse, sexual precocity, stealing. Pete had shown me the prospectus for the academy. The kids were not allowed to wear black, nor could they wear camouflage clothing or clothing that promoted identification with drugs, alcohol, music groups, violence or sex. Instead they were required to bring what was called wilderness gear — a backpack, sleeping bag, heavy duty all-day hiking boots, a headlamp, ice skates, skis or snowboards. Pete wasn't concerned with any of these details. Language was the only thing that interested him. He would meet with the Austrian woman who had written the book, go through the translation with her, iron out various editorial points, but he probably wouldn't look much further than that. They might just as well meet in Chaveny Road but apparently she couldn't leave the school.

In the same way that he wasn't interested in the kids at the school, Pete never asked about my animals. He liked the idea of me running the kennels but when I tried to tell him about the day-to-day problems with the individual pets, he seemed to switch off. I began to suspect that maybe he didn't actually like animals and I wondered how much of a problem that was going to be.

In fact the only person in the Murphy family who had ever shown any real interest in my animals was Warren. Warren never ceased to amaze me. I came home one day and found him in the 'playground'. He had a rather skittish red setter out of her cage and he was grooming her. As I looked around, I saw that he was working his way round all the dogs. Several had been hosed down and shampooed and a variety of grooming items were lying about the yard.

'Warren, what's all this? Why aren't you at work?'

'I am at work. Can't you see?'

'Won't they miss you down the salon?'

He stopped what he was doing and looked at me.

'Where have you been? I'm starting to think you're not part of our world any more. I mean, hello? Are you still living here in Chaveny Road or is this just your body I see before me? Has your spirit gone drifting off into the stratosphere? Ever since you came back from America it's like you're a different person. You need to come down to earth and notice what's been going on around here. I haven't worked at the salon for over a month now. I quit.'

'Well what on earth are you doing instead?' I was stunned.

'This,' he said, holding up the setter's head and outstretched tail, 'doesn't she look great? I switched from styling old ladies' hair to grooming animals. Hairdressing pets. Your dad showed me what was needed when I helped him out at the kennels when you were away.'

'He never said.'

'Well, did you ask him? How much have you two talked since you got back? It seems now you're out with Pete every evening I'm the one who spends time with him. We reckon you've grown out of us.'

'Oh, don't be ridiculous.'

'I'm not being ridiculous. We were only saying the other day that we were going to have to book time with you in order to be able to ask you how you felt you could best contribute to Murphypets. We were wondering if you would be free a week next Friday, but of course if that's inconvenient, maybe some time next year?'

'Oh, shut up!'

He was triumphant. 'You don't even know what Murphypets is, do you?'

'All right,' I admitted, 'I don't know. So are you going to tell me or are you going to spend all day crowing about my ignorance and how I've been neglecting you all?'

Up at the house Warren pointed to a navy blue van parked off to the side. From the back, it looked perfectly ordinary to me, just two doors like any other van. But Warren told me to look on the side and I saw the lettering. MURPHY-PETS. Murphy's Mobile Pet Care. Then he pressed a leaflet into my hand. *I come to your* home *in my specially fitted van to provide you with Medicated Shampoo, Flea Rinse and Conditioner. Turbo Drying Advice for pet care. I make your pet look beautifully groomed in a stress-free environment.*

I couldn't believe it. Warren had set up an entirely new line of work and I hadn't known a thing about it. But he wasn't finished yet.

'Wait till you see my website. That's how I get most of my work.'

He took me indoors and I made to climb the stairs to his room but he drew me away to the back of the house. In a little room with a view of the pool, he had set up an office.

'Dad built this workspace for me,' he gestured to a long counter against one wall on which stood a computer, printer, two phones and a fax. He switched on the computer and within minutes he had logged on and was pointing to the screen in great excitement.

'Look, see, Murphypets.com. Everything you need to know about dogs, cats, fish, birds, ferrets, reptiles, small pets.'

I sat down and stared at it.

'Ask a question, go on,' said Warren. 'Type in that Search space there then hit Go.'

'What kind of question?'

'I can't believe you're so computer hopeless. What do you feed the dogs on at the kennels?'

'Well, it varies. Whatever their owners have been feeding them.'

'And do you ever have a problem finding a particular brand for a particularly fussy little pomeranian or something?'

'Well, yes, but then I ask Dad.'

'Well, you haven't recently, have you? Or you'd know about Murphypets.'

'Dad's in on this as well? In fact, I do need to find out where to get a certain kind of cat food . . . '

'Go on then, type it in. I bet Murphypets.com will be able to help you.'

'Can't you just tell me?'

'Well, I'd have to ask Murphypets.com. We have a mass of information but I don't know it off the top of my head. And if we can't tell you then I'll find out and add the details to the website. That's why I need you involved, to broaden our information base.'

'But what's all this — Today's Features. What's 'Ask Frank'?'

'Click on it and see.'

I did and up came Dad's name. *Need to know what's wrong with your pet without a trip to the vet's surgery? Ask Frank Page, M.R.C.V.S.'*

I was hooked. Half an hour later I was still scrolling around the Murphypets site, delighting in my finds. *Futons for dogs. Sisal rug scratcher with built-in mouse for cats. The best way to keep your pet calm when administering a pill. Do you want your pets to have legal rights?* Then I saw a feature that stopped me dead in my tracks. *The best kennel in your area.* Warren saw what I was looking at.

'Go on. Hit it. You might like what you see.'

I saw my own name.

'Now hit the mailbox. Here, I'll do it for you.'

I was greeted with seven e-mails from people

wanting to book space in my kennels later in the year. One even asked why I hadn't got back to them.

'How could I get back to her when I didn't even know the site existed?'

'And why do you think you came home and found me in your back yard today? I want you to become part of Murphypets like your dad. You run kennels. I do grooming. He's the vet. We're a great trio.'

'But how long have you been working on this, Warren?'

'About six months,' he said, amazing me afresh with his coolness. 'Originally I had the idea for a hairdressing website but I found I was becoming bored with hairdressing. I really took advantage of having access to Pete's laptop to surf the net and see how it all worked. I only needed a few thousand pounds to get the site up and running and Dad was happy to provide that so I suppose he's involved as well. Anything to get me away from hairdressing as far as he was concerned. A mate I was at school with turned out to be a whizz when it came to designing a website so I roped him in, for peanuts, needless to say, but he'll get something later on. Dividends are paid out of profits and all that. Where the salon really came in handy was networking. I had built up a really good client base, they'd become friends and I could trust them to keep quiet. I began to quiz them about their animals and all the things they needed to know and what I'm doing now is building the site, adding new stuff to it every week. Which is where you and your dad come in. The more services I can offer the better. Now I've got to go out and raise money to keep us going and expand. I need to find potential partners and investors. I need to solicit product reviews. I need help in research.'

'But I thought the dot.com bubble had burst,' I said, trying to sound knowledgeable.

'Maybe the e-boom's died down a bit, sure, but I think this could work. I want to make it a very personal, almost a neighborhood site. You have the only decent kennels for miles around, play on that, make a name for yourself with personalized advice and push the fact that your dad's a vet and part of the team. We have more than the website to rely on, we have a business. I've been talking to your dad about turning the front of your house into a proper reception area and office for Murphypets. OK, so huge companies have millions to spend on marketing and developing their sites but they don't have the localized appeal that we have. That's what we have to play up. Everyone knows us round here. That has to mean something.'

'But how many of them are online?'

'More than you think. It's the thing you'd never expect retired people to understand but they do and it's perfect for them. They can shop online, they can surf the net and keep in touch. And most of them have pets. As part of our service, I think we should offer free computer lessons to help old people use the net to their best advantage. As often as not there's a computer in the household somewhere.'

'It's just the Page residence that's a little lacking in hardware,' I laughed.

'Don't you believe it. I went with your dad to buy a home computer yesterday. I've been training him with the one at the surgery and he's a fast learner, I'll give him that.'

That evening, over dinner at a new Mexican restaurant that had opened off the High Street — Mexican food coming to the Chaveny Road area, whatever next? — I opened my mouth to ask Pete if he knew about Murphypets and then closed it again. Something told me to keep it to myself, that he might dismiss it and then I'd be depressed. Instead I asked him how much he used the Internet.

'I send e-mails. I don't surf or any of that nonsense. I hate all that information being thrown at you. I never know where to look. It's all so messy and bitty. I'm afraid I'm a bit old-fashioned in that department.'

He was too dreamy. He was practical when he had to be, like sorting out his new living arrangements, but the rest of the time he was in another world. It was one of the reasons I liked him, but I couldn't help being secretly impressed by how entrepreneurial Warren had become. And his enthusiasm was infectious. I couldn't stop thinking about Murphypets and how much I wanted to be involved. I had already answered all the e-mails about the bookings and now I couldn't wait for Dad's new computer to be installed.

Dad's new computer. Dad and I needed to have a little talk about who was going to be using this computer and when. In fact, Warren had set a date for the first Murphypets meeting between the three of us a week hence and I was really looking forward to getting to grips with my new role. God knows, I needed to sit down and have a chat with Dad anyway. Warren had made me realize how far away from home I had drifted in my head.

But our first talk was not about Murphypets, as it turned out. Something happened before the meeting that provoked a talk about a very different matter.

I came in from giving the animals their evening feed to answer the front doorbell and found a strange woman on the doorstep.

'I've come for Frank Page,' she said.

'The surgery's not here. You go down the High Street, turn left at the lights and you can't miss it.' She didn't have a pet with her but what else could she want Dad for? I gave her a quick up and down. About forty-five. Nice brown hair with a touch of gray at the temples, tied back in a loose knot. Good skin, warm brown eyes, very wide mouth. Didn't much like her choice of nail colour. The dark blue trousers and jacket were a bit frumpy for my taste but she had a good figure.

'Oh, no, it's Frank I want. He's expecting me. We said seven o'clock at his place.'

'Then you'd better come in. He should be home soon.'

I was in the process of making her a cup of tea when Dad came home and to my utter amazement walked straight up to her and gave her a kiss on the lips.

'You've met Peggy,' he said cheerfully. I hadn't seen him so animated for quite a while, but then I hadn't seen that much of him, had I?

'Yes, I'm Peggy Marshall,' said the woman pointedly. I hadn't introduced myself and I hadn't asked her what her name was. 'And you are?'

'This is is my daughter,' said Dad, glaring at me, 'you know, the one I've told you about.'

As if he had any others. And what had he been saying about me?

'We're going to try out the new Mexican place,' Dad told me.

I tensed. This was a date. He'd kissed her on the lips. They were standing rather close to each other. Something was going on, something else I'd missed.

'Well, you won't be needing your tea then,' I said, pouring it down the sink in a rather churlish manner. 'Try the margueritas. They're to die for.'

I called Dad at the surgery the next day. He hadn't come in till nearly one o'clock in the morning.

'Will you be in this evening? I thought I'd make macaroni cheese.' His favorite and I'd written down how Delia Smith made it on TV. 'Unless you've got something else on, of course.'

'Wouldn't miss macaroni cheese,' he said quickly. 'Be home around seven.'

Had he heard the silent subtext? *I want to talk to you.*

I took the direct approach. Two mouthfuls and

he held his fork in mid-air when I asked, 'So who is Peggy Marshall?'

'You know who she is. You met yesterday.'

'Yes, but who is she to you? How long have you known her? What does she do?'

'Is she after my money?'

'What money?' I pounced on it, then had the grace to look a little sheepish. What money indeed? No one would ever go after Dad for money.

'I met her at the surgery. She brought a patient in. A very nice little Sealyham terrier with the most foul-smelling breath I think I've ever encountered. Worms. Had to be dosed with vermifuge immediately. I used something that's just come on the market. It's really good, it's called — '

'Dad!' I warned, 'You were telling me about Peggy Marshall.'

'I was, wasn't I? She's a widow. Her husband had a heart attack. She's barely forty-five.'

'So you asked her out on a date?'

'Not right away. She brought her dog in a couple of months ago and I was still seeing Nor — '

He stopped. Of course he did. He hadn't actually told me he and Nora had been an item.

'All right, Dad. Cards on the table. What about you and Nora Murphy? Warren e-mailed me about it while I was in America by the way so don't pretend nothing happened.'

'I wasn't going to pretend.' He looked a bit hurt and I had an instant pang of remorse. I was the one who had allegedly been neglecting Dad.

Maybe he had been searching for the right moment to talk to me and I had always been far too busy running around with Pete. 'It's very simple. You remember when Warren first turned up on our doorstep with that dead canary?' I nodded. How could I forget. It was my first introduction to the Murphy family. 'Well, when Nora came after him I took one look at her and thought she was the most beautiful creature I had ever seen. I'm afraid that goes for your mother, too. Virginia scored high in the looks department but to me Nora Murphy was out of this world. And she turned out to be a sweetheart to boot. You seemed to like her. Her husband was a boorish oaf. I am not exactly the type of man who relishes the notion of adultery but I have to admit that with Nora Murphy, I was tempted.'

I waited. I had never experienced Dad in such a confiding mood. He'd given me odd snippets about my mother and Mitzi but never much about himself.

'I think I knew almost from the start it would be a waste of time,' he continued. 'I'd bump into her in the High Street, we'd go and have a coffee, then, as we got to know each other, she'd invite me up to the house for some supper, or I'd take her out for a pizza. She'd talk, I'd listen . . . '

I'll bet you did, I thought. You're so good at listening, but when does anyone ever listen to you?

'And . . . '

'And inevitably we grew closer. We kissed

339

goodnight a few times, very chaste, a peck on the cheek, but that's as far as it went. Nora Murphy is in love with Pat Murphy and always will be. I don't think she realized what she was doing but she talked about him all the time. I'd say something about what I'd read in the paper and she'd immediately relate it to something about Pat Murphy. The thing I liked about her was that she wasn't feeling sorry for herself. She wasn't about to go to him and beg him to come back. And she didn't run him down. I liked that too. She accepted that he'd done her wrong but she still managed to remember the good things about him. I knew if he ever came back of his own accord, that would be it as far as I was concerned.'

It occurred to me that Nora had not said anything to me about her meetings with Dad. She obviously didn't view him in any kind of romantic light. Poor Dad. Unrequited love, just like mine for Billy. Well, thank God for small mercies, he didn't appear to have made a fool of himself like I had done.

'So then you met Peggy Marshall?' I prompted.

'If there was one thing Nora did do for me, it was to open my eyes to the fact that I wanted someone in my life. The time had finally come to replace your mother. I confess I had been using you as an excuse not to do anything about it. I had to be there for you, etc. etc. But my experience with Nora changed me. I found I was more receptive. I noticed women in the street and when Peggy came in with her dog, I found my attention was on her rather than the dog which was a first for me. I think it was the fact that she could take my mind away from my work that made me realize I was seriously attracted to her.'

I wanted to ask, *Have you done it with her? Have you done the business?* But you can't ask your own father for details of his sex life. Except he wasn't my father. Still . . .

'Well, I liked what I saw of her,' I said to reassure him and he rewarded me with a huge smile. He was seriously happy and I was seriously happy for him.

'And Warren's been telling me about Murphypets.'

Another huge smile.

'Isn't it exciting? That's the thing about Peggy. She knows all about this Internet stuff and she's been teaching me. She's going to give me lessons on my new computer. At the moment I give her the answers to the Ask Frank Page questions and she e-mails them for me but all that's going to change. You're joining us, I hope?'

We spent a happy hour discussing plans for Murphypets. My mind wandered periodically back to Nora. It seemed like only yesterday that she had been my heroine, my role model. There had been a time when I had wanted nothing more than to be like Nora Murphy, married with a large family. Now my dreams had changed. I wanted to be part of Murphypets. I wanted excitement in my life. Marriage and kids could come later. There was plenty of time.

So it came as an almighty shock to discover one month later that I was pregnant with Pete's child.

341

22

I went into instant panic.

I told Pete.

But first I told his mother. I don't know why I told Nora first. I suppose deep down she would always be some kind of substitute mother for me. I had less in common with her than I had once had. With my new Murphypets persona, I felt a little guilty that I was now rather contemptuous of her stay-at-home-wife-and-mother approach to life, given that it had been my approach once. Amazing how much I'd changed after just one summer with Mitzi. I didn't really have all that much in common with Mitzi either. I was sort of in-between the two of them. But I forgave Nora everything because she was sweet, understanding Nora and I knew she would be there for me.

You can tell a lot about how you feel about someone when they turn out to be the first person you want to run to when you're in a jam. And my first thought was to run to Nora.

But I'd overlooked something. Nora was a good Catholic girl and even in this day and age, her first assumption was that Pete and I would get married so the baby would have a father. She did not even stop to consider the possibility that I might have an abortion, which would have been Mitzi's immediate reaction. Mitzi, my godmother. My other substitute mother, as different from Nora as she could possibly be.

342

The person who had been around when my mother had got herself pregnant.

Pete proposed in the sweetest way.

I was spending the night with him and I woke up around dawn to find him fumbling with my hand. He was trying to slip an engagement ring on my finger so it would be the first thing I would see when I opened my eyes. I had ruined it all by waking up but it was still unbelievably romantic. He held me in his arms as the sun came up outside and raised my arm so the ring on my finger caught the early morning light.

'O let us be married! too long we have tarried: But what shall we do for a ring?'

'The Owl and the Pussycat' whispered in my ear in Pete's rich voice was heaven.

'I bought this ring from a Piggy-wig, you know that, don't you?' he tickled me and I screamed. 'He had it at the end of his nose.'

'And he sold it to you for only a shilling?' I couldn't help wondering where Pete had found the money to buy me a diamond ring and I didn't want to ask because I suspected the answer would turn out to be something to do with Pat Murphy, and I didn't want to know I was wearing something he'd paid for.

And even if he really did want to get married, did I want to? It was extraordinary how just the day before I had been convinced I was madly in love with him and as soon as the word wedding came up, I began to think twice about the whole thing. Did I really love him? I found myself questioning all the things I had been so sure about. If you liked going to bed with someone and they could be relied upon to call when they said they would did that mean you loved them? As days went by a horrible splinter of doubt began to sneak into my thoughts. I loved Pete but he wasn't exciting. But then husbands weren't meant to be exciting, were they? They were supposed to be the solid, dependable, kind — like Pete.

Needless to say the baby was the deciding factor. To my amazement, I didn't hesitate for a second about whether or not to have the baby. It was an immediate yes.

Dad guessed. Did it have something to do with him being a vet? Or maybe it was the sound of me being sick morning after morning. We danced around each other tentatively for a while. I wasn't sure how to tell him. He wasn't sure if he should say something. In the end I don't think I actually ever came right out and said the words 'I'm pregnant' — he just came into the bathroom and held my hair away from my head one morning as I was throwing up and then we sat at the kitchen table and discussed it.

That was when I knew I had to marry Pete. I had to give my baby a father. I listened to Dad chatting away. I loved him so much. I couldn't deny the child growing in my womb the chance to have a dad like him. Pete wouldn't be like Dad, of course, but the baby might love him as much as I loved Dad.

And of course I couldn't bear to see Pete's unhappiness if I said no.

I let him smother me with attention. I used my pregnancy as an excuse to do nothing. We decided we ought to get married as soon as possible, as far ahead of the baby's birth as we could. We'd have the reception at No. 57 because our house wasn't big enough but Dad would pay. Definitely.

We picked the day and booked the church and rushed to tell Nora.

I couldn't understand it. She looked completely shattered.

'Mum, what is it?' Pete put his arm around her. 'You want us to get married, don't you?'

She nodded. ''Course I do. You're sure about this date?' She looked at him.

'We're totally sure. It's pretty soon but the sooner the better as far as I'm concerned. Please, Mum, smile. Be happy for us.'

She did smile. She was happy for us. But something was worrying her.

Warren set me straight. I cornered him in the kitchen at No. 57.

'What's up with your mother? Ever since we set the date she's been really unhappy about something.'

'It's the fifteenth? She can't handle it.'

'It's too soon?'

'No, no, no. Fifteen. One and five. It doesn't add up to seven. She can't understand why Pete's picked a date that doesn't add up to seven. She's superstitious, I've told you. She thinks it's a bad omen.'

'Our marriage will fall apart?'

'Who knows? It's all in her mind. But I think the real thing that's upset her is that Pete isn't superstitious any more. He's grown out of it.'

'Well, we can't change it now.'

''Course you can't. It'll be fine.'

I didn't tell Pete. It was all a load of nonsense anyway. Yet another thing I had to forgive Nora for. But it niggled away inside my head. What could go wrong?

The baby had settled down and I began to feel normal again. I humored Nora by happily entering into lengthy discussions about brides-maids (I didn't want any) and music for the wedding service — she had a cousin in Limerick who could play the flute so that it haunted you, she said. Well, ask him if he wants to play at our wedding, I suggested, and she beamed happily and went to the phone to call him right away.

It was when Pete reminded me that he was due to leave for Montana the following week to work on his new book that I realized didn't want him to go. I would miss him. This had to mean I loved him.

'Well, come with me, why don't you? I have to level with you, the ring cost so much that I can't afford a honeymoon as well so let's make this our honeymoon. We can take advantage of the fact that the publishers are paying my expenses. Let's be eccentric and have it before the wedding. We'll go hiking in the mountains and we'll go to Glacier National Park and you'll come back glowing with health and look completely wonderful when you walk down the aisle.'

'You mean I wouldn't otherwise?'

'Well, now it will be guaranteed.'

I hit him playfully. I was rather relieved to hear

346

that he had bought my ring himself. Montana. The Rocky Mountains. The Wild West.

'What about the baby?'

'You'll be fine,' he reasoned. 'You're not far into your pregnancy. You're fit. You're healthy. By all accounts you've had it pretty easy so far, just a little sickness early on. Look at it like this. We may not get another chance to go there. This way the baby will visit Montana and later on you can tell him/her all that he or she experienced. You will have shared it, it's just the baby won't have actually seen it.'

It was a bit dippy. Very much dreamy Pete's way of looking at things, a bit New Agey for me. But why not?

And so I, who had spent all my life in a suburban offshoot of London, found myself going to America for the second time that year, flying once again to New York and then on to Kalispell in Northwest Montana, changing planes at the Twin Cities. I was so proud of myself, calling them that. St Paul/Minneapolis — but everyone called them the Twin Cities.

Montana — Big Sky Country, they called it — was an eye-opener. Not just the fact that it never got dark. You could draw back the curtains at three in the morning and it would still be light. Not just the breathtaking vistas laid out before us. Jagged mountains with snow-capped peaks. Rolling green plains. Crystal clear lakes with the mountains reflected upside down in their calm surface. Streams and waterfalls running down the mountains. And the glaciers! Great slabs of ice rivers lying like white blankets down the sides of mountains. I was becoming almost blasé, the way I was abandoning my trolley at Sainsbury's in the High Street one day and casually getting on planes that transported me to somewhere like this the next.

But the most extraordinary change was in Pete. That was the real eye-opener. The thing about him you wouldn't have discovered if you never saw him outside Chaveny Road. It was as if you could show him a mountain and he became a different person. Never would I have thought that quiet, reflective, poetic Pete would be such an outward bounder. Billy, yes. He was speedy and active. Warren, maybe. He'd shown himself to have a lot of energy even if it was of the Internet entrepreneur variety — and that reminded me, I had to send him a postcard as soon as I could. Needless to say it was Warren (and Dad) who was once again responsible for the animals at my kennels. But Pete, never. Yet he couldn't wait to be out there. From the minute we arrived he was poring over all the brochures detailing such intrepid activities as white water rafting, mountain biking, rock climbing, trout fishing. He was right in the middle of one of his favorite movies, *A River Runs Through It*. And I couldn't help thinking of *The Horse Whisperer* and pretending he was Robert Redford. He showed me the details about Glacier National Park, how we'd stand on the Continental Divide and drive along the romantically named Going To The Sun Road. He couldn't wait to get up to the top of the mountains and he was so excited, like a little boy, that I knew I couldn't dampen his enthusiasm in any way. I loved this new Pete. We called each other Lewis and Clark, after Meriwether Lewis and William Clark, the two explorers who had been sent by President Jefferson at the beginning of the nineteenth century to discover Montana, travelling more than 8,000 miles by horseback and boat, scaling mountains just to see what was on the other side.

The real challenge would be hiking up into those mountains. Was it really wise for a pregnant woman to walk up steep rocky slopes with a heavy rucksack on her back? Absolutely, I insisted. What I didn't tell Pete was that I was more worried about my own nerves than the safety of the baby. My doctor back home had told me it would be fine to take exercise. But what I hadn't bargained for was the effect the mountains had on me.

To begin with they were stunning, when they were far away in the distance and I was safely down on the ground in the middle of the Flathead Valley. The sun was strong and the endless pine forests didn't seem at all gloomy. To be honest, on the horizon the mountains didn't seem threatening to me because they didn't seem real. It was just the picture on the postcard I had remembered to send to Warren and Dad.

Even when we went for our first visit to the Lost Horizon ranch to see Pete's Austrian professor and talk about her book, I was relaxed. We had a forty-mile drive in our hired car along the highway to the academy and turned off it to take a seven-mile drive up into the foothills. It wasn't even a proper road, just a dusty dirt road that had to be impassable in winter. Arriving at the ranch it seemed like we were entering an Indian reservation. A lake, creeks, ponds, endless pasture flanked by mountain timber and meadow. There was a little wooden ranch house that served as a cookhouse and dining hall; another that served as the schoolroom, a multi-purpose barn housing a gym and additional classrooms and four log cabins that were the dormitories. An intimate, functional campus for the disturbed kids far away from the city life that had screwed up their lives. The sheer grandeur of the wild around them soon left them awestruck and the outward bound activities were a far cry from urban temptations like drugs and alcohol. And if they did decide to run away, it was forty miles to the nearest town.

The official title of Pete's author was Admission and Family Liaison Director. It was part of her job to assess the kids whose parents applied for enrolment in the academy. Often they were the children of divorced parents, fiercely independent children who were used to living on their own terms and getting their own way and filled with self-destructive impulses, children who could not conform to regular classes, free spirits who ran away from home at the drop of a hat. One sixteen-year-old girl wept openly as she told me how she had already tried to kill herself four times but now she felt she was beginning to turn a corner.

What I kept coming back to was the fact that I had a baby growing inside me, a baby I was determined should never have to experience what these kids had been through. Pete and I would never divorce. And given Pete's dreams of a large country house with kids playing on the lawn and his sudden display of passion for outdoor activities, it was highly unlikely that we would wind up living in a city.

Poor Pete. It was clear that he had a full day's work ahead of him with his author. He would be shut up in one of the cabins. But, he insisted, I shouldn't waste a minute of our trip. He arranged for someone to take me to a place called Jewel Basin which was apparently spectacularly beautiful.

And that's when I got my second eye-opener.

I had agoraphobia.

I was fine to begin with. There were five of us, me and four of the teachers at the Academy — young men and women from various parts of America who told me they went hiking in the mountains regularly because once they'd finished their stint at the Lost Horizon Ranch, who knew when they'd have a chance to return to Montana? And it was a while since they'd visited Jewel Basin. But I'd love it. The views were breathtaking.

We drove out of Kalispell towards Flathead Lake, the largest natural lake west of the Mississippi, but we turned off the highway before we reached it and cruised along Foothills Road, so named because the Rocky Mountains towered above us. This particular range was called Swan Mountains and further on, beyond a town called Bigfork, was Swan Lake. The names were all magical but none more so than Jewel

Basin. I imagined a pool of mountain water with diamonds of light glinting in the sun. I rubbed my tummy surreptitiously, trying to take it all in so I could tell my baby later where he or she had been.

The weather was perfect. A sheer expanse of blue sky stretched out over the Flathead Valley behind us as the car began its ascent of the mountain road. Shafts of sunlight pierced the pine forests on the lower slopes as the road began to twist and turn and double back on itself. And all the time we were climbing.

I'm not sure exactly when I noticed I was cold. I was so busy looking out of the car window at the view that I reached for a sweater and tied the arms loosely around my neck without being aware of what I was doing.

Then it hit me. I was freezing. The temperature had dropped right down and there were no more pine trees. In fact there was no green at all. We were having to navigate more and more bends and it dawned on me that below the road was a sheer drop to the bottom of the valley.

I was becoming nervous. I was aware that I was holding my breath. Every now and then we had to drive around a pile of fallen rocks in the middle of the road and this brought us very close to the edge.

What if another car came round the bend at that moment?

Where were the other cars? Were we up here on our own?

What would happen if we broke down? Would anyone find us?

I clamped down mentally on my growing anxiety. I was having the time of my life. I mustn't let the others see that I was anything other than beside myself with excitement.

We had been climbing for over half an hour, half an hour's drop to the ground if we did go over the edge. Eventually we arrived at a clearing and got out of the car in a deserted car park. One of the men went to a wooden post from which a book was hanging, tied on by piece of string.

'Damn,' he said, 'has anyone got a pen?'

'Why?' I asked.

'There's nothing to write with. Usually there's a pencil tied to the post as well but the string's broken. It's gone.'

'Write what?'

'We have to register our party in this book at the start of our hike so that if anything happens to us the Mountain Rescue team know we're up there.'

No one had a pen. I looked at the book. The Walker family from Des Moines had signed it two weeks ago. Had they made it back down? Or were they still up there? I shivered.

I looked up at the massive gray wall above us with a cloud hanging over it. No more sunlight, no more greenery, no sign of life whatsoever. Just hard, unwelcoming granite.

My companions wore sturdy hiking boots. I only had sneakers.

'Doesn't matter. You'll be fine in those. We won't have to tramp through much snow.'

'Snow?' I was incredulous. 'In August?'

'Take a look.' He pointed to the distance and I saw snow-capped peaks.

'We're going all the way up there?'

'Almost. And then back down again to Jewel Basin. Two hours there, two hours back.'

One of the women looked me up and down. 'I'm more worried about the fact that she doesn't have keys to jangle. And we should have got her a whistle.'

'In case we get separated?' I asked.

'In case you meet a grizzly bear. You're supposed to wear something that jangles so they hear you coming. If you surprise them, they're more likely to pounce on you.'

'Well, I've got this if they do,' said another man, and produced an evil-looking knife from a sheath attached to his belt.

The good news was that I was a strong walker. I exercised the dogs at my kennels every day and even though I was in the early stages of pregnancy, I was pretty fit. We set off and I had no trouble keeping up with them as we trudged up the wide mountain trail.

But then everything changed. Suddenly the trail narrowed to a path barely more than three feet wide, cut sharply into the cliff face. As it had been when we were in the car, we rounded bends and were faced with rock falls. What if these rocks fell on us as we were hiking and we had to move quickly out of their way? We could fall over the edge all the way down to the valley below.

I couldn't move fast because I was scared that I would stumble and trip. And whenever I looked out at the view, as the others urged me to do at frequent intervals, I freaked.

We were so high up.

I was cold. It was bleak. And the grizzlies were watching me.

I began to feel sick. I glanced back. Big mistake. Behind me was an endless stretch of granite bends and a death-defying path twisting like a snake around them. The path I had already traveled and the only way I could return to safety.

And then I looked ahead and saw where we were going. Far away I could see the path winding down the mountain to a dark, threatening pool of black water.

Jewel Basin.

I began to feel seriously dizzy.

Was I completely and utterly mad? Why was I risking my unborn baby's life like this?

I turned my face to the wall of granite and breathed deeply, resting my head against the jagged rock. Behind me, just beyond my heels, was an eight thousand foot drop to my death. Mine and my baby's.

I couldn't move or I would fall.

I closed my eyes.

I could feel my heels inching towards the edge and knew there was nothing I could do about it . . . They told me the next day that it had taken them an hour to talk me down. I recalled hearing their voices through a fog of cotton wool that had taken up residence in my head. They were discussing what to do with me, whether to try and coax me forward in the hope that I would get over my fear or whether to abandon the day's outing and somehow get me back to the car.

It didn't take them long to figure out that it would be pretty hard to get me to move either way. One of them had to hold my hand all the way back to the car. Progress was at a snail's pace. I barely remember any of it.

I owed these people my life, although they laughed in my face when I said as much. It wasn't unheard of, they told me. The mountains affected people that way sometimes. I'd probably find I felt hemmed in even now I was on the ground. They were right. Now the mountains seemed oppressive. I wanted out. I wanted to go home. I wanted to be back in Chaveny Road.

But I couldn't deny Pete his adventure. He had worked like a demon throughout the day in order to be able to finish ahead of schedule and spend the rest of his trip doing all the things he had planned.

He had heard all about what had happened to me, of course, and that night we lay in bed and he hugged me to him.

'I should have been there. You wouldn't have been frightened with me there. You'll be fine today. I can't wait to share it all with you.'

I kissed him over and over again on his neck because I couldn't think what to say. It hadn't occurred to me that he would still expect me to go with him after what had happened. Didn't he understand how petrified I was? How nothing would make me go up those mountains again? But if I didn't go, would it spoil it for him?

'I never knew you had this thing about outward bound stuff. I never knew you were such an adventurer.'

'Tell you the truth, I never really knew it myself.' He pulled me even closer. 'I think you've liberated me in some way. I really believe you love me and it's given me courage, confidence, all the things I had a problem with growing up.'

'Your mother loves you,' I pointed out, wondering what he would say to that.

'My mother loves me,' he repeated slowly, 'and I love her, but you know what, I never thought I'd say this but I think Dad can take care of her now. I think that's what I never wanted to face up to. I wanted to be Dad's substitute and it just wasn't possible. Mum loves Dad for whatever reason, and even though Warren and I disapprove of the way he's behaved, we have to accept that Mum needs him. More than she needs us. That's what hurts. I'm OK. I have you. But I worry about Warren.'

'How can you be worried about Warren? He's going to do so well. Murphypets is a brilliant idea. You're talking about my colleague, don't forget.'

'I know, I know. It's just his private life seems to be a great big zero. He's not gay. We've established that with Ferdy's help. But he doesn't seem to have anyone in his life. Come to think of it, I don't think he ever has.'

'That's so sad. Why?'

Pete hesitated. 'I know why,' he said, 'but I don't really want to go into it now. There are going to be problems and I don't want to spoil our holiday by talking about them. I'll tell you one day, OK? Maybe when we're back home.'

Very mysterious. But Pete was right. Why spoil what little fun we had left? Although would it be fun for me if I were forced to return to the mountains?

'I wonder if our baby will have a direct mix of our good qualities and failings?' I mused out loud.

'Good qualities and failings?' Pete kicked me gently under the bedclothes. 'Name a few. Start with my good qualities and your failings.'

Now it was my turn to kick him.

'Seriously,' I said, 'you're much more adventurous than I. You're raring to go up these mountains, you're courageous, fearless, intrepid,' I knew I was laying it on a bit thick but I had my reasons, 'whereas I am a scared little mouse. Pathetic really. One day up there and I'm a goner. Nothing's going to get me up there again.'

He raised himself on one elbow and looked down into my face.

'You mean that, don't you? Oh, don't do this to me. Please come with me. It'll mean so much to me to have you there.'

'You're such a romantic, Pete. I hope our child will grow up to be a romantic like you, especially now you've toughened up a bit. But please try to understand when I say I'd rather die than go with you. When I'm up there, it's the most awful thing but I have this weird urge to throw myself into the void. I could literally feel my feet being pulled over the edge.'

'You need a good night's sleep. You'll feel different in the morning.'

But I didn't. I felt worse. I had nightmares.

First the car careered over the edge and began to fly through the air and I woke up with a start before we hit the ground. Pete was fast asleep and I watched his face for a while. It always scared me a little to do this because in repose his pale, poetic face seemed almost lifeless. Pete never stirred in his sleep, always lay totally still, and sometimes I even shook him to see if he was still breathing.

Tonight, however, I left him to sleep. He would need all his energy for the next day. I spent a long time thinking about what I had experienced. Maybe it would be different with Pete there. I had gone with strangers and maybe that was what had made me nervous. Pete would give me strength. I would look upon it as a test for the way our marriage would be in the future, facing things together. I would be terrified and he would be there for me. Maybe it would be like this when the baby was born. Terrifying pain in the delivery room but Pete would be there beside me. It would mean a lot to me to have him there so I must start thinking of the times when it would mean a lot to him to have me with him. And it was obvious that he wanted me to share his new-found adventurous spirit in Montana. I wouldn't let him down. I would go with him up the mountains.

But then I fell asleep again and had another nightmare and this time I was back on the ridge where I had gone into a state of panic and clung to the rock face. In my dream, unlike reality, I was facing out, looking across the valley. I was

359

being pulled slowly forward, I had my arms out as if I were reaching out to embrace someone. I took one step and then another.

I woke up screaming so loudly Pete actually stirred.

There was no way I was going with him.

He set off for Jewel Basin at eight o'clock the next morning. They had decided to return there to make up for the abortive trip the day before and Pete was to go with them. To make up for disappointing him, I fussed around him, attaching jangling keys to his belt, teaching him to whistle through two fingers. I was now the expert. He'd gone out and bought himself a pair of proper hiking boots at some point.

'You're all set,' I told him proudly. 'Don't pet the bears.'

Today they had a different car. A big SUV with a four-wheel drive. Pete sat in the back and waved out the window, jangling his keys and whistling at me for all he was worth. I blew him kisses until the van disappeared.

I had a blissful lazy day. We were staying at a little place called the Duck Inn in Whitefish, a smaller, older town at the foot of Big Mountain, something else that was appropriately named. I wandered along the river and picked flowers and I lay on the river bank and dreamed of how life would be with my newly established family. Pete, the baby and Dad as Grandpa. And, I supposed, Peggy Marshall.

By six o'clock they had not returned. Pete and I had planned to go and eat supper in a little café in Whitefish. The mountain air made me hungry and I hoped I wouldn't have to wait too long.

I heard the van draw up at around nine by which time I was ravenous.

He wasn't with them and I tried not to show my impatience.

'How was it? Did you get all the way to Jewel Basin without a Scaredy Cat like me to hold you back? Was it wonderful? Did Pete have a great time? Where is he?'

That was when I noticed they were lined up in front of me, everyone in the party except Pete. They were looking at each other as if no one knew who should speak first.

When someone did find the words to tell me, I screamed louder than I ever had in the mountains.

23

Mitzi took the first plane out of New York the next morning and arrived at Kalispell by lunchtime.

Just as I had turned immediately to Nora when I had discovered I was pregnant, now my first thought was that I needed Mitzi. It was instinctual. She was the only person I knew in America apart from Billy. But I never even thought of Billy.

Mitzi, to whom I had not even talked since I left Long Island. Mitzi, who didn't even know that I was back in America, let alone pregnant. Yet when I called her she responded immediately. Her ear had to have been attuned to the hysterical tone of my voice.

They had had to sedate me. Apparently I didn't stop screaming for twenty minutes. After that I turned down the volume a little and settled into a pattern of intermittent moaning. I literally ached with pain. They were worried about the baby, of course. What the shock would do to my system.

By the morning, after I had finally collapsed and had a few hours' sleep, I was able to grasp what had happened.

Pete had been reckless. He seemed to have adopted the persona of a mountain goat, leaping ahead of them along the trail, moving much too fast. They said he never stopped talking about me and the way I had changed his life. How he felt like a new person, how he felt liberated, how he would never have dreamed he could be up a mountain like this without a care in the world.

My one tiny consolation was that that was how he died. Happy, in love, without a care in the world. A recollection shifted bizarrely in my head: how I had heard about someone's father who had been on vacation in the Caribbean, floating on their back in the aquamarine sea, when they had a heart attack — literally out of the blue. *What a way to go*, everyone had said. It was a bit like that with Pete.

It was just a tiny slip, apparently. He stumbled, tried to regain his balance, failed and it was all over in a second. One minute he was there, ahead of them, shouting into the cold mountain air about how wonderful I was, and the next time they looked he wasn't.

I couldn't bring myself to ask, 'Did you look down, did you see him falling?'

Mitzi arrived just as they reported that his body had been found and at that point I totally lost it. I barely recognized Mitzi but luckily I allowed her to take charge. After all, these people who had been with me barely knew who I was. They didn't know who to call.

Someone had to tell Nora. I managed to get this much across, found the number in my book, but when they handed me the phone I couldn't go through with it.

So I called Dad.

I don't remember what I said but we talked for a long time and then Warren came on the line.

'I'll tell Mum.' He was firm, decisive, exactly what I needed somebody to be. 'I'm coming out there to get you. We'll bring his body back together. Hang in there. This is the worst thing that could possibly happen to anybody but you have to hold it together.'

What impressed me, even in my distraught state, was that he didn't say, 'Think of the baby.' I could tell everyone around me was worrying about the fact that I was pregnant. I'd been checked over. The baby was fine. They just seemed to be worried that I might do something stupid.

Mitzi spoke to Warren, told him where we were, how to get there, said she would organize the release of the body to be taken back to England.

Then she turned her attention to me. She must have spent hours just sitting with me and rocking me in her arms and when I was ready to talk she just said simply, 'Tell me about Pete.'

And I began to talk about him.

'The first hint I ever had of what Pete was like was when Warren told me, 'Pete just dreams and watches.' And then he elaborated. He said Pete watched *me*. We were at school together and I'd never even noticed him.'

I gulped. *I'd never even noticed him.*

That's when I knew how awful Pete's death really was.

'Mitzi, before we came out here I was fretting because I was having these funny feelings about Pete, that I shouldn't be marrying him. I was actually asking myself if I really did love him and

I thought if I had to ask something like that, I more or less had my answer. But then I'd always find a reason to persuade myself that I was being ridiculous. I found out he was coming here and I realized how much I would miss him, so that meant I loved him. Stuff like that. And I did love him. As a friend. A friend with whom I shared great sex. If I'm really honest, the sex was the most exciting part about him. Pete was a wonderful person. Rare. He was sort of other worldly, incredibly sensitive, but he was making such progress. I can totally understand how he felt liberated being out here. He was very close to his mother. He had just moved into his own apartment away from her. He was really trying to distance himself from her, for my sake. In the most gentle way he could. I guess when he arrived here, he probably felt he had really got away. He was a translator. He went traveling when he came down from university but I don't think it quite severed the bond he had with Nora. But the truth is, Mitzi, now that I think about it, I'm not sure he was ready to get married. He was mature in so many ways because he was so responsible, but emotionally I think he was still needy. There was still the element of the little boy who had just cut loose from his mother's apron strings. Did I really want to be his new mummy?'

It was true. I realized I had buried all sorts of doubts about our relationship. Pete had always been in love with me and that was what had drawn me to him. He was the first man who had ever loved me and I had felt some kind of heady power over him. But now, faced with the tragic aftermath of his death, I found I was more shocked about the fact that such a wonderful man had died so young than I was about losing my fiancé. I was more sad on Nora's behalf than my own. Hers was a far, far bigger loss, hers and my unborn child's. I cared. I cared desperately but never for one second did I think my life was over.

And surely that was what I should be thinking.

'I feel unbelievably guilty,' I told Mitzi.

'You have no need to,' she said. 'He wasn't here because of you. He was coming here anyway because of work, so I understand. He would have felt liberated and climbed those mountains whether you were here or not. Or do you feel bad because you didn't go up there with him?'

I hadn't even thought of *that*.

'I feel guilty because a tiny, tiny part of me is saying, 'Now you don't have to marry him, now he won't ever know how you really felt.' I feel guilty because I feel I used Pete. I was in love with the idea of being in love and he was the perfect person for me to indulge myself with. He was so romantic. He was such a timely antidote to the whole Billy fiasco. Does it shock you to hear all this, Mitzi?'

'I've heard worse,' said Mitzi. Of course, she was a shrink. I was getting free treatment. She was helping me get it all out. 'You're going to feel guilty for quite a while. It's natural. What's great is that you can recognize it so early. Does it matter whether you really loved him or not? He thought you did and it made him happy. And you certainly cared about him. What is amazing is that you are not glorifying Pete. You are being realistic and that's important when it comes to telling your child about its father. It sounds like he gave too much and took too little and you know, in a way, he had a problem there. It sounds like you were already irritated by his devotion to you. You saw it with his mother and it didn't worry you too much because it wasn't really your problem, but the way I see it, you'd have been marrying a saint and that's a hard act to live up to.'

Everything Mitzi said was true but there was one thing about Pete no one could take away from me.

'No one will ever have a more beautiful voice,' I said. 'Where's the phone? I have to call London. What do you dial?'

'We've made all the necessary calls. Everything's taken care of.' Mitzi put her hand on my arm. 'Who do you need to call?'

'No. Please. Give me the phone. I want to call Pete.'

To her credit, Mitzi didn't stop me but now she was looking very worried indeed.

I called his flat and got what I wanted. His voice on his answering machine.

'This is Pete Murphy. I'm not here at the moment but please leave me a message after the tone. Thank you.'

I hung up and dialed again. And again. And again.

I had to make the sound of his voice resonate

367

around my brain until I knew I could conjure it up at will. I went on dialing and listening until Mitzi gently took the phone away from me.

'Oh, Mitzi,' I said, leaning against her, 'have you ever lost someone?'

'Oh yes,' she said quietly, 'I lost your mother, remember?'

When Warren arrived I had another shock but it was a positive one. Encountering him out of context, away from Chaveny Road, I saw him in an entirely different light, or so it seemed. He was taller and older and very much in control of the situation. He had a haunted look about him — it was his brother who had died, after all — but he was sensible and practical at all times.

'That young man is extraordinary,' Mitzi commented. 'If Pete was anything like him, I can see why you were drawn to him.'

'Pete was like no one,' I said. 'Warren's a regular guy. Pete was on another planet.'

'Well, as earth men go, I think Warren's pretty special. He's the youngest, right? He's been in the shadow of his two older brothers all his life. I'm probably the first person to notice him. I'll bet he stays in the background most of the time and just gets on with things. Am I right?'

Funnily enough, she was. Billy was a show-off who craved attention and got it at whatever cost. Pete had been the center of Nora's life for so long, so in a way he had always been noticed somewhere along the line. But Warren was always just Warren, hovering in the background just like Mitzi said.

Warren had not let go of my hand since the

minute he had arrived unless he absolutely had to. It was as if he thought his grip would somehow glue me together until I was able to get through this awful time and come out the other end. It occurred to me that he might want to take a look outside, see a bit of glorious Montana. Warren had never been out of England before, as far as I knew.

'Who the hell cares where we are?' he said, and it made total sense. We needed to be together. Montana would always be the place where Pete had died. It was hardly a tourist attraction for him.

'Today's Monday. We'll fly home tomorrow. The funeral's Friday.'

'How's your mother? How's Nora?'

'Terrible. As you might expect. But something's happened. You won't believe this but Dad has been amazing. He and I took care of all the funeral arrangements and it kind of brought us together. And he's been right there for Mum. He never had much time for Pete. It was always Billy, Billy, Billy, till it made you sick. But it's like what's happened to Pete has humbled him in some way. I've seen a different side of him, maybe it's what made Mum fall in love with him years ago. They're inseparable. Isn't it awful, but I think it might be the making of them? She never said a word to me. She turned to him. Straight away.'

Poor Warren. Lost in the background.

'I'm here for you, Warren. You know I am.'

He cried then. Big baby tears, just like the ones he'd shed when his blessed canary had

369

died. I hugged him to me.

'I know,' he said, 'I know. You've always been there. Next door. I loved knowing you were there at the end of the drive. I loved it when you came in with me on Murphypets. When your Dad called, for one awful moment I thought it might have been you who had gone over the edge. Do you know when I learned it was Pete I actually felt a tiny stab of relief. Isn't that awful?'

You and me both, I thought, but I didn't have the nerve to tell him. Something had become clear to me. Pete had said we would have to face a problem with Warren when we got back. I hadn't understood what he was talking about but now I knew. Just as I knew that the problem had gone away with Pete's death.

Warren let go of my hand for half an hour so I could say goodbye to Mitzi. There was no point in her coming over for the funeral. She had never known Pete, although she probably felt like she did now. I hadn't told her about Dad not being my real father. If I knew one thing it was that Mitzi and Frank Page should be kept apart. They were on different continents. It wouldn't be hard. Pete had been the only other person — apart from Ferdy, who had disappeared into thin air after delivering his thunderbolt — who knew the truth. One day I might want to find out who my real father was and that might mean visiting Mitzi on Long Island and embarking upon an investigation amongst the fisher folk there. But now was not the time.

But I knew I wanted to keep Mitzi in my life. She shared something with Warren. She was someone who brought me alive. She helped me to see the real me, to change, to move forward. Without Mitzi would I have embraced the notion of joining Warren in Murphypets quite so readily? I don't think so.

'How are you, Mitzi? I haven't even asked.'

'I'm grateful to you, is what I am,' she told me, smiling. 'It took your sweet presence to make me see that I was a mess. A drunk making a fool of herself over men. I've taken the first step. I've joined a program. My name is Mitzi Alexander and I'm an alcoholic.'

'Mitzi, that is completely wonderful. I'm proud of you. Why didn't you tell me before? Why didn't you write or call?'

'Why didn't you?' she challenged.

'Touché.'

'We needed space,' she acknowledged.

I nodded. 'Mitzi, I have something to ask you. You don't have to say yes right away but will you think about it? I'm your goddaughter, even though I'm not Jewish like you. Do you think that rules out the possibility of you being godmother to my baby as well?'

The look on her face told me her answer.

'Maybe because you're Jewish I wouldn't expect you to show up at the christening.' That way she and Dad wouldn't have to come face to face.

'I'll be a special kind of godmother and we'll have a special American baptism on Long Island,' she said. 'Now I'm going to hand you over to Warren. I have no qualms about that. None whatsoever.'

And nor, I realized, did I.

On the flight home I began to worry about how I was going to get through the funeral, although to be honest I was more worried about how Nora was going to cope. I envisaged a lot of sobbing and wailing. It wasn't really my style. I knew I was going to mourn Pete for a very long time but I wanted to do it privately. I didn't want to be in the middle of a lot of shrieking and wailing. It was bad enough when we landed and just by chance I happened to look down and see the casket being offloaded slowly down a gangplank. It was an awful, shocking sight and one that would stay with me for a long time. It was so final. Pete was in that coffin and he was never coming out of it. I think that was when I said goodbye to him, silently, sitting in my cramped airline seat waiting to disembark. And then I stood up and dissolved into Warren's arms. He had to more or less carry me off the plane with a blanket over my head so the other passengers wouldn't be able to gawp at my grief.

If I could lose control like this, how bad would it be for Nora?

But she surprised me.

Warren came down to the house the day after we got back and he had delivered me safely into Dad's care to tell me that the funeral was going to be a private mass for the family only, but of course that included me. 'Then what Mum wants to do is this — and I know you'll like this part — she wants to have a big Irish wake in the garden in about a month's time. We're going to plant a tree and have a little memorial plaque right near where Natasha was buried, and we'll invite everyone who ever knew Pete. It'll be grand.'

It was the perfect solution. No embarrassing public displays of emotion and a chance to celebrate Pete's short life with dignity, although from what I had heard about Irish wakes, there wouldn't be anything dignified about it.

'Billy's in trouble,' said Warren, looking mischievous. 'Ooh boy!'

'How come?' I was intrigued.

'Told Mum on the phone that he wouldn't be able to make it to the funeral mass. Went on and on about his career. Seems he's got a big break in a TV series that started shooting last week. He won't get any time off for a month. Funnily enough Mum didn't really seem to care but Dad hit the roof. I've never seen him so angry. He grabbed the phone from Mum and yelled at Billy. Called him a bunch of names that shocked us all, said he didn't want him back home until he'd learned a bit of respect for the dead.'

'Well, it is pretty disgusting,' I pointed out.

'I think Billy realized what he'd done because he called back within the hour. Said he was going to try and get compassionate leave, something he should have asked for in the first place. But Dad stuck to his guns, told him to stay where he was. Mum's having quite a time persuading him Billy can come back to read at the memorial service. But guess who's flavor of the month in Dad's eyes now?'

I smiled at him.

'I can't remember when Dad last spoke to me

direct,' Warren went on, 'now he won't leave me alone. It's almost as if for the first time in his life he's noticed he has another son. And it seems he genuinely cared about Pete, although you'd never have known it. He came into my little office yesterday and sat down and asked if I'd mind if he had a little chat with me about Pete. And you know what? It was really nice. All our sentences began 'Do you remember the time when . . . ?' and it was amazing the amount of stuff Dad could recall. He's quite a nice guy when it comes right down to it, not a great brain but he's got a kind heart underneath all the bravado. But I think what's happened has made him realize he wants to be the one to take care of Mum. He kept going on about marriage, bit sickening really but maybe it's for the best. He went on and on about security, kept asking me about Murphypets and did I have a girlfriend?'

'And do you?' I held my breath. Was the mystery of Warren's private life about to be solved?

I regretted asking him as soon as the words were out of my mouth. He looked so awkward.

Then he looked straight at me. 'I'm not sure, to be honest,' was all he said.

What kind of an answer was that?

Dad and I went to our local church and said a prayer together for Pete. The vicar was a little surprised to see us and quite rightly so. We never went to church, maybe once a year on Christmas Day, if that, but Pete and I had been to see the vicar recently to post our banns and arrange a date for our wedding so he knew how devastating Pete's death was for me. As we sat in the church I thought of the significance of that wedding date and how Nora had been convinced that it was a bad omen. How right she had been and how wrong that I should be condoning superstition while sitting in church. And then another thought occurred to me. Nora wanted to have a mass for Pete because they were Catholics. How come she had not insisted that Pete have a Catholic wedding? Did she somehow know that we would never be married? I banished such an awful thought as soon as it popped into my mind.

I don't know what I would have done without Dad in the weeks that followed. Of course, I don't know what I would have done without Dad my entire life but he was especially understanding in the time running up to the memorial service. He had lost my mother and every now and then, always at exactly the right moment — I've no idea how he knew but his timing was perfect — he would give me a snippet of his own experience and how he dealt with getting over her.

He came upon me one day crying quietly while I was feeding the animals. It was a time when I knew I could count on some privacy and I used it every morning to allow the tears to fall, to find some kind of release. Dad had come out to give me a telephone message. With anyone else it would have been an intrusion but Dad just wandered around the yard, silently helping me until he came out with, 'You know you forget and yet you never forget. There'll be a time when you find you haven't thought about them for a whole day and you suddenly remember and you feel guilty. Then you realize it's OK because you can still remember everything about them, it's just that you don't suffer so much pain all the time. Your life has resumed its daily pattern but they are still there in the background. You never let them go. They'll always be with you. You were lucky to know them. They were lucky to know you. And sad. Like a love affair that's over. You find it hard to accept at first but then you do. It's bearable. You move on. And it's OK, sweetie. It's allowed. You just have to be allowed to do it at your own speed. No one's rushing you. Least of all me. I've been there. I know.'

That's how I was lucky to have Dad. He understood and that was a wonderful thing in itself, but I think what was really astonishing was the way in which he was able to express himself so explicitly when it really mattered. For most of the time he was the strong, silent type. He saved his words for when they were really needed. It seemed Warren and I were both rediscovering our fathers.

And I saw how happy he was with Peggy Marshall. The fact that I didn't feel jealous of her in any way told me that she had to be a nice person. We didn't really have much in common, there wasn't that strange instinctive bond I had immediately felt with both Nora Murphy and Mitzi, even though those two women were total opposites. But Peggy was polite and gentle and considerate and she adored Dad. The ultimate proof of her sensitivity came when she said she wouldn't be coming to Pete's memorial service.

'What do you mean you're not coming?' I was astonished.

'I don't want to intrude. I barely knew Pete and you'll need Frank by your side. You don't want me coming between you at a time like this.'

'Peggy,' I said, 'I think Dad would like to have you by his side and he can have me on his other side. Have you thought of it like that? Because from where I'm standing it looks like that's the way it's going to be from now on. Has he popped the question, by any chance?'

I hope she appreciated *popped the question* because, God knows, that was a Peggy expression if ever there was one. She went bright red. She really was rather girlish for a woman in her forties.

'How did you know?'

'I didn't. I was just asking. And you've given me my answer.'

'Oh my God, he should have been the one to tell you.'

'Who cares who tells me? I couldn't be more delighted.' And I hugged her just to show I meant it.

And to take our new relationship a step further, I invited her to come and help me select what I would wear to the memorial service. I was beginning to show a little and I had spent a whole morning trying on maternity clothes in a shop in the High Street. In the end I decided to root around in my wardrobe and dig out some of my old clothes that I had set aside following a highly successful diet a couple of years ago. I was pleased the ever practical side of me had made me hang on to them because they were outfits I had always liked and now they fitted me again. Peggy and I laid them all out on the bed and one by one I tried them on. I was aware that I was going to great pains to remember the type of thing Pete had liked me in. He loved rich, somber colors like plum and bottle green. I was in the process of trying on a maroon dress with a jacket to match when I heard Warren shouting up from downstairs.

'Anyone home?'

'Up here. Just trying to find something to wear.'

'Well, please don't wear that,' he said, coming into my bedroom. 'Hello Peggy, how are you? It makes you look a hundred and two.'

I looked in the mirror. He was right.

'Try this.' He picked up a vivid turquoise A-line shift, shot silk. Someone had brought it back for me from India and I had never worn it because it had been too big. Now, to my surprise, it fitted perfectly. And it looked stunning.

'Pete hated turquoise. I never wore turquoise with him,' I said nervously.

'Well Pete won't be there to see it,' said Peggy, and then froze. She could do that occasionally, say something unbelievably tactless and then grope around, trying helplessly to retract it.

'Quite right, Peggy,' said Warren, coming to her aid. 'Wear it,' he told me, 'I think you look completely fabulous. Take a look at yourself in the mirror. It's your color.'

I looked and he was right and somehow it felt good being admired by Warren. It would be a little chilly but then I realized I could slip a beautiful cream-colored pashmina shawl around my shoulders. It had been a present from Pete but one way or another it had been somewhat overshadowed by the engagement ring. Now I could please both Pete and Warren. And myself.

The sun shone. The sky was royal blue, not a cloud in sight. What do you call people attending a memorial service? Guests? Whatever, Warren and I met them in the hall of the Murphys' house and directed them through to the back garden where Nora and Pat were waiting for them. Nora had adorned the hall with huge arrangements of tall white lilies and their scent wafted all the way through the house.

The garden had been transformed. The pool was covered and all the garish patio furniture had been put away. Nora had hired little gilt chairs and placed them in rows on the lawn in front of a small podium with a microphone. Just beside it was the little mound and plaque that was Natasha the canary's resting place.

It was, I couldn't help remembering, at her funeral that I had first encountered all the Murphys. Who would have guessed we would all be gathered here together in such similar — and yet at the same time so very different — circumstances.

It was tough seeing Billy again. Not because I harbored any residual feelings for him. Quite the opposite. He was as gorgeous as ever, probably more so dressed in what looked like an extremely expensive suit, probably Armani. His new TV series must be going well — or had he found himself a rich mistress? Why did I automatically think it must be the latter? But what I found hard was having to accept that there had been anything between us. I wanted to wipe my association with Billy Murphy from my past, but it just wasn't possible. He was there, larger than life, green eyes as devastating as ever, and he was embracing me and coming out with garbage like, 'Gee, Babe, I've missed you so much. I'm so sorry for your loss. If I'd known where you were I'd have come straight to you. If there's anything I can do, you know all you have to do is . . . '

As if I could ever count on Billy for anything. He was probably the last person I would ever turn to. To our horror, Warren and I realized he wanted to be part of the welcoming committee at the door. We managed to get rid of him by suggesting he go and rehearse for his reading.

Warren was the MC, if you could have such a thing at a memorial service.

He began by greeting everyone, thanking them for coming and thanking God for blessing us with such a wonderful day. I was sitting with Dad, Peggy and all the Murphys in the front row and Warren explained to those who did not know that I had been Pete's fiancée.

'Now I want you to welcome someone many of you already know. My brother Billy who has made a special trip from New York to be here with us today to remember Pete. As you know, Billy is now an actor and for that reason we have asked him to read a poem to us today. Billy?'

It was awful. Quite, quite awful.

We had decided that Billy should read the poem that Pete had read at Natasha the canary's funeral. Keats' 'Ode to a Nightingale'. But what we had overlooked was the fact that what had made that rendition so special was Pete's extraordinary voice.

Billy leapt up on the podium and beamed down on everyone as if he expected applause. He proceeded to tell everyone what he had been doing since he had been away and what a hit his TV show was going to be.

'I hope you guys get it in England,' he said. Everyone waited for him to say something about Pete but he didn't, just launched straight into the reading. No explanation as to why he was reading that particular poem, no little anecdote about the time Pete had read it and why. Nothing about Warren and Natasha which would have made everyone laugh and broken the ice a little. It would have been so easy to do. But Billy didn't think like that. He might be at his brother's memorial service but as far as Billy was concerned, this was all about Billy.

He was performing. He was 'on'. It was his show, not Pete's.

'Darkling I listen; and for many a time I have been half in love with easeful Death, Called him soft names in many a mused rhyme, To take into the air my quiet breath, Now more than ever seems it rich to die, To cease upon the Midnight with no pain.'

On and on he went, his voice far too dramatic for the delicacy of the poem. He waved his arms around, he played to the crowd, small that it was, and when he was finished, he clasped his hands together and bowed. When he raised his head he looked around expectantly, again waiting for the applause that was not forthcoming.

They didn't love him. They didn't get him. They didn't exactly boo him offstage but it was a sure bet the reviews would stink.

Warren joined him.

'Thank you, Billy,' and with that Billy had no option than to relinquish the limelight and join the rest of us in the front row.

'I'd like to say a few words about Pete,' said Warren, and I could sense a collective sigh of relief. Warren knew what we were here for.

He spoke from the heart. He remembered all the intimate details about Pete from their boyhood and he brought his shy, sensitive brother to life in a way that I could hardly bear. It was as if Pete had been the baby and Warren his older brother, protecting him from the harsh reality of the world outside. Nora had fretted about Pete and she had made a big show of watching out for him but it was Warren, I realized, who had been his real savior.

I was so lost in my own memories of Pete that I didn't notice when Warren began to look straight at me. Dad had to murmur in my ear.

'Warren's talking to you now, I think he has something to say to you.'

'I want to tell you something that I think will make you realize just how much you meant to Pete.' He smiled down at me. 'You can all laugh at what I am about to tell you, if you want,

382

because believe me we all did. Pete was superstitious. He had that from Mum. I'm not that way myself but I accept that other people can be. Pete's lucky number was seven. I remember him coming home from school one day and announcing that from that day forward he would be getting up at 3.04 a.m. We waited for an explanation. Had he suddenly taken it into his head to deliver a paper round? No. He had noticed a wonderful girl sitting in his class and decided it was love at first sight. He had noted the time — 3.04 — and as these digits added up to seven he felt it was a good omen. He would be setting his alarm clock to 3.04 a.m. every morning in honor of you.' Warren looked at me again and I could feel everybody craning their necks towards me.

'My bedroom was next door to Pete's. The walls were thin. I heard that damn alarm go off every morning until we persuaded him to reset it to 3.04 every afternoon. He wouldn't hear it, he complained, so you know what we had to do? We had to buy him one of those alarm wristwatches for his next birthday so he could set the damn thing off for 3.04 every day and it wouldn't disturb anyone. I think even he was embarrassed by that but it didn't stop him doing it.'

I had to laugh. And the truth was I did recall Pete's wristwatch going off at odd moments, and maybe it had been at 3.04 and I hadn't realized.

'The important thing is,' Warren went on, his voice softening but still perfectly audible, 'he died knowing he loved you and that you were waiting for him at the foot of that mountain. In a way, loving someone brings us more happiness than being loved. The saddest thing is that he will never see his child, but what I want you to know is that I will always be there to be a father to that child. I can never replace Pete's love for you but I shall love you and your child in my own way if you will let me.'

His eyes met mine. Pete had known about this, that Warren loved me too. He had known it would be a problem had we returned from Montana and married. Warren would have had to deal with it. In a way, Pete, a man given to making sacrifices for others, had made the ultimate sacrifice. He had died so that Warren and I could come together. He had not done it deliberately. He had not killed himself. It was almost as if it were meant to be.

I looked at Dad. He was smiling. He had known Warren was going to say what he said. He squeezed my hand as Warren came down off the podium to his seat beside me. All around us people were clapping and saying, 'Well done, Warren.' And Billy sat and sulked.

Nora stepped up to the microphone.

'I'm not going to say anything because if I do, I'll just break down and cry and ruin this beautiful day so I'm just going to sing for my Pete.'

I remembered the last time she'd sung for him at his birthday party. This time he wasn't even here but somehow I knew he would have a better chance of hearing her.

She looked more beautiful than I had ever seen her. I sensed Dad sitting up sharply when she took the stage. He was going to be very happy with Peggy but he would always keep a little corner of his heart saved for Nora.

She was wearing blue. A soft misty blue with a hint of violet in it. A long dress, chiffon swathed around her elegant figure, billowing sleeves. Her hair was loose and blowing around her face. She reminded me of a young Joan Baez. I listened to the words as she began to sing and she had chosen something that allowed her voice to swell and render the air with such emotion that I could tell everyone was succumbing to the release of tears.

> *Amazing Grace*
> *How sweet the sound*
> *To save a wretch like me*
> *I once was lost*
> *But now I'm found*
> *Was blind*
> *But now*
> *I see*

The words spoke to me in a way no others had for a long time. I *once was lost, but now I'm found, was blind but now I see* . . . The audience was standing, clapping and stamping their feet. Nora had finally become the singer she had always wanted to be, but most important of all I could see Pat Murphy looking up at her adoringly and this, I knew, would mean more to her than anything else.

As for me, to say I had been blind was an understatement. Now that I could see I

385

understood just one thing. As I joined in the applause with Dad on one side of me and Warren on the other, I knew I was standing between the two men I wanted to be with for the rest of my life.

Part Five

SHRIMP

Long Island, 2001

24

Mitzi didn't get it. Why would Shrimp McCarthy want to rent her house?

She'd never met him but she'd always wanted to. He was the fishing correspondent for *The East Hampton Star*. She read his column every week. It was early May and only the other night Shrimp McCarthy had alerted her to the fact that there had been reports of alewives and squid in the area which meant that migrating striped bass could not be far behind. Now that she was about to move out to Long Island full time, Mitzi was determined to master the art of surfcasting. She was looking forward to purchasing a surf rod. The striped bass season — when anglers were allowed to keep the bass they caught — would begin on 8 May. The minimum legal size was 28 inches and that was what Mitzi had set her sights on.

It had come as no surprise that Loretta Rothstein had declined to rent the house for the summer. But what could Shrimp McCarthy possibly want with a fancy mansion on a bluff when as far as she knew he wasn't even married and must have a home out here anyway? It was a mystery, as indeed was Shrimp himself.

By all accounts he was a loner who never invited anyone to his home, so no one really knew where he lived. But at some point in the late Eighties, his name was on everyone's lips when a book he had written — narrative non-fiction about his father's rumrunning days, wonderful local fishing detail combined with an exciting seafaring story — had become a bestseller. The editor of *The Star* had invited him to write a few pieces and out of this assignment had grown a regular column. Shrimp had been covering the waterfront on the East End of Long Island for several years now. Everyone knew him, except, it seemed, Mitzi.

He was due at eleven. She had planned to go up to the house and check that all was in order before she showed it to him. She had made Loretta pay for the massive clean-up operation following the disastrous benefit last summer. After all, it had been the collapse of her stupid porch that had caused most of the damage. But it was already ten to eleven, he would be here soon if he was punctual — and journalists usually were.

She needed to rent out the house for top dollar this year. Giving up her practice in New York was a big step, but sitting here in the calm of the boathouse, she knew it was the right one. She felt a little guilty about the fact that she had ploughed money into the boathouse in preparation for living there all year round. A new kitchen, an indoor bathroom, a new roof, central heating. Molly probably wouldn't even recognize it. I ought to have spent this money on the big house, Mitzi thought, some fancy addition to attract rich renters.

And she should have found somebody by now. Only three weeks to Memorial Day, the Season was almost upon them. But she had been so busy shifting her life from the city to the island, selling her apartment, getting rid of her New York furniture, extracting herself from the agonies of her bereft patients who did not appreciate being suddenly abandoned.

But she was a new person, Mitzi knew. She was ready to start a new life.

She heard the sound of a vehicle approaching above her. She stepped out on the deck and looked up. She could see the big wide fender of a pick-up truck and above it a line of fishing rods sticking up out of their holders.

Shrimp McCarthy wasn't at all how she had imagined. She had envisaged a fair-skinned burly fisherman, slightly balding maybe, with ruddy cheeks and a sunburned pate. But the man coming down the walkway was the opposite. His long legs encased in jeans were the first thing she noticed about him. He was lithe for his age. He had to be close to fifty. *About my age*, she thought. He had dark hair and lots of it. It was white at the temples but other than that there was no sign of gray.

The thing she liked most about him was his easy grace. He almost glided towards her across the deck, hand outstretched. As she took it, she noticed the long tapering fingers, more like those of an artist than a fisherman. But then he wasn't just a fisherman, he was a writer. And a damn good one.

'Shrimp McCarthy,' he said, and when he grinned she couldn't take her eyes off him. He had a beautiful face. Long straight nose, dark

391

brown eyes with thick black lashes. But it was his mouth that she found most attractive. It was very wide and humorous. His eyes gave away the sadness he had known but his mouth laughed it all away.

She wanted to kiss him.

Oh shit, thought Mitzi, *I thought all this would go away when I stopped drinking.*

But it wasn't the kind of feverish longing for sex that had accompanied her former desire to kiss fishermen once she'd been sitting at a bar for a few hours. She might want to kiss Shrimp McCarthy but she knew she'd rather die than make the first move. It was a different kind of longing, one tempered with respect.

'We've never met,' she said, 'my family have had the house for twenty years.'

'I know,' he said. 'Where are they now?'

'Oh, they passed away four or five years ago. My father first, then my mom. And they hadn't been out here for some time. So, shall we go up and take a look or can I offer you a cup of coffee first?'

He looked puzzled.

'Where are we going? I can see everything right here. You've made a lot of changes but it doesn't matter. It'll suit me fine. I'll take it.'

'What are you talking about?'

'I'll take it. The boathouse. Right here. Where are you going, by the way?'

'I'm not going anywhere. I'm staying right here.' Mitzi was utterly bewildered.

'With me? I didn't realize that was the deal.' He grinned again.

'No, you'll be up at the house. And I'm afraid the walkway's off limits to renters. You can come to the edge of the bluff and look out over the bay but no further.'

'But I've come about renting the boathouse. Someone in the office said Mitzi Alexander's looking to rent her house to someone new this year so I wrote down the number and called right away.'

'Sure, but it's not the *boathouse*, it's my parents' old house up there. You must have passed it when you drove down here.' Now she understood. The boathouse and the jetty with its mooring rights for his boat would suit him fine. 'But why would you want to rent anyway? Don't you have a place to live?'

'I always rent and it's time I moved.'

She waited for him to apologize for his mistake and be on his way, but instead he was looking around him in wonder.

'You've really done some work on this place.'

'You know it?'

'I used to live here.'

'That's not possible. No one's lived here except us. My parents converted it from the original boathouse when they bought the property.'

'I know. They did me out of a home.'

'You lived in the *boathouse*?'

'That's right. Slept in the boat.'

'What about in winter? It wasn't heated.'

He looked around. 'There used to be a wood burning stove.'

He was right. She'd had it removed to make

more space. She didn't need it now she'd had heating put in.

'I only used the house in summer.'

'I know,' he said, 'I've seen you many times from my boat when I've been out fishing in the bay. You fish too, don't you?'

Strangely, she didn't feel spooked by the thought of him watching her. It was oddly comforting, as if he'd been watching out for her.

'Yes. Where did you go after you left here?' She noticed he made no effort to hide the fact that he had been trespassing when he lived at the boathouse. Maybe he had gone on sleeping there in the winter months before she'd removed the stove. Slipped the catch on one of the windows, climbed in and made himself at home, always keeping one ear open for the sound of her car at the top of the bluff.

In any case he didn't answer her question. 'I used to watch you at night, too.'

And he was watching her now, she thought, waiting to see her reaction.

'Where from?'

'There's an empty shack further along the bay, about five minutes' walk from here, on the curve. From the deck there I have a clear view of your jetty. You've had quite a lot of action in your time.'

From anyone else this would have been unforgivable. But she could tell Shrimp knew he had her. And he wasn't threatening, or rude. He was direct, and exactly what she needed most, gentle. And above all he was showing an interest in her and it gave her confidence.

'I have had quite a lot of action in my time,' she repeated slowly. It seemed pointless to deny it since he had clearly seen everything. 'But that's all over now.' She looked him in the eye. 'I am an alcoholic. But I've stopped drinking and I've stopped the action, as you call it. No night-time visitors. How long have you had this shack?'

'Ever since I moved out of here. It's falling apart. I've never done too much to it in case the owners noticed. I think it's a case of they got old and didn't use it any more and their kids probably go to Europe or Hawaii or Florida or someplace for the summer. I keep waiting for a grandchild to turn up and claim it. If anyone bought the property, the shack would probably be a tear-down anyway. But it's getting to the stage where I really ought to find someplace else. That's why when I heard you were renting, I figured it would be perfect. I'd just move back in.'

'Sorry,' she shrugged, 'no can do.' She was somewhat staggered by his bravado. How could anyone live like that? Yet she had to admit she was intrigued. At least he appeared to have reached the stage where he was prepared to pay for his lodging. 'I'm moving out here full time,' she added.

'That's the right thing to do.' He was serious for a minute. 'You need the calm of this place. When you sit out there on the jetty and gaze out to sea, you look like you're really at peace with yourself.'

'Have you been watching me through

binoculars?' Mitzi laughed and then stopped abruptly when he said:

'Sure.'

'Why?'

'Because I think you're beautiful.'

He said it so simply and it was so obvious he was speaking the truth, Mitzi swallowed hard. She could feel her face twisting with emotion.

'Go ahead and cry,' he said, crossing to put an arm around her shoulders. 'It can only do you a lot of good. I noticed you because you were so striking and yet so sad. And so self-destructive. Allowing all those men to take from you and give nothing in return.'

'Why didn't you ever introduce yourself?'

'I was in no hurry. I knew I would when the time was right. An opportunity would present itself. And it has.'

'I'm just amazed we've never met before.'

'Well, we did once.'

She looked at him, astonished. He didn't look familiar. Surely she'd have remembered that face.

'You were pretty distraught at the time. I don't think you even *saw* me, though you were looking right at me.'

'When?'

'You had a friend who drowned.'

'Virginia.'

'Virginia,' he confirmed.

'You knew her?'

'I met her years ago when she was out here staying with her uncle. So here she was again. At your house. But she was on her own. You weren't there.'

Mitzi didn't say a word. She knew what was coming.

'I was about to go over and see her. Maybe renew our acquaintance. But before I could get there she set off in your little rowboat. She had on these huge waders. She didn't need them. It was crazy. You know what happened. I told you at the time. You heard what I said even though you didn't take into account who was speaking. She stood up in the boat and she overbalanced, right out there by Cartwright Shoals. I went out there immediately and dove into the water. The current was very strong that day. I thought she must be halfway to Montauk, although I heard her body was washed up over in Napeague.'

'She was my best friend,' said Mitzi. 'She was the best friend I ever had — before or since.'

'That's a pretty lonely thing to say.' He still had his arm around her and his hand came up to gently press her head to rest on his shoulder. 'Tell you what, why don't we pay her a little homage. It's a beautiful day, let's take a boat out — could be yours, could be mine, doesn't matter — and say a little prayer for her out there on the water.'

'Why don't we?' Mitzi disengaged herself from his arm. Her heart was beating like thunder. This was all moving much too fast for her but there was no way she wanted to put the brakes on. 'Let's take my boat since it's right here.'

'Now that I've met you, we can go fishing together,' he said as he rowed out across the bay. He said it as if it were the most natural thing in the world. She sat in the prow of the little boat, opposite him, trying not to stare at his beautiful face. The boathouse and the jetty before it were becoming a diminishing dot on the shore behind him.

'Will you teach me surfcasting?'

'Of course. Tell me something. You had a young girl staying with you last summer . . . '

'You saw her too? You know who she was?'

'Tell me.'

'Virginia's daughter.'

'I know.'

'You do?'

'Well, I guessed. You see, Virginia let me into a little secret that time I first met her when she was staying with her uncle. She told me she thought she was going to have a baby. She wasn't quite sure, she hadn't had it confirmed, but . . . '

'Molly was born nine months after that summer. Virginia was at Cambridge. She and Frank had to get married pretty quickly, but guess what?'

'What?' He had stopped rowing, had rested his arms on the oars and was staring at her intently.

'Molly has a baby of her own now, a little boy. They'll be out here this summer to stay with me. I'm Molly's godmother. You'll get to meet her, if you'd like to?'

'I'd like to very much,' he said, taking her hands in his.

'Did you ever get . . . I mean, do you have any children yourself?'

'I have a daughter,' Shrimp said slowly, 'and it's the most wonderful thing. I just found out I have a grandson.'

We do hope that you have enjoyed reading this large print book.

Did you know that all of our titles are available for purchase?

We publish a wide range of high quality large print books including:
Romances, Mysteries, Classics
General Fiction
Non Fiction and Westerns

Special interest titles available in large print are:
The Little Oxford Dictionary
Music Book
Song Book
Hymn Book
Service Book

Also available from us courtesy of Oxford University Press:
Young Readers' Dictionary
(large print edition)
Young Readers' Thesaurus
(large print edition)

For further information or a free brochure, please contact us at:
Ulverscroft Large Print Books Ltd.,
The Green, Bradgate Road, Anstey,
Leicester, LE7 7FU, England.
Tel: (00 44) 0116 236 4325
Fax: (00 44) 0116 234 0205